RECIPE FOR LOVE

ANNE MALCOM

Cover Design: TRC Designs
Editing: KimBookJunkie
Proofreading: All Encompassing Books

For all the compulsive ~~worriers~~ *warriors.*

FOREWORD

I had so much fun writing this book. If you follow me on any of my social media platforms, you may have seen snippets of my messy kitchen while I was baking. I have dubbed myself 'The Chaotic Baker,' since whenever I bake, our kitchen explodes. Not literally. Luckily.

An idea bloomed from that. About a story with a woman who has a lot of quirks. Who loves sugar. Who is wildly successful. Who battles with anxiety daily. Who falls for a grumpy badass who has loved her since the moment he laid eyes on her.

Nora was born.

It seemed like a no-brainer to have recipes to go along with each chapter, since I wanted to give my fellow chaotic bakers a chance to try fun and different things. Not all of the recipes are my own. In fact, most of them aren't. I do tend to make little changes here and there to original recipes, so if I did, I was sure to note it.

If you do want to bake as you read, I highly recommend this book, *Dessert Person* by Claire Saffitz. Most of the recipes you'll find come from there.

We'll start with a treasured favorite, just in case you want some cookie dough with your smut.

I know I do.

Us Kiwis will know and love the humble 'Santé Biscuit.' These cookies (as you Americans say) bring so much nostalgia to me. I remember making them with my mum, my nana, my girlfriends. There have been many times in my life when I was heartbroken, sad, stressed, overwhelmed, and I turned to these cookies to get me through it.

Full disclosure: I make the cookies purely so I can eat the dough and very few cookies actually make it into the oven.

This isn't me recommending you eat raw cookie dough, of course. That's up to you.

Okay, let's get to the recipe so we can get to the book.

Also, if you're making this for a bunch of people (and not just for yourself on a Friday night, which I do regularly) I recommend doubling the recipe for higher yield and more dough to eat during the process.

Sante Biscuits

- 1/2 cup of butter, softened
- 1/4 cup sugar
- 5 Tbsp sweetened condensed milk (the original recipe calls for three, but I always add more)
- 1 1/2 cups flour
- 1 tsp baking powder
- 3/4 cup chocolate chips
- 1/2 tsp vanilla

Preheat the oven to 350°. Line a baking tray with wax paper.

Cream together butter, sugar and condensed milk until light and fluffy.

Combine all of the dry ingredients in a separate bowl, then sift them into the creamed mixture, mixing until combined. Add the chocolate chips.

Roll the mixture into balls, place them on the baking tray and then flatten them with a fork.

Bake for 15 mins or until golden at the edges but still soft.

Leave on the tray for 5 minutes, then transfer to a baking tray to cool (even though they are best eaten warm).

CHAPTER
ONE

Recipe: Tan Slice

My name is Nora Henderson, and I am currently having a pulmonary embolism.

If you didn't know, a pulmonary embolism is when a blood clot develops in the body then travels to a lung where it disrupts air flow.

The symptoms are a sudden shortness of breath, chest pain, a feeling of anxiety, lightheadedness, heart palpitations and sweating. If you have deep vein thrombosis you will also have pain, swelling and warmth in your leg.

If not treated, it can cause serious problems, ultimately leading to death.

Death.

Right now, I could be *dying*.

"Nora, do the muffins have peanuts in them?" a voice asked, interrupting visions of what my funeral might look like.

I thought it would be small but well attended. The flowers would be white. Lilies. Or roses. At the church down by the water, even though I wasn't a particularly religious person. It was pretty there. A nice place for a funeral.

I blinked my pink, girly, magnificent, orderly kitchen into focus and sharpened my attention on the fresh-faced, blonde-haired Australian who had just asked me a question.

"What?" I asked, my voice scratchy and dry. Likely from the trouble I had breathing. Caused by the blood clot *clogging my arteries.*

"The muffins," she said. "I would've just lied and said no if the customer in question hadn't stressed their life-threatening peanut allergy. I don't want to get sued if they like, keel over and die or something."

My breathing evened out, my heart slowing now that I had something to focus on.

Fiona was obsessed with being sued. Apparently, you couldn't sue people in Australia like you could here.

"No, there are no peanuts in the muffins," I reassured her.

She chewed her lip. "Can you come and tell the customer? I think I kind of shattered my credibility with them. I told them that no one had died from our products... that we know of. It would sound better coming from the person who actually *baked* the muffins. And liability would shift to you." She winked before her blue eyes flickered over me. "Plus, you look like you're spiraling back here. What is it today?"

Fiona was one of the few people who knew about my health anxiety. About my worrying about anything and everything. She didn't judge me for it. Didn't tell me I was crazy—which I often thought I was—didn't try to reassure me that if I just 'calmed down,' everything would be fine. She took me in stride, stayed composed when I couldn't, and didn't act like I was a massive hypochondriac, which I was, to put it lightly.

She didn't understand completely, of course, because *her*

brain didn't torture her daily. At least not like mine had since before I could remember. My life has consistently been punctuated by worry. Bookended by anxiety and panic.

"Nothing," I replied weakly. I was embarrassed, hyper-embarrassed about this little idiosyncrasy. I did not *want* to be like this.

I did not thrive on ill health. I didn't run to the doctor or the emergency room, didn't lie in bed day after day with my imagined maladies. No, I continued to function, just quietly spiraling until I didn't die from a pulmonary embolism. That was the only way to lessen the anxiety... continue living until the next wave of panic, the next life-threatening illness.

I did not want the attention, though my mother had thought that's where this little quirk originated. I was the last person in the entire world who would actively *want* attention.

Not like Fiona. Even though she didn't want it or strive for it, she attracted it in a natural way and flourished off it. Bloomed like a flower in situations where people were attracted to her like honeybees.

Whereas I shriveled up, tried to make myself look as small as possible.

I sighed, looking down at the cupcakes I had been frosting. They were chocolate peanut butter with a fudgy frosting. I called them the PMS special since they were the perfect degree of chocolatey and sugary and comforting when you were craving them. I was sure indulging those cravings by consuming copious amounts of sugar, butter and chocolate wasn't the best way to serve your hormones. You should probably eat nuts, fruits, smoothies... whatever.

As much as I believed a healthy lifestyle was a cure for a lot of ills, and that processed foods full of sugar, chemicals and preservatives were the reason for a lot of our health problems, I also believed that a little chocolate wouldn't kill you.

Or even a lot of it.

Plus, I imported all of my ingredients from France. It was really costly and not at all fiscally responsible, according to my accountant, but you couldn't deny that the ingredients were more wholesome, without the additives that were commonplace here in the US and illegal in Europe. You could taste the difference.

My business was all about taste. And it was worth it since people literally traveled across the country to come and get these cupcakes. People paid exorbitant shipping fees to have them made, shipped in climate-controlled packaging and trucks so they arrived fresh the next day.

"Yeah, I'm done here," I said, looking from the cupcakes to Fiona.

Her eyes flared as she looked down. "Okay, you better not be shipping those out anywhere or putting them on sale before I have at least two."

I grinned, leaning over to grab the plate I'd set aside for her. "Way ahead of you." I winked, wiping my hands on my apron before brushing my cheek with the back of my hand out of habit.

Though I'd been baking for years—my whole life pretty much—I still had not perfected the art of looking like Nigella Lawson after I was done, all flawless and goddess-like. No, my auburn hair was usually escaping from the tight bun at the top of my head, chocolate was staining my fingertips, and flour ended up... pretty much everywhere.

When I first opened the bakery five years ago, I'd tried really hard to not only be the baker but also the face of the place, painstakingly crafting my appearance after spending hours in the kitchen. I'd battle with my wild burgundy locks, trying to wrestle them into a slick bun. I'd attempt to put on makeup, slathering it over my freckles, wear white dresses that molded over my considerable curves... the whole thing.

But that quickly went to shit.

You could not wear white and be a baker. Or maybe other bakers could. You couldn't be *me* and wear white.

I wasn't exactly the kind of person who would talk myself up, but even I couldn't escape the wild success of my business and my food, so I knew that I was a good baker. Maybe even a great one. But I was not orderly, put together nor organized like a lot of my contemporaries at pastry school had been. In every other aspect of my life, I was meticulous, careful, purposeful. In the kitchen, I was not. Sure, I adhered to correct measurements— most of the time, at least—but other than that, I was like a hurricane.

I'd gotten the nickname 'the chaotic baker' in school which was an apt way to describe me.

Trying to fight it had almost driven me mad, so I'd embraced the chaos and no longer tried to make myself look perfect. My hair was clean, brushed and somewhat tamed when I made it to the front of the house. Makeup was a thing of the past. The closest I got was the tinted strawberry lip balm I swiped across my lips after I'd wiped the flour off my face, or if I had extra time in the morning, I'd brush mascara on to accentuate my large green eyes.

Fiona was leaning on the arch between the kitchen and the front of the house, regarding me with perfectly manicured brows.

Fiona, despite spending her day waiting on people, looked like she could've just strutted off a runway or from a *Sports Illustrated* shoot. Her blonde hair brushed her shoulders with perfect beach waves which never turned frizzy, never stuck up or out of place and always looked intentionally mussed. Her tanned skin was always glowing like she'd just spent a week sunning herself in the Caribbean, even in the dead of winter. She was tall, much taller than my 5'5" and had curves that seemed to defy physics itself. On top of all that, she had a sweet tooth that should've wreaked havoc on those curves but did nothing but improve them.

Even though she was only wearing a plain white tee and worn blue jeans, she wore the simple outfit like it was couture or something.

I liked to think that the hordes of men who frequented the bakery came because of my superior baking skills—which I was sure was part of the reason—but I knew that Fiona was an important ingredient, luring in men outside my target audience. The ones who weren't likely to be drawn in by chocolate, peanut butter and buttery light croissants—which were the best you could get outside of Paris.

"Are you sure you don't want to tell me about the latest malady?" she asked, folding her toned arms across her ample chest. The black lace of her bra was showing through the thin white material, looking sexy, chic and effortless at the same time.

I could never pull that off. I *wanted* to pull that off, but I didn't have the effortless, sexy thing going on. The best I could go for was cute with an anxious edge.

I wore high-waisted pants from Paris. I had them imported because they never wrinkled, fit my pear-shaped body like a dream, were comfortable enough to wear all day, and made me look halfway presentable. My chiffon blouses were the same. Feminine with delicate flower prints on them, the fabric not clinging to my curves like the cheap stuff did.

"I'm sure," I told Fiona, straightening my shoulders and

6

trying to push away thoughts of a blood clot traveling to my heart or brain. After having this affliction my entire life, you would think I'd be very good at convincing myself I wasn't dying from a blot clot or some infectious disease. But when it came to this, practice, it seemed, did not make perfect.

I had not become good at convincing myself I was okay, but I'd got pretty damn good at hiding it from the public at large.

Fiona lingered, as though the customers asking about the peanuts weren't waiting at the counter. Presumably because she knew they wouldn't be mad, irritated or irate. Fiona had a way of charming even the most difficult of customers. It was impossible to be irritated with the woman with the enchanting accent, electric blue eyes and the warm magnetism that seemed to exude from her very pores.

I had yet to meet someone who was immune to her charms.

"You don't *look* sure," she prodded.

Fiona, who was endlessly patient and caring, did not find this part of my personality to be annoying, weird or off-putting. My ex-fiancé had found it to be all of those things. Which I supposed was the normal reaction. I hated dealing with my own idiosyncrasies; I couldn't expect anyone else—even the man supposed to love me unconditionally—to want to deal with them.

I let out a sigh, blowing a rogue strand of hair from my face. "I'm sure that the customers would like to know whether the muffins are going to kill them or not," I told her. "Now, let's go."

"You need to get laid." Fiona pursed her lips as I brushed past her and walked to the front.

Despite spending every single day in this space for the past five years, the impact of the effect the bakery had on me had not dulled. Not in the slightest.

The windows were frosted at the bottom, but the top half

showed the beautiful New England coast, which at this point was working toward brooding as we said our last goodbyes to summer. The interior was painted a soft pink, so soft it was inching toward beige, creating a warmth that made me feel cozy even in the dead of winter. The walls were cluttered with mismatched, vintage frames and paintings that I'd picked up at thrift stores. The tables were round, a darker shade of pink. The chairs were velvet, comfy, inviting customers to stay a while. Round pendant lights hung from the ceiling, contrasting with the vibrant green hanging plants that Fiona had managed to keep alive. A pink neon sign reading The Chaotic Baker glowed on the wall.

The glass display of baked goods was giant and full of pastries, cakes, cookies and sugary filled goodness. Baskets of fresh baked goods were scattered across the surface.

Cake stands littered the counter, all of which were half full of fudgy chocolate tortes, apple pies and strawberry shortcake at this time of day.

Our coffee machine, imported from Italy because I knew the importance of good coffee, which was espresso, not what the US had brainwashed us into thinking was coffee—sat next to the cash register. I had that painted pink too, with The Chaotic Baker written in my own sloping script.

My heartbeat slowed as I made it to the counter, reassuring the patient customer that my muffins wouldn't kill them, ringing them up, then getting their order ready.

Few things could calm me when I was spiraling, but the smell, the feel, the rhythm of the bakery that I'd created tended to do that.

Though I liked being at the back of the house, doing all of the baking, the task that made me feel safe and comfortable, it was nice to have the distraction of customers filing in, getting lost in the gentle rhythm of making small talk, preparing plates and takeout orders.

My health concerns dissipated with my own version of hustle and bustle in my bakery.

My adopted hometown, Jupiter, Maine, was a little, sleepy, seaside town that tended to keep generations of residents living here, residents who looked out for each other, who shopped small, and who had a penchant for sugar and coffee.

In addition to that, our town was charming and picturesque, therefore, there was a lofty tourist trade pretty much any time of year. And my place was on the list of 'must see' town attractions on every brochure in every inn, hotel, and bed and breakfast in the area.

Then there was our social media presence. Fiona took care of all of that since I abhorred any and all kinds of technology. She thought it was psychotic that I had no social media of my own. Which made sense since she was obsessed with all forms of social media and incredibly proficient at making us somewhat popular on platforms.

She was always filming me baking or decorating cakes. I was fine with that until she told me to "up the cleavage," then I'd banned her from putting me in any pictures or videos.

I definitely did not need *that* kind of business.

Anyway, we were busy. Consistently busy. But even consistently busy, successful bakeries had lulls.

Because I was meticulous about tasks, charts and cleanliness, there wasn't much to be done in said lulls. The cookies for when the kids got out of school and their moms took them here for a sugar fix were already in the oven. The counters were cleaned. The dishwasher was going. Plates were cleared from tables. Takeout boxes were stocked.

Free time.

It was an enemy that I usually battled off.

Free time meant thinking. Thinking meant second-guessing what I had previously thought were sound decisions or convincing myself I had a life-threatening health condition.

I'd had my near-death experience for the day, so now it was time for questioning decisions.

"Did I make a mistake?" I asked myself in a small voice, biting my lip as I packaged up a cake. I smoothed my hand over the script, 'Innocent pleasures – food without morals' logo in bright pink, sloping script, a little cherub eating a cupcake below it. The Chaotic Baker was in small serif font below it.

My eyes found Fiona's. She was leaning against the pink granite countertop that cost way too much but was worth every penny. "Breaking up with him," I clarified.

"Fuck no!" she replied loudly.

I quickly hurried to the counter to give the older couple their cake, smiling in apology for my employee's outburst—one that was not at all uncommon but somehow didn't seem to offend anyone because it was spoken in her endearing accent.

"He was a piece of shit," Fiona continued, inspecting her nails. "He cared only about himself yet was really good at making it *look* like he cared about you... except in all the places that mattered. For example, making sure you had all the orgasms you deserve, which, my darling, a fuck of a lot... minimum."

My cheeks warmed as I looked around, thankful for the lull, all of our customers seated around tables, out of earshot.

Fiona, for her part, wasn't the least bit embarrassed about discussing orgasms—granted mine, not hers—at her place of work.

"Yeah, but he was handsome, had a stable job, owned his own home," I rattled off the qualities, my stomach swirling with unease. "He treated his mother well..." I struggled to find more positive examples. "I've never seen him hit a dog with his car," I offered weakly.

Fiona rolled her eyes. "Oh wow, he was a decent human being who didn't murder animals. *That's* the bar, babe?" She shook her head. "No. He was an asshole when you told him, gently, that he needed to make a little more effort in the bedroom. Too gently, likely," she added with narrowed eyes, knowing me far too well.

I had told him gently. With the same flaming cheeks I was sporting now, with a vague sensation that I was going to throw up, with sweat pooling underneath my armpits and my heart thundering in my chest.

I did not like confrontation. At all. I'd had to hype myself up to have the conversation for about three weeks, ruminating on it, trying to convince myself that it wasn't really a big deal. Of course, it was Fiona who gave me the push and decimated my attempts at being in denial, saying "Yes, it was a really fucking big deal, and a real man would welcome a healthy conversation about sex and his woman's needs."

"You were direct enough to get the point across that you are not just a masturbatory aid, you are a woman with desire, with needs," Fiona continued, her eyes blazing with passion and fury for me.

She was protective, even though she was two years younger than me and technically my employee.

"But—"

"No," she interrupted. "No fucking buts. When you tried to tell him what you wanted, what you needed, he blew up on you, gaslit the shit out of you, and then said that you'd better buy a vibrator because he wasn't going to change."

I bit my lip. Shit, he had said that.

I felt cold at the mere memory of the tone he'd spoken to me in, the indifference in which he'd uttered the words. The way he'd tried to spin the conversation, shame me, tried to make me feel crazy, needy, demanding.

I wasn't really the kind of girl who got angry, and I hadn't even been angry then, I'd been more shocked... and hurt. Deeply, deeply hurt. To have someone you love speak to you that way took the breath right out of you. Took the fight right out of you.

Well, I supposed it wouldn't take the fight out of a woman like Fiona. She'd never let a man speak to her like that. Shit, she'd never even let herself get into a situation where she said yes to a man who didn't care enough about her to meet her needs.

Fiona reached down to swipe some frosting off her cupcake, licking from her finger. "You see, the worst thing about fucking men is they want to do the bare minimum and for us to treat them like gods," she said when she was done. "They pretend to be clueless when you tell them you didn't actually come in the one minute and fifty seconds of sex—no foreplay, by the way—then they act hurt and humiliated when you discuss it with them because they're manipulative little fucks."

Her dark brows knitted together in fury as she swiped more frosting. I knew better to interrupt her when she was on a roll.

"When really, they're smart enough to know, of course, you're not getting off without foreplay and one minute and fifty seconds of penetration." She rolled her eyes before narrowing them at me. "Your piece of shit ex was not angry about *that*; he was angry about you pointing it out. Because you fractured his bullshit fantasy that a woman should not have real, visceral needs and desire. All of your fucking American sitcoms with the dopey, overweight, below average, misogynistic husband with the hot wife who they treat like shit tells them that women don't have needs. We, in their eyes, exist for them. And if we dare to communicate our needs, we're bitches, our expectations are too high, we're reading too many romance novels... whatever the fuck." She waved her hand, not at all perturbed that two customers had just walked in. Two male customers that were now within earshot and looking at Fiona with equal parts awe and fear... as they should've.

Fiona's eyes flickered to them, and she grinned. "But in reality, they're scared of a woman not just knowing what they want but being brazen enough to demand it." She shrugged. "Well, that and they're just really fucking lazy. They want to come with the least possible effort, and if you do too, that's nothing but an unrequired bonus, not the goal. You are better off without that prick. You need a guy who will make you come so hard, you can't walk for an hour afterward."

She spun to face the counter. "Now, what can I get you blokes?"

It was only after I'd packaged up the men's orders that I realized Fiona had deftly distracted me from my pulmonary embolism that had never really existed in the first place.

TWO

Recipe: Almond Croissants

From 'Dessert Person'
see note in the 'recipe' section for additions

Fiona had well and truly put my mind at peace over my decision to break my engagement two months before the wedding.

Not that I was truly doubting it anyway.

I knew I'd made the right decision.

Even though I had broken out in hives for weeks because of the stress over what I was doing, what people would think, who I was letting down et cetera, et cetera. I was a people pleaser with an anxiety disorder who hated conflict. And canceling a wedding that was just months away, being organized by my would-be mother-in-law—who happened to run the town, or thought she did, at least—was pretty much the most conflict-heavy moment of my life. And would've made the most well-adjusted person experience anxiety.

Hence the hives.

And the insomnia.

Panic attacks.

But I did it.

Something, despite my misgivings in my weaker moments, I was very proud of.

Almost all of the deposits put down were refundable, and I paid for what wasn't. All of my friends understood. The woman who would thankfully never be my mother-in-law seemed to have finally given up on leaving nasty messages on my answering machine.

Unfortunately, the man who I was supposed to be marrying —today, in fact—had not gotten the memo.

Nathan had left his fair share of nasty messages too, but now he'd transitioned into 'trying to win me back,' a ritual I was not unfamiliar with. When I had first told him that I wasn't happy or satisfied in the bedroom, we'd had a terrible fight where he said some truly nasty, ugly things to me.

Though I could almost be considered a doormat—it was clear that's how he thought of me—even I had a line, so I'd broken up with him then and there. That was the first breakup. It had lasted a week. A week of him groveling, buying presents, declaring his love for me, making promises.

Then we had make-up sex, sex that I actually enjoyed. That communicated he'd heard what I'd said and was going to change.

Except he didn't.

He snapped right back into old routines less than a week after that.

A week.

As if he thought two orgasms from me and a semblance of effort from him was all it took, and I'd forget about my own needs. Or maybe he didn't want me to forget. I'd done a lot of thinking, and I'd come to the conclusion that he wanted me to repress those needs. Become like one of those cliché wives on the sitcoms who read romance novels, hid vibrators from their husbands, using them when they weren't home, and drank a bottle of wine a night to dull the reality that their husband didn't much care about them being a sexual being who existed outside of their need for pleasure or procreation.

And I'd almost done it too. I'd doubted myself. I'd almost been convinced that was how real relationships were. Fiction was fiction. Sex, passion, desire didn't have to be everything. Slowly, I'd cut off pieces of myself, switched off the parts I couldn't cut, and repressed all of those feelings.

I baked relentlessly, ate cookie dough like it was a food group, stayed up until the wee hours of the morning reading steamy romances, pretending I was one of those heroines the heroes worshipped every which way. I drank more wine than I should've. I smiled through tears and pretended I wasn't beginning to hate the man I was supposed to spend forever with.

Until I couldn't anymore.

Until I knew that if I kept this up, I was going to turn into a bitter, sad and angry woman.

Until I called off the wedding.

Now I ate less cookie dough. I didn't cut it out completely, though, because what would life be without cookie dough?

Of course, I read romance novels because they were amazing, but I got more sleep. And I still drank wine but didn't do it to escape reality; I did it to enjoy good food, good company.

And no way was I going to let Nathan grovel his way back.

I pressed ignore on his name as it flashed on the screen of my phone sitting on the counter.

Tina, another one of my longtime employees, looked away from our espresso machine and scowled at my phone.

"Why haven't you blocked him already?" she asked in her deep, gravelly, no-nonsense tone.

Tina was in her fifties, rode a Harley Davidson, and loved rock n roll, something she made known by her band tees, the silver adorning her body, the tattoos on both of her arms, and her penchant to rock out to Iron Maiden and The Clash when she chose the bakery playlist. Tina, much like Fiona, swore like a sailor and didn't take bullshit from anyone.

Tina also loved her wife of twenty years, Tiffany. Yeah, Tina and Tiffany.

Tiffany loved everything pink. And leopard print. And faux fur. Her hair was bleached blond, and always hair-sprayed within an inch of its life. I'd never seen her without bright pink lip gloss.

I loved both Tiffany and Tina endlessly. They were kind of like my surrogate parents... or big sisters since Tiffany told me she'd drown me in the Atlantic if I insinuated that she was old enough to be my mother.

"I can't block him." I sighed, arranging the display of almond croissants I'd just taken out of the oven.

At first, I'd baked one batch in the morning and that was it. Except they sold out within thirty minutes of opening, and things had gotten violent when customers found out there weren't enough for everyone.

So now I made a batch in the morning and a batch in the afternoon. To curb the riots.

To be fair, these croissants were out of this world. I'd gone to

Paris for three months to learn to perfect them. They were light, pillowy with baked almonds on top, and a creamy almond custard filling running through them.

"Yes, you can fucking block him. Don't be nice to that fuck," Fiona chimed in, her lips pursed. "And you're not even *trying* to be nice, you're being literal since you're literally unable to block him because you don't know how to use your phone," she pointed out with a grin.

My shoulders stiffened at how well she was able to read me and how utterly hopeless I was. Yes, I hadn't blocked him because I didn't quite know how. And because it felt unnecessarily cold to do to a man who I had previously promised to spend the rest of my life with.

"Give me your phone," Fiona demanded, holding out her hand. "I'll make sure—"

But I'd stopped moving. Stopped breathing.

"Shhh," I hissed, waving my own hand at her. "My boyfriend is here."

Her eyes flickered to the entrance as if she was just realizing he had walked through the door.

Impossible.

The *second* he opened it, the air changed. Became charged. The hairs on the backs of my arms stood up. My stomach swirled with anticipation and nerves. My palms went clammy.

It was like the entire atmosphere changed. Like the world stopped spinning.

It didn't actually stop, of course. Tina continued to frown at the espresso machine—the one she declared her undying hate for daily—the customer in the corner typed furiously away at her laptop—she was writing a zombie romance screenplay—while nursing the same cup of tea she'd had for an hour. Maddie, a regular, shouted at whomever she was on the phone with while waiting for her skinny cap.

But customers still noticed him.

You couldn't not notice a rugged Adonis walking into a rather girly bakery. It shouldn't have been possible for a man with that much testosterone to walk into a bakery decorated to look stunning on any and all social media feeds. Not with the neon signs. Soft pinks. Delicate teacups. Artful lattes.

But he walked in here. Every day. Well, not *every* day. He didn't come on weekends. Except that one time three weeks ago when he came on a Saturday.

He was a muscled construction worker, always covered in paint, dirt or grime, and he wore it like it was fucking part of his outfit. He wore the *shit* out of it. His midnight hair escaped from the baseball cap he always wore. He took it off whenever he made it to the counter, a gesture that was oddly old-fashioned and one of the many little gestures of his I loved. Like how he glowered at everyone as a default but winked at small children if they were behind him in line, and opened the door for everyone.

There was always dark stubble shading his angular jaw. It never turned into a full beard. It was always rough, rugged, manly... like the rest of him. My fingers itched with the need to run my hands along that stubble.

His eyes were blue. Strikingly blue. Like a Siberian fucking Husky. I'd only locked onto them a handful of times even though he'd visited the bakery every weekday.

Five days a week he tortured me with his pure masculine allure. With the ludicrous reaction I had every time.

"You know, you can't call someone a boyfriend when you've never actually spoken to them before," Fiona commented, her eyes on him as he settled at the end of the small line.

"I've spoken to him," I hissed, my eyes jerking down to the

cupcakes I was arranging on a tray before he could glance my way.

"Asking him 'cash or card' doesn't count," she countered dryly.

I knew she was still staring at him without shame. Fiona could stare at whomever the fuck she wanted because she was comfortable in her own skin. Because she was movie star gorgeous but in a way that didn't make you hate her since she was so down to earth, friendly and utterly confident. You wanted to be her best friend.

Like Blake Lively.

Fiona was my best friend and lived up to all the expectations you had of her upon first glance. Then she exceeded them.

"You're not engaged anymore," she continued, still staring. I knew that because my gaze flickered from him as it did when he got too close—when those Husky eyes locked with mine—and I focused on Fiona, who was not at all worried about meeting his gaze or having him see her staring at him. She was not worried about him thinking she was some kind of deranged stalker. Because no man would think Fiona was a deranged stalker if she was staring at him; he would think God had somehow shined luck upon him and he'd be counting his blessings, likely melting into a puddle of masculine muck, ready and willing to do anything to make her his.

I knew this because I'd seen it happen. Many times with many men. They all fell at her feet. The ones who weren't married or gay, and a disappointing amount of married men discreetly tried to fall at her feet too.

Fiona did not get tangled up with married men. The rest she was more than happy to get tangled up with.

But this man, this man who I'd imagined was my boyfriend long before I ended my engagement, the man who I looked at, fantasized about, and ran away from when he got close to the counter... He did not fall at Fiona's feet.

I knew that because when she served him, I spied on them from the kitchen. She had tried, when he first started coming in, to flutter her eyelashes, just being the sex goddess that she was because anyone with an attraction to the male sex would be tripping over themselves in order to try to get close enough to that man to lick his biceps.

But he appeared to be immune to Fiona's charms. The first man in history. Sufficiently rattled that a man did not find her mouthwatering, she had lamented over that, swearing he must've been gay.

She'd seen the disinterest as a challenge, ramping up her flirting to no avail... until she realized that I was infatuated with him. She realized this because of the way my entire chest, neck and face reddened when I was forced to interact with him, when I would practically sprint out the back when he walked in the door, muttering about ovens and timers going off.

Then, because Fiona was my best friend, she'd immediately ceased flirting and changed tactics, relentlessly trying to get *me* to commence flirting, even while I was engaged to Nathan. She'd given me a grace period since I broke the engagement and turned into somewhat of a mess, letting me run off to the back whenever he came in.

Which was exactly what I was about to do, after I'd bathed in his near presence for another handful of seconds.

I took a deep breath, imagining that I could smell him... a masculine musky, salty, outdoorsy scent that no cologne could replicate. On the few occasions I'd found myself brave enough to actually interact with him, I'd inhaled that scent. It had made my knees weak.

Or maybe my wobbly knees were caused by his eyes zeroing

in on mine, so intense, so unnerving, it had been impossible for me to hold eye contact.

I dreamed of him. That scent. Even while Nathan was lying in bed next to me, smelling of expensive aftershave and the matching body wash I came to despise.

It was not healthy... For me to be infatuated with a man I'd only had a scant amount of interactions with. Who likely barely knew I existed, the intense stare just his default.

Rowan Derrick was somewhat famous in Jupiter. Not just because the construction business he'd opened with his best friend Kip was wildly successful and in demand, but also because everyone wanted the two muscled, badass, rugged, insanely gorgeous men to work on their houses. Kip was a notorious ladies' man. He was handsome, for sure. Dirty blond hair that was always mussed. Striking green eyes. Tall. Ripped. A cheeky grin. A charm that came out of him as easily as breathing.

I appreciated all of that. But at a distance. It was Rowan who made my insides twist.

Interestingly, Kip and Fiona had never found their way into bed together, despite them both being devastatingly attractive and only ever after casual flings. Maybe that was why...They were just too similar.

That didn't matter at this moment though.

"I'm just going to..." I pointed to the kitchen. "Check on the flour levels," I said lamely, my eyes purposefully avoiding the place in line he was taking up.

"Nope," Fiona replied as she stepped back, holding her hands up with a wicked grin. "I need to go on my break."

My palms started to sweat as a customer stepped in front of the register. "No, you don't need to go on your break," I told her, my pulse spiking.

She leaned toward me, hands on her hips. "Yes, I do. It's the law. I could sue you." She looked purposefully at the place in line I was studiously avoiding. "You've gotta start doing things for you now, babe." Then she winked and sauntered off.

I gaped at her in disbelief and horror.

Panic crawled up my throat as I dealt with the next customer on autopilot.

I looked at Tina who was banging at the espresso machine. "Why don't I take over there, and you take the cash register?" I offered, my voice dry and scratchy.

He was getting closer in line.

Tina glanced at me with a twinkle in her eye. Normally, she would thankfully switch since she had a love-hate thing going on with the espresso machine, and she was firmly in the hate phase today.

"Nah." She grinned. "Think it's time."

Then she turned her attention back to the machine, giving me no other option but to continue serving customers. I considered just leaving them there and running out of the room, but though I might've been a little eccentric, flighty and anxious, I was also a businesswoman who would not just run out on paying customers like that.

I rolled back my shoulders, working to plaster a smile on my face and continued working as he got closer. I took great care in plating cakes, cupcakes, croissants... taking much longer than I normally would've. But then Angelina—the teenager we'd hired to wait tables and take food out—took over, leaving me no other option but to man the cash register.

Fiona's words echoed in my mind as I gave the last customer his change, my hand shaking in anticipation of my next one.

I set my palm flat on the counter so I could hide the shake and steady myself.

This is ridiculous, I thought. *You don't even know this man.*

You're acting like some idiotic lovestruck teenager just because he has good bone structure. And disarming features. And dark hair that curls out from underneath that backward baseball cap. And broad shoulders. And arresting, silvery-blue eyes. And the hands. Large. Long fingered. Clean but always speckled with paint. If they went over my skin, his calluses would be rough, textured.

My eyes met his silvery blues.

As always, his jaw was covered in stubble.

His mouth perfectly formed, those lips never turned upward into a grin but not angled downward in a scowl either. He was stern, masculine and somber but not entirely terrifying. Well, I was sure to the general public he wasn't *entirely* terrifying. To me he was.

It occurred to me that he'd been standing in front of me for at least thirty seconds, and I hadn't said a word. I'd just been staring at him, at his jaw, at his lips.

To be fair, he hadn't said anything either. Actually, he was staring at me too. My nipples pebbled underneath my shirt in a way that was incredibly inappropriate in a place of business.

My place of business.

I had to do something.

Say something.

"Has anyone ever told you that you have a Kacey vibe?" I blurted.

He didn't answer, just blinked once very slowly, likely wondering if I was having a break from reality.

"From *Yellowstone*," I added quickly.

Another blank look.

"The TV show," I continued lamely. "It's about cowboys." I drummed my fingers on the counter, wishing I could hide beneath it. "Well, not just about cowboys. It shines a spotlight on the commercialization of family ranches, the theft of land from Native Americans, and yes, it's got a sufficient amount of badass scenes and great romantic subplots. It's the best show on television. Multifaceted."

Oh my god, what are you talking about?

My ears flamed in embarrassment as I waved my hands manically. "Anyway, it's great. You've got a Kacey vibe. He's a former Marine." Why I couldn't just shut the fuck up and ask for his order was beyond me, but I was in too deep now.

His brows were furrowed a tad, and the corner of his mouth turned upward in what looked like amusement. I couldn't tell for sure, though. I was spiraling now.

"A Kacey vibe mixed generously with a Rip aesthetic," I continued to blather. "Rip is the best and most complex character on the show in my opinion. He has a tragic backstory and can be ruthless and violent, yet he's gentle, kind and patient with Beth."

Oh my god, I want to die.

I seriously considered cutting my losses, turning and running from the counter, going through the kitchen, through the back door, getting into my car, and driving out of town never to return.

But I couldn't abandon my business, my home. And my car was almost out of gas.

So I stayed put, likely flaming red, definitely sweating and utterly mortified.

"Beth is a badass," I explained for no other reason than I must've lost my damn mind. "She's tougher than any man and ten times smarter. You think she's got a cold heart, but it's a ball of fire for those she loves." I continued to thrum my fingertips on the counter, hearing my pulse thrashing in my ears as well as the sensible, mortified part of me screaming from somewhere deep down to shut the fuck up.

25

Though I could be considered to be somewhat dramatic, I was also shy. Timid even, Nathan had said. I was not known to babble about characters on my favorite TV show to complete strangers.

Yet, there I was.

For the life of me, I couldn't figure out what else to do at that moment but stare at the man who I'd made my pretend boyfriend for months and who would likely never come here again because he'd been accosted by the insane owner.

I forced my lips shut, gripping on to the counter for dear life, waiting for him to say something. Maybe something polite, or hopefully he'd just ignore me altogether, place his order, giving me something to do other than stare at him like an idiot.

"I'm Rip, so that makes you Beth?" His voice was low, throaty, but with a warmth threaded through it. A warmth that sparked fire in my belly and places much lower than that.

Holy. Fucking. *Fuck.*

Did he just say that?

He just said that.

I let out a burst of laughter that sounded like it came from a hysterical teenager.

"I own a few sundresses and a couple of pairs of cowboy boots because I am a Midwestern girl, but that's as close to Beth as I'm ever going to get," I said, going for a casual, joking tone yet failing abysmally.

I wanted greatly for the earth to swallow me up.

He kept looking at me with a warmth in his mesmerizing eyes, with a slight upturn to his plump lips.

"Would like to see those sundresses and cowboy boots," he murmured, crystalline eyes staying on mine.

My heart was hammering away in my chest, my feet felt like

26

they were glued to the floor, captured by his stare. I was surprised that I hadn't melted into a puddle yet.

He'd just told me that he'd like to see me in a sundress and cowboy boots. And he'd said it in a way that made it seem like, after that, he'd liked that sundress and those cowboy boots on his bedroom floor. The words had been dripping with sexual interest.

But that was insane. A rugged, manly man like him could not be interested in an eccentric bakery owner who babbled about TV characters, was virtually afraid of her own shadow, always thought she was dying of something, and was generally just a complete dork.

No, he definitely needed a Beth type. Strong, sexual, unable to be rattled or scared by anyone or anything.

"I, um..." I cleared my throat, looking to Tina for help.

She had abandoned all pretense of making coffee and was staring at the two of us with folded arms and a wide grin I really wanted to hate her for.

Get it together, Nora.

I straightened my spine and forced myself to look at him. Or rather the general shape of his face. Getting trapped in his gaze was how I got in this situation in the first place. This situation would be ingrained into my brain for the rest of my life.

"Coffee, black and an almond croissant, right?" I asked him, tapping at the screen of the register.

I'd thought that focusing on business would extricate me from the embarrassment that was burned into my bones until I realized that I hadn't actually asked him for his order. I'd made it obvious that I'd memorized his order. Not just memorized it, I knew that at certain times of the day, he ordered different things. A croissant first thing in the morning, a lemon poppyseed muffin if they were sold out. Croissants at this time if he hadn't gotten

27

one in the morning. Sometimes, he'd come for brownies if it was late in the afternoon. I'd never seen him get cookies. Once, he'd ordered a cupcake. Lemon curd. He liked lemon flavored things. Not too sweet.

I collected all the little tidbits about him, hoarded them like they were going to be useful for something. Like they were going to be mine. Like *he* was going to be mine.

Ridiculous... I truly was a ridiculous person.

"I mean, what do you want?" I spluttered, my chest tightening, sweat beading between my breasts.

Yes, I tended to sweat when I was really nervous. Which, of course, made me even more nervous, worrying that someone would notice aforementioned sweat, therefore making me sweat more.

So now all I could think about was the hottest guy to walk the earth seeing my boob sweat.

The edges of his body were starting to blur as I ramped myself up for a full-on panic attack for being the biggest dork on the planet.

The corner of his mouth twitched, and his eyes might've twinkled with amusement. But I also could've been hallucinating.

"I'll have a black coffee and an almond croissant," he said, deadpan.

"And I'll have an almond croissant, two macadamia and white chocolate cookies, and a brownie," the man standing behind him added, grinning ear to ear.

Kip. His business partner.

Kip was blond, almost boyish, a little more tanned, and he had a lighter energy than Rowan. They were an unlikely pair.

I was infinitely thankful to Kip for reminding me that other people existed in this world. Other people to yes, witness my break from reality, but also to focus on.

"Got it," I told him, focusing on his friendly and attractive but not dangerous face.

"And a latte," he continued, still beaming with glittering eyes while looking from me to Rowan. "Caramel. Oat milk. To go."

I nodded once, vaguely noting it was amusing and kind of adorable that a macho man construction guy was ordering an oat milk latte with caramel.

I made myself busy, putting their pastries into our signature pink and white striped boxes, taking a lot of extra care and time with the boxes and the bows I tied around them.

Unfortunately, no matter how long I took on their orders, I would actually have to give them to them at some point.

By the time I was done, Tina had already made their coffees, and both men's hands were fastened around our pink takeout cups.

Rowan's fingers were long, masculine. I wasn't sure that fingers could actually be masculine until this moment. Those hands would look so large and rough against my pale skin.

Why I was thinking about those hands on me right then was anyone's guess.

I shook myself out of it and slid the boxes across the counter toward the men, not wanting to risk any kind of brush with those hands.

Far too cowardly to look upward, I focused on the cash register, tapping at the screen with trembling fingers. No one spoke. Well, no one in the immediate vicinity spoke. Of course, people in the café spoke. Florence and the Machine played from the speakers, mocking me with all of her divine feminine strength, with her utter confidence and strong sexual energy.

I turned the screen to Rowan, my lips pursed together, my eyes downward again.

There was a visceral energy in the air, like the atmosphere carried an electric charge. It was quite possible I'd been imagining that... I had a very active imagination.

Instead of turning his attention to the screen as I was willing him telepathically to do, he kept staring at me, his eyes twinkling and penetrating at the same time. That same sexual interest that had dripped from his tone a few minutes ago leeched from those stunning eyes of his.

It was becoming increasingly hard to stand on account of my trembling knees. I hadn't known that a stare could make my knees tremble. I hadn't known knee trembling was an actual thing that happened in real life.

Yet there it was.

There I was. Trembling, sweating and almost fucking panting because of the way the man was staring at me.

It was different from the times I was brave enough to serve him before. Sure, he'd been polite and sexy, always making eye contact when I found enough courage to look up. But there hadn't been any of the burning, twinkling thing. There hadn't been any flirting.

But then again, before, I hadn't rambled on about *Yellowstone* either.

Still, I knew this was different.

For a moment, a terrifying yet glorious moment, I thought he was going to say something else. Ask me something. Like on a date. Or to be his girlfriend... Like a fucking rugged, brooding, alpha male was really going to ask me to go steady when we'd barely interacted. It was completely wild and unrealistic, yet I thought it, nonetheless.

I held my breath.

But then he broke eye contact, moving his attention to the screen and tapping at it, no doubt giving me an unnecessary tip since he did every time.

"I'll be seein' you," he promised, and then he and Kip—who winked at me—turned around and walked out.

I couldn't be sure if I was disappointed or relieved.

CHAPTER
THREE

Recipe: Santé Biscuits

ROWAN

"Y ou gonna shoot your shot?" Kip asked as we exited the bakery, my entire body tightening up as the crisp air greeted us. There was no more smell of sugar, cinnamon... whatever the fuck the mix of shit was in there that made all my muscles relax, made my dick harden just a little.

Yes, I was a sick fucking fuck for getting hard at the smell of baked goods. But technically, it wasn't the baked goods that got me hard. It was the woman doing the baking. The woman who from the first fucking moment I'd laid eyes on her had sparked something inside of me. And yes, it was my cock first because I had still yet to gain total control over my animal instincts. Though I think you would have to be fucking dead not to have a reaction to her.

She was drop dead gorgeous.

Dark ruby hair that was thick, long and always escaping from whatever bun she'd piled it up in. Peaches and cream skin that flushed pink whenever I was around. Freckles dusting across her delicate nose. Full red lips that made any man think about what they'd look like around his dick.

Eyes sharp, angular, strikingly green. So green they glowed. But only when she was having a good day. They fucking changed color. It sounded insane, but it was true. When she was happy, excited or whatever, they glowed a vibrant emerald. When she was having a bad day, when she wasn't happy, they were duller, almost hazel.

Her body was a fucking dream. Curves to die for. Curves I wanted to worship.

And then there was her voice. Low, raspy yet delicate at the same time. I felt it in my dick whenever she spoke.

And today, when she'd started fucking babbling about some TV show, the apples on her cheeks seemed to grow larger, making her freckles look darker against her skin. It had almost spelled the end of me.

Her hair had been falling around her face, her emerald eyes glowing with what looked to be panic but still made me want to yank her across the counter and finally taste her rosebud mouth.

Especially now that she wasn't wearing that fuck's ring. Now that I wasn't in danger of spending fifteen to life in a state penitentiary for killing him after laying his hands on what was mine.

And she *was* mine. Whether or not she was wearing that ring. I knew that was fucking insane since I barely knew her, but I felt like I did. I knew that she was shy, that she showed every single emotion on that face of hers. Knew she blushed easily. That she smiled at children. Knew that she donated all of the leftover baked goods to the homeless shelter at the end of every day. That she was soft-spoken and a little goofy. Knew that everyone in town fucking loved her. That she was a goddamn treasure in this town. I knew that she had no fucking clue just how indescribably gorgeous she was.

She didn't go out... I never saw her at the bar. Knew she spent almost all her time at that bakery of hers. Which she'd built into a nationwide fucking sensation.

"I don't know what you're talkin' about," I said to my best friend as we climbed into the truck.

"Bullshit," he returned, his voice muffled by the huge bite of brownie he'd taken. Which was followed by a groan I really didn't need to hear from my best friend. Though I knew it wasn't voluntary; there was no way you could eat that shit without having some kind of physical reaction. I didn't eat sugary shit. Not until I found myself in that fucking bakery three years ago.

Now I had dreams about the fucking *croissants*.

Well, Nora was usually baking them in my kitchen, and she was usually naked, but the croissants were there.

Kip chewed noisily as I placed my coffee in the cup holder of the truck, still staring at me, wordlessly calling bullshit.

"We're not talkin' about this," I barked, turning the truck on. "We're talkin' about the house we've got to finish by the end of the week and the renovations we've gotta start next week, the quote we've gotta give tomorrow, and the scheduling conflicts we've got with two big clients," I said, willing myself not to stare at her from the windows like a total fucking stalker.

At least not when Kip was watching.

"We need to hire more guys," Kip said.

He was not wrong.

"Or girls," he added. "Women are just as capable, if not more capable, than men at any and all things."

He was not wrong about that either.

"If we hire women, you cannot fuck them," I told him,

sipping my coffee to distract me from not taking one last glimpse at her before the bakery was out of sight.

Kip huffed beside me.

"It's a lawsuit," I informed him.

"That's what lawyers are for," he muttered around the brownie. "Nora doesn't work for us, she works for herself."

"Since we don't bake fucking cookies for a living and she doesn't build fucking houses, I think that's goddamn clear." Fuck... Now I had the vision of Nora in a hardhat and nothing else in my head.

"So, you have no lawsuits to get tangled up in when you fuck her," he rambled.

A car honked as I pulled the truck over to the side of the road so I could glare at my best friend without getting into a wreck.

"You are not gonna talk about me fuckin' her ever again," I growled, pointing my finger at him.

Now it was not something I was particularly proud of, but I could be a scary guy. Most of the time I was a scary guy. Kip knew that it was more than just a glower, too, because he'd been with me. He knew the look in my eye when I had left part of myself behind, when I was ready to hurt someone without regret or mercy.

Similarly, I knew that behind those easy smiles of his, Kip could kill a man in less than ten seconds without spilling a drop of blood. I knew that those easy smiles were just a fucking farce, that he was forcing them with everything he had because otherwise, he'd have to think about what he lost four years ago.

His teasing smile lingered despite the promise of violence I knew he saw in my eyes. Kip was fearless... He'd faced things regular people feared only because they were foreign, unknown. We both knew horrors most people couldn't even dream of. Him more than me.

35

"So, you like her," he deduced, tapping his chin. "I've never seen you go all psycho serial killer over a chick before."

I gritted my teeth. "This subject is closed."

He was right.

I was not a monk. Far from it. I dated. Fucked, more accurately. Women only stayed overnight if I was too tired to kick them out after sex. I did not cook breakfast, did not eat meals beyond dinner. It was only fucking. That much was clear. The second I got an inkling that a woman was getting attached or she got it in her head that she could 'change' me, it was over.

I wasn't an asshole. Or at least I tried my best not to be an asshole. Made sure they always got off before I got off. But I was well aware I could not be described as warm, fuzzy, romantic or any of the other shit women wanted.

"Okay, okay," Kip held his hands up in surrender. "I'm done."

"Good," I grunted.

"But I would get in quick," he added before I could pull the truck out. "She's single now. A lot of men are gonna try and get in there."

"They can try," I clipped out, my blood burning at the thought of some other piece of shit touching her.

Touching what was mine.

NORA

"That was bad," I whispered, staring at the door that Tina was locking.

After Rowan left, I'd hightailed it straight to the kitchen and didn't speak to anyone for the rest of the day. I retreated into my safe space and baked three different batches of almond cookies and a peanut butter cake with double chocolate frosting.

Fiona stared at me and then the cake I'd just arranged on a

cake stand on the counter for tomorrow. The cake itself would be gone before ten in the morning. It was kind of famous. And only made on certain occasions—when I was deep in some kind of anxiety spiral or personal drama.

"It must've been bad since you made the Crisis Cake," she observed.

"It's a peanut butter cake with double chocolate frosting," I countered, chewing my lip.

Fiona rolled her eyes. "That is the Crisis Cake." She pointed at the cake stand.

I continued to gnaw on my lip, unable to argue with her. It was the Crisis Cake. Everyone in the bakery knew that. It was famous. Delicious. Decadent. It cured things only peanut butter and chocolate could cure. I only made it when I felt like my life was spiraling. I'd made it far too often when I was with Nathan. Since breaking up with him, I hadn't made it once. Until now.

"You weren't there," I told her.

"Yes, I was," she chirped happily, dipping her spoon into the bowl of leftover frosting she'd snatched from me before I could clean it. "I was watching from your perch in the kitchen, usually reserved for your spying whenever Rowan comes in."

I glared at her. "I do not spy."

"You totally do."

I gritted my teeth. "Okay, I bake crisis cakes, I spy on hot guys, and then I make a complete ass of myself in front of hot guys!" I huffed, hiding behind my hands.

Fiona grinned. "You didn't make a *complete* ass of yourself."

I ignored that and snatched up the bucket and brush I had prepared earlier in order to get down on the floor and scrub our pink tiles.

"What are you doing?" Fiona demanded from above me.

I reveled in the satisfaction I got from the brush reaching the dips in the grout, far more effective than our mop was.

"I'm cleaning," I answered, pointing out the obvious.

"I understand that you're cleaning," she huffed. "I just don't understand *why* you're cleaning since we mop every day and scrub that floor once a week. Which we did yesterday. Beyond that, when you're not baking, you're running around cleaning like a toddler on cocaine."

I screwed up my nose. "I don't like to think of a toddler on cocaine," I informed her. "And even if I were to think of one, I don't think a coked-up toddler would be cleaning."

"Whatever," Fiona sliced her hand through the air dismissively. "What I'm trying to say is you're scrubbing a floor that is honestly probably cleaner than my dining room table."

Although Fiona wasn't quite the neat freak that I admittedly was, I highly doubted that was true. Her small cottage on the beach was cluttered in that delightful, Nora Ephron kind of way. Cluttered but clean.

"I'm scrubbing the floor to distract myself because I'm likely going to sink into a deep depression when I do think about what an ass I made of myself today," I grunted, scrubbing harder.

"Jesus Christ, can't you deal with depression like a regular woman, and use your vibrator until you lose feeling in your clit, drink wine, and eat your weight in imported chocolates?"

I glanced up from where I was scrubbing. "Do regular women really do that?"

Her eyes damn near popped out. "Of course, they do. Self-pleasure, French wine and Swiss chocolate. Not all of *this*." She gestured at the bucket.

I looked from her to the bucket, pausing to consider such a course of action. It seemed self-indulgent to do such things. Sure, I had a vibrator. Sure, I owned a good amount of wine and Swiss chocolate—I wasn't completely unhinged. But I hadn't combined all three things to deal with a crisis. I hadn't had the luxury to deal with my problems in that kind of way. So, I'd figured out a way to turn something that always needed to be done—cleaning—into my own form of meditation.

During my contemplation over how I'd spent my life dealing with trauma, Fiona had taken the opportunity to snatch the scrubbing brush from my hands and pick up the bucket of water.

"Hey!" I protested weakly, trying to grab them back. But I was on the floor, and she was standing, and much taller than me.

"Nope," she said, popping the 'P.' "You're going to go home and engage in all of those activities that will actually make you feel better. And I swear to fuck, if you pick up any kind of cleaning implement in your house, I'll know." She wagged her finger at me.

"Cleaning makes me feel better," I balked, rocking back on my heels.

"Bullshit. Now get up," she ordered, holding her hand out to me.

I pouted, thinking of arguing with her and deciding not to. She wasn't exactly wrong... Chocolate, wine and my vibrator did sound pretty good to me right now.

"Fine," I conceded, grabbing her outstretched hand and letting her pull me up.

"He's never going to come in here again," I whined once I was on my feet.

Fiona squeezed my hand before letting me go. "Well, then he's a fucking idiot," she declared. "Even when you're making a dick of yourself, you're hot as fuck," she informed me with a wink. "And I know for a fact that there is a man out there who will find you hot when you're making a dick out of yourself."

I forced a smile and didn't argue even though I wasn't entirely convinced.

I had a feeling that I would never see Rowan again.

* * *

It turned out that staying late at the bakery, cleaning it from top to bottom, would've been the safer option.

I should've known... The universe wasn't exactly well-versed in giving me a break. Not that I wallowed in that. The universe had given me plenty. Or I had made the most of every single, however small, opportunity it vaguely flung in my direction.

My life was good. Great even. But that didn't mean I was going to be the girl who could catch a break.

That was made apparent when I walked into my kitchen and my ex-fiancé was sitting there.

"What are you doing here, Nathan?" I sighed.

I wasn't entirely surprised. He'd been calling me nonstop, not getting the message. And today was the day we had planned on getting married. Before I called off the wedding, that is.

He was the last person I wanted to deal with right now. I was still sufficiently rattled and mortified by the interaction with Rowan, still trying to convince myself that I'd imagined the interest in his gaze.

I was confused. Amped. But also exhausted. My day started at four in the morning, as it had for years. It was second nature to me now, getting up, making coffee. Stretching... if I could force myself to act like I was a little bit interested in exercise. Driving to the bakery, opening up, tying on my apron and getting to work. Mornings were my favorite. No one else was up. It was just me. Me in my element. In the place I felt safe, confident, secure.

But because of those early mornings, I was in bed by nine.

Ten at the absolute latest. I could function off six hours of sleep, but I preferred a minimum of seven. I worked until the bakery closed at four p.m., then spent another hour shutting things down. It was a long day. Work I adored, but it took a lot out of me.

My evenings were mine too. When I would pour a glass of wine. Make something to eat or pick at whatever was in the fridge. I'd turn on the TV, sink into the cloudlike cushions of my sofa, let the last of the sun stream through the windows of the home I'd created. The home I loved.

The home that Nathan was polluting with his presence.

"How did you get in here?" I asked before he could answer my original question. He had been sitting on one of the barstools at my kitchen island, again, polluting one of my favorite rooms in the house. The largest because, well, it needed to be. The kitchen was my heart and soul. Where I created, where I entertained, where I found calm amongst chaos.

The room with windows that looked out onto the rugged seascape. The room that always had fresh flowers sitting on various surfaces. Recipe books were lined up along the counters, the hammered white backsplash peeking out from behind them.

All of my appliances were sleek black, top of the line, worth obscene amounts of money. The kitchen of my dreams.

"I still have a key." Nathan held up the silver object which glinted in the light.

I frowned as I hung my purse up on a hook beside the light switches.

A key. Yes, I'd given him a key. Not because I'd wanted to but because he'd pressured me to. Because he'd given me a key to his apartment, so why would I withhold one from him? Because we were meant to be spending the rest of our lives together.

It had filled me with a sour unease, giving him unregulated

access to a home that was my sanctuary. Was mine alone. A home that I had worked for, that contained my blood, sweat and tears. The first safe home I'd had in my entire life.

"You need to give me that key back," I said, settling myself on the other side of the island, desperate for distance between us.

I hadn't seen Nathan since I broke off the engagement.

He looked good, I supposed.

His short blond hair was combed over to perfection, not a strand out of place. Tanned skin was smooth except for the slight wrinkles in the corner of his eyes. The cornflower blue eyes that were nowhere near as arresting as the translucent ones that had landed on me today.

That had branded me today, it seemed.

Nathan was still wearing his suit, blue tie loosened slightly. His jacket hung on the back of the stool, indicating he'd been here a while.

The whisky glass in front of him also hinted that.

"We need to sort things out," he countered.

I closed my eyes for a second, trying to find the strength, the patience. This was not out of the blue. Nathan had been calling, texting, sending flowers and gifts trying to 'win me back.' Except you can't win someone back who had decided they didn't want to marry you.

You respected that decision. Maybe you hated or resented that person for the rest of your life. Maybe you spent thousands of dollars on therapy to repair the damage they did. Maybe you took a trip to Europe to rediscover yourself and fall in love with some Italian. You did not constantly call them, send them gifts, and act as if their decision was some small disagreement that could be rectified. Like their decisions meant nothing.

"There is nothing to sort out," I told him, opening my eyes

and rolling my shoulders back. "We broke up," I said firmly, meeting his eyes.

He sighed, much like he always had when he'd found me slightly irritating, when me exerting my opinion on something was an inconvenience.

"No, we didn't. We had a fight."

I gaped at him. "Me calling off our wedding is not a fight." My words came out through gritted teeth. "Me calling off our wedding was me making a decision about my life which was long overdue. I'm sorry I didn't make it earlier, I truly am. But I don't want to be with you."

Nathan narrowed his eyes at me, looking irritated but not like he was getting the point. Nathan with his blue eyes, his expensive suit, his looks and family name was not entirely used to people saying he couldn't have something.

Which was why he was here. Not because he really loved me or wanted to spend his life with me. Because I was suddenly more desirable to him now that I'd told him he couldn't have me.

Men.

I sighed, turning to the cabinet behind me to retrieve a glass to fill with large amounts of wine.

"This is not acceptable, Nathan," I said to the wine cabinet. "You can't come into my home. You cannot keep calling me. I've made my decision. We both need to move on with our lives."

I retrieved my glass, placing it on the counter. But before I could close the cabinet, hands settled on my upper arms, whirling me around.

My body let itself be whirled around because I was frozen in shock. I hadn't heard Nathan round the island—on account of the Italian loafers he wore—and I certainly hadn't been expecting him to grab me.

The grip itself was much too tight. Much tighter than I'd

thought his soft, manicured hands were capable of. Something I'd lamented over when it came to our sex life but something that currently alarmed me, given the situation.

Given that we were alone in my home, my closest neighbor a seventy-year-old woman who was three miles away.

Nathan's eyes were blazing with anger now. "I'm not moving on with my life," he snapped. "I made a decision to make a life with *you*." His grip on my arms tightened. To the point of pain.

Fear sparked in my belly.

Nathan was not an overly large man. He was lean, with more of a swimmer's body, but he was tall. Much taller than me. And definitely able to overpower me, manhandle me as he was right now.

I was a woman living alone. I was a curvy yet petite woman who did not have any fighting skills to speak of. At that moment, I realized I should've prioritized training to fight back. Defend myself. So I would not feel so helpless when a man had his hands on me.

But I was lucky enough to have never been in a situation where a man had put his hands on me, so I hadn't thought I'd need to learn such things. I thought—stupidly—that the universe had fucked with me enough and wouldn't add being physically hurt by a man to the list of my traumas.

"You need to get your hands off me right now, Nathan," I told him, willing myself to meet his eyes, to not let my voice shake. "And then you need to get out of my house."

I was proud of the steel in my voice.

The steel that had absolutely no effect on Nathan, apparently.

"No," he gritted out. "I'm not leaving until we sort this out. Until you're mine again."

Fury and fear mingled together inside me. "I was never

yours," I hissed at him. "Evidenced by the fact that you don't respect my decisions, you don't take your hands off me when asked, and you think I'm someone *to be owned*."

The tips of Nathan's ears reddened in indignation and his lips turned down with a scowl. "You don't mean that," he muttered, gripping me tighter. "I just need to show you." Then he yanked me forward, our lips crashing together, his tongue forcing its way into my mouth. A tongue that I immediately bit.

Which, thankfully, made him rear back in pain, letting go of me.

Not thinking, I turned, intent on getting as far away from Nathan as possible. Unfortunately, amidst my fight or flight response, I forgot that I had left the cabinet open, and I ran right into it.

Now I wasn't what could be called a runner by any stretch of the imagination, but when the guy you broke up with—the guy who you'd become repulsed by—forced his way into your house then into your mouth, you became a runner. And I had installed these cabinets myself. Not to toot my own horn, but they were damn sturdy. Which was something I had been very proud of up until that moment.

If I had been subpar at cabinet building, the door would've likely just come off its hinges. But I wasn't subpar. So, the door stayed firm. I, on the other hand, after slamming into it at full speed, fell right to the ground. Pain exploded in my left eye as my head slammed into my Italian stone floors.

"Nora!" the voice came from somewhere far away. It was muffled.

Then there were hands on me. Hands that I had literally ran into a cabinet door trying to escape.

"Get your hands off me," I hissed, my own voice tight and

thin from pain. I forced myself up, hating the vulnerable position on the floor with Nathan anywhere near me.

My head swam as I sat up, my face throbbing, and the vision in my left eye almost entirely obscured as I glared in Nathan's general direction.

"Nora—"

"Get the fuck out of my fucking house," I snarled at him, my voice unrecognizable.

Nathan paused for a split second. I doubted it was from any kind of actual concern, likely because I'd never spoken to him like that before. I'd always been delicate, agreeable, submissive. And I'd never cursed in front of him. He'd found it 'unbecoming.' Ugh. How in the fuck had I let this man put a ring on my finger?

"I'll call the police if you're not gone in the next thirty seconds," I threatened. I really would've called the police if I thought I'd be able to get up and reach my purse, which I knew I couldn't. The point was to make sure Nathan didn't know I couldn't.

Nathan's self-preservation won over, and he reacted quickly, his shape moving away from me and footsteps receding as he ran from the house. I didn't breathe easier until I heard my front door open and close. And even then, I didn't breathe easy. On account of all the pain.

Though I was a neurotic hypochondriac, I had a rather high pain tolerance. I'd broken my arm once, and no one believed me because of the hypochondria, so I was forced to go to school for a week with a broken arm. And run our school's cross-country race. I actually came in second, the one and only time I had run because it was forced upon me. My mother had felt sufficiently guilty, so that ended up being the one time in my life when she was kind to me for an extended period.

It took every single ounce of my willpower to grit my teeth

against the agonizing pain in my head and face, clawing at the counter to get myself upright. The room spun, my vision blurred, and I felt like I might hurl all over my lovely quartz countertops. But after a few minutes—or maybe more than a few, who knew? —there was no vomit on my countertops, and my vision improved somewhat. Dark spots still danced around the room as I gripped the counter, using it to help me along to the cabinet above the fridge where all of my medicine was housed.

I fumbled with various bottles, cursing myself for being obsessed with health and wellness and swearing off most traditional painkillers.

Again, after a few minutes—that quite possibly could've been more—of my head feeling like it had grown three times its normal size while grabbing blindly at bottles, I found a bottle of Advil.

Tears running down my face, my hands shaking, I managed to spill some into my palm and retrieve a bottle of water from my fridge.

Then I spent the rest of the night lying on my sofa, staring at the ceiling, and willing the throbbing in my eye to go away.

On the plus side, I did not think about what an ass I'd made of myself with Rowan.

Every cloud, and all that.

FOUR

Recipe: Peanut Butter Cake with Double Chocolate Frosting (the Crisis Cake)

"I'm going to fucking *kill* him!" Fiona screamed when she walked through the door of the bakery.

I winced at the tenor of her tone which seemed to exacerbate the throbbing behind my eyes. That and the sunlight streaming through the windows. Usually, I adored the way the bakery was bathed in the morning sun... I'd lean against the counter, sipping my coffee, watching the way the light hit the magical space I'd created.

None of that today.

"It's easy to buy a gun, right?" she scowled, dumping her purse on the counter, eyes zeroed in on the left side of my face. "A fact that we really hated and have been rallying against for the longest time, but something I am currently thankful for."

"You don't need to buy a gun," I told her quickly, horrified.

"Right, we've got plenty of knives in the back," she nodded once, heading in that direction. I snatched her arm before she could run into the kitchen and arm herself with a knife to do who knew what.

"Fiona," I groaned. "Who are you planning on killing?"

She stopped, luckily, since I didn't like my chances if she decided to fight me on it.

Her glower deepened as she focused on my face. "Nathan," she spat out the name like it tasted bitter. "He's the one who did this, isn't he? That fucking *cunt!*"

Fiona, being Australian, used the 'C' word daily, which, apparently, was the norm for those hailing from the Southern Hemisphere. She'd also educated me on the use of it. A 'soft T' was meant to be some kind of compliment, like "he's a good cunt," and the 'hard T' was meant as an insult, like "he's a fucking cunt."

This was certainly a 'hard T' moment.

"Nathan didn't do this, if he's the cunt you're referring to," I informed her.

Her brow lifted. "*Rigggght,* like there is some other man who is small enough and disgusting enough to use violence against a woman who dumped him instead of taking it like a man," she ranted. "Or I should say, taking it like a woman since men never take rejection or any kind of setback well. Women are the ones who properly deal with shit. Continue on."

"Nathan didn't do this," I repeated.

Her glower did not waver in the slightest. "You mean to tell me that Nathan was not in your presence when that happened?" She motioned to what was a pretty impressive black eye.

I chewed on the inside of my cheek. I could not tell her that.

Fiona took my pause as some kind of confirmation that Nathan was the one who'd hurt me.

"I'm going to fucking kill him," she seethed.

I gripped her harder to ensure she did not go in search of weapons again. I'd never seen Fiona truly mad before. It was scary and touching. She would go to battle for me, in an instant. As I would for her, of course. But she'd be a lot more successful.

"Fiona," I said gently. "Nathan was in my presence when this happened, but he didn't do it... technically."

Fiona narrowed her eyes. "You better explain quick, or I'm going to get some knives."

So, I did. Explain. Which didn't really do much to quell Fiona's fury. In the end, she was still set on killing Nathan. As was Tina, who didn't help at all because she actually owned a firearm, but luckily, she had a somewhat cooler head about it.

Tina's solution had been contacting an outlaw motorcycle club she was in touch with and letting them deal with Nathan.

So, I had to talk her down from that too. Luckily, the bakery needed opening and customers needed serving, so there was ample distraction for them. Both of them had been muttering threats all day, though. They weren't worried that Nathan technically hadn't laid a hand on me.

It had been a whirlwind day. I'd slept in, which was unheard of for me.

The classical music of my alarm clock was much too soft to pull me out of the deep unconsciousness I'd lapsed into after finally falling into a restless sleep last night. I supposed the amount of booze I'd consumed had helped that. I wasn't a spirit girl usually, but that was mostly because I hadn't experienced a situation that called for spirits. Unless I was making my bourbon pumpkin pie with pecan streusel for Thanksgiving.

So, because I overslept, my entire schedule was out of whack.

I was an hour behind on everything, rushing to get muffins, cookies and croissants out of the oven. And because I was in a rush to leave the house, I did not have the presence of mind to slather concealer all over my eye.

Luckily, I had snatched a cardigan from my closet which hid the angry fingerprints on my upper arms.

I hadn't exactly forgotten about my black eye. I couldn't forget about it since there was a dull throb behind my eye the entire day. But I got caught up in the business of the café—serving customers, running coffees, replenishing the bakery displays—a familiar and comforting rhythm. People asked, of course, about my face. It was a relatively small town, and word of such things spread like wildfire, so I'd hidden out in the kitchen after a morning of well-meaning questions and comments.

Dot, one of my beloved retirees, casually mentioned that she had her ex-husband's kneecaps shattered when he thought he could lay hands on her, and she was still in possession of the baseball bats that achieved that feat.

I had politely declined her offer, equal points horrified and impressed that the woman who wore cat sweaters and had a purple rinse in her hair shattered her ex-husband's kneecaps.

We were a tight knit town; people looked out for each other. Small town values remained here in Jupiter, despite the rest of the world going crazy.

It was nice, something I loved, especially since I'd never had that feeling growing up. I was well liked and respected here. Of course, a part of that was because I was the one who made all the sugary stuff and had a top-of-the-line espresso machine. But part of it was also because I tried my best to be a good person. I donated both my time and my money to various town projects. I was involved in every town event. Helped out wherever I could.

So, I was well liked.

Nathan was not.

Therefore, most people put two and two together when they saw me. Two and two being me looking like I'd been punched in the face, and the fact that I'd broken up with someone who people generally thought of as an uptight asshole who didn't take rejection well.

It was exhausting, explaining that I'd had an accident at home to everyone. Fiona and Tina were the only ones who knew that Nathan was in my house when the aforementioned accident happened. I was planning on them being the only two people in possession of that little gem of knowledge since the town's rumor mill had been running relentlessly, and the intricacies of the truth had been lost along the way.

Because I was flustered, exhausted, in a lot of pain and generally off-kilter, my body didn't recognize the change in atmosphere when he walked through the door. In fact, I didn't even know he was there until I looked up from the cash register to see him standing right in front of me.

Kip was also there, though I paid no mind to him.

I couldn't. Not when Rowan's eyes found mine.

For the life of me, I couldn't tell what his expression or posture might've been in the seconds before I lifted my head and presented my bruised face to him.

Usually, those eyes were warm, inviting. But seeing them right then, I couldn't believe that they were capable of being anything but two glittering holes of fury.

The phrase, 'if looks could kill' was rather trite and cliché, but I couldn't think of anything else. Sure, I was still standing, and my heart was still beating, meaning the look he gave me didn't literally cause me to drop dead, but it would've made me take a step back... If I hadn't been frozen in place.

"Who did this to you?" Rowan's nostrils flared, his jaw was set in a rigid line.

I blinked at him, unnerved at the pure menace in his tone. I knew this guy could be dangerous—that was communicated by his muscles, his size and the general way he carried himself—but being presented with it were two different things.

My hand went to the spot he was glaring at on reflex. It shook. His eyes widened at my shaking hand, so I quickly yanked it back down to my side.

"No one," I squeaked. "I just... walked into a cabinet." It was the truth. Leaving out some important details and one important asshole, but the truth, nonetheless.

A truth that Rowan, apparently, wasn't buying.

He made this known by rounding the counter in a handful of quick, powerful strides and advancing on me. I was entirely unprepared for him to break the barrier between us and come into my space, therefore, I didn't have time to escape.

I didn't have anywhere to escape to anyway since the espresso machine was directly behind me which I hadn't thought about until my back slammed into it.

Rowan didn't stop, his hand grasping my upper arm in a firm, purposeful but not painful grip before he began to drag me toward the kitchen.

Or he would've had I not let out a little whimper of pain.

You see, the grip itself would not have been painful had I not had bruises on the exact spot he gripped. But I did. Therefore, the whimper I couldn't control.

The whimper that stopped Rowan dead in his tracks and made him let go of my arm like it had burned him. His eyes zeroed in on the spot that was thankfully covered by cashmere. Delicate cashmere that thankfully could not be dissolved by the fury in his gaze.

I froze, unable to stop staring at him, unable to say anything. Rowan was quiet for a moment too. It seemed the entire bakery held its breath.

Well, until his palm landed on my lower back—feather light, barely there, yet I could've sworn the imprint of it seared into my skin—and gently guided me to the kitchen.

I let myself be guided because I didn't know what else to do. Because it seemed the safest option, away from all of the spectators. I was not used to being the focus of town gossip, and I knew the black eye plus this interaction with Rowan would have people talking about me for days.

The kitchen was my safe space. And here he was in it. All large, imposing and furious.

"Take off your sweater," he said quietly. He may as well have roared it for the impact it had. Although his tone was velvet smooth, it was threaded with pure fury. The fury that shone in his eyes, that made the cords of his neck stand out, made his hands fist at his sides.

It was the fury that should've had me shrinking into a tiny, terrified ball. Not just because of last night but because of who I was as a person in general. Skittish. Afraid of most things. Anxious to submit to most situations.

But inexplicably, I folded my arms across my chest, jutted my chin upward and narrowed my eyes at him. "No," I snapped.

He blinked slowly, once, regarding me. The fury did not dissipate, not in the slightest. The air seemed to vibrate with it. "Nora." My name came out through clenched teeth. "Take off the fucking sweater."

It was the first time he'd said my name. And although he was doing the whole intimidating, alpha male thing, the thing that should've turned off the staunch feminist in me, it made my fingertips tingle. And not entirely unpleasantly.

"Rowan," I seethed right back. "Do not order me to take off pieces of clothing like you have the right to."

His body jerked. "Oh, I have the fucking right," he said, voice low.

My knees trembled of their own volition.

"You have a black eye." He motioned to my face.

"I'm aware," I told him.

"A black eye," he repeated as if I hadn't spoken. "And because this town is a huge fucking gossip mill, I know that yesterday was the day you were supposed to marry that piece of shit."

The venom in which he referred to Nathan surprised me. As I had mentioned, Nathan was not well liked. And I definitely didn't think he was the kind of guy Rowan would ever hang out with. But I didn't think he knew him well enough to speak with such passion.

Apparently, he did.

"Yesterday, when I saw you, that perfect skin was flawless," Rowan continued, voice threatening, posture tight. "Today, the day after your scheduled wedding day, that perfect skin is marred. And you just yelped in pain when I touched you. Which leads me to believe that that," he nodded to my face, "is not your only bruise."

"I did not yelp," I argued, my mind still processing what he said about my perfect skin and the tone in which he'd said it.

Rowan pinched the bridge of his nose, taking a long, audible breath before speaking. "You take off the sweater, or I'm calling the station and gettin' Finn down here to take your statement."

I worked to swallow the lump that had formed in my throat. "My statement?"

He nodded once. The gesture was violent.

"I don't need to make a statement," I whined. "Nothing happened."

Panic had begun crawling up my throat. The thought of police coming here, into my beautiful bakery, my safe space, forcing me to talk about what I was trying my best to repress... Forcing all the attention on me, then onto Nathan whose mother would make it her life's mission to ruin me if I marred her perfect son's perfect reputation any further made me want to faint.

"Those are your options," Rowan shrugged, not taking his eyes off me. "Either you take off your sweater, or I get the cops down here."

"This is insane," I hissed. "You can't march in here and give me ultimatums."

Rowan didn't say anything. He just kept staring.

He wasn't touching me or restraining me in any way. I was well within my power to turn around and walk away. There was a whole bakery of people within yelling distance, my best friend being one of them. And Tina, I knew, would not hesitate to go head-to-head with Rowan if she thought I was being threatened in any way.

But I wasn't being threatened.

That I knew.

In spite of his anger—which had become a physical thing—in spite of our huge size discrepancy, even in spite of his commands, I knew that Rowan would not hurt me. This thought did not have evidence to back it up, yet I knew it just the same.

"If I take off my sweater, you're not allowed to call the police," I informed him for reasons unknown.

Rowan's jaw stiffened, and there was a long pause before he finally nodded.

I slowly took off my sweater, bunching it in my hands, suddenly feeling very uncomfortable and small under his gaze.

What I was expecting when he saw the bruises, I didn't

know. Maybe some kind of outburst. Swearing. More of the glowering, the glittering fury. But none of that came.

Instead, an impossibly gentle, barely there touch ghosted over the skin of my upper arms.

My body electrified under that touch. I was frozen as he delicately trailed the spots where Nathan had grabbed me.

One of those fingers found their way to my chin, tilting it upward so I was no longer staring at the sweater bunched in my hands. My eyes got lost in his.

"Tell me what happened, cupcake," he murmured softly.

Not that furious soft like before. Just plain soft.

He called me cupcake.

His fingers were still brushing my upper arms. His eyes were melty, warm... safe.

There was no other option but to tell him everything that had happened.

Those eyes didn't stay soft once I explained everything. Actually, they hardened the second I said Nathan was inside my house when I got home, then turned to stone when I said the rest.

But his hands stayed on me. The grip never tightened. Not even a little. His fury did not leech onto my skin.

The fury that needed to be explained. He didn't know me. Not beyond the scant interactions we'd had. Yet he was there, touching me in a way that could only be described as intimate. Calling me cupcake. Making my insides liquefy.

"You're gonna stay here," he said once I was done. "Gonna finish out your day. Not gonna do that alone." He jerked his head to where the counter was. "Your spitfire Australian friend is gonna stay. Probably Tina too. I'm gonna come back, either here or your house."

That was a lot of information. A lot of orders. Orders that

made no sense for a litany of reasons, the most of which being I did not believe that a man had a right to order a woman around. Ever.

And because Rowan and I were practically strangers.

There were questions to be asked. Arguments to be had. Lectures to be made on feminism and the rights afforded to me as a strong woman and human being who was his equal.

Yes, all of those things needed to be said.

But I didn't say them. I blinked at him dreamily then said, "'Kay."

Rowan's eyes went melty again.

He did not move. His fingers were still gently brushing my arm, my chin cradled in his other hand. His delicious scent was imprinting all over me, and I was either having a mini stroke or a mini orgasm... Maybe both.

A moment, thick with tension and tenderness, hovered over us.

"Rowan," I said in not much more than a whisper.

"Yeah, cupcake?"

"What is this?"

His mouth turned upward ever so slightly before he leaned in and kissed me gently on the forehead. When he pulled back, our faces were inches apart.

My heart thrummed.

"This," he murmured, eyes glued to mine, "is the beginning of us."

Then he just turned and walked away.

ROWAN

"Kip," I barked, striding out from behind the counter. I ignored everyone staring at me, though Tina's sharp gaze was hard to ignore. That woman scared me more than any man could. It was clear that she was protective over Nora, which made me happy. And it was also clear that, if she wanted to, she could fuck up whomever she decided to. She could fuck up Nathan with her eyes closed. I would've put money on the fact that she was planning something at that coffee machine.

She got one look at my face then back to where I'd dragged Nora into the kitchen, obviously formed some kind of conclusion about what I was doing, then she nodded. In approval, I assumed.

Kip jumped up from where he'd been leaning his elbows on the bar, probably trying to flirt with the Australian who wanted nothing to do with him. The Australian who was also giving me a sharp, protective stare.

The stares from the two women comforted me since I knew both of them loved Nora and would look out for her.

"We're goin'," I snapped at him.

Kip, to his credit, instantly got my vibe and did not try to argue with me or question me until we got in the truck.

Though there was a low thundering in my ears and a fire burning through my body, I'd managed to lock down the worst of my fury.

"Where we goin'?" he asked.

I looked to my best friend. "We're going to fuck up the piece of shit who laid hands on my woman."

CHAPTER
FIVE

Recipe: Chocolate Chip Cookies

From 'Dessert Person'

NORA

I was pretty much useless at the bakery for the rest of the day. Luckily, there wasn't much of the day left, and both Tina and Fiona could run the place in their sleep. They were more than happy for me to putter away in the kitchen, making chocolate chip cookies to calm my nerves.

I had a recipe for every situation, every ill, every season. But my browned butter, sea salt, chocolate chip cookies—made with three kinds of chocolate: dark, semi-sweet and milk—were my default. Though even the cookies—the three batches—didn't work their usual magic.

The tequila shot that Fiona forced me to pound once Rowan had left helped a little but wore off by the time we'd closed the bakery.

Rowan was not back. I didn't know if he was even going to come back. I had no idea what he was doing. No idea why he was doing it. My mind kept running over everything he'd said, the fury, the way he'd looked at me. And most importantly, his parting phrase.

"This is the beginning of us."

The words bounced around in my head over and over, making me feel warm, jittery and absolutely freaked out all at once.

The thought of going home—to my lovely, clean, quiet house —was not enticing in the slightest... I'd be alone with my thoughts, and then I'd probably try to take down the ceiling fan in order to clean it or something equally crazy.

Luckily, I didn't have to face that because I had a best friend named Fiona. A best friend who had, without asking, followed me home, linked her arm with mine and walked into my house with me, chattering about anything and everything under the sun, not giving me a moment of silence.

She went to my speaker system and hooked up her phone to it, the sounds of Fleetwood Mac filtering through my house. Fiona had a knack for knowing which band, which song, was required for any situation. Kind of like me with baked goods. And I never could have known that Stevie Nicks singing "Landslide" was the exact thing I needed to calm my nerves, but Fiona did.

"You get the wine, I'll get the glasses." She nodded at my wine fridge.

The dining table was made of reclaimed wood, rustic and perfect with an antique chandelier hanging over it and pink backed, vintage, French chairs surrounding it. The faded pink rug underneath it covered dark hardwood floors—the original hardwood floors, of course.

Thankful to have a task, I did exactly as she said, picking a bottle from the fridge, going through the process of opening it, and throwing the cork into the large glass vase that was sitting on a shelf in my bar. The vase was filled with other corks. Any time anything big was happening in my life—good or bad—I saved the cork from whatever bottle of wine I was drinking to either deal with or celebrate that life event.

I liked the ritual of it, collecting moments in my life. Both to learn from and to relish in. I wasn't quite sure what the events of today would mean, but I knew for certain that they were pivotal. That this was a day to be remembered. This was, as Rowan said, the beginning of something.

I felt giddy just thinking about his tone, the look in his eyes when he uttered those words.

Fiona had gotten two glasses out and put them on the counter.

"No, those are Pinot glasses," I told her. "This is a French Burgundy. You need those glasses." I pointed to the Burgundy glasses on the second shelf.

Fiona stared at me with a blank look on her face, two glasses dangling from her fingers.

"You are such a fucking grown woman," she groaned after a beat, returning the glasses to the cabinet. "I mean, different glasses for red wine?" She shook her head. "And fancy ass glasses too." She held one up in appreciation, twirling it in the light. "I drink my wine from teacups, water glasses or a vase in a pinch."

I laughed, taking the glasses and pouring from the decanter.

"I swear, you make me feel like I'm twelve years old," she muttered, taking her glass and sitting in the window alcove, settling amongst the cushions that had taken me six months to find.

"You have fancy cushions that probably cost you a hundred dollars a pop." She fingered the fringe on them.

I took a sip of my wine, settling beside her. More like two hundred a pop... Not that I would tell her that. I was slightly ashamed that I'd spent that much money on pillows. Then I reminded myself that I'd worked fricking hard to be able to spend two hundred dollars on pillows and not bat an eyelash. I'd spent years counting every penny I spent, living in a crappy apartment that smelled of mold. Then more years living in a construction zone as I slowly did this house up. I had my own bakery that made a lot of money, after two years of barely breaking even. Not to mention the childhood with empty cupboards, electricity being shut off, different houses every six months, clothes that were always two sizes too small, shoes with holes in them.

Yes, I deserved the pillows. The expensive hand soap in the glass bottle, the rugs, the six different kinds of wine glasses, the French Burgundy.

I'd sacrificed my twenties for my dream home, for my successful business, for security. Financial and otherwise. Because I was yearning for something else, something more, I let myself pretend I was falling in love with a man who was completely wrong for me. Because I desperately wanted to be a mother and wife, I'd said yes to that man when he presented me with a ring that said nothing about the person I was, showing me that he had not thought about me when picking it, merely what people would say when they saw it.

Luckily, I didn't let myself dwell on that. For too long, at least.

My thoughts strayed from Nathan to Rowan. Who was doing God knew what. He said he was going to come back. To what end, I did not know.

"Today was... a lot," I said, taking a huge gulp of my wine.

Fiona was regarding me. "One way to put it."

"I mean, let's not even talk about the drama with Nathan last night," I continued, taking yet another large sip. "But then Rowan got all..." I trailed off, thinking about the way his face had tightened in fury, the searing heat on my skin where he'd touched me. I blinked rapidly so I wouldn't get lost in that memory. "I don't even know how to describe all of that," I shrugged. "But it was too much. It makes absolutely no sense."

Fiona scrutinized me. "No sense?"

I nodded, watching the wine swirl in my glass.

"Yeah, he doesn't even know me. And the few times he's spoken to me, I've been taking his order or you know, blabbering on about *Yellowstone* sounding like I need to be medicated." Embarrassment from that memory still burned hot.

Fiona didn't reply right away, she just studied me, her lips pursed together, her eyes squinting in focus. "You're being serious."

My body should've been feeling light and relaxed as I'd drained my first glass of wine, but that wasn't the case. I was still tense. Strung out. Especially with Fiona looking at me like that, without humor, with an intensity that wasn't exactly characteristic for the normally lighthearted woman.

"Yes, I'm being serious," I told her, getting up to retrieve the decanter from the bar. I'd left it over there like some kind of rookie, trying to lie about the volume of wine I would need to process the events of today. And last night.

"Oh, for fuck's sake," she sighed the second I sat down, refilling both of our glasses.

Her harsh tone surprised me, as did her skeptical gaze.

"Now, sweetie, I love you," she said, taking the glass. "I adore you. All of your quirks and your weirdness only make you a more incredible person. One of the most incredible people I know."

"You're saying a lot of nice things but in a mean tone," I

informed her, leaning back against the cushions, chugging more wine in an effort to relax.

I wasn't in the habit of chugging wine. Especially expensive bottles of Bordeaux.

Fiona tilted her head, scrutinizing me. "Well, I think you need some tough love," she hiked up a shoulder, her tone not gentle but not quite harsh either. "I never liked Nathan."

"Shocker," I muttered.

"I know I didn't hide it that well, but I also managed not to punch him in the face."

I bobbed my head in affirmation. "You did manage that."

"I tried. My best. Even though I hated the way he treated you. Hated that he magnified all of your insecurities, that he erroneously confirmed to you all of the bad things you thought about yourself. That you still carry that. That you're still blind to how wonderful you are." Her eyes flickered over me. "That you don't realize what a fucking babe you are."

"You have to say that, you're my best friend," I told her, giving her a playful shove.

"I do not." Her eyes rolled toward the back of her head. "Maybe because I'm your best friend, and I love you unconditionally, I'm biased. But everyone sees it." She pointed at me. "You don't. You don't realize that every single man in this town would jump over their grandmother's corpse to get a date with you."

I screwed up my nose, wincing at the pain that came from the gesture. I did not like that visual, nor did I agree with it. But it was definitely dangerous to argue with Fiona right then.

"I see you don't believe what I'm saying," she tsked, showing that we were close enough that she could read my mind, or at least my facial expressions. Or she knew me well enough to understand I would not believe that every man in town wanted to date me.

Because every man in town wanted to date her.

"It's going to take a lot of work to unlearn the shit that Nathan reinforced inside of you. Shit that took root long before you left that fucker."

She took another sip.

I took a gulp.

"I have faith that you will learn just how beautiful you are, how hot you are." Fiona murmured. "How all of your weirdness only makes you more attractive." She was saying the nice things in a softer tone now. "And I know that you don't need a man to do that work. But..." She played with a loose thread on one of my expensive pillows that should not have a loose thread. "The muscular man who has been staring at you like a lovestruck teenager, who quite obviously finds your weirdness ridiculously cute, who wants to rip your clothes off and do very bad, very good things to you, and who is out there somewhere, defending your honor." She pointed in the direction of my front door, gesturing wildly. "Now I do not think that a woman needs a man to defend her honor."

She was on a roll now. Fiona talked fast and when she was on a roll there was no point in trying to stop her.

"A woman can defend her own honor. Or a woman can be without honor, if she likes it that way." She winked. "But even I think his caveman stuff was pretty damn hot. And I only experienced it secondhand."

"Yeah, it was pretty damn hot," I agreed, my body tightening when I realized what I'd said. "I'm not supposed to admit that, am I?" I cradled my glass against my chest. "I'm a strong woman. I hate toxic masculinity and the damsel in distress stuff." I put the heel of my hand to my forehead. "I'm a mess."

"We all are, baby," Fiona squeezed my knee. "But do not get yourself bent out of shape because for once in your life, someone wants to protect you without wanting anything in return." She considered that. "Well, I'm sure he wants things from you," she amended. "But things you will likely want too. And if you don't want them, then I'm sure he'll still do the defending of your honor thing because he just happens to be that kind of man."

I stared at my best friend, who was not known to mince words. But she also was not one to dole out that kind of truth. Not all in one go, at least. Throughout the duration we'd been friends, she had tried to chip away at my warped self-image, trying to make me believe in myself more.

And I had done a bunch of work on myself too. Work I was very proud of. But I was still weird, fucked-up, anxious and a result of the traumas of my past. No matter how much work I did, I'd always be a little eccentric and a lot anxious. I was okay with that. Or at least, I'd accepted that.

I opened my mouth to argue about one of the many things she'd said, especially the part about Rowan wanting something from me. In my own narrative, that made absolutely no sense. He was a strong, insanely handsome man who should not be interested in me.

But I wasn't completely blinded by my own neurosis. And I did remember the way he'd looked at me. The way he spoke to me. What he'd said before he walked out... Yes, he did want me. For whatever reason.

"It's scary," I admitted reluctantly.

Fiona nodded, her eyes soft. "It should be."

"Can we maybe take a break from talking about all of this and just listen to Stevie, watch the sun set and get a little tipsy?" I asked hopefully.

Fiona grinned. "Fuck yes, we can." She held her glass up to

me. "Only if we toast to you letting yourself feel happy that you've got a hot hunk of alpha out there doing shit for you because you're a hot piece of ass."

I sighed dramatically but held my glass up. Of course, she had to add that in there.

"To you," she said as crystal clinked together.

"To me."

* * *

LUCKILY, our conversation got lighter and veered away from childhood trauma and Fiona trying to change what I saw in the mirror. There was only so much a girl could take. Especially a not so mildly neurotic anxious mess such as me.

The wine helped. And the warm, comforting presence of my best friend.

I was almost back to normal when there was a booming knock on my door.

Okay, it was most probably a regular knock, but considering I had a really good idea of who was knocking on the door, it boomed. Through my head, at least.

I jumped at the sound, some of the wine escaping from my glass as I put it down much harder than I needed to. I absently used the sleeve of my shirt to wipe the small amber puddle away.

"He's here," I whispered, standing quickly, staring down the hall in the direction of my front door.

Fiona stood too, but much more gracefully and without the look of terror I assumed was on my own face.

"He could be," she raised a shoulder.

"Who else would it be?"

"Amazon delivery guy, UPS guy, FedEx guy, serial killer who's finally chosen his moment to strike." She listed the options on her fingers.

I inhaled deeply, wondering if I would've preferred to take my chances with a serial killer than the man I thought it was.

"You have to answer the door," I told Fiona.

She winked at me. "I agree. I would be the cliché first victim of the serial killer on account of the blonde hair and big tits."

I didn't say anything. I was too busy having a mini freakout, convincing myself that I had bought a pair of expensive shoes last night and paid to have them delivered at nine o'clock at night. But I hadn't. Not last night, at least. I did not order a man either, but I would bet my—rather impressive—shoe collection that it was a man.

My man.

I frowned at that intrusive thought.

He was not my man.

"You're not going to answer the door, are you?" Fiona deduced.

I shook my head slowly.

She sighed dramatically but was still smiling. The bitch.

Not that much of a bitch though, because she turned around and walked down the hall. To answer the front door, I assumed.

CHAPTER
SIX

Recipe: Coffee Coffee Cake

From 'Dessert Person'

There was a ringing in my ears. My face still throbbed faintly, though the wine had taken most of the edge off. Thankfully.

I had an overwhelming need to run upstairs to my bedroom and curl up in a corner of the closet and hide behind my dresses.

Unfortunately, my feet wouldn't move. And despite my fear, despite the dryness in my mouth and the pit in my stomach, there was something else. A kind of excitement that made me feel like I wanted to vomit. I wanted to see him. Rowan. Craved the way I felt when his eyes were on me. Wanted to see him in my home, even though that meant that I would never not be able to imagine the space without him, and eventually have to move because I could not live with the ghost of a hulking, handsome man I was half in love with haunting me with what might've been.

But it was not a hulking, handsome man who walked down my hall.

No. It was a large brown blur whose nails clicked along my hardwood floor.

The dog did not jump up on me as its wagging tail and outstretched tongue made it seem like it might. No, it stopped right in front of me, sitting obediently and staring up at me with a smile on its face.

Now, I was aware that many people were of the opinion that dogs could not do things such as smile, but in my opinion, they were very wrong.

"Hi," I said to the dog.

Obviously, the dog, a chocolate lab, did not say hi back. Its tail thumped steadily on the rug, tongue continuing to sway as it tilted its head up at me.

I liked dogs. I had always liked dogs. And children. At somewhat of a distance. I knew I wanted both of them someday, but I'd never been in a situation to be up close and personal with either, so I wasn't quite sure how to act with them.

I had a small circle of friends, only three who I spent a lot of time with: Tina, Tiffany and Fiona. None of them had dogs or children.

I didn't have any contact with my family, apart from Ansel, and he did not have a child or a dog. And unfortunately, he lived thousands of miles away.

"You're very cute," I informed the dog, gingerly holding out my hand for it to smell. The dog sniffed it for a moment then rubbed its cheek against my palm, communicating what it would like me to do. I obliged, scratching its head and behind the ears. Its tail thumped harder.

I'd been so preoccupied with the dog and with petting it that I had not noticed its owner striding down my hall.

Not until two sock-clad feet stopped beside the paws of the dog.

"Maggie," the voice said, warm and hoarse at the same time.

I held my breath, concentrating on the socks for a moment more before wondering why he didn't have shoes on before I found the courage to look up at him.

Yep, it was Rowan standing in front of me. Not wearing any shoes. With his dog. He was still wearing worn jeans, a tight tee that accentuated his large, muscular biceps. His hat was on backward, his sexiness driving me insane.

"Her name." He motioned down to the dog I was petting. "Maggie."

I tried to figure out how this rugged, hulking alpha came to own an adorable and sweet chocolate lab called Maggie.

"She's cute," I said, my voice frustratingly thin and high.

"She likes you," he replied, eyes warm yet intense.

My shoulders felt strained, carrying the weight of that gaze. My heart thrashed in my chest then moved up into my throat.

Fiona was still here somewhere. I swear, her presence still lingered. But I had blinders on. All I could see was Rowan. And Maggie.

We didn't talk for a long moment. Or maybe it wasn't that long. Maybe it was only a handful of seconds. Time seemed to lose its meaning when I was in Rowan's presence.

"What are you doing here?" I finally asked.

"I'm stayin' here," he declared in a gruff tone.

My eyes would've popped out of my head if I were a cartoon character. Since I wasn't one, they just bulged in disbelief.

"What?" I stuttered, clutching my wine glass for dear life. It seemed as if the world had turned upside down in the space of one day. About thirty hours ago, I'd been making a 'dick of myself'—as Fiona would say, and aptly, might I add—in front of this man. Sure, he'd been friendly and almost flirty, but he was quite obviously being polite because I was the woman who made the croissants and had the fancy coffee machine. He enjoyed his croissants and fancy coffee.

Him humoring me and vaguely flirting made sense, then.

Him manhandling me—tenderly and in a way that inexplicably made my toes curl—stroking my skin gently, calling me 'cupcake' and then going off to presumably defend my honor did not make sense.

And him turning up at my house, with his dog, announcing that he was going to be staying in my house *certainly* did not make sense.

Rowan Derrick was in my house. Amongst all of my books, my cushions, my girly yet classy rugs and ornaments. My ceilings were high—with the gorgeous, original crown molding—yet somehow he looked too large for my open plan room. Like my entire house had shrunk with him in it.

"We're stayin'," he reiterated, looking down at the dog that was sitting obediently at his side. His eyes then went around the room, to my pink velvet sofa, the cream armchairs. "That's if you allow dogs in the house. Probably should've asked that first."

My mind was running at a hundred miles a minute, trying to catch up, trying to gauge how likely it was that I was having some kind of break from reality or extremely vivid dream. Maybe I'd been in a really bad car accident, and now I was in a coma.

I focused on the dog, who was tilting her head at me inquisitively. "Yes, I allow dogs in the house," I replied, still staring into those curious eyes. "I'm not a monster."

Somehow, my gaze had drifted up to his, where his eyes were... I hated to say sparkling, but there was no other word to describe them. Cue pebbled nipples and uncomfortable heat in my nether regions. Not uncomfortable bad, but uncomfortable because it was highly inappropriate to be experiencing that heat in front of a dog, my best friend and the object of my sexual fantasies.

"It's settled then."

Again, my eyes attempted to pop from my head. "It is not settled," I snapped, putting my hands on my hips. "There is absolutely no reason for you and your dog, no matter how adorable..." I stifled the groan inching up my throat, "I mean the dog, *the dog* is adorable," I corrected quickly. "Despite that, there is no reason for either of you to stay here."

Rowan's gaze hardened as it focused on my eye, the throbbing part of my eye. "That right there is a reason."

I tilted my head to regard him, but not in the same way Maggie had. There was a little more hostility in my head tilt. "So, you're here to ensure that I don't run into any cabinets?" I asked dryly.

The twinkling in his eyes disappeared. "To ensure that the man who was responsible for the bruises on your arms and you running into a cabinet to get out of his grip doesn't return."

Though my body was still hot with... anger? Attraction? Confusion? A sliver of ice crept down my spine. I was not accustomed to feeling fear in my own home. I'd been staying in houses alone since I was five years old. Creaks and darkness and silence that only an empty house could provide did not scare me. Plus, I didn't let myself watch any scary movies, any true crime documentaries or pretty much anything that could bring all that kind of bad energy into my home.

But there was a thread of fear at Rowan's mention of Nathan. I would say he wouldn't hurt me, but there were bruises on my arms to contradict that statement. He wasn't taking no for an answer. Men who didn't take no for an answer were dangerous. And there was no limit to what those men might do to convince themselves that they could make a woman say yes.

"You seem like you're sorted here," Fiona said, jerking me out of my own head. I watched her drain her glass then walk it to the sink where she rinsed it.

"What are you doing?" I asked, a hysterical edge to my tone.

Yes, Rowan's presence in my house and his presence in general was unnerving to say the least. But Fiona was here. Fiona was my anchor to reality. My buffer. She was what I could cling to when things became too much.

Fiona could fill awkward silences. Fiona knew how to deal with really hot, ultra-masculine, hard-ass men.

Without Fiona, I was fucked.

She looked up from the sink at me then to Rowan then Maggie then back to me. And she smiled. She fucking smiled.

"I'm going home to listen to the new Taylor Swift album and eat an entire rotisserie chicken," she chirped.

"No, you're not!" I half shrieked.

"Yes, I am." Fiona's smile stretched wider before snatching her purse off the counter and winking at me.

Then she walked out.

Of my house.

Leaving me alone with Rowan.

And Maggie.

Maggie, although cute, did not provide an appropriate buffer and could not fill awkward silences that would quite obviously stretch their way into every corner of this house because... how was I meant to keep up any semblance of conversation when Rowan was in my house?

I stared in the direction of the front door, the one that had just opened and closed.

There was only so long I could mentally will Fiona to come back before I had to focus on the problem at hand. Being Rowan. And his dog. Well, the dog wasn't a problem. Actually, I was quickly falling in love. With the dog.

"You don't need to stay here," I told him when I'd found the strength to look in his general direction again. "I mean, it's very... I don't want to say polite because forcing yourself into my house for the night in order to protect me from cabinet doors isn't actually polite, it's more over the top, insane, and more than a tad misogynistic."

I folded my arms across my chest, annoyed enough now that I wasn't too scared to look him in the eyes.

The eyes that were twinkling once again.

And the twinkling made my breath hitch again. I'd never experienced so many conflicting emotions at one time before.

"A tad misogynistic?" he repeated, his voice no longer hard and scary. It was soft... like molasses.

I struggled to hold on to my anger. It was slipping through my fingers in response to his melty tone, twinkling eyes and his overwhelmingly masculine beauty. And the way his dog just sat at his side obediently.

I nodded with pursed lips. "Yes. Because you coming in here and saying you need to stay in my home because I couldn't possibly be able to stay in my home alone, me, a thirty-three-year-old woman who has lived on her own her entire adult life without sticking my fingers in any light sockets."

His lips twitched. Maggie, who was now obviously sick of this whole thing, abandoned her post at her master's side and padded over to my fireplace, plopping herself down in front of it like she owned the place.

I was momentarily distracted by the dog and the way she made my home feel... complete.

Yes, it was the dog, not the man who gave me that feeling.

I needed to get a dog.

"Maggie can stay," I decided, looking back at Rowan. "But you, sir, have to leave."

Rowan's lip was no longer just twitching. He was now smirking. I'd never seen him smirk. He looked really, *really* good smirking.

"Maggie goes where I go," he informed me.

"Everywhere you go?" I countered.

He nodded.

"But you work construction."

"I'm aware."

I let out a puff of air. "You cannot take a dog on a construction site."

"Tell that to Maggie," he replied. "She's been on site with me since she was a puppy."

"That's got to be against code."

"We really talkin' about construction code?" Rowan asked, obviously amused.

"No," I frowned. "We're talking about you. Not staying here. Nathan is not a problem."

All twinkling and smirking ceased. "He's not," he shifted his position. "I watched his taillights leave town limits less than an hour ago."

I blinked at him several times. "Excuse me?"

"Watched while he packed a bag then watched him get in his car and leave Jupiter."

I tried to digest all of these details.

"Wait, you drove him out of town?" I asked. "You literally *drove him out of town.*" It wasn't quite a question because the intensity in his eyes told me he wasn't bullshitting, nor did he strike me as a man prone to hyperbole.

Rowan hummed in agreement. His demeanor was still somewhat intimidating, with the tight shoulders, the stiff jaw, those stormy eyes. But there was no longer that simmering intensity that had taken over the bakery earlier today. That still lingered on my skin. Something else had replaced it. Something slightly softer but no less powerful.

"But Nathan's family has lived here for years," I spluttered. "They were some of the founders, if you believe his mother, which I do not."

Fiona and I were of the opinion that his family were the ones who likely pushed out the rightful settlers of this place—either with force or bribes... I thought it was the former—then buried the truth down deep in order to lord their power over everyone.

Rowan didn't respond to this. Not so much of a shrug of his shoulders. Nothing. Just that intense, unwavering stare.

"He's gone?" I repeated.

A nod.

Nathan had always been a big fish in a small pond. He'd spent all of the time we'd been together talking about how he was better than Jupiter. How this town was backward and stuck in the past, how the people were all small-minded idiots. I did not agree with him on any of that. Though I wasn't one to push back on much, I pushed back when he talked shit about the town that had become my home and the people who had become my family.

So, he didn't talk shit about the people in my presence. Not often, at least. But he had made it known that he was better. He always talked about moving to the city, to New York, L.A., where he could reach his full potential. Except I always knew he wouldn't because then he wouldn't be a big fish in a small pond. He'd be a tiny fish in a vast ocean. He wouldn't be the richest, the Ivy League educated, important—in his eyes, of course—person in town. He wouldn't be important at all. On some level, he knew this. Because he never left. He never would leave.

Except he did.

Tonight.

With Rowan following him.

"I'm struggling to digest this information," I informed him, turning back to my unfortunately empty glass in search of some relief.

Though it did give me something to do, and I was thankful for that. I was sure if I stayed under Rowan's stare for much longer, my feet would burn holes into my lovely, restored hardwood floor.

I gave Rowan a wide berth while walking to the bar where the decanter was. Such a wide berth that I slammed into my console table, almost knocking over a vase. It toppled for a couple of moments before righting itself once more. I mentally cursed my klutziness, especially considering my audience. I continued my journey to the bar, feeling Rowan's eyes hot on my back.

I focused on the act of opening the bottle of wine, not bothering with the decanter... There was no time.

My hands shook as the amber liquid splashed into my glass.

It occurred to me that I was feeling somewhat tipsy. Fiona and I had cracked into the bottle of wine as soon as we walked in the door. Normally, I would've arranged an extensive charcuterie board at the very least. But I was off-kilter. So, we'd polished off an entire bottle of wine between the two of us, without consuming anything to soak up the alcohol.

Therefore, I was tipsy.

When I turned around, Rowan was still standing where he'd been previously, except now he was facing in the other direction... Toward me. Eyes on me. He stood in the middle of my house, looking like something an ancient Greek or French artist might use to make a sculpture from.

"Although you are an uninvited guest, I cannot physically have you in my house without offering you a refreshment," I told him, my voice somewhat breathy. I didn't want it to be breathy because I wanted to be firm and adult-like, and sober.

But one could not be looked at the way Rowan was looking at me and not be breathy. Sober or not.

"So would you like a glass of wine?" I nodded to the bottle I just opened. "Though you don't exactly look like a guy that drinks wine," I squinted at him. "I've got a plethora of spirits... I could whip you up a cocktail. I don't have beer, unfortunately. And you look like more of a beer guy than a wine guy... or a cocktail guy."

Yes, Rowan was a beer guy. He could've been the face of any and all beer companies. He was what advertisers were trying to sell when they made beer commercials. Masculine. Rugged. The look of a guy who knew how to build furniture and eat pussy like a champ.

Fuck.

Why was I thinking about Rowan eating pussy?

Rowan didn't answer. Instead, he walked to the glass-fronted cabinet—the one responsible for my black eye—got out a glass —the correct one, it was important to point out— then walked back toward me.

I held my breath as he approached, my entire body stiffening. His eyes were intent on me, full of promises that shouldn't exist.

For a second, an extremely long one, I had the insane thought that he was going to kiss me.

But of course, he didn't. He brushed past me and picked up the wine bottle I'd just opened.

He was holding the bottle, inspecting the label. "This needs to be decanted," he observed, eyes flitting upward to me. "It's a good vintage."

I blinked rapidly. "It is a good vintage," I agreed, stunned that the rugged, masculine man knew what glass to use for what wine, and recognized a good vintage.

I stored that information away, clutching it internally.

His gaze lingered on mine before he poured it. The moment was incredibly surreal. Rowan here, pouring himself some wine, like it was natural. Like he did this every night.

I took a large swallow of my own wine, even though it likely wasn't the smartest decision given my current state of near inebriation.

"Can I offer you something to eat?" I asked, realizing that I was hungry. "I'm guessing that with all the returning to the early 1900s and running someone out of town, you probably worked up somewhat of an appetite." There was a bite to my tone now, I was proud to say.

Rowan did not bristle even the slightest at my tone. In fact, he smiled. It was more than a little unnerving. Not just because he was showing off white, straight teeth and the smile itself was really hot. It hit me that he'd smiled more in the past few minutes than he had in all the time I'd known him.

Granted, I only knew him insofar as how he liked his coffee and baked goods. Maybe he smiled all day, every day when he wasn't around me. But I didn't think so. He didn't come off as a cheerful guy. Some people might even go so far as to say he was a grump. Not in a bad way. But in a very sexy way.

Grumpy men were somehow more often than not regarded as broody, dangerous or mysterious.

Grumpy women were more often than not regarded as bitches.

"I have worked up an appetite," he replied. "But I'm happy just to order pizza. Don't want you runnin' around after me. Not after you've been working all day."

It made me feel warm, that line. No man I'd been with had ever considered what I'd done with my day prior to their arrival. They certainly didn't think whatever I'd done—be it opening a bakery or remodeling a house or working a double shift—meant that I wasn't able to fulfill my duty of serving them.

I had terrible taste in men, I realized.

"You are not ordering pizza," I gasped.

The smirk returned. I decided I loved the smirk. I decided that I wanted to have an oil painting commissioned in order to immortalize the smirk.

"I said order a pizza, not decide to cook Maggie," he scoffed.

I looked at the dog who was now snoring peacefully on the rug, horrified. "That is a gross visual."

"Well, the look on your face when I said I was going to order pizza was as bad as sayin' we were eating the dog," he said blandly.

"I might've shed almost all of the weird and horrible routines of my childhood," I explained. "I don't scrimp, or use coupons, I light candles for the mood, not because I have no other option." I nodded to my fireplace. "That is for décor, not because there's no heating. And I buy $200 pillows. But for whatever reason, I cannot bring myself to engage in the luxury of ordering in. Not when there's food in the pantry, in the fridge. A whole bunch of it."

I hadn't intended on saying all of that. I had intended on

just telling him that the one and only pizza place was likely closed by now. Or that George, the delivery driver, was probably much too stoned to drive all the way out here if they weren't closed.

But I didn't say that. I spewed a whole bunch of personal, embarrassing details about my background at him.

As a result, Rowan was no longer smiling.

Shit.

His features were tight, eyes blazing with seriousness, mouth a thin line.

Before he could say anything, or look at me with some kind of pity, I stomped over to the kitchen, placing my glass on the countertop so I could open my fridge and peruse.

My fridge was behemoth and immaculately organized. There were rows of various soft drinks and sparkling waters in glass bottles, organized by size. Glass bottles of homemade dressings were in the doors along with my homemade nut milk. I had three different kinds of butter: salted, unsalted and PDO Charente-Poitou Butter imported from France.

If you took a look in my refrigerator, you'd think I was organized and completely nuts with no social life to speak of. Which would be right.

"Grilled cheese," I decided, snatching up three kinds of cheese, mayo and butter.

Rowan had migrated from where he was standing to the kitchen. But not to perch on one of the barstools as was the norm for any visitor in my house. I cooked, arranged cheese boards and they watched. It was a rhythm. A comfortable rhythm, one I enjoyed. I loved people coming into my home, looking after them, feeding them.

Those dusty pink barstools had set me back a bomb, so I was glad I got my money's worth.

But Rowan did not follow the rhythm I had established in this kitchen. Of course, he didn't.

Rowan was there, right there when I closed the door of the fridge. So close that my body brushed against his before I knew what was happening. And before I could stop myself, I inhaled audibly, reveling in his clean, masculine scent.

Then I realized that I'd just *sniffed* this man, so I jumped back, arranging my ingredients on the counter before stepping back so I could get a chopping board and some fresh bread from the walk-in pantry.

My hand was shaking when I grabbed it.

Rowan was still there when I turned around.

"You need to sit over there." I pointed to the pink barstool.

Rowan did not look to where I was pointing. He continued to look at me. Which just wouldn't do. "Why do I need to sit over there?" he asked, his tone smooth. Deep.

I swallowed, battling both arousal and discomfort. "Because this is my kitchen, and I can't have a man in my kitchen."

He raised his brow. "Not very progressive of you."

I suppressed a groan. This man was infuriating and far too attractive for his own good.

"How are you suddenly in my life, demanding to stay the night and in my kitchen?" I demanded, folding my arms.

He didn't answer immediately. No, he just kept staring at me. No one stared at someone that long without speaking. Not unless they were about to rip their clothes off.

And Rowan wasn't about to rip my clothes off.

Was he?

Sweat beaded between my breasts.

No, a man like Rowan wasn't going to rip my clothes off when I got boob sweat whenever I got nervous. Or turned on. Which I was. Even though I was also terrified. But that good kind of terror. Like when you were on a rollercoaster and you knew that the restraints were most likely going to be effective.

But there was a tiny percent chance that they wouldn't be. That your ride would be the time that someone didn't fasten them correctly and you'd go tumbling to your death. But that was part of the fun, wasn't it? To get off and feel as if you'd cheated death.

"I'm in your life because I want to be in your life," Rowan answered, still not breaking his devastating eye contact. He took a step forward. A small one. But any closing of the distance between us caused my throat to constrict and the boob sweat to intensify.

"You tell me that you want me to leave, that you really want me to leave, and I will," he offered in a low, throaty voice.

My heart thundered. I had just been arguing with him about him being here. I'd been doing so passionately. But that was when Fiona was here as somewhat of a buffer. That was before he started staring like he did and talking to me in a tone that was like melted chocolate.

Say it, I urged myself. *The chance of falling with him is a fuck of a lot more likely than on a rollercoaster.*

I opened my mouth. "I need to make the grilled cheese," I said instead of telling him to leave like I should've.

For one, terrible, glorious moment, I thought he might not give me the space to make the grilled cheese.

But then he stepped back. I let out a breath of relief. Or disappointment. I couldn't tell which.

"I want to help." His voice was rough now.

"I need you to be over there." I pointed to the barstools. "Because I just... I need you to be over there. I have been through *a lot* in the past twenty-four hours."

Rowan pursed his lips, frowning at me for just a moment

before he strode around the island to sit on the barstools. My heartbeat did not slow down with the giant slab of quartz between us.

But it slowed enough to make the grilled cheese.

Rowan Derrick was in my house.

It was insane.

But what was even more insane was how natural it felt.

How right.

CHAPTER
SEVEN

Recipe: French Hot Chocolate

W e didn't speak for a while as I arranged our sandwiches then got my cast iron pan from where it hung on a hook over the gas range.

My kitchen was an adorable mix between modern and rustic, leaning toward a farmhouse look with the mixture of pots and pans hanging above the stove, merging with my more eccentric style—the pink barstools, the brushed brass fixtures and the large vases of flowers on each surface.

"What will Maggie have?" I asked, breaking the silence. "I don't have dog food."

I mentally told myself to pick up some dog food. Then I mentally chastised myself for thinking about picking up dog food. Picking up dog food was working under the assumption that there would be a dog here to eat it. I was not planning on getting a dog—though Maggie's presence seemed to complete the house and was making me seriously consider it—and there was no reason for me to get dog food unless I was going to get a dog.

Maggie would not be having another sleepover here.

Because her master would not be having another sleepover here.

"I could whip her up some scrambled eggs," I offered, forcing away those thoughts. "Or I've got tuna in the pantry. I'm sure that will be good for her. Choline and omega three."

"She's got food," Rowan said quietly, an indescribable look on his face. His features had softened, but his eyes flared with something I couldn't decipher. "It's in the truck. Came prepared."

I tugged on my lip. He'd come prepared. Ready to stay the night here. After he ran Nathan out of town.

I didn't think about the Nathan part. I couldn't. It was too huge and confusing.

"Why didn't you bring it in?" I asked him.

He tilted his head. The gesture was overwhelming in and of itself. That coupled with his nearness and general presence in my home was more than I could take.

"Didn't want to seem presumptuous," he said with a straight face.

I stared at him then let out a giggle. Then another.

He watched me with that same tilt to his head.

"You didn't want to seem presumptuous," I repeated amongst my giggles.

He nodded.

"But walking into my house and announcing you were staying here was... subtle?" I asked, putting a hand on my hip.

Rowan was smiling now.

I didn't like it.

Or actually, I did. Which was the problem.

"Are you going to get your dog's food and let me finish our dinner?" I asked him with faux impatience.

What I needed was space to take a breath that didn't smell like him.

For one heart-stopping second, I didn't think he was going to give me that respite since he just kept staring at me. And for the second time tonight, I was sure he was going to kiss me.

But he didn't.

He put his wine down on the counter and walked around me to retrieve the dog food.

He was going to stay.

As was Maggie.

* * *

THE REST of the night passed in something resembling harmony.

Not *complete* harmony.

Because I was still freaking out on the inside, my foundation cracked. I was hyper-aware of my every movement, my every breath, the way that I was eating, walking, sipping my wine. The wine buzz helped me a little with that self-consciousness. Enough so I could get through our meal of grilled cheese without choking.

Maggie had happily chomped away at her own food. Especially after I topped it with a can of tuna.

Rowan had regarded that with a raised brow before I'd gone on what could only be called a rant about the chemicals they put in food—even dog food—and that we needed to adjust Maggie's diet so she could live a long and happy life.

At the end of my rant, I realized I'd overstepped my bounds by judging the food he fed his dog and insinuating that it was any of my business.

Rowan did not seem bothered at all, though. He had a soft, intense, vaguely amused and incredibly handsome expression on his face.

At that point, I focused on my wine and my sandwich, which turned out to be an incredible combination.

Rowan had sat directly beside me at the breakfast bar with his own two sandwiches. We were close. So close that his thigh actually brushed against mine a couple of times. I'd stiffened, the sandwich pausing on its journey to my mouth before I forced myself to act chill. Or as chill as someone like me could manage.

Once I was done, I shot up to do the dishes. Or tried to. Rowan took them from me, standing much too close once more. "Cook doesn't do the dishes," he said, voice low and thick.

"I don't mind doing the dishes," I whispered.

"Didn't ask you if you minded," he replied, taking the plates from my hands. But he didn't walk to the sink immediately. Didn't even move. He just stood there, the plates between us. "You make a kickass grilled cheese, cupcake," he murmured.

I looked down at the plates, no longer able to hold his penetrating gaze. I did make a kickass grilled cheese.

"Thanks," I responded in a small, shaky voice.

At that, he stepped backward and moved to the sink. I watched the muscles of his back move underneath his tee, hypnotized. I was overcome with the need to walk up behind him and reach my fingers underneath that tee and trace every one of his muscles with my fingertips.

I quickly shook away those thoughts, reminding myself that would make an already complicated situation that much more complicated.

Instead of doing what almost every instinct in my body was telling me to do, I just sat back on the barstool and watched him work. Normally, I wouldn't do something like that. I would've grabbed my phone, a book, any instrument of distraction that I could hide behind. But I had a good amount of wine in me at that point and a male specimen who redefined the word handsome, so I just stared at him. In my kitchen. Doing dishes.

When he was done, he wiped his hands on a kitchen towel and turned back around.

I think I fell half in love with him right then, standing in my kitchen, drying his hands on my kitchen towel.

"You're not going to leave, are you?" I asked in a sigh.

"No way in fuck," he said, not on a sigh. I would say it was closer to a growl. Up until that very moment, I hadn't thought men actually growled things. I thought it was creative license taken by some of my favorite romance authors. And I loved it. In fiction.

Because I had not encountered such a thing in real life. Until that moment.

And it was safe to say I *adored* it in real life.

"I have the guest bedroom made up," I whispered, my voice shaking. What I really wanted to say was that he could sleep in my room. The words got stuck in my throat, though, too gnarled with fear.

I got off the barstool without any kind of grace. But I didn't fall down, at least.

"I'll show you," I said quickly, almost running out of the room.

I didn't look back to see if he was following, I knew he was from the low thump of his feet against my floor and the tap of Maggie's nails.

Though I didn't think you could 'feel' someone checking you

out, I couldn't help but think Rowan's eyes were focused on my ass.

Until I tripped over a step.

"Woah, you okay?"

His hands were at my hips, and his heat behind me nearly knocked me over. Yet he was behind me, and something instinctual in me told me this was a man who wouldn't let me fall.

"Fine," I rasped out.

He didn't let me go. Not immediately. We lingered there, his hands on my waist. We might've lingered there a lot longer if Maggie hadn't whined in protest from somewhere behind me.

We were caging the poor pooch on the stairs.

That got me moving. Once free, Maggie brushed past me and waited at the top of the stairs for both of us, tail wagging.

I scratched her head on the way past, walking to the guest room on unsteady legs.

The floor lights lit up with motion, the sconces on the walls already on. Photos from the past five years lined the walls in the hallway in a mishmash of vintage frames. Me outside the bakery, before it was redone, posing with the 'sold' sign. Various group shots of Tina, Tiffany, Fiona and me. Ansel was in a few from when he came to visit. It was my very curated timeline of my life with large chunks noticeably missing. Namely my entire childhood.

I didn't know whether Rowan was inspecting them or not because I didn't look back. I didn't trust myself to.

The guest bedroom was beside my study and had a window that looked onto my vast property before the rugged seaside took over.

I'd taken great care in outfitting it in the same kind of elevated, vintage style as the rest of my house.

"So, there's a bathroom in here." I walked in, switching the light on, checking that it was appointed with towels even though I knew it was.

The walk-in shower was tiled in forest green slate. The waterfall showerhead was brushed brass as were all the fixtures.

"Extra toothbrushes in here." I opened the cabinet in the vanity, pointing to the toothbrushes, still in their packages along with various mini versions of my favorite toiletries. All manner of things a person sleeping over at my house might need.

I liked to be a good host. Liked to separate myself from my childhood as much as I possibly could.

On that thought, I slammed the cabinet shut and walked out of the bathroom, moving to switch on the lamp that sat on top of the bedside table.

"TV." I pointed to the large armoire against the wall. "Inside there. Remote in the drawer." I patted the bed with the plush green, velvet comforter and ornate brass headboard. "Fresh sheets. Everything you might need, I guess."

I was so entrenched in going through my hostess motions—or maybe I was clinging to them so I didn't have to focus on Rowan—that I hadn't realized the way he was looking at me.

His hands were clenched by his sides, so tightly the cords in his forearms were protruding. His posture was rigid, tight. The expression on his face could only be described as hungry.

Ravenous.

And I was the feast he was craving.

My fingers bit into the inside of my palms. Need thrummed in between my legs.

"Nora," he ground out my name as if he were grappling for control. "You need to get out of this room right now."

My knees shook. I stayed rooted in place. "Why?" I asked in a low whisper.

He swallowed. Visibly swallowed. I watched his Adam's apple bob with the motion.

"Because I'm in a room with you. Where there's a bed." He nodded to the bed in question. "Because your cheeks are flushed, because I've been dreaming of what your lips taste like. Because I can barely fuckin' control my need to claim them. Taste you."

Holy. Fuck.

Did he just say that?

Yeah, he just said that. All of that. I was sure I was having some kind of out of body experience.

I stepped forward on shaky legs.

Rowan's body visibly stiffened even more at my approach. His jaw was granite.

"Nora," he warned.

His low rasp was like fucking catnip to me.

What I was intending as I continued to approach him, I wasn't sure. I was not the initiator. I did not have sexual confidence. Sure, I harbored a lot of fantasies where I did have sexual confidence. Where I was unafraid to take charge, to let myself believe I was desirable to any and all men.

But I'd never put those fantasies into practice. I'd never been with a man who made me feel safe enough to explore that part of myself. Not with any of my long-term boyfriends. Especially not with the man I had agreed to marry.

But Rowan... The man I'd barely said boo to prior to the past forty-eight hours... he made me feel that way. Desirable. Powerful. The man looked like he could shatter from the force it was taking him not to claim me.

"You don't need to control anything," I told him, stopping inches from him. My bare toes almost touched his socks.

He straightened his stance, appearing even stiffer now. If it were possible for a man to turn to stone, I think he might've then and there. But he was flesh and blood and intoxicating.

"You can taste me," I invited, licking my lips.

A vein in Rowan's neck pulsated. His brows were bunched together, and I could see him gritting his teeth from my very close vantage point.

"Fuck," he ground out. "You're makin' it really fuckin' hard for me to do the honorable thing."

I grinned, going up on my tiptoes so our lips were almost touching. "What if I want you to do the dishonorable thing?" My voice was almost unrecognizable. Sultry even.

And it was working. I could see it in the way Rowan's expression went from hard, controlled to something else entirely.

Something primal. A man getting ready to claim a woman.

My body hummed with expectation and need.

I closed my eyes, preparing for the kiss and whatever else came after it.

But instead of hands grabbing my neck, waist or ass, instead of lips crashing against mine, Rowan's hands went to my shoulders, firmly and purposefully pushing me back. He wasn't gripping me hard enough to hurt, but the sting of rejection was more excruciating than anything else.

My muscles coiled with the need to run, fight or flight mode engaged.

But Rowan's hands were still on my shoulders, holding me in place. He was frowning at me, and the tears that were filling my eyes.

I cursed myself for not being in control of them. My body's first response to almost anything was tears. Anger. Frustration. Rejection.

It was bad enough to try to seduce a man and fail, but to have him see you cry after that failure was something else entirely.

Rowan raised one of his hands in order to wipe a tear from my cheek with his thumb.

"This is possibly the most embarrassing moment of my life," I croaked. "Beating out the time that I ran into a screen door at Jasmine Floyd's party in tenth grade and everyone, including the boy I liked, laughed at me."

"That can stay at the top. This is not embarassin'."

"I tried to be sexy yet failed." I was sobbing now, blubbering like a fool with snot running from my nose and everything. "And now I'm crying. Trust me, it's embarrassing."

"You did not fail at bein' sexy," Rowan grumbled. "You're sexy by fuckin' breathing. And I should be getting some kind of medal for resisting you right now." The way he looked at me stopped the tears. "I'm hard as a fuckin' rock right now, Nora. I'm gonna go to sleep tonight thinking 'bout what it would be like if I was a slightly worse man. If I was the man who took advantage of the woman he's been wanting for years when she's had too much wine, when she's wearing a bruise another man put there."

I opened my mouth to argue about that minor detail since Nathan didn't technically put the bruise there. But Rowan's finger drifted to my mouth to silence me.

"Not gonna let you defend him, cupcake," he said softly. "And he's not gonna be in this moment." He tucked some hair behind my ear. "This isn't rejection, Nora. This is me being greedy, wanting you to have all of your faculties... The first time we fuck, at least." His lips hovered inches from my mouth. "Some time after that, I will gladly watch you drink wine, knowing that I'll be getting this later." His hand ghosted down the side of my body in a barely-there touch.

"Now go," he whispered. "Before I forget every fuckin' thing I just said."

The restraints on my rollercoaster creaked, and though part of me wanted them to fail, I held on tight. Meaning I turned on my heel and walked out of the room.

CHAPTER
EIGHT

Recipe: Chocolate Buttermilk Cake

From 'Dessert Person'

I expected him to be asleep when I entered the kitchen. Most everyone in this time zone who didn't work the night shift somewhere was still asleep before five in the morning. That was part of the magic.

It was *usually* magic, at least. Not when I'd spent the night tossing and turning, knowing that Rowan was in a bed not three doors down from me. In my house. Beneath my sheets.

Naked.

Well, I couldn't be *sure* that he slept naked. But he didn't come prepared, and I seriously doubted that he was going to sleep in jeans.

So, he was likely wearing underwear.

Or nothing.

I didn't think he was a briefs type of guy. Maybe boxers. Or at the least boxer briefs. And he definitely wasn't wearing a shirt. That meant my sheets were going to smell like his torso. The torso that was likely as chiseled as the rest of him.

I had wondered, for the majority of the night, exactly what he was wearing in that guest bedroom. Then I'd wondered what he would be wearing if he weren't in the guest bedroom. If he wasn't so fucking honorable and had carried me to my bedroom as I had longed for him to do.

I replayed his words in my head over and over again. There were a lot to replay.

"You're sexy by fuckin' breathing."

"This is me being greedy, wanting you to have all of your faculties... The first time we fuck, at least."

"If I was the man who took advantage of the woman he's been wanting for years."

Years.

He said he'd been wanting me for years. That might've taken up more real estate in my head if I were thinking logically. But I wasn't. I was overcome by desire. Maddened by it.

My need was almost uncontrollable. I was totally preoccupied. Incredibly turned on. I needed a release. Badly. But I didn't reach into my bedside table for my vibrator, though it was extremely tempting.

I was too worried the gentle hum of the vibrator would carry, then he'd hear me. Which was impossible, really. The low hum would have to carry through my comforter, my closed door, down the hall and through his closed door. Every wall in this house had been reinsulated. I'd seen to it myself. Noise didn't carry the way it used to in old houses.

I could quite easily have given myself the relief my body sorely needed, and Rowan would've been none the wiser.

Except I hadn't. For whatever reason.

So, I had barely slept. And although I'd showered and put on clothes for the day, I was no less awake.

My goal was coffee. A lot of it.

Because I had a one-track mind, and I was pretty much a zombie when I descended the stairs, I didn't notice that the kitchen lights were on, and the aroma of coffee beans was filtering through the air.

Not until I walked into the kitchen.

And saw Rowan.

Not asleep.

And unfortunately, not naked. He was dressed in the same clothes from last night, sans baseball cap. I'd never seen him without his baseball cap, except when he took it off at the counter, but I'd never let myself look then. And he always put it back on quickly.

Now it was impossible not to look at him. His hair was mussed from sleep in a way that was incredibly sexy... in a way that I knew men like Nathan spent far too long in front of the mirror trying to replicate. My hand twitched with the urge to brush away the midnight strand that had fallen across his dark eyebrow. The stubble on his chin was thicker than the five o'clock shadow that was normally there. It only made him more ruggedly handsome.

"Mornin'," he said, voice thick and throaty.

"Good morning," I replied reflexively. "You're awake."

"Figured you were gonna be up at the ass crack of dawn." He squinted out to the windows, where it was still dark outside. "Well, not even the ass crack of dawn." He looked back to me, and I lost my breath a little, overwhelmed by the force of his attention. He was definitely awake and aware but still somewhat sleepy, the corners of his eyes crinkled, and he was regarding me with a hooded gaze.

I was seeing Rowan Derrick without his baseball cap, *sleepy* in my kitchen.

His dog was sleepy in my kitchen too. Maggie was napping in front of the French doors, her head lifting up to stare at me in good morning before it flopped back down onto the floor.

Memories of last night rushed toward me. It wasn't like I'd forgotten last night... I wasn't wasted; my inhibitions were just loosened. But they were in full force now. And embarrassment, hot and thick, rushed up my throat at the memory of just how brazen I'd been.

My eyes darted away from his, finding the coffee machine. "You made coffee?" I asked even though he obviously had, my voice croaky.

Out of the corner of my eye, I saw Rowan's head swivel toward the machine. "Attempted to. Gotta admit... after tastin' the coffee at the bakery and realizing what shit I'd been drinking for most of my adult life, I shelled out for an espresso machine. Not one as fancy as this, though."

I smiled at that. The coffee machine was similar to the one at the bakery, just not on an industrial scale. It was my pride and joy. Stainless steel, shiny, serving as both a piece of art in my kitchen and an instrument necessary to my survival.

His large hands entered my field of vision as they fastened around a steaming mug. "Don't know if it's shit. Don't know how you take it either."

I focused on the mug then quickly took it from him. Despite my best efforts, our fingers brushed, and my body heated once more. Not with embarrassment this time.

"I take it black," I replied, thankfully taking a large sip.

"You, the queen of sugar, take your coffee black?" Rowan clarified, obviously surprised.

I grinned into the mug, still not brave enough to look him in the eye. "Well, every other part of my life is sweet to the point of sickly. Gotta even it out a little with some bitter," I joked lamely.

Oh god. There I was... the dork.

But Rowan did not think I was a dork. Or if he did, he did a good job hiding it behind his warm smile.

"Can I make you some breakfast?" I offered after taking another sip of the coffee, which did nothing to warm me up like Rowan's smile did.

"You're always offering to feed me."

"Well, you're always in my kitchen at mealtimes," I countered.

"Wouldn't call this a mealtime." Rowan glanced out to the darkness once more.

"Touché." I took another sip of my coffee, feeling more human by the moment. "I don't eat this early either. I usually eat at the café once I've done my first round of baking."

He nodded slowly, then we lapsed into silence. I couldn't tell whether it was comfortable or awkward. I couldn't trust my judgment right then.

Especially with Rowan's eyes on me.

I was wearing white today—which was playing with fire considering the amount of chocolate I handled. My tailored pants were high on the smallest part of my waist, an emerald green, chiffon, flouncy blouse tucked in. The sleeves came to my elbows, long enough to cover my bruises but not long enough to get in the way while I was baking.

Rowan took his time assessing my outfit. He did not hide that he approved. Of my outfit. My body. His tongue ran over his lips as his eyes roved over me and I suppressed a shiver, trying my best to hide my need for him.

Last night was not rejection, no matter what I tried to tell myself. Because even I couldn't deny that Rowan wanted me. He wasn't hiding it. Not even a little.

Just when I thought I couldn't handle another second of his attention, he cleared his throat, breaking the moment.

"Remember this place," he said, cupping his mug while looking around the kitchen with an assessing eye. An experienced eye. He was moving out of sultry Rowan mode into construction guy mode.

Which was a disappointment in some ways but intriguing in others. I liked seeing these versions of him, wanted to know how many more there were.

"The last owner called me and Kip in for a quote to refurbish it. Didn't like what we had to say."

I chuckled, thinking of the crotchety old man who used to live here, who was incredibly bothered by the fact that I, an unmarried woman, was buying his house with her own money. But it was me or no one since the place was crumbling around him and would've cost him a small fortune to fix up. It had been on the market for a year when I bought it, and the owner's children were anxious to get him out of the farmhouse that was almost falling down around his ears, and into a retirement community in Florida.

"Who did the work?" Rowan asked, moving around the room, running his hands along the wall and over to the archway that led into the hall. I loved arches for transitions. They made a house warmer, a little more unexpected and modern without compromising the history of it. Well, at least that's what I thought. Who could tell what Rowan was thinking.

I was enchanted by the way his hands moved across the smooth surface. Confident, strong.

"Um, I did," I replied, thinking I may need my head examined for getting turned on by watching a man caress my house.

Rowan's attention turned from the walls to me, his eyes wide with shock. "You did all of this?"

I nodded, looking down into my coffee in embarrassment. I had no idea why in the hell I was embarrassed. I'd been proud up until a few seconds ago.

I shifted uncomfortably on my feet. "I'm sure there are plenty of things you'll be able to tell me I did wrong." I shrugged. "The genius who had just started a new business the year prior then decided to sink most of her remaining savings into this place." I gestured to the ceiling with my hands. "I certainly couldn't afford a contractor, so I watched a lot of YouTube videos. I had plumbers in, of course, and Tina got some of her friends to come help me from time to time."

I thought about the burly, terrifying bikers she'd sent to my house. With tattoos, leather vests and their Harleys, they were imposing as all hell. And a good amount of them were incredibly handsome. Fiona had been in her element.

And they'd all turned out to be polite, good men... outside of the bedroom, Fiona let me know with a wicked grin.

"I roped my brother into coming down here for the first summer after I bought the place." I smiled fondly at the walls, at the floors, at the things I had created with my brother. "He did the heavy lifting. And the electrical stuff."

I missed my brother terribly for a second. Like a missing limb. Of course, the distance between us always hurt, but there were moments when I felt incomplete, like I made a terrible mistake, moving so far from him. But I'd done it because I'd had to. I couldn't be in the same city as that woman. And for whatever reason, Ansel couldn't leave her.

She had her hooks in deep.

"Your brother's an electrician?" I was thankful that Rowan's question jerked me out of my thoughts.

"He is. Got certified a few years ago. He's back in Chicago."

"He older?"

My lips lifted of their own volition. "By two minutes... something he lords over me any chance he gets."

Rowan inclined his head as he regarded me, a gesture I now recognized as his way of showing he was not just listening but hanging on my every word.

"You're twins?" he asked, surprise evident in his tone.

That amused me for some reason. "You seem shocked. Do I not seem like a twin?" I teased.

He rubbed his hand over his jaw, brushing at the thick stubble. "No," he replied instantly. "You seem like one of a kind."

Holy crap. What did someone say to that?

I cleared my throat, not knowing what to do with my body, so I just chugged the rest of my coffee, scalding my tongue and throat in the process.

"I've got to get to the bakery," I announced, wincing at the burn.

Rowan watched me for a beat before nodding. He returned to the kitchen, not just to rinse his mug and leave it in the sink for someone else—meaning me since there was no one else—to take care of like Nathan had done with every single one of his glasses, mugs and plates. No, he rinsed it, putting it in the dishwasher.

Such a simple act of common courtesy shouldn't have seemed so big to me. But it did. And it highlighted yet another concession I'd made for Nathan. Another way I'd given him permission to walk all over me.

Even with Rowan in my space, I retreated into my mind as I went through the motions of getting my purse and closing the house up for the day.

Maggie rubbed her head against my thigh, as if she could sense that I was spiraling. I scratched her ear, grateful to her for simply existing. I needed a dog. The companionship. The unconditional love they provided. Except I was gone from five in the morning every day. And I could not bring a dog into a bakery since that was a health code violation. So no, it didn't make sense for me to get a dog. I would just have to make the most of this one.

Maggie trotted happily beside me as I walked to the front door where Rowan was sitting on the reclaimed wood bench at the entryway, putting on his boots.

There it was. Another act of courtesy. Taking off his boots because he didn't want to dirty my house. Granted, Nathan wore expensive loafers that he went to great pains to keep clean so they wouldn't make any mess, but it was the principle of the matter.

Comparing one man against the other was not healthy. Not even a little. But there was no comparison. No competition. Of that I was certain.

Rowan didn't say anything as we walked out the door. Me, Maggie and him. Not as I locked it either.

I thought we'd get in our separate cars and drive off, pretending last night never happened.

Did I hope for that? Maybe. The fearful part of me certainly did.

But another part of me couldn't imagine going back to whatever we were before, when Rowan was nothing but a man I pretended was my boyfriend. When he wasn't a man with a dog he loved and a smile that was mine alone.

But I shouldn't have worried about such things. Because while I was in my head, Rowan was most definitely not in his.

He approached me before I registered what was happening. And when I realized what was really going on, I backed away on instinct, not because I was scared... exactly.

"Nora," he murmured, caging me against the back of my car, his warm, muscled, impressive body pressing up against mine.

He still smelled like him but with a hint of the soap I kept in the guest shower. The same soap I used. Lavender. Imported from France, where they didn't pump their personal care products full of chemicals like we did here.

I liked his smell. *Loved* his smell. But the mixture of his scent and my own? It was much too dangerous. It made me think of... other things mixing together.

That and the fact that his hand was now on my hip, his lips were inches from mine, and he was murmuring my name in what could only be described as a sultry tone.

"What?" I wheezed, my eyelids fluttering rapidly at the vision of him that close up. Unfortunately, there were no gross imperfections, nothing at all to put me off.

"You're not drunk anymore." He slowly ran the back of his knuckles along my jaw.

I shivered at the intimate gesture.

"I was never drunk," I argued, or at least tried to. My voice was thin and weak, barely above a whisper. "Tipsy at the most."

"Fine." His eyes searched mine. "You're not tipsy anymore. So..."

"So?" I asked, barely audible.

"So, me kissing you wouldn't be takin' advantage of you."

My heart drummed double time, and it was already pounding pretty damn hard. For the first time in my life, I did not assume my physical symptoms were due to some life-altering or

107

ending disease. I didn't think of anything, actually, apart from the way Rowan smelled, the warmth of his body against mine, and the way his words vibrated through me.

"Technically, I-I'm not in full possession of my faculties until I've had my second cup of coffee," I stuttered. I wasn't sure why I was saying that, weakly trying to argue against him kissing me.

I had been imagining this man kissing me ever since I laid eyes on him. But now I was stalling. Because I was scared. Terrified of what kissing him might mean. I was sure, utterly sure, that once he kissed me, nothing would ever be the same again.

Rowan didn't kiss me, though. His grip on my hip tightened some, his other hand clasping the back of my neck.

"You want me to kiss you or not, cupcake?"

The ground rocked underneath me as the question bounced around in my head. I scrambled to grab a hold of it so I could keep it, revisit it later, file this moment away.

"I would very much like for you to kiss me," I said, so quietly I wasn't certain he'd heard me.

Apparently, he did because the second the words were out, his mouth was on mine.

I thought he'd kiss me gently at first. Ever since he saw the bruise on my face, he'd been handling me with great care. Like I was breakable.

But he wasn't doing that now.

Our lips crashed together, his tongue plunging into my mouth, hand at my hip yanking our bodies as close as possible.

I clutched on to the sides of his jacket, holding on for dear life and kissing him with a kind of ferocity and hunger I hadn't known was inside me.

I'd never been kissed like this before in my life. A kiss had never made me feel like this.

Like I was being claimed. Like I'd be on my deathbed and still taste him, feel him.

A little moan escaped from the back of my throat, needing more, anxious to get rid of the layers of fabric separating us. I needed his naked body. Needed to drag my fingertips over the peaks and valleys of his muscles.

I slipped my hands underneath his tee, reaching around him to do just that.

Rowan lifted me up, a growl rattling his chest. I didn't hesitate to wrap my legs around his hips, raking my nails down the skin of his back. Not hard enough to puncture it, of course. Though I did have an unfamiliar need to do that. To draw his blood.

That was not something I'd ever been in to. Any kind of violence, any kind of rough sex... Maybe I'd never trusted a man enough to give in to that particular desire.

The way Rowan was kissing me, holding me—just to the point of pain—gave me the inkling that he would be into the rougher kind of sex. And that soaked my panties even further.

I was ready for it. For him. To take me right there. On the trunk of my car.

But he obviously was thinking clearer, detaching then resting his forehead against mine.

We were both breathing heavily, neither of us saying anything for close to a minute.

"Been imagining doing that for a long time," he rasped. "And I like to think I have a pretty vivid imagination, but... *fuck*."

My skin tingled, and I was still having trouble seeing clearly, thinking clearly. Most of my attention was on Rowan's lips and getting them back on mine as soon as possible.

"You've got a bakery to open," Rowan told me when I didn't say anything.

"I vaguely recall owning a bakery," I whispered, my voice not sounding like my own.

His lips turned up. But not in the same smile I'd been treated to previously. No, this one wasn't light or soft. His expression was still harsh, features held tight, eyes clouded with hunger.

Rowan was trying to hold on to control. Because he wanted me.

Him kissing the absolute fuck out of me also communicated that, to be fair. But the way he was holding himself together, seemingly by a thread, made me feel... powerful.

Rowan glanced to his side, so I did too.

Maggie was sitting a few feet away from us, tongue wagging happily.

I let out a half hysterical giggle at us nearly having sex on my car at five in the morning with the dog watching us.

Rowan lowered me down before leaning in to kiss me gently on the nose, in direct juxtaposition with the deliciously brutal way he'd just claimed my mouth. Then he stepped back, lifting his cap to run his hand through his hair before placing it back on.

"Gotta get you to the bakery." It wasn't a statement. There was an unsaid question there. An invitation, maybe?

My house was right there. Steps away. There were beds. But if I let my desire guide me, we definitely would not make it to the bed upstairs. We'd be having sex on the vintage rug in my entryway.

My nerve endings sang at the mere prospect of that.

And I almost did it. Took the lead. Gave in to those carnal instincts.

But at the last minute, I wussed out.

"Yeah, gotta get to the bakery," I sighed.

He didn't look disappointed. Or at least not that I could see.

He nodded, gave me one last panty melting look then whistled to Maggie.

She promptly got up and jumped into the truck when he opened the door for her.

I got in my own car, and Rowan followed me all the way to the bakery, idling there until I unlocked the door and made it inside.

Because he was the kind of man who waited until I was safe before he let me out of his sight.

The problem was, I knew, even then, my heart wasn't safe with him around.

Recipe: Fall Loaf

From 'Dessert Person' (written as Spiced Honey and Rye Cake)

"So," Fiona said, leaning against the counter.

I looked up from my dough. "So what?"

"Don't play coy with me, bitch," she snapped. "I left you last night, half pissed with the man you've been drooling over since forever, standing in your house declaring he was spending the night. What the *fuck* happened last night?"

I pursed my lips, focusing on the dough in front of me. "Nothing happened last night."

"Nothing happened?" She sounded incredibly disappointed.

I nodded, leaving a few beats of silence between us, trying to figure out whether I was going to kiss and tell.

Who was I kidding? No way I could keep this quiet.

"We did almost have sex on my car this morning."

Fiona let out a low shriek and hit me on the arm. "You sneaky bitch!" She looked me over. "What do you mean 'almost'?"

I abandoned the dough once more, giving her my full attention while dusting flour from my hands. "Well, Fiona, do you really expect me to have sex with a man I've been obsessing over on my car? A man I haven't even been on a first date with?"

"Of course, I fucking do," Fiona replied instantaneously.

I studied my nails, scraping flour out of my cuticles. "Okay, well, I might've. Had he not cut it short."

"He cut it short?" she repeated. "What was he, on drugs?"

I chuckled. "No, he... I don't know. It's confusing. He's confusing. He went from being nothing to me to staying at my house, saying things. Doing things."

I shook my head, trying to shake it free of the intrusive thoughts that had been swirling since I walked in.

"This is too much for a human being to deal with." I threw my hands up.

Fiona squealed, squeezing my arm. "No, honey, this is exactly what you've needed all this time. You need someone to take over your mind so thoroughly that you don't have the time, space or energy to talk yourself out of it, doubt yourself or convince yourself that you're dying."

Though I wanted to argue with her, I couldn't.

Because beneath all of my anxiety, dramatics and protests, I knew that Rowan Derrick was indeed what I'd needed all this time.

And that scared the crap out of me.

ROWAN

I knew she was special the second I first saw her.

Three years ago. When I first came into the bakery after hearing all that shit about her coffee and all the baked goods.

I wasn't typically interested in sugar or food in general. Not at that point, at least. Food was a thing that kept me alive. No more, no less. That's what got me through eating MREs or whatever shit was on base when we were there. I'd turned off that part of my brain. Even after I came back, haunted by all the shit I'd seen and done over there, I'd kept that mindset.

And control. Control was important. Controlling my body, what I did with it. What I put in it. What it became. A weapon.

So no, I did not go there planning on becoming fucking addicted to pastries. The exact opposite, actually.

I'd gone for the coffee. And because Kip wanted to hit on some waitress there. Even then, four years ago, he was fucking everything in sight in order to get away from reality. I'd been worried about my friend then, watching him closely at the same time as trying to deal with my own shit and start our business in a new town.

My mind was on a million other things.

But then I saw her. With fucking flour on her face. With hair escaping from the bun on her head. With a smile and a face that would launch a thousand ships. And it was clear she didn't know it. How god damn stunning she was. Women who knew they were good looking held themselves differently. Not that it was bad. Not with all of them, at least. But some of those women used their beauty as a weapon... as they should've because I'd seen a lot of fucking men think that a woman's beauty was theirs to own, take or destroy. No, I never judged those women.

But Nora... she didn't acknowledge her beauty. She was shy,

easy to blush, and her smile was small, uncertain but warm and genuine. I didn't know her then, aside from what I could glean from her body language. But I knew enough.

And I knew she was too fucking good for me. So, I kept coming back for the coffee. For those glimpses of her. So I could eat the things she created.

Even when she was wearing a ring that another man bought her, one that was flashy, obviously expensive and didn't fucking suit her at all. She was better suited to something original, vintage, unexpected. Not some huge, cold rock without any warmth or story behind it other than the six figures it was worth.

But there was no ring on her finger anymore. And I was fucking desperate to make her mine in every way I could.

That's why I was there. For another glimpse of her. Another taste. But not of the sugary shit she'd gotten me addicted to— well, that too—but her lips. Because those were the sweetest things I'd ever tasted. Because I had no intention of letting her go. Letting her get in her head like I'd seen last night and this morning. Her nose had wrinkled, her eyes went far away, and she shrank into herself.

At first, I thought I might have to treat her with care. Give her space. Time. But I had an inkling that space and time were my worst enemies with her. They gave intrusive thoughts too much fuel. Room to grow.

Which was why I was going to the bakery. Before work.

Maggie enjoyed it since she got an extra-long walk this morning. I didn't mind it either since I got to taste Nora's mouth. Claim it. Claim her.

Yeah, it was the best morning I'd had in a while. A long fucking while.

Yet I needed more.

Hence me walking into the bakery before work, just after seven. Because I needed more. Of her.

I hadn't been up this early in a long time. Six thirty was closer to when I got up for work. Sometimes seven. I considered that to be early enough.

Nora, though, got up at fucking five in the morning and looked absolutely fucking stunning.

It was hard to believe, before this morning, I'd been sleeping in my bed while this beautiful fucking creature was awake. I vowed to be up with her as often as I could. Even though it would be a fucking effort. I had not been up at five in the morning since I couldn't sleep at all after I got back, back when the nightmares kept me prowling around the house at night, looking for intruders, looking for ways to silence the screams, the gunfire that echoed in my head.

But it wasn't her I got.

It was a feisty Australian who grabbed my upper arm the second I walked through the door of the bakery. The bitch moved quick, rounding the counter and making it to me in only a handful of seconds. I guessed because she didn't want Nora seeing my entrance or her advance on me.

Now, she was a force to be reckoned with. Tall, but not as tall as me. Few were. And though she was stronger than she looked —couldn't have been more than a buck forty soaking wet—she was not strong enough to drag me from the bakery if I tried to fight her.

But she was close to Nora. That I knew. And she was a woman, one that impressed me. So, I didn't fight her.

The bakery was busy, even at six thirty in the morning. People in this town tended to get up early, especially when there was a limited amount of those almond croissants Nora made. Those people looked amused by Fiona dragging me outside. And also interested since this was a town that knew everyone's business.

Fiona did not seem to care about her audience, her sharp gaze focused squarely on me as she shoved me around the corner of the building, away from the entrance and the windows.

Bitch did not fuck around either. She dove right in.

"She's not soft," Fiona informed me, folding her arms as she lectured me. "She looks it. She looks kind and good and soft. She's all of those things. But she's a lot more. A fuck of a lot more. She's special."

I bristled at the hostility in her tone. "I know."

She shook her head violently. "You *don't* know. Because you're a man. Because you think she's special because she's beautiful. Because she has nice tits. And she looks delicate, perfect for big, hulking men like you to protect."

Her eyes grazed over me... not in appreciation, but in judgment. A fuck of a lot of it.

"Which I know all men want to do," she hissed. "Even the ones who proclaim to be feminists. *Especially* the ones who proclaim to be feminists. But then they find that the soft, small, beautiful, shy, dorky girl who owns the bakery can take care of herself. Can tear down and put up drywall. Can change her own tires. Can do about a hundred things that I would have to pay someone to do. She's impressive as fuck. To women, of course. To men, when she renders them useless or inferior, it fucks with them. And that's when they decide it's time to start taking things from her. Small pieces but enough to shrink her down. She's strong in so many ways, but she's also fragile. She's apt to think the worst possible things about herself, if people encourage that. And *he* encouraged that."

My blood boiled. It had been boiling. Since the second I saw that fuck with his hands on her in the bakery. Then when I saw his ring on her finger. Again, when I saw that fucking bruise on her face.

But this was different. Because as tough as the Australian chick was trying to be—not *trying* to be, she *was* one tough bitch —I knew underneath all of that anger was hurt too. She loved Nora. Fiercely. Enough to come out here, willing to go toe to toe with me. Enough to hurt when she saw her friend being taken apart, and unable to do anything about it.

"If you're looking for a damsel in distress, you can piss right off," she narrowed her eyes on me. "She's saved herself. From shit you couldn't even imagine. So, if you're looking to fix her life for her... look around, buddy." She waved at the bakery behind us. "She's done that too. She doesn't *need* you. And if that's why you want her, then go. Now. Because I'm not gonna sit on the sidelines this time when a man tries to cut her down so he can stand taller, pretending he's lifting her up too."

"You done?" I asked her when she didn't speak for a few seconds.

She scowled at me. "If you hurt her, I'll peel the skin from your face and roast it on my barbeque in front of you."

I nodded, trying very hard to restrain my urge to smile. Not because she was trying to be funny... She was dead fucking serious, which was why I needed to smile. It made me happy as shit that Nora had someone to go to bat for her like this. Said a lot about the kind of person Nora was.

"Wouldn't expect anything less," I told her. "Get why you want to protect her. She deserves that. Also get men are assholes. I've been one in my time."

I inwardly winced, thinking about how badly I'd treated women when I first got home. I never had nor would I ever put a hand on a woman. But that didn't mean I hadn't hurt them. By using them. Being callous, cruel because I needed sex to silence my nightmares but also couldn't handle another human being near me.

I regained my focus on Fiona. "But I'm not gonna hurt her." It was a promise. More to myself than Fiona.

She stared at me intently, measuring my words, weighing them. I suspected that Nora didn't have a whole lot of experience when it came to men, and it seemed—from what Fiona told me and from the small amount of Nora I'd experienced—that she was trusting. Kind. She didn't expect men to lie to her.

Fiona did. Because she knew us too well. And she knew most men were in the habit of making promises in order to get what they wanted.

She nodded slowly after a long silence. "Fine," she relented. "But I've got my eye on you."

"Wouldn't have it any other way."

NORA

When Rowan walked through the door, I lost my breath. My heart hammered in my chest, my knees trembled. My lips burned with the reminder that he had been kissing me this morning.

Marking me. Making me his. But I already was. I always had been.

But in the time between the kiss till now, I'd managed to convince myself that I'd somehow dreamed it. Or that I'd over-hyped the way he'd touched me, looked at me, the way his voice went raspy and full of promise.

As had been established, I was very good at convincing myself of all manner of things.

But seeing Rowan saunter in, his eyes instinctively finding mine, it became an inescapable fact that I had not imagined anything at all.

He had changed. He was wearing a flannel, black and red, unbuttoned with a black tee underneath, molding to his abs. The jeans he was wearing were worn, splattered with paint, and he had on his work boots. And of course, his trademark baseball cap on backward.

I found it very hard—almost impossible, if I'm honest —to do things like serve the remaining customers in front of him in line.

My fingers were numb, stomach swirling with butterflies and my body urging me to run. That's what I did, ran away from things that made me feel fear, uneasy, a little too alive.

And Rowan made me feel all of those things.

But that stare... That froze me in place.

"Hi," I breathed when he stood in front of me.

He didn't say anything, just kept looking at me in that way that wasn't fit for public consumption.

When my lower lip trembled, his eyes followed the movement.

Then he stopped staring.

He took action. Purposefully coming around the counter, he passed Tina at the coffee machine heading straight for me.

"What are you—"

I didn't have time to ask the rest of that question since he was kissing me.

In the middle of my bakery.

With witnesses.

Like, a lot of them.

And I knew this town. My regulars. They were nosy. And they would very much be enjoying the show. I was not into PDA. Not at all.

Except for right now.

The kiss lasted longer than was appropriate for my place of

work and business, but there was nothing else I could do but kiss him back.

I was clutching on to the sides of his shirt for dear life.

Rowan pulled back, mouth still inches from mine. "Hi."

I blinked rapidly, trying to get my bearings after that kiss while simultaneously analyzing the roughness of his voice while uttering that one word.

Then the sounds of the bakery rushed back in, and I realized what had just happened.

"Rowan, you cannot just kiss me in the middle of my bakery," I hissed as I stepped back, brushing my hands over my hair which had been messy before all of this.

I had tried to sound stern and pissed off, but it obviously didn't work since Rowan was grinning with a twinkling gaze.

"I think he just did, sweetheart," Tina answered for him, sounding amused as she poured milk for a latte.

I glanced over to Tina, who not only sounded amused but looked it too. Her own green eyes were sparkling with warmth. Which was definitely uncharacteristic since she wasn't exactly known for being warm and fuzzy with anyone but her wife.

She had been cold and straight up hostile with Nathan.

Apparently, she already approved of Rowan. Which made no sense. Tina was a hard woman to impress, and she certainly wouldn't be swayed by masculine good looks. Yet there she was, eyes shining, not threatening Rowan with her eyes or words.

I turned my gaze back to Rowan. "I need to work," I informed him, my cheeks still flaming with the heat of his attention, lips burning in response to his kiss.

"I've got it!" Fiona sang, pushing past the both of us to situate herself at the counter, serving customers.

I had no idea where she'd been, and I hadn't even seen her approach. I was both thankful and resentful for her presence.

This was far too much attention from Rowan in a concentrated amount of time. I wasn't capable of coping with this.

Rowan took Fiona's presence as an opportunity to gently grasp my upper arm and lead me to the kitchen.

It smelled like apple and cinnamon since I had decided to make my fall loaf, full of spices and drizzled with local honey right out of the oven. It went amazing with warm apple cider or a pumpkin spice latte—with pumpkin syrup made in-house.

I was going to tell him that he couldn't come behind the counter and kiss me. That I was overwhelmed right now and wasn't ready for a relationship... or whatever the heck this was. But he spoke first.

"I'm takin' you to dinner," he declared.

His hands were no longer on my upper arms, they were on my hips. It was hard to concentrate with them there, but for the life of me, I wasn't capable of stepping out of his grasp.

"W-What?" I stuttered.

"Dinner," he repeated. "Tonight. Carlisle's. Seven."

Carlisle's was the fanciest place in town. For good reason. The chef, and the restaurant's namesake, Carlisle, had owned some fancy restaurant in New York, was rich and famous, and a huge star of the culinary world. Then he stepped out of all that, for reasons the town's busybodies loved to speculate on—but had never got to the bottom of—and came here to Jupiter to open his restaurant.

The food was out of this world. They didn't take reservations; it was first come, first serve. It was always packed. No matter what.

"You want to go on a... date?" I asked him.

"Want to fuck you," he replied bluntly.

My body jerked with a shock that was not even a little bit unpleasant.

"Want to fuck you," he repeated, his grip tightening on my hips as his eyes dropped to my lips. "Had to stop myself from doing it last night. And this morning." His eyes lifted, looking behind me to where the sounds of the bakery were filtering through. "And right now," he added.

Sex in public has never been a fantasy of mine. I was a shy, private person who didn't much like being the center of attention. But right now, I was ready for Rowan to fuck me in my kitchen with an entire bakery of people a few feet away.

"But," he gritted out. "Wanna do things different with you. Wanna take you on a date. Give you what you deserve. Show this whole town you're mine." He lifted his hand to brush my cheek. "And then, I want to show you you're mine."

My stomach flipped as I sucked an unsteady breath through my mouth.

Rowan was regarding me intently. "If that's what you want." It wasn't exactly a question. More like him verbalizing a forgone conclusion.

I couldn't speak. I was too busy trying not to melt into a puddle at his feet. Or try to climb him like a tree.

"I'm pretty good at reading people, Nora," Rowan murmured. "Really fucking good at it. And I've made it my business to read the subtleties of your expressions over the years."

Another stomach flip. My heartbeats stuttered.

"In addition to that, you were pretty fucking enthusiastic this mornin' and a few minutes ago," he continued. "So, I'm rather confident that you want this too. Us," he clarified. "But I'm gonna need to hear it from that pretty mouth of yours."

"People d-don't talk like this in real life," I stuttered. "Men especially don't talk like this in real life."

Rowan's lip quirked. "This is real life, cupcake."

I digested his words. He was right. This was real life. Everything was much too stark for it not to be. And my pounding heart, the throbbing in between my legs, the tingle of my fingertips (that made me worry I was having some kind of stroke), confirmed that yes, this was indeed reality.

"Need to hear you say you want to be mine," he requested gently.

I tilted my head, eyes roving over him. His angular jaw covered in stubble. Those lips that were perfectly full and masculine. The dark brows framing his smoldering gaze. Inky hair that brushed his forehead. Broad shoulders. Muscular arms. Sinewy forearms exposed from the way he'd pushed up the sleeves of his flannel. Large hands covered in calluses, proof of the work he did every day.

I'd cataloged all of this before, of course. But from a distance. Or with fleeting glances when I was brave enough to actually engage with him.

"Do you want to be *mine*?" I asked him instead of heeding his command.

I was forcing the staunch feminist in me to the forefront. Because I was embarrassed at how much I wanted to be his. Even though, two nights ago, I'd been cursing another man for thinking I was something to own.

But Rowan was saying it was like I'd be something to *worship*.

Still, I was pushing back. Because how was I to know that he truly wanted to be mine? It was one thing to *have* a woman, but it was quite another to be *had* by a woman, belong to her in the same way you expected her to belong to you. A lot of men didn't think like that. Thought the rules were different.

"Cupcake, I was yours the second my steel-toed boot set foot in this pink fuckin' bakery," he said without hesitation.

My lungs seized as he stole all the oxygen from them.

Rowan didn't rush me to respond when I just stared at him,

unblinking, trying my best to fathom what he just said. To believe it.

"Carlisle's will be packed by seven," I said finally, unable to find the strength to say anything else.

Rowan didn't look disappointed that I did not utter I was 'his', presumably because that was pretty clear. "I'll make a call, get him to put a table aside."

"Carlisle doesn't just put tables aside," I replied. "Not even for Tom Hanks, and he's a national treasure."

It was true. The movie star had come to town when he heard one of his favorite chefs was working again. And when he turned up, there were no tables. Carlisle did not make exceptions.

With all of his good nature, Tom had taken it in stride and had stood in line with the rest of the patrons the next night.

That was three years ago, and the story had already become a town legend.

Rowan leaned forward to kiss the top of my nose. "I'll pick you up at seven," was his only explanation.

Then he walked out of my bakery like he hadn't just rocked my world.

CHAPTER
TEN

Recipe: Malted Chocolate Brownies

From 'Dessert Person'

I was driving home, thinking of what I could wear out for dinner tonight. I'd barely been able to concentrate all day and had taken solace in the predictable and safe rhythm of baking. Even that hadn't done much to calm my nerves, though. Not even the malted brownies that were known to work like a charm against nerves and heartbreak.

I was thinking about my red dress and the Valentino Rockstuds that went with it. I hadn't had the occasion to wear them in a while. Though I did wear designer heels to work—I usually slipped into cozy Uggs while I was baking, I wasn't a masochist—I saved my special designer pieces for dates or special occasions.

And I hadn't had either of those in a while. I hadn't been out anywhere in a while, come to think of it. Fiona had tried to drag me out to bars many times since the breakup, but I'd been insistent on my need to stay at home, where it was safe, where the floor wasn't sticky, and the wine was much better.

But a date. With Rowan. To one of my favorite restaurants in town. In the world, really. Yeah, that was something to break out the good shoes for.

Thoughts of shoes and dates and even Rowan went out of my mind when my eyes found the parking lot of the store.

Slamming on my brakes was instinct more than anything. As was pulling my car into the parking lot and getting out, running through the lot until I got between them.

Ronnie and Lori.

Lori had worked on and off at the bakery throughout the years. When she was home from school, needed the extra money. I offered that kind of work to a lot of the high school and college kids who needed money every now and then. I liked almost all of them.

Lori was one of my favorites.

She was sweet. Tiny. Petite like a fairy. Pretty like one too. Her white-blonde hair was stick straight, glossy and framed her delicate features perfectly. She was getting her PhD. She was smart, kind and bound for great things.

Ronnie was a drunk. Well known to be one. He worked at the town's one and only dive bar. He and Lori were high school sweethearts. I supposed that was why she stayed with him. For the nostalgia of it. For what they used to be. I liked to imagine at some point he used to treat her well. Before he was injured and lost his football scholarship. But whether or not he used to treat her well didn't matter much now.

Not when he had been screaming at her in the parking lot.

Pushing her around while she cowered, shrank in on herself with no one to fight for her.

Which was why I slammed on my brakes, pulled into the parking lot, ran out of my car and stood between them, facing off with a man who was much bigger than me and quite obviously violent.

"Leave her alone," I shouted at him, trying my best to get in his face. I might've been taller than Lori, but I wasn't even close to the same height or size as Ronnie.

He might've lost the scholarship and gained quite a bit of weight, but that didn't mean he wasn't still big and much stronger than me.

"This is none of your business, bitch." He scowled down at me. "Fuck off."

His stare was unfocused. Bloodshot. His breath reeked of whisky, and he was swaying on his feet.

He was drunk. Which was likely why he was laying hands on Lori. Or that's what I wanted to believe. I glanced around the parking lot, which was unfortunately quiet at this time of day. It was long after school got out and a little before most people got out of work.

I was on my own. For now, at least.

"You laying your hands on a woman you're supposed to love and cherish is my business," I spat at him.

Lori sniffled, tears streaming down her face. "Ronnie, please—"

She tried to touch his shoulder but he shrugged her off, still glaring at me.

"Get the fuck outta here before I teach you a lesson," he growled, leaning forward in an effort to scare me.

I was scared. No doubt about that. I had no weapon, no self-defense skills, and no one else in the vicinity to back me up.

Although he was in his seventies and needed a cane to walk, Henry, the owner of the store, would be out here if he saw what was going on. Henry wouldn't hesitate. So, I had to assume he was out back or engrossed in one of the many steamy paperbacks he loved to read without shame.

"Ronnie," Lori pleaded from behind me. "Please don't do this. Don't talk to Nora like that." Her voice was thick with tears. Smaller and weaker than I'd ever heard it. This was a girl who was beaten down, who had been manipulated by this asshole.

My heart broke with the instinctive knowledge that this was not the first time Ronnie got like this.

"I know you, Ronnie Cockran," I said, refusing to back down or let him think I was scared. "I know you're a drunk. And a coward. Instead of taking what life gave you and turning it into something different, better, you let yourself be the victim. And it's clear you're in denial about that because you're trying to make her a victim now." I jabbed my finger in Lori's direction, not risking a glance at her because I couldn't be sure what Ronnie would do if I took my eyes off him. "I see you. You're small and weak." I let the words fly like weapons, rage simmering inside of me. "And if I make a call to Finn, he's gonna come down here, and you're not gonna be brazen enough to get in *his* face. That, I'll bet my life savings on. Because he's got a gun, a badge, and a fuck of a lot more honor than you."

Insulting and threatening Ronnie at this juncture probably wasn't smart. He was not sober enough to see reason or think about the consequences of what would happen if he made good on his threats.

But I couldn't help it. Couldn't restrain the anger, the fury that I had toward him and men like him. My blood was boiling.

As was Ronnie's it seemed by the way his nostrils flared. "You fuckin' bitch," he snarled, lifting his hand, to do what, I didn't know.

Luckily, I didn't find out since the squeal of tires against pavement made both of our heads turn, Ronnie's hand hovering in the air.

A familiar truck screeched into the parking lot, a familiar man bursting out of it.

But the familiar dog was faster.

Maggie. The sweet dog who had napped on my rug, who had rubbed her head against my hand and followed her master dutifully, now ran ahead of him.

Ronnie started screaming as Maggie's teeth sank into the flesh of his legs.

"Get it off!" he cried.

Maggie did not get off. She was growling, tearing through his pants. I stared in both horror and a sick kind of relief.

"Maggie. Heel." The stern voice cut through the growling and Ronnie's screams.

Maggie instantly stopped her attack, sitting at Rowan's heels which weren't stationary for long. No, the second the dog let go of Ronnie, Rowan was on him.

He had Ronnie by the throat, dragging him away from me.

Ronnie didn't even try to struggle. Not even a little. Presumably because he was nursing an injured leg, courtesy of Maggie, but mostly because he was now faced with a man, a real one, one who could snap him in half in a second.

Rowan.

Coming to my rescue.

Like it was his job.

Kip was hot on his heels. I didn't know what both of them were going to do with Ronnie, but that wasn't my business. Lori was my business.

I turned to her, watching tears stream down her cheeks.

"Honey," I said tenderly. "Are you okay? Did he hurt you?"

She shook her head rapidly, hiccupping.

"Has he hurt you?"

She nodded. Slower this time.

I opened my mouth then closed it again when I realized there was nothing I could say to make things better.

So, instead, I took her into my arms and hugged her, if only so she wouldn't see Rowan beating the shit out of the man who had been hurting her for who knew how long.

* * *

In the end, the cops did not need to be called.

Lori had brothers.

Three of them.

Two of them turned up at the store and had words with Ronnie. Kip and Rowan stood close by, seemingly to ensure that they stuck to just words. At least with Lori present.

Rowan had not beat the man to a pulp as I'd expected him to. Maybe because of the audience, with Henry coming out of the store and Kip at his side. Or maybe because of Lori, sobbing in my arms. Ronnie's worst injury was the one Maggie inflicted, which no one seemed too worried about, least of all Lori's brothers.

One of her brothers was at the house the two of them shared, getting Ronnie's things out. He was moving out.

Then they loaded her in her car and put the fear of God into Ronnie.

I hoped that the threats and the shame from today were enough to get him to leave Lori alone. But the problem with abusive men—men who believed that the world had wronged them—they tended not to learn. Especially when the woman they had been abusing was succeeding where they were failing.

My stomach churned with worry for Lori, fury at Ronnie for making it so she would not be at ease with herself or with men for a very long time.

It had rattled me. A lot. I had been through crap in my life... indifference, neglect... but never straight up physical abuse. I knew men were capable of that. Unfortunately. But knowing that and seeing it firsthand, to a sweet young girl, were two different things.

And I was rattled because Rowan had avoided me. Hadn't spoken to me. Granted, he kind of had his hands full with Ronnie and then Lori's brothers.

Maggie, on the other hand, had not left my side, pressing into my leg and tilting her head for scratches. Both of our eyes were on her dad, yet to look at either of us.

But with everyone leaving, he approached me, his face a cold mask that did nothing for my unease.

"Keys." He held out his hand.

I blinked at him, at the command. My keys. He was asking for them with the single word, without any kind of please. I was well within my rights to tell him they were my keys, and I'd drive myself.

Part of me wanted to. But a larger part of me was still rattled, and as cold as he was being, I did long for him to take control. For his presence. Regardless of whether that was pathetic or not.

He grasped the keys I'd held out to him, his expression still granite.

"Get in the car," he ordered.

I bristled at his tone and his expression... detached, unfamiliar. "What about your truck?"

"Kip's taking care of it."

I pinched my lips between my thumb and index finger. I did not like this version of Rowan. But I was coming to understand that this man was protective. To say the least. And I could recognize that there were two different versions of this man. The one with twinkling eyes and easy grins, and this one. The somber, dangerous, cold, demanding side. I guessed this was the soldier, the one who turned off the twinkling eyes and the smiles in order to get through whatever he went through.

Though I understood that to a point, I didn't like it. And I definitely didn't deserve this cold detachment, most especially after what had just happened.

"Maggie." Rowan opened my passenger door for her.

I stayed rooted in place. As did Maggie. Rowan's jaw twitched as Maggie and I ignored his commands.

There was a warm satisfaction in knowing his excellently trained pooch was now siding firmly with me.

Girl power, baby.

I crossed my arms in front of me. "I get you're a big bad alpha who has... some type of *feelings* for me," I explained lamely. "I get that you just saw me almost getting hit in the parking lot, and you're mad about that. But *I* was just about hit in a parking lot. *Me*." I jabbed my own finger to my chest. "And it is not on me to tiptoe around *you* because you can't regulate your anger. And it's *definitely* not okay to take that anger out on me."

I was almost yelling by the end of that little tirade.

Thankfully, Lori, Ronnie, her brothers, and the rest of the audience that had accumulated were now gone.

Still, I didn't really want to be in the parking lot, yelling at the guy who wasn't even my boyfriend.

I wasn't a person who yelled. Or even raised her voice. Growing up, I'd understood that the best way for me to exist was to be quiet, almost invisible. And even after I got out of my mother's house, I hadn't been able to shake that. Plus, yelling at a man was risky. Dangerous. You could never know how a man might punish a woman for losing her temper.

But for once, my usually ironclad self-preservation shattered. That and despite how pissed I was with Rowan right then, he had made me feel safe enough to yell at him.

My words penetrated. I watched them go through the mask, watched his eyes flash with something resembling shame or regret. But he didn't shed all of his fury. Not even a little.

He stepped forward so he was close to me but not touching. His feet were splayed, his posture tense. He looked like a man who was standing his ground for battle.

"Ronnie Cockran is a piece of shit. And a moron," Rowan seethed. "And I would usually describe him as a harmless piece of shit. Except when you get in his face and show him what a moron he really is." When his eyes slid down my body then back up, I was surprised my clothes didn't catch fire. And not in that sultry way he'd stared at me this morning. No, in a way that was full of fury. "Especially when you're five foot nothing, and you're a fuckin' woman."

Though I was shaken, I was nowhere near shaken enough to let him get away with that.

"What the heck does me being a woman have to do with anything?" I demanded, hands on my hips.

His fury did not dissipate, but his brow twitched, with either more amusement or anger, I couldn't tell. And I didn't really care at that point.

"Not sayin' that because I think women are somehow less than men." His words were clipped. "In fact, I am of the firm opinion that women are better than men in every way, and that had I not stepped in, you could've taken him." He folded his arms so we were both in battle stances. "Which is why he's even more dangerous. He was standin' there, trying to act like a man by threatening a woman. His woman." His eyes were stormy. "Then he threatened *my fuckin' woman.* And he's been layin' hands on an innocent girl. So now he has to die."

My eyes bugged out.

When anyone else in my life made death threats, I didn't take them seriously. Fiona threatened the lives of people daily, as did Tina. For various reasons. From ordering some overly complicated coffee or looking at her wife too long—Tina—or for walking around with their phone on speaker—Fiona. Not once had I been seriously concerned about them following through on such threats. Because though both women could be scary and dangerous in equal parts, I didn't think either of them were capable of murder. Although Tina was pretty possessive over her wife, so I couldn't completely rule her out.

But that was her *wife.* They'd been married for years, loved each other fiercely. Committing murder in her defense or to avenge her would've made sense.

Rowan and I weren't married. We were loosely dating—if that's what you could call it. And that technically wasn't even true because we hadn't even had our first date yet. We'd only just consummated this thing between us this morning, if you counted kissing as consummation.

Sure, I might've had an infatuation with him that could've *maybe* been described as love. But of course, I was insane.

Rowan was, aside from this current moment, an exceptionally sane man. Therefore, there was absolutely no way he could be in love with me.

So, him threatening murder did not make sense.

Not that anyone threatening murder ever actually made sense.

But he meant it. Staring at him, into those tempestuous eyes,

I knew he was seriously going to end the life of the man who'd threatened me.

"Don't," I whispered, my previously sharp tone completely gone.

I grabbed a hold of Rowan's large, strong hand. It made me feel warm. Safe. Tethered to the earth.

"Please do not kill a man for me," I asked, begging him with my eyes.

"He would've hurt you if we hadn't driven past when we did," he ground out. "He was already hurting that girl."

"He was," I agreed, my blood still boiling with that knowledge. "But she has brothers who will make sure she's never hurt again. And then there's the possibility of Ronnie turning up dead, and those boys being accused of his murder." Half of me was joking, or at least hoping this was some kind of hypothetical conversation. But the other half was being dead serious—pardon the pun—knowing that I was speaking to another version of the man I was quickly—far too quickly—falling in love with.

Now that I was looking at him closer, without my red veil of rage, touching him, I could see just how tense he was. Felt the tremble of rage in his hands.

He had transformed into the dangerous—deadly—man I knew he could be. Who, at some point before I'd known him, he'd had to be to survive.

I had no idea how to deal with truly dangerous men. No idea how to bring him back from the brink. I just knew I needed to.

So, I worked on instinct. I went up on my tiptoes so I could clutch his face, bringing it downward to me, our lips almost brushing.

"Will you take me home?" I asked softly, looking into those savage eyes of his.

He didn't respond, just kept staring, his hands gripping my hips tightly.

I didn't back down, though I felt uncertain, unsure if I was doing the right thing.

"Please?" I whispered, brushing my lips across his.

Then he responded.

Enthusiastically.

I'd intended to give him a delicate kiss, to coax him back to the man who didn't need to use violence to avenge his woman.

He was not that man.

He was now the man who needed to claim his woman in a brutal kiss in the parking lot.

My back slammed against the car before I knew what was going on, Rowan's hands on my ass now, kissing me fiercely.

To be fair, I kissed him back just as fiercely, realizing that I had some adrenaline of my own spiking in my body.

"I'm takin' you home," Rowan growled against my mouth right when I was about to wrap my legs around his hips and put us both in danger of getting arrested for indecent exposure.

"Yeah," I agreed, trying to catch my breath.

He didn't let go of me right away, just kept me there, pressed against the car, pressed into him, my chest rising and falling rapidly.

"Scares me, prospect of you gettin' hurt," he murmured, his hand brushing against the still fading bruise on my eye.

It felt surreal, that a mark still existed on my body from a time when Rowan and I weren't this. That this relationship—if that's what this was—had yet to outlast a bruise on my skin.

"I sometimes go to a place I'm not proud of," he continued, eyes soft now. "Become a man you shouldn't see. One who doesn't deserve a woman like you."

He was punishing himself now. I could see that. Feel it.

There were a bunch of things I could've said to that. Like the fact that I wanted to see all of him, even the versions of himself he wasn't proud of. That a dark and slightly shameful part of me was turned on by this slightly unhinged, dangerous man who'd lost control at the thought of me getting hurt.

But those things weren't appropriate conversations to have in a parking lot. Or in a relationship that had yet to outlast a bruise on my face.

"Take me home," I requested instead.

He stared at me a beat longer, before he pressed his lips against mine and murmured, "okay, cupcake."

CHAPTER
ELEVEN

Recipe: Pistachio Pinwheels

From 'Dessert Person'

A romantic dinner was out of the question after the events of that afternoon.

The energy was not the kind I wanted following us on our first date. Especially considering we'd had our first fight today. Which was incredibly unbelievable, me yelling at Rowan like we were some kind of couple. Him declaring he was going to kill a man for me like we were in some kind of movie or novel.

We'd driven home in silence. You couldn't exactly say that things were tense, but there was something between us that didn't have any right to be there. It added another intimate layer to a relationship that wasn't really a relationship.

But Rowan's hand was on my thigh the entire drive home.

The *entire* drive.

It made me feel glued to my seat while also floating among

the clouds. It made me feel a part of something. That we were tangible and real, and it was perfectly normal for him to be driving me home in my car, with Maggie resting her head on the console between us, his hand firm on my thigh.

There were no words at all during the drive. Not even when he pulled into my driveway and we all got out, him taking off his boots at the front door, and Maggie trotting to the French doors, waiting patiently for me to let her out.

I did so, watching the chocolate lab sprint around my large backyard, discovering all sorts of new smells and marking her territory.

The wind blew the curtains inward, bringing with it the crisp fall breeze that made my insides relax.

I felt him behind me. Warm. Large. Unyielding.

On instinct, I leaned back against him.

He smelled of something that was utterly unique to him.

His lips found the top of my head, pressing down gently while wrapping his arms around me.

Although I wanted to stay there forever—or for a while, at least—I was me. Intrusive thoughts always found their way in. It was not in my nature to enjoy a simple moment for what it was.

"My life is not normally this eventful," I said, staring at Maggie running along the edges of my overgrown garden. "It will not require you to go into protective mode every single day."

Apparently, Rowan was not ready to have this conversation unless we were face to face. He made that known by turning me around, hands on my hips.

He was still pissed, that was clear, but his posture relaxed. Somewhat, at least.

I gnawed on my lip. He was still incredibly handsome and sexy, and I was still very mindful of the promises he'd made earlier about what we were going to be doing tonight. Technically, I should not have been so turned on by a man who had promised death and violence earlier, but I couldn't help it.

My eyes ran over him hungrily. The broad shoulders. The defined chest. The chiseled forearms. The stubble-covered jaw. That piercing gaze. No matter how many times I blinked, he was still there. Still pure masculine perfection.

"My life is not exciting," I added. "There are not normally black eyes and parking lot showdowns." I massaged my temples, trying to regain my train of thought.

Rowan didn't say anything. He just pinned me with an intense stare.

I swallowed thickly. "I think it's important to point out I'm a rather boring person," I continued. "Because you, sir, are not a boring man. And I don't want to misrepresent myself."

It was crucial that he knew this, I'd decided at some point during the ride home. I didn't know what kind of women he'd dated before me, but I didn't think I was his usual type. And I didn't want him thinking I was someone I wasn't.

"Why did you stop?" he asked instead of addressing anything I'd said.

I squinted at him. "Why did I stop where?"

His grip on my hips tightened for a moment. "At the store. When you saw Ronnie and Lori." His words were strained, tight. He hadn't completely wound down, he'd turned into something else. Someone else. That dangerous alpha guy.

And it seemed it took a while for him to find his way back to the man who smiled at me in the bakery.

"I don't understand the question," I told him slowly.

"Most people wouldn't stop," he said. "Especially women who aren't armed, who are half the size of the man smacking around his woman. If they stopped, it would be down the street, maybe, and they'd call for help."

I shook my head. "You don't have a very high opinion about people. I like to believe most people *would* stop."

His gaze remained shrewd and penetrating. "You believe that because you're you," he countered delicately. "But I've got a low opinion about people in general because people suck. Because they look out for themselves. You didn't do that. You stopped. Put yourself in danger. Were willing to take a blow for someone you barely know."

I bristled at that. "I know Lori. I know she's sweet. Innocent."

"Not disagreeing about that." Rowan showed me his palms. "But why did you stop?"

"Because it wasn't even a question to me." I shrugged. "It's not like I had some big moral dilemma. I saw it. Saw her. Instinct kicked in."

Rowan continued to eye me with that stare that made my ankles shake under the weight of it. "Jesus," he muttered.

I wasn't quite sure what he was trying to communicate with that. His jaw was still locked, posture still rigid, but his eyes were tender. His stare was almost... reverent.

"Why do you like me?" I blurted.

He inclined his head, face impassive. "Excuse me?"

I sighed, knowing it wouldn't be as easy as just asking the question and getting a straight answer. I'd have to go through the whole song and dance, humiliating myself. But I'd opened up this can of worms, and the tightness in his jaw told me he wasn't going to let this go.

"You like me," I said.

"*Like* is one word to describe how I feel about you," he murmured.

The murmur was a boom inside my head. My stomach fluttered, my thighs clenched, and I tried really hard not to let out an embarrassing girly sigh. I managed. Barely.

Then I straightened my spine and remembered what I was doing. "Well, it makes no sense. That you like me. You are this tall, muscled, incredibly handsome, enchanting man. You're a real man. Like cut wood with an ax kind of man. Women absolutely drool over you, and you don't even notice. You have some kind of... power about you, like if we were both on a plane and it was going down, I wouldn't be scared. Not at all, because I know you would somehow handle the situation. Now, I don't know if you're a pilot or whatever, but I know you'd take care of it. Take care of me."

His body visibly relaxed at my words, though his dark brows bunched together, listening to me very intently. With an intensity that was nearly impossible to breathe through.

"And I'm a baker," I added. "A good one, I'll give you that."

"A great one," he corrected, his voice thick and velvety.

I swallowed the embarrassment creeping up my throat. "Yes, well... Some call me a great baker, and I won't argue about that, but apart from my baking skills, there's nothing interesting about me."

I frowned, looking for tidbits about my life that were even worth talking about. Things that would measure up to a man I trusted to save me from a plane crash.

"I have a drawer full of planners, notebooks and journals," I continued rambling. "Not like a small, narrow, bathroom drawer. No, a big one. A huge dresser drawer full of beautiful, witty, trendy notebooks. To write plans in. Goals. Lists. Some of them have a list or two inside, but most of them are empty. Because I have high hopes for myself and imagine myself as someone who fills up journals and ticks things off lists. Every time I buy one, I promise myself that is the time I will become one of those people."

I sucked in a breath, staring straight at him without actually looking into his eyes. "I don't know how to use Excel. I know that is terrible. Utterly terrible for a small business owner who does everything herself. I have to file taxes, keep up with expenses, organize schedules, order supplies, keep inventory. But I just have a drawer. Multiple drawers actually. Full of crumpled up receipts, stained with flour and syrups. I hire someone to deal with payroll because I will never, ever fuck with someone's paycheck. My financial stuff can be a hot mess because it's my life, but I have people who depend on that paycheck to pay their rent. So that, I'm organized with. The only reason the IRS hasn't imprisoned me is because one of my stepdads—the only one I liked, the one who acted like a dad—he's an accountant. He's my accountant, and he's more than happy to be paid in cookies. I need a beta blocker just to go to Trader Joe's."

He was watching me with rapt attention, a look on his face I might've enjoyed, might've even marveled at, had I not been on a roll.

Unfortunately, I was on a roll, so I did neither. So, I did not realize what in the fuck was going to come out of my mouth next. If I'd had any idea what was going to come out of my mouth, I would've sewn it shut.

I remained unaware.

"When I get anxious or uninspired, I masturbate," I announced. The words came out of my mouth, but I didn't realize I'd said them. Therefore, I kept talking. "I do it because I like sex, pleasure too. But I get ideas for new cakes, pastries while I'm doing it. I solve problems. I relax at the same time I find more energy. I feel more alive."

When the last syllable left my lips, once the damage was done, I snapped my mouth shut, blood rushing to my face as I realized what I'd just revealed.

What I'd just said out loud.

I said that *masturbating gave me ideas for pastries.*

Please, Thor, smite me with a crack of fucking lightning.

My feet didn't work. If they did, there would've been a me-shaped hole in my lovely wall that had been repaired and painted just six months ago.

His features had changed, his expression not soft nor intense nor like any expression I'd ever seen. My whole body was aflame, especially between my legs.

Rowan didn't respond.

Not with words, that is.

He lifted me up. Over his shoulder.

I had not been expecting that. Who would expect a man to literally lift her and fireman carry her toward the stairs?

I'd let out a little squeal when it first happened, but it wasn't until we were halfway up the stairs that I spoke. "What are you doing?"

Rowan didn't answer me. He continued his ascent, walking us into my bedroom before setting me down.

I almost gasped when my feet hit the floor and took sight of his face. His face that was white hot. And hungry.

For me.

"Show me," he demanded.

I felt his voice as if it were a caress over every inch of my body. "W-what?"

Again, if my legs were working, I might've run. But I couldn't be sure. My need was quickly surpassing my embarrassment.

He didn't touch me. No... Even though I was desperate for him to.

"Show. Me," he repeated, mouth inches from mine. "Show me how you make yourself come."

My knees started trembling

"Rowan," I whispered. "I can't do that." I was a mix between incredibly fucking turned on and so self-conscious I wanted to curl into myself and disappear. It was an exhilarating and incredibly uncomfortable feeling.

Rowan's solid gaze did not abate at my words nor the unspoken plea threaded into them.

He was asking too much of me. We'd never done more than kiss. And somehow, this felt more intimate than sex. A heck of a lot more intimate. I'd never done it with another man. Ever.

"Where do you keep it, cupcake?" he asked, whisper soft.

I didn't have to ask what he was talking about. I knew what he was talking about.

"In the nightstand." I nodded over to my 'side' of the bed, paperbacks piled on the surface along with my water glass from last night, a pink, antique lamp and trinket tray with discarded earrings and crystals in it.

Rowan didn't hesitate. Didn't ask permission. He walked over to my nightstand and opened the top drawer. I squeezed my eyes shut, embarrassment washing over me. But it wasn't just embarrassment that infiltrated my system. There was something else too.

A fire that had been burning inside me. A fire Rowan had been stoking since that day at the bakery when he smiled at me and asked me if I was his Beth.

I kept my eyes shut as the drawer closed, as his soft footfalls returned in my direction.

"Nora."

My body spasmed at my name coming out of his mouth.

My eyes opened on instinct.

And there was Rowan. In front of me. In my bedroom. Holding my vibrator.

"You want to be a good girl for me?" he asked, voice silky, holding the vibrator out to me.

My pussy pulsed.

I didn't think I had a praise kink. In fact, I'd always mentally rolled my eyes whenever I watched or read about a man asking a woman to be his 'good girl'. There was much too much misogyny in a request like that. Taking away a woman's power by requesting she be 'good' by obeying commands of a man.

Or so I'd thought.

I'd never felt more powerful than I did right then. At that moment.

My hand was shaking when I took the vibrator. Our fingers brushed, but that was the only contact we had. He turned with me as I walked on unsteady feet to my bed, slipping off my heels before sitting on the soft pink comforter.

I was aware of my every movement. My every breath.

It should've felt awkward, what with me holding my vibrator and readying myself to use it in front of the fully clothed man standing on the side of my bed.

Yet it didn't.

Sure, there was a healthy sprinkling of unease, of fear, but the kind that only made my desire heighten.

I eased open my pants, lifting my hips so I could take them off.

Rowan watched my every move, a low hiss escaping his lips as his eyes found my pale white lace panties. They were completely sheer, showing off every inch of my pussy, the manicured strip of hair that I got waxed religiously even though there hadn't been anyone to see it or appreciate it since Nathan.

"Fuck, baby," he murmured, rubbing his hand over his mouth.

Sure, the image of his face painted with desire when looking at me in my panties was something to behold, but something else caught my attention... The bulge in his jeans.

The very fucking large bulge in his jeans.

My grip tightened on the vibrator as my thighs rubbed together, desperate for friction.

But I didn't move my hand, didn't turn on the vibrator and give myself the release I most desperately needed.

"I'll show you how I make myself... come," I rasped, my cheeks heating as I said the words, making eye contact with Rowan. "If you show me." I nodded to the bulge in his jeans.

I took a deep breath, trying to find the courage, the right words to communicate what else I wanted. Instead of doing that, I leaned up, pulling my blouse over my head to reveal my sheer bra, my aching nipples pressing up against the lace.

Another strangled hiss of appreciation escaped Rowan.

There was little room to be self-conscious here, even though I was lying in my bed, almost naked, and he was standing over me fully clothed. From the beginning, Rowan had made it clear he liked my body. Found it beautiful. Desirable. So, I didn't shrink away, worry about the dimples in my thighs, the extra weight on my hips and stomach. There wasn't any kind of judgment in Rowan's gaze. There was only want.

"I want you to show me how you make yourself come," I repeated, my tone husky. "Then I want you to... finish. On me." My cheeks flamed hotter with the request. I wasn't embarrassed by it, not completely. But I felt brazen saying it aloud. Not the timid baker I'd been for as long as we'd known each other.

Rowan's eyes widened at my request.

I might've felt nervous then. Might've sank back into that meek version of myself who didn't verbalize my desires.

But there was no time for that.

"It's like I fuckin' dreamed you up," Rowan growled, hands moving to his belt.

I squeezed my thighs together in anticipation as I watched him free himself from his jeans.

And it was time for my eyes to go wide as he wrapped his large hand around his length. Though I couldn't say this as a general rule, I could say in Rowan's case it was true what they said about big hands. Big hands... big, magnificent cock.

I licked my lips, thinking about touching it, having it inside me.

"Nora," he growled.

My attention moved back upward to where his intense, hungry stare was fastened on me. "If you don't stop staring at my cock and get that vibrator going, I'm gonna forget about anything and everything but burying my cock inside you." He sucked in a ragged breath. "And as much as I wanna do that, I want this to happen first."

I almost abandoned the vibrator and climbed up to him. The severity of his features, the low and strained tone to his voice told me that he would not fight me on it. Even a little bit. We both wanted him to be inside of me. To the point of insanity.

Sexual tension raced between us like charged particles in an electric force field. But there was another kind of erotic charge there too. Getting ourselves off, in front of each other.

So, I pressed the button on the vibrator, barely hearing the hum over my roaring heartbeat.

I cried out when it hit my clit, at the same time that Rowan started pumping his cock. My eyes followed every stroke. Well, they did until Rowan spoke.

"Look at me," he commanded, his voice rough, thick, almost animalistic. "Give me your fuckin' eyes, Nora."

My gaze instantly heeded his command, looking upward. My body spasmed as I met his eyes, the pure, feral hunger magnifying the already maddening pleasure my body was experiencing.

My back arched against the bed, my toes digging into the comforter. I felt the telltale buildup of an orgasm as my body coiled, readying to explode. But this was not the same as when I used this alone. And when I used this alone, it was pretty damn good. This vibrator was the best on the market, in mine and thousands of reviewers' opinion. It had a soft suction head that one had to feel to understand.

I had yet to meet a man able to replicate even a quarter of the pleasure I experienced from this machine.

Until now.

I knew my body well. Thought I'd explored the pleasure that I could experience with this vibrator. But I hadn't. Hadn't even scratched the surface.

Rowan wasn't even touching me. Rowan was standing above me, watching me, touching himself, and he was giving me the most erotic experience of my life.

"You're so fuckin' gorgeous," he ground out, still working himself.

That was when I exploded, my body releasing all its tension, all the pleasure pent up inside of me. Maybe I cried out. Maybe I made some kind of sound. I couldn't be sure. My body was my own, and it was Rowan's, his eyes never leaving mine as my orgasms rushed over me, blending into each other.

Then he growled, and I felt him, releasing onto the naked skin of my stomach. My body let go again with the carnal, primal act of having him doing this to me. Doing this on me.

The world blurred, the ground underneath me shifted, and my body turned limp, my limbs heavy.

Rowan's belt rustled as he righted himself. I noted that from my spot, still reveling in the aftermath of one of the most intense experiences of my life.

Rowan's form moved as his feet thumped faintly on my floor.

Again, I noted this with detachment, my chest rising and falling rapidly.

When he came back, he had a washcloth, and he was gently cleaning himself from me.

The act itself was tender, intimate.

Before, I'd been so hot, I thought my body was going to burst into flames from his attention, from him getting off on watching me.

But the only way to describe how I felt now was warm. Comfortable. Him taking care of me, treating me with reverence.

I looked at him through my lashes, still unable to fathom that this was real. He was real. But he was real. This was real.

"Cupcake, that was the hottest thing I've experienced in my whole fuckin' life," he told me in a rough voice, taking me even further from what I'd thought reality was.

"Can't wait to get my cock into that pretty pussy of yours," he continued. "Know it's gonna be sweet, tight... fuckin' heaven."

And although I thought my body was spent, all pleasure inside of me sated, my thighs pressed together at his words, need for him blooming in my stomach.

Rowan's eyes were blazing as he leaned down and laid his lips between my legs, on top of my soaked panties.

Then he inhaled. Deeply. Me. The smell of my pleasure, of the aftermath of what we'd just done. What I'd just done.

His eyes found mine, sending my heart into my throat.

"Sweet," he murmured.

My mouth was dry, every single one of my limbs tingling from the word, from his gaze. From him.

Then, from somewhere outside, a bark sounded, Maggie yanking us back into reality.

Though a large part of me was disappointed, I was somewhat relieved too. There was only so much a girl could take. I needed to regain my bearings.

"I'll go check on her," Rowan said, standing up.

"Good idea," I replied lazily.

He didn't go right away. He stayed there for a moment, staring at me like he was committing me to memory or something.

"I'll be down just as soon as I've regained use of my legs," I informed him.

A grin cut through the hunger in his gaze, and he chuckled warmly. I liked the sound of it, the way it brushed against my already sensitive skin.

"Take your time," he said. "Let me know if you need me to bring you down the stairs the way you came up." He winked then walked out to check on Maggie.

I watched him leave, unable to connect the winking, chuckling man with the one who, just an hour ago, had been threatening to kill someone who might've hurt me.

They didn't seem like the same person.

But they were.

Rowan was both of those men.

And maybe he was mine.

CHAPTER
TWELVE

Recipe: St. Louis Gooey Butter Cake

From 'Dessert Person'

I could've felt awkward in the aftermath of what had just happened in my bedroom. Lust burned hot and quick, and getting lost in the moment was one thing, but holding on to that intimacy after the embers had cooled was quite another.

I'd had a quick moment of paralyzing fear while I was in the bathroom getting myself together while Rowan was downstairs checking on Maggie. My heart had started hammering, and I was vaguely certain I was having some kind of cardiac episode. It was not uncommon for me. In my experience, a spiral like this would normally take at least an hour to come down from. If not longer. But I heard Rowan downstairs with Maggie. Felt his presence. My body still thrummed with what we'd just done. So my 'episode' came and went.

Then I got dressed. In cashmere sweats, fixing the hair that had escaped during our... activities before rubbing some errant mascara from underneath my eyes.

My cheeks were flushed, my eyes bright, glowing, emerald green. They did that when I was happy, excited, well rested. I hadn't seen them like that in a while.

A post orgasm glow really was a thing, and something that no amount of beauty products could replicate. An orgasm a day keeps the dermatologist away.

Rowan was pouring wine into a decanter when I found my way into the kitchen, my lips stretched into what was surely a cheesy smile. I was still floating on somewhat of a high from the orgasms, everything soft around the edges.

My heart stuttered in my chest, seeing Rowan standing at my bar, hat off, pouring wine while Maggie had claimed what I'd already come to understand as 'her' spot.

"Thinking we might have to do a raincheck on dinner tonight," Rowan told me after his eyes slid up and down my body.

My skin tingled from the look of hunger and appreciation on his face as he took in my simple cashmere sweater set. It skimmed over my curves, showing off my generous hips and ass, but it wasn't something I considered 'sexy'. But the way that Rowan was looking at me, you'd think I'd walked down here in lingerie.

Then again, he knew what I looked like in lingerie.

My cheeks warmed at the memory.

Rowan's lips brushed the side of my mouth as he handed me a glass of wine. "Love that you still blush after I've seen you come hard and hot, after my cum has decorated that perfect skin."

Jesus fucking Christ.

I clutched the stem of the wine glass so hard I was surprised it didn't snap in half. My knees almost buckled, and my chest heaved. Literally fucking heaved.

I didn't know what to say to that. What did someone say to that?

I didn't know, so I focused on doing what I could to keep standing and breathing.

Rowan lingered much too close for much too long, but I was very disappointed when he stepped back.

I looked from him to Maggie. "So... if we're not going out for dinner, I can whip us up something to eat," I suggested, my voice still breathy and thin.

Rowan tipped his chin as he assessed me. "I have a feeling that you're always looking after people when they come here."

I shrugged. "Well, it is my house."

"It is," he agreed, nodding and walking into the kitchen. "But I also have a feeling you rarely find yourself in situations where someone else is looking after you. Feeding you."

A pleasurable ache formed between my legs.

"*Feeding you.*"

Of course, he was talking about food.

Except he wasn't. I could see from the way his lip curled upward, his eyes flickering with the hunger I'd seen in my bedroom.

"I, um..." I cleared my throat. "I haven't had the occasion to have people... feeding me."

Rowan continued staring at me, this time with a wrinkle appearing between his brows. "Yeah, well, consider this the occasion." He looked to my fridge. "Am I gonna get in trouble for touching anything sacred in this kitchen?"

I let out a chuckle. "Why would you be in trouble?"

Rowan opened my fridge door, motioning to the organized shelves. "Never seen a fridge like this before, cupcake. I'm afraid you might chop off an appendage or somethin' if I put stuff back in the wrong place.

My lips stretched up in a smile. He was teasing, but he was doing it good-naturedly. Warmly.

"I like things a certain way, including all of your appendages." I hid behind my hands for a moment, realizing what I'd said. I swallowed my embarrassment then continued. "But I promise, I'm not going to punish you for not adhering to my slightly eccentric organization method."

His eyes flared. "I've got a feeling being punished by you is something that I'd enjoy very much."

My pussy throbbed with need even though I knew my body wouldn't be able to handle another orgasm. Okay, my body definitely could. My overstimulated mind on the other hand? No. I needed time to process.

We stared at each other for a handful of seconds before Rowan broke the spell between us.

"You got a book you've been wanting to read or a show you haven't had time to start watching?"

I blinked at the change of subject before I got my bearings. "Um, I have multiple shows and books that have been put on the backburner."

Though I enjoyed binging TV shows, and starting and finishing a book in one sitting, I'd been doing that less and less these days. My days were busy because I made them busy. Less time to be idle meant less time to overthink and convince myself I was suffering from whatever condition it was that time.

I hadn't suffered from anything but whatever the female version of blue balls was since Rowan had come into my life.

"Not that cowboy show, though," he said. "We're gonna watch that together. From the start."

I gaped at him. "You mean *Yellowstone*?" Dumfounded that he remembered my blithering episode about Rip and Kacey and Beth.

He nodded.

He wanted to watch *Yellowstone* with me. Again, considering what we'd just done upstairs, this shouldn't have felt as intimate as it did. But there was something domestic, permanent about watching a show together. Maybe not as romantic as whatever romantic gestures existed before the advent of streaming on demand, but it was to me.

"Go watch or read," Rowan ordered, arching his head to the sofa. "Let me cook for you."

Unable to argue with the man, I went and did what he ordered.

Maggie dutifully followed me.

I was certain after I curled up on the sofa, with Maggie lying against my legs and Rowan clanging away in the kitchen, that I would not be able to concentrate on the show I switched on.

But somehow, I did.

* * *

Rowan made spicy vodka pasta.

It was incredible.

I had two bowls of it, without feeling self-conscious that I was supposed to act demure and nibble at my food or whatever. Nathan had ordered salad for me whenever we went out, would scowl in disapproval whenever I ordered dessert. Although it stung, I never called him out like I should've. But I also didn't cancel the dessert order. I was comfortable with my body. I was never going to be the woman who wore a size zero, or even a size six. That wasn't how I was designed. I had curves. My stomach would never be completely flat, my hips would always be wide. I would always like sugar and wine, and I despised most forms of exercise. Nathan had known all of that when we got together.

Yet he still wanted me smaller, to fit in with all of his old fraternity brothers' wives, starve myself like his mother did.

Such a fucking asshole.

Rowan did not frown at my second helping. No, he made it bigger than the first.

And he did the dishes.

"But the chef doesn't do the dishes," I argued.

Rowan considered me with an arched brow. "You do the dishes when you cook for people?"

I pursed my lips. "It's my house, it doesn't count."

He snickered. "Uh-huh. I'm doing the dishes, cupcake, that's all there is to it. Before I do that, gonna light a fire."

He gestured toward the window, to where night had fallen, my solar lanterns illuminating my patio. All of my wicker furniture was centered around a large fire pit in the middle of the area. Fiona, Tina, Tiffany and I often sat out there as winter approached, cuddled up in blankets, drinking wine and talking through the night while the fire chased away the worst of the chill.

"You're gonna sit out there with your wine, and I'm gonna come join you when I'm finished," Rowan informed me.

"You like to give orders, don't you?" I teased.

His gaze darkened. "Oh, cupcake, you have no fuckin' idea."

My throat tightened and my pussy hummed with need. Again.

I swallowed roughly and gripped my wine.

"Now get that sexy ass of yours outside," Rowan ordered gruffly.

What was a woman to do? I got my sexy ass outside.

* * *

THOUGH THERE WERE plans of a grand romantic night at one of the best restaurants in the state—if not the country, in my humble opinion—and though those plans were somewhat ruined by a violent asshole, I found myself almost glad.

Not glad that Lori had been traumatized yet again—if I could've wished that away, I would have—but glad that the conventional date plans had been derailed.

Not just because of what had happened upstairs.

But because of what the night turned into. Sure, we might've skipped a bunch of steps—the unwritten dating handbook had some kind of time limit before a man was supposed to be in your space cooking dinner, but I didn't give a shit. That handbook had been thrown out the window. Not that Rowan was a man to stick by any rules in a handbook, written or unwritten.

And although, prior to this, I was a woman who stuck to rules, who believed in the stages of dating, boundaries—both physical and otherwise—in a relationship, I couldn't help but admit that this was the best date I'd had in my entire life.

We were sitting outside, the fire going. I was curled up against him on the wicker sofa, the fire flickering in front of us, wine in my hand.

"You've done good on this house," Rowan broke the comfortable silence. He was looking up at the exterior, the crisp white paint and the pink window shutters and detailing. If the man I bought it from knew I was planning on so much pink, I bet he would've burned it down rather than sold it to me.

"Fucking great," he amended. "I'm so fucking impressed with you, Nora."

My face, neck and ears heated at the compliment, still unused to how easily he gave them out, how sincere they were.

"Well, I'm sure you could've done it a lot better and in a much shorter time frame. And there're still a couple of things I need to work on."

"Don't do that." His tone was no longer warm and easy. It was stormy, like his pinched gaze.

"Do what?" I asked, feeling nervous, on guard.

"Cut yourself down. Your work. Try to make it smaller. This is as good if not better than I could've done. You're fucking amazing, Nora. A wonder."

My blush deepened, and I shifted uncomfortably in my chair.

"Thank you," I responded quietly.

I looked up at the house, at my work. Sure, I'd had help. And I'd cried plenty over the work, how hard it was. The mistakes I'd made and having to start all over. But it was pretty darn impressive.

"I've always wanted this area to be a greenhouse." I gestured around the patio. "Like in *Practical Magic*." It hit me then that I was talking to an Army vet turned construction worker and all-around alpha. "*Practical Magic* is a movie—"

"Know what *Practical Magic* is," he interrupted gently. "Seen the movie. Coupla times."

I jerked my head back in surprise.

He shrugged. "Got sisters. They love that fuckin' shit."

"You've got sisters?"

He nodded. "Two hellions. Well, one is a married hellion now, Kendra, which hasn't changed her one bit. Keith, her husband, worships her. Which of course, is the only way he's still breathing." He smiled as he sipped his beer. "Calliope is off in New York working on Wall Street, makin' far too much fuckin' money."

You could hear it. The pride in his voice. The love.

I hadn't known he had two sisters because I hadn't asked. It struck me I hadn't asked barely anything about his life. His family. The things you normally asked when you were dating someone.

But then again, we weren't dating in the normal sense of the word. We were too intimate for strangers. Which was what we were. Strangers. But not.

It felt uncomfortable to feel like I knew him, his body, but not his background.

"You're close with your family?" I asked.

He smiled, but it was a melancholy kind of smile. "Yeah, always have been. I'm the oldest. Though my sisters cluck over me like they know better than anything I've ever learned." He shook his head good-naturedly. "My father had his own construction business back home in a small town just outside of Bangor. He was the boss. Except in our house. That was my mom. My sisters. Not that either of us minded. Though they couldn't stop me from deploying. And each one of them tried."

I could imagine. Not from experience, mind you, but I could feel it in his voice. A loving family. Tight-knit. Two men, both alphas—because Rowan didn't come from nowhere. I would bet good money his father was one too—submitting to the women they loved. The family that saw their one boy—not that I could ever imagine Rowan being a boy—say he wanted to ship off to a war zone. One where he could be hurt. Maimed. Killed. At worst. And at best, he'd come home changed forever.

"Caused tension. A lot of it," he continued. "But they were proud. Mom had the bumper stickers, she put up signs in the yard. Sent care packages." He shook his head again. "Like if she did all that, she'd will me into coming home safe. And if anyone could, it was my mother."

My throat burned. Not with jealousy over Rowan having

that, but with joy. That a mother's love, pure and good, existed and created this man.

Rowan looked into the fire, something in his eyes telling me he wasn't seeing the flames but something else, was somewhere else.

I'd not seen that stare on him before. The thousand-yard stare. The one that told me he'd seen things I wouldn't believe and that those things had followed him. Marked him.

"We went from talking about *Practical Magic* to me." He smiled crookedly as he moved his gaze away from the fire.

He wanted off the subject. I understood that. If I stumbled into my past traumas on a night with the crisp fall air, a warm fire and good company, I'd want to stumble right out. There were nights to talk about such things. Then there were nights to relish, enjoy and appreciate that those traumas resided in the past.

"Well, if you know *Practical Magic* then you know the green-house. I want to replicate it... as much as I can." I nodded to the French doors off my kitchen, where we could see Maggie sleeping peacefully, the curtains blowing gently against her.

"I've done a lot," I admitted, my gaze running over the house, looking through the windows to all that I'd created. "But I don't know if my skills really translate to adding an entire addition onto my house."

"Could see it. Move this patio area across." He gestured to the doors off the living area where I currently had a small vegetable garden. "Because I plan to sit out here with you on many more nights," he added, making my insides flip.

Plans. Future plans. Ones that warmed me much more than the fire ever could.

I didn't quite know what to say to that. So, I snuggled closer into his warmth and didn't say anything at all.

* * *

AT SOME POINT, I must've fallen asleep out there because the last thing I remembered was the warmth of the fire, Rowan's body against mine, and the overwhelming feeling of contentment washing over me.

The next thing I knew, I was pressed against a warm chest, strong arms around me, and we were ascending the stairs.

The clink of dog nails against hardwood floors told me that Maggie was coming with us.

"Did I fall asleep?" I mumbled up at Rowan.

He was grinning as he walked us both into my bedroom and set me down on my feet. "Like a fucking rock," he replied, brushing hair from my face. "Never seen someone go down that quick or that deep."

"That's what she said," I muttered without thinking.

Rowan stared at me deadpan for a couple of seconds before bursting out laughing. Not just the chuckles I had come to adore, but a full-on belly laugh.

I'd never seen the man laugh before. The smirks at the bakery were what I'd collected over the years. And I had an inkling that this man didn't laugh often. It was the morose mood that hovered around him that gave me that inkling.

But here he was.

Laughing.

Because I made a stupid joke.

"Fuck, you're adorable," Rowan murmured when he'd finished laughing.

I could've melted at his feet right there.

But he wasn't done.

"I'm stayin' again tonight, Nora," he said softly.

I blinked sleepily at him.

"Don't think he's that stupid, but you pissed Ronnie Cockran off tonight, humiliated him," he continued, voice no longer soft. "Not takin' any risks with you." He cupped my cheeks. "Not putting you in danger."

Though he was mighty serious and speaking like he was uttering a vow, I couldn't help but grin. "Are you ever gonna stop the protective, alpha routine?"

His gaze was so intense, I was surprised it didn't scald me. "Never."

There it was. Another vow. One that felt heavy and permanent.

I took a moment to digest this. Though he was being over the top protective, he wasn't entirely wrong. I had humiliated Ronnie today. And he'd stared at me with cold hatred and anger. If he wasn't ready to take responsibility for his actions, he was likely ready to blame whomever was closest. Punish them.

And that was me.

It should've worried me more than it did.

But it didn't.

Not with Rowan in front of me.

"You're not sleeping in the guest room this time, though," I whispered.

His posture stiffened, and I watched his jaw flex. "Not a good enough man to fight you on that, Nora."

I didn't hold back my grin, going up on my tiptoes so I could lay my lips against his. "Good," was all I said.

THOUGH I WAS STILL INCREDIBLY sensitive between my legs from the use of my vibrator, I had plans for Rowan tonight. He was going to be in my bed. And he was going to be wearing... whatever he

164

wore to sleep. I was going to see that naked, muscular torso. Touch it.

My hunger for him burned brightly and fiercely, even though exhaustion made my limbs heavy and slack.

I went through my skincare routine as quickly as I possibly could, my eyelids getting heavier and heavier as I did so.

"I've got an extra toothbrush," I told Rowan when I emerged from the bathroom.

Then I stopped short.

Rowan had taken his shirt off and folded it neatly on one of the plush armchairs facing the doors to my balcony. There were two—large, linen and cozy, complete with ottomans. Putting two there was my version of manifesting, I guessed since my bedroom was one of the first rooms completed in my home, and I'd been single at the time.

There hadn't been anyone for me to sit next to at that time, watch the sunset with glasses of wine before retiring to bed. It had made no sense to spend an obnoxious amount of money on not one but two chairs when I had no evidence the second chair would get any use.

So of course, Nathan coming into the bakery not that long after I finished my bedroom and asking me out was something I took as a sign.

And it was only just now, in my sleepy state, I realized that was why I had held on to him so tight, ignored so many of the blazing red flags.

All because of that fucking chair.

Although it was a huge breakthrough, I didn't linger on that epiphany for long. Because Rowan was in my bedroom.

Shirtless.

And he was perfection.

My eyes took him in hungrily. As I expected, he was ripped.

All muscles. Biceps, shoulders, pecs. As if carved from marble. And the ridges of his abs... I had a very strong urge to run my tongue between them.

On closer inspection, I saw them. The scars. Not a lot, but enough. Enough scars marring the smooth, solid skin of his torso. Scars that communicated he had lived a violent life. That he had been in situations where people were trying to kill him.

My heart bled for him, for the man who'd had to experience that and come back to a family that loved him but wouldn't understand what he'd become.

I swallowed, thinking about all of that while still taking in his naked torso.

His jeans were unbuttoned, and he looked like he was just about to step out of them.

I licked my lips.

"Gotta stop doin' that, cupcake," Rowan said as he closed the distance between us, rubbing my bottom lip with his thumb.

"Doing what?" I whispered.

"Looking at me like that." He grasped my hips, pulling our bodies flush together. "Makes me want to fuck you right here on this floor."

It was a good thing he was holding on to me because I didn't quite trust my legs to hold me up after that little statement.

"I wouldn't be... adverse to that," I replied, my voice rough and full of need.

"Neither would I," he murmured as he yanked me even closer to show how much he wanted that. Me.

Need coiled through me.

"But you're dead on your feet, cupcake," he continued, smoothing back some hair on my face. "You were up before the sun today, on your feet all day, and I've got a hunch you got about as much sleep as I did last night because I was imagining this." He pressed his lips against mine. Soft at first, but then harder, hungrier.

I met his need with a hot hunger of my own.

Rowan leaned back, hands biting into my hips with a mixture of pleasure and pain. "I'll tell you that my imagination pales in comparison to the real thing."

My lips were swollen, my heart thundering, and my body his to command, despite the exhaustion creeping to all of my limbs.

"I want you, bad right now, Nora," he murmured against my lips. "But I want you rested. Because later, I'll want you up for hours. Want to take my time with you." His hand skimmed down my side. "Want to learn every inch of your body."

My breathing was quick and shallow as Rowan's hard-on pressed into my stomach.

"I have a feeling that no matter how late I'd keep you up tonight, you'd get up at the ass crack of dawn."

I nodded slowly. "Of course, I would."

Though I wouldn't like it, though my day would likely suck—because he was right, I didn't get any sleep the night before and would be a zombie after two nights without rest—and getting in late wasn't an option. I took pride in my business, my bakery.

I'd never resented my early mornings or my responsibilities. Never considered that a responsibility. Not until that very moment.

Rowan nodded, kissing my nose. "So, I'm not gonna be the reason my woman is losing sleep she can't make up. Especially when I can't convince her to play hooky."

"It's not playing hooky when it's my business, and I have employees, customers and my reputation to think of," I bit out, not feeling as warm toward this man as I had moments before.

There was nothing that would get my hackles up quicker than a man I was dating trying to get me to change the way I conducted my business, trying to take it away from me, in any kind of way. It was irrational and possibly unfair to get so snippy with Rowan so quickly, but he'd hit a nerve. One I didn't even know was so exposed until this moment.

Instead of looking pissed at my tone, Rowan grinned. "Yeah, there's no convincing you. So, you should point me in the direction of that toothbrush."

Whatever irritation that had sparked inside me disappeared quickly. I did what any sane woman might do, and I showed him where the toothbrush was, leaving him in the bathroom to do his business.

But not before I took a mental picture of him in my totally girly bathroom, complete with a claw-footed tub, brass fixtures, perfume and skincare arranged on the polished stone, double vanity.

Maggie had already claimed her bed as one of the chairs facing my balcony. I smiled at her, curled up and peaceful, scratching her head as I walked past.

Though I was growing more and more tired with every step, I couldn't resist slipping into a pink silk nightie with lace edging before I got into bed.

I had plans. To seduce Rowan, who seemed like he wouldn't need that much seducing. He was just trying to look out for me, after all. And I was willing to have a night without sleep for him to fulfill his promises.

Except I was asleep the moment my head hit the pillow.

CHAPTER
THIRTEEN

Recipe: Minty Lime Bars

From 'Dessert Person'

I had been planning on letting him sleep.

It was cruel to wake someone up this early two days in a row when they weren't accustomed to waking at that ungodly hour. I understood that there weren't many humans who could enjoy this hour. Fiona got to work an hour and a half after me, and she complained daily about the 'torture' it was, getting up with the sun.

Rowan did hard physical labor all day... He did not need to be up this early. I didn't expect anyone to keep the hours I did. That was an unfair expectation.

Plus, he looked so peaceful.

The sun was long from rising, but the dark of night had receded enough to illuminate his handsome face.

Rowan was a cuddler, something that delighted me. I'd slept encircled in his arms the entire night, my back to his front. Though I wasn't exactly what anyone would call slim, he was so large that he made me feel that way, tucked into him like I was made to be there.

At some point in the night, we'd both moved, him on his back and me half on top of him, using him like a pillow.

So, when I woke, I got to see him sleeping. Half-naked.

What a sight to see.

Though his face was still harsh, masculine lines, everything was softer now, relaxed. His hair brushed across the faint creases of his forehead—which only made him more attractive, same with the tanned skin—from working outside, I assumed. His full lips were slack, as was the rest of him. He was sleeping deeply. And he deserved it.

I took a handful more seconds to drink him in, to process that Rowan Derrick was truly asleep in my bed, then I got out of bed.

Or at least, I tried to.

Just as I turned to get out on my side, an arm grasped my hip and pulled me back to him.

I let out a muffled cry of surprise and delight as Rowan tucked me into his warmth.

"Like the nightie, cupcake," he murmured sleepily, running his hands along my bare thigh then upward, across the pink silk.

My body tingled with need.

"Thanks," I whispered, breathy.

"It was a special kind of torture, coming back to bed and seeing you wearin' it, fast asleep," he rasped, nuzzling my neck.

More body tingles.

Actually, I was pretty sure my body turned to jelly then.

"I didn't mean to fall asleep," I grumbled.

His hand spanned the silk just underneath the swell of my breast. "I figured as much. But you needed the sleep."

He was right. I had needed the sleep.

I was a routine girl. An early night girl.

Both my routines and early nights had been thrown out of whack since the moment Rowan entered the picture.

Not that I was complaining.

"You need your sleep too," I informed him. "It's much too early, and I didn't want to wake you."

"Haven't had the pleasure of sleeping next to you. So, I definitely notice when you're tryin' to get out of bed." He held me tighter, voice still thick with sleep.

My throat constricted as his hardness pressed into my back, showing me just how awake he was.

Though I thought that morning sex was something invented by Hollywood directors—because who really wanted sex when they first woke up, having not brushed their teeth or emptied their bladder—I was not averse to it. Even though I really would've liked minty fresh breath.

I broke out in chills as Rowan dropped soft kisses below my ear. "Could get used to wakin' up to you every morning," he said, inhaling. "And the way you fuckin' smell."

My spine prickled delightfully. He smelled pretty darn good himself. And even though I hadn't been interested in sleepovers before, I found myself realizing it was because I'd never slept with the right man.

There was a rustling of a collar then the clinking of nails against the hardwood floor.

Rowan groaned against my neck. "Apparently, Maggie is already accustomed to your schedule."

As if to agree, she put her two front paws on the bed, pushing herself up to say good morning.

It was the most adorable thing I'd ever seen.

"I'll go down and let her out, start the coffee." Rowan squeezed me once more before rolling out of bed.

I stared at his back, the pockmarks of scars on it, tracing the way the muscles moved as he did.

The urge to run my hands along every inch of his skin, press my lips against those scars and learn where they came from, hit me hard and quick.

I didn't know where they came from. What he'd gone through to get them. I knew what he'd endured had been dark; I'd heard it in his voice last night. But there was so much unknown about the man I'd let into my life, into my bed.

And he didn't know anything about me. We were still strangers, doing domestic tasks like letting the dog out and making coffee.

But it was far too early to be thinking about that. So instead, I watched them leave the room, Rowan with one long, lingering glance at me in bed that set my skin on fire. Then, once they went downstairs, I got myself in the shower so I could get ready for my day.

* * *

ROWAN'S EYES had been on me since I came downstairs in my dress. And yes, I might've put it on for him.

It wasn't really normal for me to wear a dress to work. Not unheard of since I dressed mostly based on my mood, and every woman should be able to wear a nice dress whenever the fuck she felt like it. But yes, this one might've been for Rowan's benefit.

It was a Diane von Fürstenberg wrap, black with tiny little

daisies all over it. It gave me great cleavage, skimmed my hour-glass figure perfectly, and ended mid-calf.

I'd paired the dress with a pair of wedges that had straps going up my ankle.

I'd spent a little more time on my hair this morning, trying to make my messy bun look effortless and sexy. And everyone knew an effortless looking bun took about three times longer than normal. Then I'd pulled strands down to look casual around my face. I swiped on some tinted moisturizer that made my pale skin look glowy and blush high on my cheeks.

Yes, I'd dressed for Rowan. Sue me.

Rowan liked the dress.

He made that known with the look he gave me. And by the way he grabbed on to me the second I made it to the kitchen, kissing the absolute heck out of me.

Then he'd made it known by murmuring, "Fucking love the dress, baby."

It seemed Rowan was not the kind of man to hide his feelings, nor was he the kind of man to keep praise to himself.

And he made me coffee.

Great coffee.

I cupped the mug he gave me, and we drank in silence until he went upstairs to finish getting dressed, and I got my things together so I was ready to leave.

I was used to the mornings being mine. Quiet. Feeling like I was the only person in the world. I'd liked it like that. It was one of the many excuses I'd used to make sure Nathan didn't stay over. Which wasn't a stretch anyway since he was a 'light sleeper' and would always complain about me waking him up too early.

On the rare occasions when he did stay over, my mornings

didn't feel sacred. I was aware of him, up there, sleeping, having to tiptoe around my own house.

It was not like that now. I was hyper-aware of Rowan's—and Maggie's—presence in the house. But it was not a bad thing. It made the place feel full, complete.

Especially when I got to see Rowan descending my stairs, dressed in the clothes from last night, putting on his cap, backward.

"Kip's picking me up from the bakery," Rowan said as I did my best not to drool all over him.

"Wouldn't it be easier for him to pick you up from here? You can go back to sleep. I assume you get up early, but not this early, and you have a long day of manual labor ahead. You need the rest."

Rowan's eyes twinkled. "Appreciate the concern, baby, but you're up, I'm up. There's no fuckin' way I'm going back to sleep in that bed without you in it."

My chest bloomed with warmth at that statement. Like he was planning on sleeping in my bed with me again.

Soon, I hoped, even though that bowled through all the sensible rules I had about dating.

No sex until the fourth date.

No sleepovers two nights in a row until we'd been dating for longer than two months.

That kind of thing.

I'd been steadfast about those rules, clinging to them for a variety of reasons, all of which stemmed from my childhood.

The rules existed to protect me. Although none of the men I'd dated could really do real damage. Because of the rules, because I held them at arm's length, because I picked men I could never truly fall in love with, I never really got hurt.

If there was ever a time to cling to those rules, it was now. If there was a man who could truly hurt me, it was this man in front of me.

"You don't start work for hours yet," I argued. "I'll drop you off at home first." I didn't want Rowan and Maggie having to hang around at the bakery for hours with nothing to do. I also was incredibly curious to see where Rowan lived.

"No," Rowan argued back. "You're not gonna be alone in that bakery on a street that's not gonna wake up for another few hours."

I frowned at him. "I'm there every morning on my own."

He nodded stiffly. "Yep, but every other morning you hadn't pissed off a man who we already know doesn't have a problem hurting women."

My throat went dry. I hadn't thought about Ronnie. Not once. Nor had I ever thought about me being alone and vulnerable in my bakery in the morning. Rowan was right. It was hours before the other business down the street opened. Even the early risers who ran on the beach waited for the sun to come up, especially with the weather cooling down.

I'd liked that. Loved it. Feeling like this was my time, when no other responsibilities existed. Just the measuring of sugar, butter, flour and chocolate.

I would not let anyone pollute that.

"I highly doubt that Ronnie Cockran is motivated enough to get up at five in the morning to teach me a lesson," I countered. "I doubt he's up before noon."

The worry about him was a niggle in the back of my head, no different than the niggles every woman had in the back of her head about the creepy guy at the grocery store who stared at her too long, the guy at work who was always asking her out, the ex-boyfriend who didn't take the breakup well.

Ronnie could hurt me, that was not something I was

deluding myself about. Sure, the chances were slim now that he knew he had a whole bunch of people watching him, ready to teach him the lesson he sorely deserved.

But I wasn't going to change the way I lived my life, and I wasn't going to make Rowan feel like he needed to be my bodyguard every second I was alone.

"You're not gonna change my mind, Nora."

Maybe I should've fought more. Told him that he couldn't barge into my life, home and business, declaring he had to protect me from one thing or another.

But I didn't. Because I didn't want to fight him.

Rowan went into the bakery first. Did a 'walk through,' whatever the fuck that meant.

Maggie and I waited in my office, her going to sleep on the sofa across from my desk. She was not at all perturbed by new spaces and was quick and happy to claim them as her own. I liked that. No, I loved that.

Rowan appeared in the doorway with a brisk nod that I guessed communicated everything was clear. It was good timing too. My caffeine high was wearing off, and the espresso machine was calling my name.

But before I did that, I had to get some dough ready for the first batch of croissants. That's what I was thinking of when I walked past Rowan into the kitchen.

"You can go now," I told him. "There's no one here. Ronnie isn't hiding in the pantry," I joked.

But Rowan was not in the joking mood, it seemed.

He stepped forward, purposefully.

The look in his eyes glued my feet to the floor.

"Gotta have a taste before I go anywhere," he murmured.

Then he was kissing me. Claiming me.

My body responded immediately, viscerally.

Rowan let out a low growl from the back of his throat, and my whole body vibrated with pleasure.

His hands found my hips, then he lifted me up onto the counter, objects clattering to the ground somewhere far away.

I opened my legs for him to step between, for his hardness to press up against the lace of my panties as he pulled my dress up my thighs.

I let out a groan of pleasure as I ground myself against him, desperate for the friction of his jean clad cock against the thin placket of my panties. The need was overwhelming; I felt ready to climax from just that.

"You don't want me to fuck you right here and now, you gotta tell me," Rowan rasped against my lips.

"If you don't fuck me right here and now, I'll go crazy," I whispered, clinging to him.

I'd barely gotten the words out of my mouth before Rowan shoved my dress up to my hips.

I was thankful for the stretchy fabric as I lifted my arms upward, and he yanked it off, throwing it to the floor before bending his neck to suck my aching nipples through the lace of my bra.

I let out a low curse, and my body electrified with need, an orgasm already building up inside of me from his teeth brushing against my sensitive nipples.

My hands clutched his head, throwing off his baseball cap and running through his hair.

"Rowan," I pleaded

He lifted his head, eyes dark with need.

"I need you," I whimpered, my hands moving down to push at his jacket.

He didn't hesitate in discarding the jacket on the floor. My hands went to the bottom of his tee, yanking it up over his head.

I was desperate, wild... near insane with need. I wanted his skin against mine. Wanted him inside of me.

Rowan seemed to be seized by that same madness as he reached to unclasp my bra, discarding it then cupping my breasts, kneading them, massaging them. My eyes rolled back in pleasure, then he grasped the back of my neck, pulling me forward for one more brutal kiss before he pressed me downward. My back found the cool surface of the counter as he arched my hips up in order to get my panties off.

Rowan let out a low hiss of appreciation as his gaze ran over my naked body.

"Need to taste you before I fuck you," he declared, pushing my thighs apart before feasting on the apex of them with his eyes.

I'd never been presented to a man like this before. Never felt so desired.

Rowan stared at me a moment longer, then he dove in. His hands were underneath my ass, lifting me upward to him, giving him the angle he needed. The angle I needed.

He was relentless, tongue working expertly against my clit, making my body sing to him. I'd thought that he looked like a man who could eat pussy like a champ, and I had thought right.

No man had ever made me feel like this with his mouth before. No man had ever fucking *feasted* on me before. I writhed against the cool surface of the counter, arching myself upward to his mouth.

"You taste so fuckin' sweet," he growled, his words vibrating against my pussy.

I was almost at my breaking point when my eyes met his.

"You gonna come for me like a good girl?" he asked as he pushed a finger inside of me.

My teeth sunk into the flesh of my lip, so hard I tasted blood.

His finger moved inside me, slowly, torturing me. I knew from the wicked look on his face it was intentional, that he could feel how close I was to climax.

"Nora, are you gonna come for me?" he asked again, low and thick.

I nodded rapidly, barely able to move, desperate for release.

"Tell me you're gonna be my good girl."

My body spasmed against his finger, seconds away from exploding but needing his mouth.

"I'm gonna be your good girl," I rasped.

He smiled wickedly before his lips found my pussy again.

My first orgasm washed over me, hot and quick and over-whelming. My body was plagued with aftershocks, and I barely noted that he was standing, reaching into a pocket or a wallet until I heard the telltale crinkle of a foil packet.

At least one of us was thinking. Condoms were not even on my radar right then. Not even a little. I wouldn't have asked him to put one on. Furthermore, I wanted him inside me without one.

Except I wasn't on the pill. Didn't want to disrupt my hormones like that.

I was clean, and I was pretty sure that Rowan was too, but that wasn't enough to risk my health and a possible pregnancy.

So, I was distantly glad that Rowan did the thinking for the both of us.

He got the condom on and lifted me upward from where I was lying. Our faces were inches apart, his eyes burning into mine. "Want to look at you when I fuck you for the first time," he murmured, lips brushing mine.

And then he was inside me.

I cried out in pleasure, my body still sensitive from his lips, still recovering from my first orgasm.

Rowan didn't ease in. Didn't take me gently. He held on to me, thrusting hard and slow.

My body met each of his thrusts, hungry, ravenous for more.

"You're gonna feel me inside you all day, cupcake."

My pussy clenched around him in response to his words.

"So fucking hot," he continued. "Such a sweet. Fucking. Pussy." He enunciated his words with harder thrusts, each one bringing me closer to the edge, with me toppling off at the word 'pussy'.

He kissed me then, likely tasting the blood from how hard I'd sunk my teeth into the skin of my lip.

My body opened up to him, moved in tandem with his as he continued fucking me with the perfect force, with the perfect rhythm.

"You're mine," Rowan grunted, the veins of his neck bulging.

My body soared as another orgasm rocked me. This one more intense than the last. More intense than anything I'd ever experienced in my life.

Suddenly, Rowan stopped. Completely. Gripped my hip with one hand and the back of my neck with the other. "Say it," he gritted out.

His body was stiff, his stare cold, almost feral. Rowan was holding himself still with great effort. "Say you're mine, Nora."

"I'm yours," I gasped.

His eyes blazed with satisfaction as I tightened my legs around him. "Now say you're mine," I demanded.

He grinned. "Oh, I'm fuckin' yours, Nora." Then he began moving again. And he took us both over the fucking edge.

* * *

AGAIN, there could've been awkwardness in the aftermath of getting fucked on the counter. Especially with two people who weren't familiar enough to know each other's after-sex routine.

But just like everything with Rowan so far, all rules and expectations were broken.

He stayed inside of me after we were done, breathing heavily, holding me to him tightly. I was clinging to him for dear life, my limbs lead, my heartbeat thundering and my mind in pieces. I'd never had an experience that sexual, that explosive.

Rowan pressed his forehead against mine, eyes locking on me, unwavering. Though he was literally still inside me, the act itself, of that unbroken eye contact, felt far too intimate, too meaningful. But also, far too right at the same time.

"You we're fuckin' made for me," he murmured. "Never came that hard in my fuckin' life. And I already get hard whenever I smell cinnamon. I'm done for now."

Though he was speaking very seriously, his voice a low rumble, I couldn't help but let out a little giggle.

"Cinnamon?" I repeated.

A lazy grin spread across his face as he dropped a kiss on my lips. "Let me tell you, baby, any time I smell baked goods, I think of you. Naked." He grabbed my hips, pulling me closer, proving he was still hard inside me.

I let out a little gasp of pleasure.

"Yeah," Rowan hissed in satisfaction. "So now, any time I smell cinnamon or chocolate, I'm gonna think of this right here, and I'm gonna be fucking done for."

Warmth spread through my belly as he gazed at me intently, not speaking for a handful of seconds.

"Yeah, fucking done for," he murmured, kissing me hard before he gently pulled out of me.

"Stay right there," he ordered. "Gonna take care of the condom and be back."

"I couldn't move if I wanted to," I told him honestly.

He gave me another lazy grin, staring at me like he was imprinting a photo to memory before walking in the direction of the bathroom.

Another time, I might've gone straight into panic mode or started overthinking everything. But in an act almost unheard of for me, I just laid there, thinking of nothing but how relaxed I felt. How every cell in my body felt satisfied.

The low thump of Rowan's boots announced his return to the kitchen. As if pulled by some magnetic force, my eyes fixed on him of their own volition, roving over his strong body, his thick muscles, the shadow on his jaw. I found it incredibly hard to believe that this man was just inside me. That this man had just vowed he was mine while giving me the best sex of my life.

Rowan grasped my hips then gently put me on my unsteady feet, reaching down to retrieve my dress from where he'd tossed it onto the floor.

I took it from him wordlessly, slipping it back on.

Rowan watched me as I wrapped the dress back around me, tying the tie firmly. With my dress settled back on my body, reality rushed back in.

"I can't believe we just had sex in the kitchen," I whispered, my cheeks warming.

One side of his mouth turned up in a devilish smirk. "I can't believe I just fucked you like I did, and you're still blushin'."

My hands went to my cheeks. "I can't help it."

"Don't want you to help it," he replied. "Don't ever want you to stop blushin' with me."

"I don't think I'm ever going to be in danger of that," I responded.

He kissed my nose then ran his hands down the side of my dress.

"You go about your morning," he commanded, stepping back.

"What are you going to do?" I asked, straightening my dress. "It's going to be incredibly boring for you to spend the morning watching me."

He settled himself on a stool right by the counter. "Like fuck it is."

I felt myself blush again. I couldn't help it.

He did that to me.

And he stayed there, on the stool, nursing the coffee I brought him while watching me begin the day's preparations, making all of our morning treats.

He especially liked that he was the first one to get them out of the oven.

It was not long before Fiona arrived, yelling about how this hour of the morning should be illegal, and I should be sued for unfair working conditions—pretty much the same shit she said every morning until she'd had her first coffee.

She stopped short, though, when she made it into the kitchen and saw Rowan sitting there.

To her credit, she didn't look surprised. Not even a little. She looked like it was the total norm to walk into the kitchen at six thirty in the morning and see a sex god in a backward baseball cap sitting there drinking coffee and watching me work.

Watching me work on the counter he'd fucked me on earlier.

To be fair, I'd disinfected it three times. And Fiona did not know we'd had sex on the counter.

"So, you know what it feels like to be up this early, and you still like her?" she asked, striding forward to snatch a muffin from the rack where they were cooling and then my coffee cup out of my hand.

"You could say that," Rowan replied, looking at me with a gaze that was entirely inappropriate and entirely panty-melting.

Fiona's eyes darted between the two of us. "Ugh," she groaned, stomping to the fridge for my homemade coffee creamer. "It is too fucking early for the two of you to be so damn cute. I demand you stop."

I smiled. As did Rowan.

And that's how the day started.

CHAPTER
FOURTEEN

Recipe: Double Apple Crumble Cake

From 'Dessert Person'

I floated on a cloud the rest of the day. A sex cloud.

Fiona commented on it after Rowan left, after she'd had her second coffee and regained the ability to be somewhat human and observant.

"You got laid!" she screeched.

Luckily, we'd only just opened, so it was just me, Tina, and Joanne, a customer who came in for muffins after her morning runs with her headphones still blasting.

Fiona loved Joanne because she didn't have to make any conversation with her, and she got the same thing every time. She also loved Joanne because she ran six miles every morning and finished that run with a full fat caramel latte and a huge chocolate muffin.

It was safe to say my best friend was very happy about the turn of events. Even more so when she found out the deed happened in the bakery.

"You don't think it's... I don't know..." I shrugged.

"Super hot?" she suggested. "One for the books? Straight out of a porno written by a woman?"

I didn't fight the grin pulling at my lips. I should've known better than to think my very sex positive and open-minded friend would place any judgment on me fucking a guy for the first time in our place of work.

"This bakery is your life." She waved her hand around. "It makes sense it would happen here. Makes it more meaningful." She waggled her brows. "And hot."

She wasn't wrong.

"You two already looked cozy this morning. Like a couple," she added. "Him sitting there watching you bake like you invented the process." She shook her head. "Vomit inducing."

I giggled at that. "Is it too fast?" I verbalized the question that had been gnawing at my gut, biting my lip. "I mean, we haven't even been on a real date—"

"Who needs a real date when you can get fucked on a kitchen counter?" Fiona interrupted.

"Conventional dating rituals are designed to keep women chaste, submissive, and in pursuit of some bullshit puritan identity... all invented by men," Tina offered from the coffee machine.

"Amen to that." Fiona bumped knuckles with her. "Don't overthink this," Fiona demanded, pointing her finger at me. "Don't sabotage it. You deserve this. Just enjoy the ride, baby." Her eyes twinkled. "No pun intended."

She knew me too well. I was going to overthink and search for a reason why this wouldn't work, why this was too good to be true. That's what I did, to protect myself from being hurt.

But I was going to try this time. To just let myself be happy. To believe I deserved this happiness.

* * *

Rowan made one more visit than usual to the bakery that day. He greeted me as he had the day prior, by rounding the counter and kissing the heck out of me. He got cheers from the afternoon rush, who obviously approved of this new relationship.

I had hidden my face and muttered about PDA but had leaned into the warm, hard space of his chest.

Despite the PDA, Rowan hadn't mentioned anything more about a date. I might've been self-conscious about that, thinking that he'd abandoned the need to wine and dine me to get me into bed since I'd already gotten into bed.

Or on the counter, if you wanted to get technical.

Rowan was not giving me vibes that he was just in it for the conquest; he was giving me long-term, commitment kind of vibes. But I wasn't experienced enough to see the truth of the situation, certainly not when I was so infatuated with this man.

So, when I didn't hear from him after the bakery closed, my mind ran to a bad place. I was a mess during my drive home, even more so when it occurred to me that I didn't even have the man's phone number.

Which of course, was incredibly dramatic and over the top since I'd already seen him three times that day. He'd literally fucked me in the kitchen in the early hours of the morning. It was greedy of me to expect him to structure his entire life around me after less than a week.

This was good, I told myself. This was getting closer to the way a regular relationship operated. Space. It was important. So I didn't lose myself. So this didn't burn out hot and quick.

Yet there I was, driving home with an ache in my chest, a familiar, burgeoning panic taking root in my stomach. It was foolish of me to think that any man, even Rowan, could fix something that had been off in me for years.

I couldn't start to expect things from him. Couldn't start relying on him.

Which was really fucking hard to do when I pulled up to my house to see two trucks parked in the driveway with the script 'Derrick & Goodman Construction' on the doors. The signage was in a large black font, very masculine and strong yet still elegant and artful.

The ache in my chest subsided as I got out of my car and walked through my house.

"What are you doing here?" I asked, staring at the space where my patio furniture used to be.

Now there was a collection of timber, Kip looking at some kind of blueprints with a pencil behind his ear.

He looked up at me and gave me a chin lift in greeting before turning his attention back to the blueprints.

Rowan didn't answer me. He instead put down the tools he was using and strode over to me, taking my face in his hands and kissing me hard and quick.

"Hi," he mumbled against my lips.

"Hi," I whispered, forgetting myself for a moment.

"This is your gentle reminder that you have an audience," Kip called from somewhere behind us.

I stifled a groan and tried to step back, having in fact forgotten that Kip was there.

Rowan's palms moved to my hips, keeping me in place, close to him.

I knew trying to fight him wasn't going to get me anywhere. Plus, I liked his hands on me. I'd missed him. In the scant few hours we'd been apart, I'd already begun missing him. A lot.

That scared me. Polluted the warmth that had settled deep in my belly. I'd learned that good feelings were fleeting, unable to be trusted. Something bad was always on the horizon. That's why I worried. If I didn't have something to worry about, it meant something bad was coming soon. So, I always had something to worry about, even if it was a made-up terminal illness.

"What are you doing?" I asked again, doing my best to push those fears away.

"Building your *Practical Magic* greenhouse," he answered, as if it were obvious.

I blinked at him. "You're building my greenhouse?"

He hummed in confirmation. "Kip's got the plans. You want to alter them, let me know. But it's gonna get cold soon, so I want this done for you before winter sinks its teeth in."

He squinted at the house. "Got as close as I could to the layout in the movie, having made some adjustments."

I struggled to comprehend this. "I told you about this last night."

His lip twitched. "I was there."

"I told you about this last night, and today, the next day, you're just... building me a greenhouse?" I needed to ask the question out loud.

"Not gonna take too much time," he shrugged. "Maybe a week. Two. We're gonna spend a few hours after work each night, a full day on the weekends, an hour here and there whenever we're between jobs."

I just stared at him.

"You're building me a greenhouse," I repeated, but this time it wasn't a question.

Rowan's expression softened. "Yeah, cupcake. I am."

I battled against the tears filling my eyes. I battled against the numerous emotions fighting for supremacy in my body right then.

The man I was kind of dating, the one I'd been attracted to for years, the one who had fucked me on the counter of my bakery earlier that day was now at my house. Building me a greenhouse.

How did one even begin to process that?

"I'm going to get a glass of wine," I blurted out, turning then all but running from the area.

Rowan's chuckle followed me.

* * *

ONCE THE WINE was opened and I'd downed the first glass in record time, I did the only thing I could do. I called the person I always reached out to when I didn't know how to feel. When I was off-kilter, outside of myself.

He answered on the second ring.

"I have a guy," I blabbered into the phone.

"In your basement?" my brother asked without missing a beat. "Make sure the handcuffs are secure."

I smiled, cradling my glass of wine against my chest. "I always make sure the handcuffs are secure," I told him deadpan. "But this one doesn't need to be restrained."

Though it was incredibly inappropriate, my mind went to what Rowan's opinions on restraints in the bedroom would be. Sure, he was an incredibly dominant guy, and I was more than willing to submit to him, but something hot sparked inside of me at the thought of him being completely at my mercy.

Then I remembered I was on the phone with my brother, and

I was a terrible, sex-crazed woman to be thinking of that in that moment.

"Oh my god, you're thinking about restraining the guy you don't currently have restrained," Ansel exclaimed, reading my mind in that uncanny way of his.

The uncanny way of ours, I guessed since I could do the same with him. It made sense... We knew each other *that* well. We'd shared a womb. And we'd also shared a life full of traumas. We had only had each other for the longest time. There was no me without him.

"The sex must be good if you're thinking about restraints while on the phone with your brother," he snickered.

"Stop," I hissed, grateful that he couldn't see my expression. "He's building me a greenhouse."

I watched both Rowan and Kip moving about, purposefully, with the fluidity of two men who had worked beside each other for years.

"A greenhouse?" my brother repeated.

I nodded, watching Maggie run happily around the backyard. "Like in *Practical Magic*."

"Holy fuck," my brother breathed. "You've been seeing a guy long enough for him to know you and love you enough to build you a fucking greenhouse, and you're only *now* just telling me?"

"I only just started seeing him," I rushed to explain. "It's happened... fast."

"Fuck yes, it has," my brother agreed.

"Is it too fast?" I asked, biting my lip. "I mean, I was engaged not that long ago."

"To an asshole," my brother scoffed, not one to mince words.

I winced at the memory of the one and only time Ansel had met Nathan. Sure, my brother was protective over me, even though historically, I had been the one who took care of the both of us. Boyfriends, and men in general, were when he didn't fuck around.

He didn't go completely crazy like a dad with a shotgun. He made an effort to get to know them. To be polite while giving off the energy he wouldn't hesitate to put them in the ground if they hurt me.

My brother was not a violent man. Not even a little bit. Sure, he looked like he was since he spent a lot of time in the gym, building considerable muscles. He boxed three times a week. Mostly because he wanted to be strong. Because he wanted to be able to take care of himself, make sure he would never be a victim again.

But the thing with my brother was he'd never turn anyone into a victim.

The other thing with my brother was he knew me better than I knew myself. He knew people. He believed that he could 'read their auras'. I'd always inwardly rolled my eyes but couldn't fault his judge of character.

He'd instantaneously disliked Nathan. I knew, not because he'd made it known, but because I knew him. He'd tried his best, tried to be polite when Nathan subtly spoke down to him about his lack of education, money, his trade, and especially about his spiritual beliefs.

Ansel had, in turn, subtly spoken about how rich, white families were the downfall of society.

Safe to say the visit hadn't gone well. It was definitely the beginning of the end for us. I could never be married to someone who wasn't right with Ansel. Because if you weren't right with Ansel, you weren't right with me.

"Okay, he was an asshole," I conceded.

"Oh, this guy must be good if he's making my little sister finally say something well deserved about the asshole she dumped. It was all, 'oh, we were wrong for each other,' 'we wanted different things,'" he mimicked.

I grinned again. Ansel wasn't wrong. I'd made excuses for Nathan until I couldn't. But I also hadn't been able to find it in me to verbalize how I truly felt about him.

"You'd like him," I said to Ansel, leaning against the counter and watching them work. "Rowan. You'd like him."

"I know I'd like him," Ansel agreed without hesitation. "I can hear it in your voice. He makes you happy."

He knew me too well.

"I want you to meet him," I said impulsively.

It was too soon to meet each other's family. That was another important relationship milestone that had a timeline on it. Six months or so. Enough time to decide whether you really liked the person enough to put up with their family. To risk having yours ask about them if it didn't work out.

But I didn't have a family. Except for Ansel.

Tina. Fiona.

That was it. He'd already met two thirds of them. And they'd already given him their stamp of approval.

But my brother was important. My brother meeting him made it real. My brother would be able to see... Feel. Reassure me that I wasn't dreaming this up. That I wasn't missing something.

Ansel was my North Star. The only person in the world I trusted.

"Of course, I'm gonna meet him," Ansel replied. "I'm shit on my vacation days because we just took a trip to Joshua Tree to commune with Mother Nature."

I rolled my eyes but continued to smile.

"Is the end of the month too soon?" Ansel asked.

My heart lifted. "No, that's not too soon!" I half yelled, almost ready to jump up and down with excitement.

I hadn't seen Ansel since he flew down to be with me after I called off the wedding. Two months may not be that long to other people, to other siblings. It was a fuck of a long time when it was your best friend, your other half.

"Good," Ansel said. "I'll book the tickets."

"Don't be silly," I chided. "I'll book them."

"Sis, I am not going to keep letting you buy my plane tickets for me," he turned serious.

"I don't mind doing it." I sipped my wine. I really didn't. Part of me worked so hard to be financially independent, to have money. Sure, being able to pay my bills and afford good health insurance was great. Along with the fancy pillows, wine and the nice things.

But my biggest accomplishment was being able to look after my brother. Though he was older—technically—smart, talented and could achieve anything he wanted, his road had been a little rougher. He was finally getting better, building a good life, but I wanted to help him. Especially wanted to get him free from the shackles of my mother.

"Really, Nora, I can pay," Ansel told me firmly. "I'm getting paid well now. In fact, I'm getting transferred to Arizona. Getting full benefits."

My mouth dropped at that piece of news. "Arizona?" I asked, sad that it wasn't closer to me but understood that he needed to find his place in the world.

"Sedona, to be exact," Ansel clarified. "Full of vortexes of spiritual energy."

"Of course, it is."

"Don't laugh at me," he ordered.

I pressed my lips together, trying to swallow my smile. My eyes met Rowan's for a beat. The corner of his lips turned up as he glimpsed me through the window.

Maggie came bounding in from outside, her tail wagging maniacally as I scratched her behind the ears.

"I'm not laughing," I told him truthfully.

"Yeah, yeah," he muttered.

"I can't wait for you to get here. To meet Rowan," I told him excitedly, being sure to keep my voice down so it didn't carry outside. "I think he's it. The real thing. My guy." I never would've said this to anyone else. Not even Fiona. Not this soon, at least. But I needed to bounce it off Ansel.

"I'm sure he is," Ansel responded.

"It's too soon for me to know that," I argued with him.

"It's not too soon when you know," he countered. "I know our life hasn't exactly given you good reason to believe that good things happen, that the future is something to look forward to. I know it's hard to trust your instincts when your traumas are polluting them. But believe it, honey. It's time to shed old skin. Old habits."

I breathed in his words. He was right. We'd been dragging our pasts along with us for long enough. He was coming out the other side, finally getting his life together and getting away from Chicago.

"Does she know?" I asked, my body tensing at the thought of her.

There was a pause on the other end of the phone. "Not yet."

"She's going to try and stop you," I said, pinching the bridge of my nose.

"She can try." My brother's voice was strong. Resolute.

I was still uneasy at the thought of my mother trying to find a way to get her hooks back in, but I had to trust this. Him.

"Things are going to work out for the both of us," Ansel reassured me. "I promise."

"I'll see you at the end of the month," I said, even though

we'd definitely be talking before then. We spoke almost every day, even if it was just sending silly videos to each other.

"You bet your ass you will." I could hear his smile through the phone.

"Love you," I whispered.

"And I love you more," he repeated the phrase we'd uttered all our lives.

My brother's words echoed in my ears as I placed the phone down on the counter then walked outside to where the men were still working.

"How do you guys feel about pizza for dinner?"

"I'm down!" Kip replied immediately. "I'll eat anything but pineapple. That shit does not belong on pizza."

I nodded. "Agree with you on that one."

I looked at Rowan who was watching me with amusement. He was likely thinking back to his first night here, when I'd acted like ordering pizza was akin to planning a murder.

"I'm trying something new," I told him in response to the questioning look he gave me.

He just flashed me his pearly whites. "Didn't say a word."

I shook my head. "Do you have any pizza preference?"

"Nope. Whatever you want, cupcake."

A surge of desire shot through me. I didn't know how he did it, but he was making ordering pizza somehow sexual.

I really wanted to do things to him. Wanted him to do things to me. But he was here with his best friend, building my greenhouse. So, I went inside and ordered pizza instead.

CHAPTER
FIFTEEN

Recipe: Chocolate-Hazelnut Galette des Rois

From 'Dessert Person'

Fiona ate with us. I called to invite her over for dinner, to watch the men building, and maybe because I had some matchmaking thoughts about my best friend and Rowan's best friend.

Fiona didn't exactly have a type, but Kip was the kind of man who appealed to everyone.

I wanted my friend to be happy. Not that she wasn't already. Nor did she need a man to define her happiness, but in the time I'd known her, she hadn't had a serious relationship. Despite her constant smile and her easy demeanor, there was something dark there, something chasing her. Something that she hadn't shared with me. But I knew it was there because like knew like. I hadn't pressed her. Wouldn't press her. She would tell me if and when she was ready. Or she'd let it stay buried and keep trying to make a life here.

I selfishly wanted that life to be permanent.

This was the longest time she'd been in one place, her family a world away. Her visa wouldn't last forever. Romance, a real, true love, meant roots.

But Fiona sensed my intentions once the pizza was consumed and I'd served a French chocolate tart for dessert—I was still me and couldn't have guests without serving dessert. We'd all settled in the living room with beer and wine, music playing from my speaker system, while Maggie napped happily on the rug.

"Just to be clear," Fiona announced, her narrowed eyes focused on Kip. "This is not going to be a thing." She waved her arms between them first, then at our little group in general. "We're not in some fucking Hallmark movie or CW show. This isn't where two best friends fall for the other two best friends." Her gaze then turned to me and Rowan. "You two are cute as fuck, I get that. You're a Hallmark movie all on your own. But I am not interested in him." She pointed her finger at Kip.

He just simpered. "The lady doth protest too much, methinks," he said before taking a pull of his beer.

I tried to stifle a giggle but failed, resulting in Fiona sending a withering glare in my direction.

"I'm serious," she hissed.

I held my hands up in surrender. "I'm not going to make you sleep with Kip."

"Oh, no one's going to have to make her," he chimed in, eyes dancing with amusement.

"There's not enough money or penicillin in the entire world," she told him sweetly.

"And there's not enough booze in the entire world to get me

drunk enough to go close enough to get those nails sunk into me," he replied without missing a beat.

All of their interactions the rest of the night had been somewhat similar. It was amusing to watch, though I was disappointed that it wasn't going to work out between them.

It felt nice, though. Sitting there together, listening to them rib each other while tucked into Rowan's side, his finger drawing lazy circles on my arm.

I started to get distracted when that finger was no longer drawing lazy circles on my arm, but slipping under the fabric of my tee and running all the way up my ribs to the underside of my breast.

We were positioned in a way that it wasn't obvious to our two best friends that Rowan's callused fingers were moving toward my nipple, but I was not exactly skilled at schooling my reactions when it came to this man and his hands on me.

I wasn't used to him and his touch, his easy affection or the way my body exploded with desire with every passing minute.

Luckily for me, the pizza was done, the tart was consumed, and the night was drawing to a close, with both Kip and Fiona needing to get back to their respective homes.

"Unless you've decided to keep lying to yourself, conquer your fears and come home with me?" Kip offered Fiona at the door.

She made a disgusted face. "If I decide to come home with you, just know I've been possessed by some kind of demonic entity and someone needs to call Jensen Ackles.'" She leaned in to kiss me goodbye, nodding at Rowan then flipping Kip the bird.

He was not perturbed in the slightest, beaming at both Rowan and me. "She's gonna fall in love with me when she least expects it." He winked before sauntering out the door.

Both Rowan and I stood in front of the closed door, his arms around me, listening to the crunch of tires against gravel as our two best friends left.

I didn't want to ask if he was going to leave too, because I didn't *want* him to leave. I knew I was supposed to want him to leave. To create boundaries, hold on to the independence I'd only recently won back from a man. But I didn't. And I felt guilty about that.

So, I just stood there, next to him, acting like if I didn't move, I wouldn't have to make any kind of decisions, act like a responsible adult.

Rowan did not seem to be struggling with any of the same kind of issues.

Luckily.

He whirled me around as the sound of Kip's truck engine retreated into the night.

My heartbeat quickened as my eyes met his, full of hunger.

"I fuckin' love your curves," he rumbled, running his hands down the sides of my body.

Despite everything we'd done, the intimate way he knew my body, I still trembled at the delicate touch.

"Good," I gulped, finding it hard to hold on to coherent thought. "Curves are an occupational hazard. Don't you know you should never trust a skinny baker?"

Rowan didn't respond to my joke. His hands drifted to the bottom of my sweater, then he pulled it up.

I lifted my arms in compliance, my nipples already pebbling, my pussy tingling with need.

From the look on Rowan's face, from the way his body flexed with need, and from the delicious shape of his cock pressing against his jeans, I thought that he was going to yank me to him. Kiss me. Lift me up and carry me upstairs to my bedroom.

I would've been partial to any and all of those things. To be honest, I felt as if I might go insane if he didn't do one or all of those things.

Except he didn't.

He stepped back so his hands were no longer on me, so I could no longer feel the heat of his body.

"Stay there," he growled as I took a step toward him on instinct.

My body froze in place at his command, my heartbeat thrashing, panties already soaked.

"Take off your bra," Rowan ordered.

Shaking, I reached my arms around to unclasp my bra, the lace tumbling onto the ground beside my feet.

Rowan's eyes zeroed in on my nipples, rubbing at his lips with his entire hand. They ached as they hardened even further.

"Pants," he uttered, his voice guttural.

Again, my hands shook as I obeyed, stepping out of my pants.

"Panties." The word was said the second I straightened.

His gaze was a physical thing. Inescapable. Unyielding.

My body was strained, coiled with the need for release as I stood there, in my foyer, completely naked, him in front of me fully clothed while devouring me with his eyes.

There was no room for self-consciousness. For doubt about the way my body curved, dimpled. No, I couldn't doubt an inch of myself when Rowan was staring at me like that.

"You're the most beautiful creature I've ever laid eyes on," he growled, grasping the bottom of his tee and ripping it off.

Where I had taken my clothes off slowly, tentatively, he all but tore his from his skin. It seemed it was only two slow blinks and his jeans were mingled with the rest of his clothes on the floor, and he was standing there naked.

In my foyer.

We stared at each other for one beat. That was it.

Then he was on me. His hands on the back of my neck, yanking our mouths together, our naked skin pressing against one another.

I kissed him back in a fury, both outside myself and more in my own skin than I'd ever been in my entire life.

Rowan fisted my hair, using his grip to pull my head back.

When our eyes met, his were pools of pure desire.

"Place your hands flat against the door and present that ass to me," he demanded, voice thick and raspy.

My stomach dipped with fear and desire, but I obeyed, turning slowly and placing my palms flat against the cool wood of my front door.

Rowan's fingers trailed down my spine, my whole body quivering.

"Legs spread, ass up to me."

Knees quaking, I obeyed.

His palms ran along the skin of my ass, moving underneath to cup my aching, drenched pussy.

But he didn't go inside as I expected him to. No, he moved back to my ass, spreading my cheeks and exposing me... there.

I let out a gasp as he dropped to his knees and dove in. With his mouth.

My knees struggled to keep me up as he continued worshiping me in a place I'd once considered forbidden, building up a pleasure that I hadn't even known existed.

Just when I thought I couldn't take any more, when I thought that my knees would give out and my body would explode in climax, Rowan stopped.

My fingertips pressed into the door, trying to sink against the wood as he raised himself up, pushing into my back, bending me over farther and pressing his hard cock against my entrance.

His hands clutched my hips, and he didn't pause, didn't wait, he just plunged into me, seating himself to the hilt.

I came immediately.

My body exploded into spasms, pleasure turning my limbs to lead.

But Rowan didn't stop, didn't pause, didn't slow down. He kept thrusting, fucking me into another orgasm, making every inch of my body his with the control he held over me.

My orgasms had split me apart, taken me off the face of the earth, but not so much that I didn't notice Rowan didn't have one of his own. He kept fucking me, stopping abruptly as I found purchase on my sanity once more.

He was out of me before I knew what was going on, whirling me around before I could process the loss of him, my heart still racing, my legs barely holding me up.

His muscles were pumped, the veins in his arms and neck defined from the force in which he was holding himself together.

"On your knees."

I obeyed without question, my sensitive pussy pulsating at the chill in his voice, the erotic lilt of it.

The rug was soft enough against my knees, but even if it was the cold hardwood, I wouldn't have complained.

"Taste yourself on me," he demanded in a guttural voice.

He was holding the base of his cock, presenting it to me. It was glistening from... me.

I didn't hesitate to take hold of him and put it in my mouth. Rowan was large, very large, so it was a tight fit, but he fit.

And he tasted of me. Of us.

My body tingled at that, at the power I had over this hulking man while I was on my knees.

I took him greedily, hungrily, running my tongue along his

exquisite, hard length, reveling in the sounds of pleasure emitting from the man in front of me.

Rowan's hands tangled in my hair, tugging at the strands then pulling me back so I looked up at him through my lashes.

"I'm about to come, baby," he warned. "You don't want me doing that in your mouth, you tell me now."

I gripped him firmer, enough for him to let out a hiss of pleasure, then answered him by leaning forward and taking him back into my mouth.

"Fuck," he roared, the gruff, gravel of his voice turning me on even more. His hand moved to the back of my head as he fucked my mouth.

His release unexpected, yet I swallowed everything he had, loving every second of it.

When he was done, I rocked back on my knees, wiping the side of my mouth and gazing up at him.

And what a sight he was. His muscles were glistening from the exertion of fucking me so hard and coming even harder, evidenced too by the rapid rise and fall of his chest.

But it was the look in his eyes that would've knocked me off my feet if I'd been standing on them.

Yes, his eyes were clouded with desire, drenched with erotic satisfaction. But there was something beyond that too. Something heavier and thicker than pure desire. There was reverence there.

I might have been the one on my knees, but he was the one worshiping me.

It was only a couple more seconds before I was no longer on my knees, no longer looking up at Rowan but in his arms.

"I'm far from fuckin' done with you, cupcake," he grated out, carrying me down the hall and up the stairs to my room.

"Not gonna rest until every inch of your skin is mine."

And he spent the rest of the night doing that, even though every inch of my skin had belonged to him since the second my eyes landed on him walking into my bakery.

* * *

I SHOULD'VE KNOWN Nathan's mother would turn up eventually.

He'd been run out of town.

Not that I didn't think that Rowan was a man of his word, I just didn't think that Nathan was smart enough to stay away. To let Rowan keep him away. I made a mental note to talk to Rowan about that. We'd never really properly addressed what had happened and why he did it. We'd been busy.

But whatever Rowan's threat had been, it had obviously stuck. From what I heard of town gossip, Nathan was in New York, working with some celebrity real estate firm.

I was sure most of that gossip came from the woman wearing the tailored pantsuit circa the Hilary Clinton presidential campaign. Ditto with the haircut.

She was doing damage control for her son. Saving face in front of the country club, making sure their precious reputation stayed intact. I knew how much those things meant to her because she'd reminded me. Reminded me that I came from nothing, of all the things that would be expected of me when I married her son. Namely giving up my business, my career, so I could get the hairstyle, the pearls, and start popping out babies.

I'd kindly told her that wasn't going to happen.

When she found out that I was not only former trailer trash but former trailer trash that she couldn't mold into something that would be palatable for her and her family, she began to actively dislike me. Of course, she never said anything outright, never did anything I could bring to Nathan. She was covert about her insults, about the ways she reminded me I was too big for the designer dresses everyone else was wearing, how my side of the church would be empty because I didn't have a family. Nathan might've noticed if he'd tried to pay attention to me. But he didn't. He let his mother treat me however she wished without stepping in or standing up for me.

And when she walked through the door of the bakery, nose turned up in distaste, I thought, not for the first time, how glad I was that I didn't have to deal with that woman for the rest of my life.

I had a feeling that I'd have to deal with her at some point, though. Not because I'd called off the wedding—she'd already spat her venom at me about that—but because Nathan was no longer in town. No longer the big man in the small town. No longer the son she could brag about at her charity lunches.

And she was going to blame me. Because she could never see Nathan for what he was, and I was the easy scapegoat for anything and everything that happened in his life since he met me.

"Why don't you go out back, babe?" Fiona asked me, her gaze on the woman in Chanel, clutching her purse to her body like she was walking through a bad neighborhood.

"No." I smiled at the last customer as Claire approached the counter. "I can handle this. Her."

I felt stronger now than I had before. Freer since I'd given myself permission to call off the wedding. And yes, since Rowan and I became a thing. He made me feel powerful. Made me see the power that was already inside of me.

It was uncanny how much this woman reminded me of my mother. Not in appearance... Claire wore her hair short and cropped, whereas my mother kept hers longer, past her shoulders. Claire was petite and half-starved, and my mother was where I got my curves from. But both of them were drenched in Estée Lauder makeup, Botoxed to high heaven, and walking in a cloud of Chanel No.5.

Both of them had perfected the way to look at someone to communicate just how lacking they found them without actually being able to move any of their facial muscles.

Tina had been muttering insults to the coffee machine as the woman approached, but she stopped once she was within eyesight.

Tina turned, putting her hand on her hip and observed my almost mother-in-law with open disdain and hostility.

It delighted me to see her pinched face tighten in something resembling fear. Tina was not impressed or afraid of the power she wielded in this town.

"Claire," I greeted her, smiling tightly but not warmly. "What can I get you today?"

"I'm not here for any of... this," Claire gestured to the glass case full of sweets with thinly veiled disgust. Which made sense since I had not seen the woman eat more than a few bites of salad or chicken since I'd known her.

"I'm here to tell you to get my son back in town." She turned her attention to me.

I frowned at the woman. "Nathan and I are no longer engaged, as you are well aware. I have no control over what he does or doesn't do."

Claire clutched her purse tighter. "I know for certain that he was at your home the night he just left without notice. I know his leaving had something to do with you. You've always had a power over him I could never understand." Her sharp gaze ran over my body, communicating she found me sorely lacking.

Or more likely, she found that there was too much of me,

since her standards of beauty came from the era where women had to practically be anorexic in order to seem desirable.

Though, unfortunately, that era had not left us completely.

I internally sighed, laying my palms flat on the counter. "I have customers," I informed her, glancing at the small line behind her. "If you're not going to order something, I'm afraid I'm going to have to ask you to step to the side."

Claire may as well have sucked on a lemon. "I'll have a coffee. Black."

"Get that, Tina?" I asked.

"Got it," Tina replied, her gaze fixed on Claire long enough to make the woman shift in her sensible, designer heels.

The coffee machine came back to life as I stared at Claire, no longer willing to let the woman look down on me, make me feel small.

"Nathan made his choice," I informed her. "I had nothing to do with him leaving town. Thankfully, I have nothing to do with him or you anymore."

Claire sucked in a sharp breath. "You are a piece of work," she hissed, abandoning all pretense of civility. "Of all the women who wanted Nathan, all the women who deserved him. Who deserved our family name. Of all the women, he chose you. He was the best thing that ever happened to you, and you threw him away. Broke his heart. Drove him out of the town he was born in."

I laughed out loud at that. I couldn't help myself.

This ticked off the woman more. She might've scowled, but who knew considering all of the toxins freezing her facial muscles.

"You really are deluded," I shook my head once I got a hold of myself. "Nathan will never be the best thing that happens to any woman. Because he was raised to think he is God's gift when really he's just another rich asshole who doesn't know where to find the clitoris."

I really wished I had a camera so I could immortalize the look on Claire's face. Fiona struggled to contain her giggle beside me, and even Tina choked out a chuckle.

The shock on Claire's face only lasted for a handful of seconds, unfortunately. Then she regained her bearings and found a toxic glower to direct my way.

"You're trash," she snarled. "And you're going to pay for running my son out of town. Mark my words."

I let out a laugh. "You sound like a *Scooby Doo* villain." Then I leaned slightly forward, narrowing my eyes at her. "Now, I understand the WASP way is to drink or dope yourself into denial about who your husband is sleeping with, where the money comes from, and the truth about the children you raised, but I think you're intelligent enough to understand that there is no love lost between your son and the residents of this town. Me, on the other hand..." I paused to peer around my packed bakery, a lot of the residents interested in this showdown. "I have a good reputation because trash or not, I try my best to be a good person. I provide jobs, sugar, and good coffee. I'm a genuinely pleasant person. So, I'd like to see you find a way to 'make me pay' without blowback from the town that even you wouldn't be able to weather."

Claire blinked rapidly at me as my words punctuated, then I watched her try to battle against the truth of them.

But she couldn't.

Everything I said was true. She'd reveled in her family's 'place' in the town and wasn't deluded enough to understand that people would be watching, people understood that she was not my biggest fan, and this town would not stand by and watch this woman damage me.

She might've said something else, something nastier, and I likely wouldn't have been able to keep up. There was only so much confrontation I was capable of. But luckily, I had a best friend who sensed my oncoming panic.

"Here's your coffee, on the house," Fiona said with saccharine sweetness as she slid the cup across the counter. "You have the day you deserve now."

Claire looked from me to Fiona then the coffee. Then her eyes went to the coffee machine where Tina was standing with her hands on her hips, staring her down, silently daring her to say more.

Claire was not a woman easily scared, but she was smart enough to understand that she was outnumbered.

She snatched the coffee and stomped out of the café.

"That was fucking amazing," Fiona screeched.

"I can't feel my face," I mumbled, the reality of what I'd just done sinking in.

Fiona chuckled. "Yeah, as impressive as that was, I don't think you have a future in bitch showdowns, you're great at them but you're apt to feel guilty after and send them a fruit basket or something."

"I would totally do that, except with that bitch," I muttered. "I'm gonna stick to what I'm good at. Baking things."

"Yes, I'll handle all bitch showdowns from here on out," she promised solemnly.

I shook my head and went back to work, not needing to run into the back the rest of the day as I might've needed to do in the past.

Things were changing.

I was changing.

And though it wasn't entirely to do with Rowan, he played a large part.

CHAPTER
SIXTEEN

Recipe: Coconut Thumbprint Cookies

From 'Dessert Person'

N ot long after Claire came in, we had another visitor.

Lori, her head down, her posture meek and guarded.

My heart bled at the way she carried herself, so different than she had six months ago when she'd last worked here. She had never been an extrovert, but she'd had a quiet, confident way about her. Soft spoken but intelligent. Witty with a dry sense of humor.

The changes Ronnie had wrought in such a short amount of time were stark and made me clench my fists at my sides, glad that Maggie had taken a chunk out of him. I wished she had taken more.

Fiona had been restocking the pastry cabinet, going stiff

when she saw Lori approach the counter, having heard my story about the scene in the parking lot.

"Lori, how are you, sweetie?" I asked, rounding the counter so I could bring her into a soft embrace.

She was stiff as I put my arms around her, which made sense considering what she must've been through. And I didn't even know the extent of what she'd been through, so people touching her could likely be a trigger. I released her quickly and stepped back, nodding to her brother who was lingering with a watchful eye over his sister.

"I just wanted to come and... thank y-you," she stuttered, looking down at her feet. I watched her take a breath before meeting my eyes. "After what happened at the General Store. I wanted to thank you. For standing up for me."

I ached to hug her again, feeling the pain in her voice, knowing that it would take her a long time to heal. That what she'd endured would impact all of her future relationships.

"You have a lot of people in this town who will stand up for you," I told her, motioning to where Tina and Fiona were standing. "And your family." My eyes dashed to her brother who was now staring at Fiona. That almost made me want to smile.

Almost.

There were things I wanted to say to Lori. A whole bunch of things. I wanted to tell her that this wasn't her fault because I could see the blame and guilt painting her face. I wanted to tell her that Ronnie was a weak coward, and that she'd find a man who deserved her, would treasure and protect her.

But it wasn't the time. Not in the crowded bakery with eyes on her. What had happened wasn't a secret. Yes, our close-knit town would come together to support her, but they would also give her attention that she did not want right then.

"Why don't you go and grab some cake to bring home with

you?" I offered. "Nothing seems quite as bad after a big slice of cake." I gave her a wink, and she smiled weakly back at me, nodding then walking to the counter where Fiona was waiting for her with an easy, warm smile.

I watched them interact with hope. With faith that Lori would recover, that she would make it through this... because she had to and because she had the strength inside her. Women did. They conquered the demons that men summoned, and they did it every day.

When the door to the bakery opened, my eyes flitted over to see who had entered.

Finn, our police chief. He was young for the position. Had to be around my age, if not a little older. His father had been chief before him and had retired when he was diagnosed with cancer three years ago.

He beat the cancer but stayed retired, Finn doing very well at keeping the peace in our small town. Not that peace was hard to keep. Our crime levels were relatively low, most of them committed by bored teenagers or drunk tourists.

Finn was amongst Rowan and Kip as the most eligible bachelors in this town. His dark hair was always kept neat and short, same with the beard that did really great things for his face. He had dark ebony skin and dark brown eyes that made women melt. He was tall, muscular and ruggedly handsome. And he did wear the shit out of that uniform.

It struck me that I was staring at our police chief, almost checking him out when I was technically spoken for. Not that I felt anything while I was checking him out; I was doing so objectively. Every man I looked at now was measured against Rowan. And even though the chief was attractive in all ways, he didn't do anything for me. Because he wasn't Rowan.

I had it bad.

As did our chief, apparently. He wasn't looking at me or anyone else, just Lori. He paused in the doorway, his jaw hard as he considered her with intensity, with something that could only be described as longing.

I was the only one who noticed it since he got a hold of himself quickly, visibly shaking himself out of it before striding over for a man-huddle with Lori's brother.

Love was in the air, it seemed.

* * *

MY ENTIRE BODY relaxed when Rowan sauntered through the door of the bakery. And it was a saunter. Not forced or on purpose. He just had a way about him. His walk communicated that he was a man in control of his body, of everyone and everything around him.

When his eyes locked on mine, an ache formed between my legs, need thrumming through my body.

I remembered last night, me on my knees in front of him, him... eating me. My whole body quivered with the memory.

Rowan's eyes flared, and his lips turned up in a smirk as he noted my blush, likely having guessed what was going through my mind right then.

Kip followed behind him, and I noted the strange, intense look on his face directed at Fiona—who was clearing tables—before a lazy grin settled over it, covering up that foreign look.

I didn't have time to ponder what that meant because Rowan had rounded the counter and pulled me into his arms for his usual greeting. I was well past protesting by then. And the bakery customers were all used to it too.

We were officially a 'couple,' by our small town's standards, at least. Rowan had informed me that at least three different people had threatened his life and limbs should he hurt me, including Dot who made sure to mention her baseball bat.

"What is it?" Rowan asked when he stopped kissing me.

He was still holding me tight, studying me intently. It was unnerving that the man could read me so well.

"It's nothing." I shook my head, trying to school my expression, not realizing I was still wearing the unease from Claire's visit.

My stomach had been churning all day, including a sharp throbbing in my side. The physical manifestations of my anxieties had taken a hiatus since Rowan and I had become... Rowan and I, but I wasn't cured. I was never going to be cured. Not unless I underwent some extensive therapy, and I really didn't want to open up that can of worms.

I could live with it. But I wondered if Rowan could. If it would affect his feelings for me. Sure, he knew I was dorky, maybe slightly neurotic, but he had no idea just how fucked-up I really was.

And no matter how unhealthy it was, I was planning on hiding that from him for as long as I could.

I tried to pull out of his grip, but as always, that didn't work. He held me tightly, watching me with concern.

"Nora." The way he said my name was a warning.

"You're impossible." I sighed dramatically, ignoring the pain in my stomach as I did so. "Nathan's mother came in."

Cue glittering anger in his eyes, tension in his jaw and narrowing of the brows.

"Relax, cowboy," I said. "I took care of it. I'm just not well versed in confrontation, so I'm a little... off-kilter."

Rowan's hold was tight on my arms, and he watched my expression for a long time before he spoke. "She fucks with you again, you let me know."

I rolled my eyes. "Aye aye, captain," I replied dutifully, knowing that arguing was useless when it came to this protective man.

He kissed my head. "You closin' up soon?"

I nodded, glancing at the clock. "Yep. You gonna hang around?"

"Yep."

Rowan and I hadn't been together long enough to establish a routine, but we kind of had one already. He didn't come to the bakery every day at closing, but he was there most days. If he wasn't, he was at my house, working on the greenhouse. There were only two nights he hadn't spent with me, and after those, he was at the bakery at five, waiting for me, to fuck me into oblivion before I started my day.

I worried he may get sick of me, that this was moving much too fast. But I wasn't worried enough to say anything. Because I liked this. Him. A lot. Dangerously too much.

I was in love with him.

And it was much too soon for that.

"I made lemon poppyseed muffins," I told him, pointing to the cake stand they were encased in.

"You tryin' to fatten me up, cupcake?" he teased.

"As if that is possible." I ran my hand along his washboard abs to punctuate my point.

All teasing left his eyes and was replaced with hunger.

I swallowed roughly, my own need awakening with a vengeance.

"Don't take too long," he instructed. "We're going to my place after this."

My heart squeezed with excitement. "Your place?"

"That okay with you?"

I nodded enthusiastically. "More than okay with me."

We'd spent every night together at my place, so I was infinitely curious about his.

"Good." He leaned in to kiss me firmly on my mouth. "Now get to closing this place up so I can take you to *my* place and fuck you in every room so your cunt is all I think of whenever I'm there."

Holy fucking *shit.*

My throat went dry when I realized Tina was only a few feet away from us. Rowan had pulled me back from the counter, closer toward the arch leading into the kitchen, and Fiona was now at the counter, bickering with Kip. Granted, the hum of the coffee machine made it incredibly unlikely that anyone had heard what Rowan had murmured in my ear, but still, my entire body was taut as a bowstring and primed for him.

He smiled wickedly, brushing his hand along my flaming cheek. "Oh, we'll be doing things to make you blush for days, cupcake." Then he stepped back, sauntering over to the cake stand to get himself a muffin.

I stared at his back. Watched him move easily and familiarly around the counter, getting himself a plate and joking with Fiona, Tina and Kip.

He looked incredibly ridiculous, wearing his work clothes behind the counter, all masculine and rugged in my girly bakery.

But he also looked right. So fucking right.

Yes. I loved this man.

I'm NOT sure what I expected.

Maybe for his house to be a log cabin in the middle of the woods. We didn't exactly have 'woods' per se, so that wouldn't really work. But something along those lines.

Rugged, built by hand with trees he'd cut down himself kind of thing.

I did not expect a cottage on the beach. On the actual beach. About ten minutes out of town proper, where the houses got more spaced out and the landscape a little more remote.

He pulled off, down a short driveway to reveal a large cottage, one that looked like Martha Stewart had designed it. Gray shingles covered the outside, roses holding on along the pathway to the front door. The wild Atlantic Ocean was moody today as we ventured deeper into fall, with winter creeping toward us. The garden around it was wild yet purposeful. When I got out of the car, the crash of the waves was what greeted me.

"*This* is your house?" I was dumbfounded and enchanted at the same time.

"Yeah," he replied, tugging me to his chest, cradling my face in his hands.

"It looks like Martha Stewart lives here," I told him.

He grinned. "Well, my mom will be happy to hear you said that."

"It's not what I expected," I admitted.

"You haven't even got inside yet."

And that was true.

"Well, let's—"

Rowan cut me off by kissing me. Hungrily. Furiously. I complied instantly, wrapping my legs around his hips, his hand going to my ass in order to press me against his hard cock in his jeans.

I cried out as he walked us forward purposefully, gravel crunching underneath us.

He must've unlocked the door, but I didn't notice that. Didn't notice anything beyond our mouths moving together, me ripping at his clothes, desperate for our skin on each other.

Clothes tumbled to the floor, shoes, keys, my purse.

It all happened in a blur.

Rowan had lowered me to the floor at some point, a soft rug underneath my back.

We were both half clothed, exposed just enough so his cock was pressing against my soaking pussy.

Rowan's face was inches away from mine. "Now I'm gonna think of this sweet pussy every time I walk through the front door," he growled, pushing into me.

I gripped on to him, crying out in pleasure.

"Gonna think of you clenching around me, taking me like a good fuckin' girl," he grunted as he moved inside of me, the cords of his neck straining.

It was safe to say that I fucking loved Rowan's house so far.

* * *

We eventually made it to the living room, our clothes all the way off for round two.

It was only after I'd slipped on his tee to use the bathroom—Rowan scrambled my brain delightfully with multiple orgasms but not enough for me to forget about preventing a UTI—that I actually got to look around his house.

And it was wonderful.

Maggie greeted me on my way to the bathroom, having been released from the mud room where she'd been hanging out while we had sex around the house.

She'd only vaguely acknowledged her dad when he let her out, making a beeline straight for me, jumping around in excitement to see me.

I was sufficiently excited to see her too, having grown almost as fond of the dog as I had her master.

Once I'd greeted her with head scratches and nose nuzzles, I went to use the facilities.

The bathroom downstairs was done in dark grays, all tiled with black fixtures. Everything else in the house was in a similar color scheme, with pops of white on the comfortable looking, slipcovered sofas cluttered with pillows in the living area. I guessed his mother picked those out. I couldn't imagine Rowan choosing tasteful pillows to complement the masculine, refined coastal vibe of the house.

The floors were polished hardwood. The living and kitchen areas were open plan with an impressive kitchen complete with breakfast bar to the left and a cozy living area with no TV, just a fireplace and floor to ceiling bookshelves. The bookshelves were stuffed, and from a quick glance, they looked well used and well loved. I tried to imagine Rowan sitting there reading. He hadn't read in my presence. Though we weren't exactly sitting in bed reading together. I wanted that, though. That intimacy. I figured he was the kind of guy to bend spines, dog ear books, mark them as his.

As much as I wanted to inspect the bookshelves, I was anxious to catalog every inch of the place.

What impressed me the most were the windows. The entire back of the house was windows. The sea moved right outside them, as if we were on a boat instead of on dry land. I walked out to where the wraparound porch had comfy looking chairs and stairs leading directly onto the sand.

"This is amazing," I told Rowan, who was pouring us wine at his bar area—shirtless, it was important to say. When done, he pulled my back to his front and handed me my glass of wine.

I took it gratefully, leaning back into him while staring at the ocean. The sky was darkening, the days getting shorter as we led into winter.

The holiday season.

It was always a busy time for me, especially in the days leading up to Thanksgiving and Christmas since I started cooking a lot of pies and cakes for people to bring to family gatherings.

I loved the fall. Loved to see Main Street decorated with lights, the sky turning moodier, the air crisp.

I loved the hot chocolates I served at the bakery, almost thick enough to be classed as a soup, inspired by the famous Angelina's hot chocolate in Paris that almost single-handedly made me gain five pounds.

I loved curling up with a good book while it stormed outside, my house encasing me in a warm hug.

Loved the fire pit nights with my girlfriends.

The holidays themselves were more complicated.

There were no family gatherings for me. I'd never experienced one in my life. No Christmas dinner surrounded by family, no home that smelled of turkey and stuffing. Not even a Christmas tree.

Though I loved to decorate and used any excuse to, I did not do it for the holidays. Not when they reminded me of what I didn't have.

Most years, Tina, Fiona, Tiffany and I ate Thanksgiving dinner together, and then Fiona and I spent Christmas together since Tina and Tiffany spent it with Tina's family. Ansel was there sometimes, but only if he could get away. Only if he'd found the energy to battle with our mother, finagle his way out of whatever she had planned.

Maybe that was why I was so bitter about the holidays... because I didn't get my brother on those days that were meant to be about family, because my toxic mother had her claws in much too deep.

Despite trying really hard not to, I resented the brother I loved with all of my heart for being so strong in so many ways yet so weak when it came to her. Even though it was much more complicated than that. For my fragile heart it was.

"Want to cook dinner for you before we go upstairs and I fuck you in my bed," Rowan murmured, jerking me out of my melancholy.

And it was a very nice way to be jerked from those thoughts.

"That sounds like a wonderful plan."

He twirled me around, being careful of our wine. "You still holding on to today?" he asked with concern. "To whatever venom that bitch spouted?"

I smiled at how quickly Rowan transitioned from his post orgasm glow to the vengeful alpha once more.

"No," I reassured him. "I'm not still holding on to that."

He surveyed me for a long moment before nodding curtly and kissing me on the nose. "Good. I'm gonna go cook us dinner." He motioned to the sofa. "You relax, read, whatever. Don't have a TV but can get a laptop if you wanna watch somethin'." He paused, tapping his lips. "We'll have to get one so we can watch *Yellowstone* when we're here."

There was a lot to digest there, namely Rowan buying a television in order to watch a show with me. After our binge watching, it was safe to say he loved *Yellowstone*.

"You don't have any TVs in the house?" I asked him in shock.

He shook his head. "Not really interested in TV. Like to read."

I mused over this piece of information. "I've never met a person who is not into television." I looked to his bookshelves then back to him. "I didn't think it was possible for little details to make you more attractive to me, but you've gone and done it."

His expression became strange then, some kind of serious intensity moving in his icy blues, his lips thinning.

I thought he might say something equally as serious as his expression, but he merely leaned forward to kiss me again.

"Or you can watch me cook?" he offered.

I glanced back to the bookshelf, incredibly anxious to check out his selection, but then my eyes went back to my rugged man and his sleek kitchen.

"Watch you cook."

His eyes cleared, and his lips turned up. "Good."

I settled on one of his barstools and sipped my wine as he moved around the kitchen, getting food from the fridge and a cutting board from a cupboard.

"I'm not on the pill," I announced as he cooked dinner.

He glanced up from the chopping board but didn't say anything.

"The past few times we've done it, you haven't used a condom, and I'm not on the pill," I continued, uncomfortable with this conversation, likely why my stomach still told me I was suffering from a tumor or something. I ignored the niggling pain, focusing on Rowan.

Rowan put down his knife and gave me his full attention. "I'll use them from now on," he replied immediately, without question, without blame or placing guilt on me.

"I don't want you to," I said quietly. "But I also don't want to go on birth control. It fucks with women's hormones."

"Know that," Rowan replied.

His response surprised me.

"Sisters," he said in explanation. "Calliope's into all that natural shit and tells anyone who will listen that Big Pharma is corrupt as all fuck, and the patriarchy are poisoning women with birth control."

I grinned, despite my discomfort. "I think I'll like your sister."

"And they'll both fucking love you." He said it with ease. As if it were a foregone conclusion that I was going to meet his family, as if it were completely natural. Which wasn't the norm with men, at least in my experience. They put off the meet-the-parents step for as long as they could. It sent the wrong message. It sent signals about commitment and monogamy.

Rowan had been sending those signals since the beginning, so his attitude made sense.

"I can get something inserted." I shifted back to the contraceptive conversation... not very sexy but very necessary. "A copper IUD that doesn't have hormones." I'd had it with Nathan, even though I also made him use condoms—something he routinely complained about—because even though I was technically committing to forever with him by wearing his ring, I knew that a child would tie me to him forever, and I was protecting myself against that.

Not once did I let it slip, did I get too caught up in the passion with Nathan—not that there was a whole lot of passion—and let him have sex with me without a condom.

But twice I'd done it with Rowan, without complaint, with full awareness of what it meant.

"If you want to do that, you can," Rowan said, eyes on me. "But if it fucks up your body in any way, if you're not comfortable with it, don't want you doin' it."

I took a long swallow of my wine. "I don't particularly like it," I said honestly. "But... I like it when you fuck me without a condom."

His jaw tightened, and I watched his Adam's apple move as he visibly swallowed. "Fuck, if I love it more than anything in this world."

Silence descended between us.

"I'll pull out," he decided.

"The show *Teen Mom* exists because of men believing in the pull-out method," I snickered, although I wasn't joking.

He didn't break eye contact as he shrugged.

Shrugged.

The man I'd been seeing less than a month didn't seem at all perturbed by the possibility of getting me pregnant.

That was a red flag. Indicating that I was supposed to pump the brakes. That I was supposed to create space.

It should've had me feeling uneasy, uncomfortable. Not warm and safe.

But it did.

So, I didn't run. Didn't pump the brakes.

I just sat there, drinking my wine, watching him cook.

We didn't revisit the subject. Nor did he wear a condom when he fucked me on the kitchen counter after dinner.

CHAPTER
SEVENTEEN

Recipe: Oatmeal Cookies

From 'Dessert Person'

It wasn't the ringing that wrenched me out of sleep. Not then. When I slept better than I had... ever. It was lucky I didn't need an alarm to wake up when I did because I would've slept right through it. I woke because Rowan's arms were no longer wrapped around me, his warm body no longer pressed against mine. He was speaking low. Barely above a whisper.

"Fuck," he muttered. "Yeah, no, thanks, Finn. I'll be right there."

I blinked into the darkness, the light coming from his phone illuminating his shape.

"What's going on?" I mumbled sleepily.

Rowan put the phone down and came back to me in bed,

226

kissing my head. "Kip's had too much to drink. Got into some shit. He needs a ride home."

"I'll come with you," I said, trying to get my bearings, sleep still clutching me. My stomach throbbed at the movement, something I noted despite still being half asleep.

"No," he countered softly. "You have to get up in a couple of hours. Go back to sleep. I'll be back soon."

I wanted to argue with him, but I was sleepy. And I did have to get up in a few hours—though he needed to as well since he had established a routine of coming to the bakery with me.

"Come back soon," I muttered, already sinking back into sleep.

He chuckled in a way that warmed my entire body. "Oh, cupcake, you in my bed, wearing my tee... I'll be back as soon as humanly possible."

He kissed my lips, hands venturing underneath my tee for a decadent moment.

I was no longer lapsing back into unconsciousness, desire waking me up.

"Later," Rowan promised, cupping my breast while peppering my neck with kisses.

"Later," I repeated, already aching for him.

I smiled at the sounds of Rowan getting up, getting dressed then kissing me once more before leaving the room.

Though I lapsed back into sleep, it was thin without Rowan there. I was listening out for him, expecting him. So I heard the gentle rap on the front door.

Maggie heard it too, her collar clanging as she growled softly, getting up from her bed.

My spine tingled with unease as I sat up in bed, holding my breath, listening.

The knock sounded again, not so gentle this time.

I heard Maggie get up from her bed and run out of the room, growling some more.

"Shit," I whispered, throwing the covers back and running after her.

I cried out as the movement caused pain to spear my side. Gritting my teeth, I ignored it, hating that my body was manifesting all of my stress in this way.

I felt a semblance of relief when I didn't hear her barking or tearing an intruder apart. Plus, I was pretty sure an intruder wouldn't knock on the front door of the biggest badass in town in the middle of the night.

Rowan Derrick had some big 'don't fuck with me' energy.

But Rowan wasn't here. And although I was pretty sure he had an impressive cache of weapons—considering his Army background and overall badassery—I also knew he was likely sensible enough to keep them somewhere safe and hidden that I couldn't find in a pinch.

At least I had Maggie, who was sitting at the front door when I crept up, still growling lowly. I took it as a good sign that she wasn't barking like mad. Dogs had a good sense for things, didn't they? If she smelled an intruder, I thought she'd act a little more concerned.

"Rowan, open up! I know you're in there, I can hear Maggie," a voice yelled through the door.

A female voice.

One sounding impatient and familiar to Rowan. Familiar enough to be acquainted with Maggie, and to turn up at his house in the middle of the night.

"Shit," I grumbled under my breath.

I could run away and hide and hope the woman went away. It was probably the most sensible course of action. She wasn't here for me. Rowan wasn't here. No good could truly come from me opening the door.

So, of course, I opened it.

I wasn't sure who was more shocked, me or her.

I'd been expecting it to be someone who looked like this woman, but I'd also been harboring a hope that it was one of his sisters coming to visit unexpectedly or an eccentric aunt who kept vampire hours.

But I'd seen pictures of both of his sisters... They had dark hair like Rowan.

This one was blonde. And much too young to be his aunt.

She was younger than me. Mid to late twenties. Wearing far too little for this time of night during this time of year. She was dressed for the club. Or what passed for the club in Jupiter.

Malley's Bar and Grill was the only place for miles with cheap drinks, a good band every Saturday, and open till three.

I'd been there a time or two with Fiona. It was fun but not exactly my scene. I was more into a wine bar and a cheese board than tequila shots and sticky floors. But to each their own.

"You're not Rowan," the woman stated the obvious.

"No," I agreed.

We stared at each other, taking each other's measurements, I guessed. She was pretty. Slim. Tall. Her black liner was slightly smudged, her lipstick had rubbed off and her curly hair was a little messy. But she still looked good. One of those magical girls who probably could run five miles and look dewy with a hint of red to her cheeks.

Her generous boobs were showcased in a strapless dress that also showed off a tiny waist that I thought Barbie was only in possession of. Ditto with the long, slim, tanned legs.

Her feet were bare.

She was holding some platforms in her left hand.

229

And she'd come here. To Rowan's. After a night out.

I was wearing Rowan's tee. No makeup. My hair was escaping the two braids I'd put it in before going to sleep. I did not have a Barbie waist or slim, tanned legs.

I should not have been comparing myself to this woman. That wasn't the kind of person I was. Nor was I the kind of person to instantly feel hostile to a woman I didn't know, purely on the basis of her connection to the man I was dating, who also seemed to be dating other girls.

"He's not here," I told her, gripping the front door. Maggie was pressed against my legs, as if in support.

The girl looked to me then to Maggie.

"I, um. I'm so sorry," she looked down, blushing. "This is really embarrassing. I got an Uber here, because, um..." She turned her head down the driveway to where her ride had left her behind before looking back at me. "Rowan is usually home, and he's usually alone, and... I'm so fucking sorry. I never would've done this if I knew he had... if I knew you were here."

The poor girl sounded completely sincere and utterly mortified. She was not some kind of harlot having an affair. She was a young girl who had an arrangement with a hot older man, and I would've said more power to her if the situation were different.

But the situation was not different.

"I'll just wait out here and order a ride," she babbled, fumbling for her phone.

I paused. Only for a second, but I felt guilty over it.

"No, come in," I offered, stepping back.

"No, I couldn't do that," she exclaimed. "This is, like, bad enough. I feel like such a fucking bitch, and I can't believe I woke you up. I promise, my ride is like..." she squinted at the screen on her phone, "twenty minutes away. I'm good waiting." She smiled tightly, but I could see the goose bumps on her exposed skin, which there were a lot of. It was cold and dark, and she was not to blame for all of this.

"Please come in," I asked. We were far enough out for the Uber to take a while, and the amount of available ride shares were slim at this time of night. "I'll make you some coffee."

She looked uncertain. "You're not gonna, like, kill me for trying to get with your man, are you?" she half joked. "Because I swear, I never would have come if I knew you were here. I wouldn't do that."

"I'm not going to kill you, Scout's Honor," I replied with a weak smile. "And I don't blame you whatsoever, I promise."

She hesitated for a moment longer before coming inside.

And that was how I ended up making coffee for the woman my boyfriend had been sleeping with in the middle of the night.

ROWAN

"I failed them, man," Kip muttered as I opened his front door.

He had a beer bottle dangling from his fingertips. One he definitely didn't need, considering the amount of booze he'd consumed tonight.

Not enough to drown it out, though.

"This is not your fault," I told my best friend, not for the first time and not for the last time.

It was like a sock in the gut, seeing him like this.

Defeated. Full of blame. Self-hatred.

"It *is* my fault," he argued, taking one last pull of the beer before hurling it across his yard where it smashed across the concrete.

"I'm the one who came home," he told me. "I'm the one who lived when I fucking shouldn't have."

He didn't sound drunk. Even though I knew he was. He sounded stone cold sober. And serious.

Which scared the fucking shit out of me.

This was Kip. The real Kip. The one the smiles and the womanizing hid. The one falling apart at the fucking seams.

I grabbed his shoulders and shook him. "Don't you fuckin' talk like that," I hissed. "You're allowed to grieve them. Fuck, you wanna drown your sorrows, do it. But you do anything to follow them, that gets you an inch closer than you are right now, you're dishonoring their memory. You may as well go and spit on their graves."

"You be careful how you fucking talk to me, man." Kip's eyes were wild and cold, dangerous.

I didn't back down. Even though I knew my friend was close to trying to beat the shit out of me.

"I'm not being careful when you're killing yourself, Kip. I ain't gonna judge any of the ways you deal with this. Until you do shit that hurts yourself. Hurts their memory." I clutched his shoulder. "I'm not letting you go away, my friend."

I saw his battle as he glared at me for a long moment. He wanted to fight me. Wanted to smash his fists against something, take out his anger somewhere. And I would've welcomed it if that was what he needed. I'd fight my best friend in the world while he was dancing with death if that meant bringing him closer to the land of the living.

But the prospect of violence left his eyes quickly, and his expression sagged. He was drained. Exhausted. Fucking haunted. It physically hurt me to see my best friend like this. Fucked with me.

"I don't know how to do this without them." Kip hung his head, voice breaking.

I reached out to grip his arm, squeezing it. "One day at a time, brother. One fucking day at a time."

He stayed there, eyes on the ground for a moment, shoulders quaking from the force of his sobs.

"You shouldn't be here with me," he eventually looked up, sniffing. "You've got a woman to go home to."

He didn't sound bitter about that, though he had every right to.

"I do," I agreed. "But she's not going anywhere. How about we go inside and have a drink?"

Kip nodded, then I followed him inside, letting him distract himself by pouring drinks while I looked for the weapons in his house, unloading every one. Just in case.

NORA

I was expecting him to arrive, of course.

Alpha males were predictable when it came to that kind of thing. So I wasn't surprised when he burst through the door of the bakery, expression thunderous, posture tight, and a furious energy that cut through the smell of cinnamon in the air.

I was making scones.

Cinnamon scones.

They were like a warm hug, made the place smell delightful, went wonderful with a pumpkin spice latte and fall breeze... and they required me to knead the dough enough to work out at least some of my frustration.

I was trying to be the woman who got angry when presented with betrayal but directed her anger outward, toward something productive. That seemed healthier than bursting into tears and eating frosting straight from the bowl like I really, *really* wanted to do.

The plan had been to ignore him. Which was incredibly immature and also totally ineffective.

It didn't matter whether I looked up from my kneading or not, if I kept my lips squeezed shut and my eyes tight so no tears fell. Not when there was a pissed off alpha in the vicinity who wanted some attention.

"What the fuck, Nora?" Rowan seethed, grasping my waist and whirling me around, pressing me against the counter.

My hands were covered in flour, so it dusted everywhere, but Rowan didn't seem focused on that.

He seemed focused on being mighty pissed off at me.

The feeling was mutual. My fury burned bright enough to momentarily distract me from the niggling pain in my stomach. This was not the longest one of my imagined maladies had stuck around, not by a long shot. My mind was a powerful thing.

"What the *fuck*, Nora?" he repeated, hands biting into my waist.

I'd seen Rowan angry. Scary angry. But that anger had always been directed at other people, not at me. And it was pretty darn intimidating to have it solely focused on me.

I almost wanted to shrink down. Submit.

Almost.

Instead, I thought of the woman at the door, the familiar way she'd spoken Rowan's name.

I jutted my chin upward. "I've got scones to finish," I replied coldly, not looking in his eye.

"I don't give a fuck about scones," he clipped out. "I give a fuck about having to deal with my best friend drunk as all fuck because that's how he deals with the demons nipping at his heels. Had to see him realize no booze in the world will chase them away." Something mingled with the fury in Rowan's tone. Something softer.

234

Concern. Emotion. For Kip.

There was a story there I didn't know. The Kip I knew was easygoing, jovial and definitely not a man who seemed haunted by demons.

But if I had learned anything about these men, it was that they were not at all what they seemed.

Though I did care about Kip, and it did hurt my heart to know there was something painful he was running from, it wasn't what mattered in that moment.

"I give a fuck about dealing with all that, expecting to come home to my woman, warm in my bed, only to find my bed empty, my woman nowhere to be found, and a fucking *note* telling me she was done with us," Rowan continued, still seething.

Fear prickled at the back of my neck, his fury coating me like oil.

The note was cowardly, I'd give him that. Especially when I knew him well enough to know he wasn't just going to accept the note, that he'd end up right here, and I'd have to face him anyway.

"I figured your bed wouldn't stay cold for long," I spat back, glaring at him.

Surprise punctured his anger. "What are you talking about?"

I rolled my eyes. "I'm talking about Kaitlyn." I hated the way her name sounded, hated that I was resenting another woman who did nothing wrong.

"Kaitlyn?" he echoed, looking confused.

My eyes stung with the tears he didn't deserve, the tears I didn't want him to see rolling down my cheeks. I turned, twisting myself from his grip and turning my attention to the dough.

"She came to visit not long after you left to get Kip," I clarified, still fighting back tears. "I'm guessing you got your wires crossed because she didn't know you weren't home, and she certainly wasn't expecting me." I tried to keep the bite to my tone, but it faltered a little at the end.

I gritted my teeth, willing myself not to cry right now.

"Nora—"

"I made her coffee," I cut him off, unwilling to let him spew whatever excuses would come out of his mouth. "She drinks it with a lot of creamer. Cashew creamer, to be exact. I know this because she told me. And because there was cashew creamer in your fridge." I forced my eyes shut for a split second before I continued. I ignored the searing pain in my side, mentally cursing my body for dealing with trauma by convincing me I was dying.

I took a deep breath, and black spots danced in my vision.

"Now I know this relationship of ours has been somewhat of a whirlwind," I ground out, "but I also know that we have been together longer than it takes creamer to expire." An angry tear escaped then. But I convinced myself it was because of the pain spearing into my side.

Rowan was close to me. Much too close, almost completely pressed into my side as I tried my best to focus on the dough.

"You don't answer the door in the middle of the night on your own, Nora." His tone was hard, eyes narrowed in anger.

"Don't turn this into more alpha bullshit about me being weak and vulnerable, and you being the strong man establishing routines for my safety," I snapped.

Rowan exhaled a long breath through his nose. "You know that's not what this is."

"Yes, you're right. This is about the woman who was knocking on your door, expecting you. And sex." I kneaded my dough with a little more force than necessary.

Rowan moved into my periphery, not letting me dismiss him and focus all of my attention on my dough.

His hand fastened around my wrist. "Nora."

I sighed, staring at the hand and debating trying to fight him. It wouldn't end well. Plus, if I continued taking my anger out on my dough, my scones would suck.

"I wasn't a monk before I met you, Nora," he told me, not unkindly. His eyes were hard, though, resolute. "I'm not gonna sugarcoat it. I fucked other women. A lot of them."

Though I was aware of that—it was pretty darn clear he wasn't a virgin our first time—it was hard to hear it. I guessed that made me weak or overly romantic or whatever.

I didn't like to think about his hands on other women's skin. Him looking at them the way he looked at me, him speaking to them in those raspy tones.

Rowan was watching me carefully, no twinkle to his eyes. There was a purposeful distance between us that made me feel cold all over. I wrapped my hands around my torso, hugging myself.

"It's important you know that. Know the kind of man I was before you." He pinched the bridge of his nose. "I came back from the war fucked-up. Without vital parts of me. I wasn't capable of being the man I am now, with you." His eyes contained so much emotion, it was hard to maintain eye contact. "Fuck, with any other woman, I don't think I would be the man I'm able to be with you."

My body warmed at his words, even though it really shouldn't have. Unfortunately, it felt like my skin was on fire, sweat beading on my upper lip because that was what happened when I got nervous, angry or overwhelmed.

"I'm sorry," he continued. "Knowing it and seeing it are two different things. You never should've fuckin' seen it."

He was right. I never should've seen it. And it was also right that it was utterly insane to think the super-hot man I was sleeping with hadn't slept with other women in his thirty-seven years on this earth.

He did not require me to be chaste, virginal and unexperienced, and I was all about quashing double standards when it came to the opposite sex.

"Kaitlyn and I used to have a casual thing. She was one of the few women in town who didn't try to push for commitment. Haven't touched her or any other woman since you became mine. Didn't think to call her because this town is a fucking rumor mill, so I figured she'd hear through the grapevine."

He was kind of right on that one. Our relationship had been the top story in our town. Literally. Someone did a piece on us in the local paper.

"The Baker & the Builder."

I kept the article, wanting to frame it but thinking that maybe a little weird so it just sat tucked in one of my many notebooks, hidden from Rowan, lest he think I was too attached. Which I was.

"And that creamer." Rowan rubbed the back of his head. "I honestly don't know what to say. I tried it once. Developed a taste for the shit. So, I have it... at home. Not here."

He looked appropriately embarrassed for a macho man admitting he liked something decidedly girly... fancy dairy-free creamer.

But it was too convenient. Men lied. It's what they did best. I had a lifetime of experience to tell me that.

A small but insistent voice inside me told me that Rowan was different. That Rowan could be trusted. But that voice was easily silenced by fear.

I sighed, looking into those blazing eyes of his. I was finding it really hard to continue to be mad at him, to continue to believe he wanted anyone but me.

"See you working this over in your head," he murmured quietly. "Tryin' to find some way to make it make sense to be mad at this. End this." He cupped my cheek, eyes looking at me and seeing far too much. "But you're not gonna find shit, cupcake. This is it. You're it for me."

My breath caught in my throat at that little admission. The one I'd been dreaming about. The one all women with square-jawed alphas who treasured them and gave them multiple orgasms were waiting for.

I opened my mouth to tell him the same. Except, apparently, my body was sabotaging me. The blazing pain in my side exploded some more, and I fell into his arms.

EIGHTEEN

Recipe: Blueberry Caramel Tart

From 'Dessert Person'

T hough it was cliché, it was the beeping and the smell that woke me up.

The hospital smell. Strong chemicals, antiseptic and sickness. Scratchy sheets against my skin. Cotton in my mouth. My brain fuzzy and eyes full of grit.

I knew a lot of people hated hospitals, and though I'd never say this out loud—lest I sound even more eccentric and weird than I was—I actually liked them. They made me feel safe. This was a whole building of people who were trained to deal with injuries and illnesses. If my insurance covered such things, I'd get a full body MRI framed just so I could see that there were no dark masses, and stop worrying about them. I'd even toyed with the idea of studying medicine for the sole purpose of making myself more capable at diagnosing myself, and more importantly, ruling out whatever sickness I'd otherwise find on the internet.

But blood grossed me out.

And I liked sugar.

Those thoughts all swirled through a cloudy and muddled mind, likely because of whatever drugs I was on.

It took a long time to open my eyes, to get my thoughts to catch up with me. The last clear thing I remembered was having an argument with Rowan. Or at least the tail end of the argument.

I'd decided to believe him, forgive him for the Kaitlyn incident. Not that there was anything to forgive. I'd jumped to conclusions and been somewhat dramatic.

What followed was somewhat jumbled. Rowan had caught me when I collapsed, of course. This was a man waiting for a bullet to jump in front of whenever we were together.

But there was no bullet, so I could only imagine how helpless that man of mine felt when there was no one to protect me from.

There were a lot of blurry images after that, and I did remember yelling. Him yelling. At paramedics. Doctors.

I remembered the fear in his voice, the desperation mingling with the searing pain in my body. I'd wanted to open my arms, comfort him, tell him that I was going to be okay, that I was just imagining it. Except even I couldn't imagine myself into that situation. Then there were a whole bunch of jumbled things: bright lights, foreign hands. And then there was nothing at all.

My room was small, private, with all the things you would expect from a hospital room. Monitors, IV bags. There was a man sitting in a chair pulled up as close as physically possible to my bed. His hand was grasping mine. His eyes were focused on me, sitting ramrod straight, face creased with worry.

"Thank *fuck*," he hissed when he came into focus.

Rowan leaned forward, clasping my hand in both of his, pressing his forehead to it.

"You scared the absolute shit out of me, Nora."

It surprised me, the fear on his face. Naked. All-encompassing.

He hadn't hidden how much he cared about me in the time we'd been together. Not even a little.

But seeing it here, with him sitting next to me in a hospital bed was something else. There was no way to convince myself that I was imagining it, that he was only with me because he wanted sex or whatever. No... This man cared about me. Deeply.

"What happened?" My throat was scratchy and raw.

"Your appendix burst," Rowan replied, letting go with one of his hands so he could lean over, pour water from a jug, and hold a small paper cup up to my mouth.

"Small sips," he instructed.

I drank gratefully, the cool water sliding down my parched throat before hitting my uneasy stomach. When he put the water down, I processed what he'd said.

Obviously, I knew there was something wrong. You don't wake up in a hospital because you've talked yourself into some kind of injury, but I also hadn't been expecting *that*.

"My appendix burst?" I repeated, feeling a dull ache in my stomach after shifting slightly in the bed.

"Yeah," Rowan gritted out. "Your appendix burst. And if I hadn't been there, you might've passed out and died right there at the bakery."

That thrust me into a sober kind of awareness. I thought I was dying of something weekly. Although that fear was a very real one, it had never been validated by anything. Death was just a concept to me, an instrument cooked up by an anxious mind.

But I'd never imagined it would brush so close.

I guessed no one did. Until it was too late.

"You almost fucking *died*," Rowan grunted, obviously haunted by how close it was.

My death hadn't just brushed this man. It had shaken up his insides.

"I didn't die," I told him in a whisper. "I'm right here."

Rowan opened his mouth to say something else, but the doctor entered the room, giving me a respite while checking my vitals. Rowan's fury didn't dissipate; he sat there all brooding, but also listening intently to the doctor.

"The surgery went well," she said, slanting a look at the chart then to me. She was only slightly older than me with kind eyes. "Since your appendix burst, we had to do a lot of work cleansing out the infection. We'll need you in the hospital for at least three days, maybe five, to monitor you."

"I cannot be here for three days," I argued with her, trying to push myself up in bed. "I have a business to run."

"You're stayin' here if I have to chain you to the fucking bed," Rowan exclaimed, his unyielding hands on mine.

"Though the hospital cannot condone that behavior, I agree with his sentiment," the doctor smiled. "A regular appendectomy is still surgery, therefore serious but nowhere near as invasive as what we had to do to you. We need to monitor you to ensure you can digest food and that your intestines are working as normal before I can discharge you. Even then, I'm going to need you to take it very easy for a few weeks. No strenuous activity for about a month."

I gaped at the woman. Days in this hospital bed? Weeks of recovery? I shook my head. "But I have a business, employees... You're telling me I can't work for *weeks*? That just won't do."

She gave me a sympathetic look "Depending on your recovery... yes. But once you've healed some more, I might be able to clear you for short periods of work. Right now, you just need to focus on getting well."

She gave me another smile, went through what would happen in the next few days then left me alone with my angry, worried alpha.

He did not give me any respite, unfortunately.

"What the fuck, cupcake?" Rowan demanded softly but with a pinched expression the second the door shut behind her. "The nurses said you had to have been in agony for hours. Days." He clutched my hands more firmly. "Not pain. Not something niggling but easy to ignore. Fucking agony. They couldn't believe that you were on your feet fucking working when you collapsed."

Rowan's concern was palpable, even if he was trying to disguise it with the usual masculine, over the top protectiveness.

"I have a high pain tolerance. I burn and cut myself regularly. Plus, I trip over anything and everything," I said, going for a joking tone despite my raspy, thin voice.

Rowan's expression didn't waver. "No one has that high of a fucking pain tolerance, Nora. Why in the fuck didn't you tell me that you were in that much pain?"

I sighed, knowing that Rowan was not going to let this go. It seemed hiding my crazy was pretty much impossible at that point.

"Because I don't know how to trust my body, and it tells me I'm dying on a biweekly basis," I admitted in a shameful voice.

Rowan's brows furrowed in confusion.

"I'm a mess," I groaned. "Not in a way that's obvious. Because I'm excellent at hiding it. But I'm fucked-up, Rowan." I chewed my lip. "It's something you should know. Granted, it should've been a little earlier than now and not a conversation I relish having in a hospital bed... no matter how ironic it is," I chuckled mirthlessly.

Rowan was not finding anything funny, his mouth curled into a grimace and his shoulders stiff.

I'd have to go all the way to satisfy him, tell him everything in order for him to understand at least a little.

"I did not have the same childhood you did," I began. "I don't have a mother who will send me care packages."

I thought fondly of Rowan's mother... the way he talked about her and his entire family, so glad that people like that existed. That they existed for *him*.

"We were born poor," I continued. "I don't remember my dad. But that makes sense since he died of an overdose when Ansel and I were two months old."

I didn't know what the man looked like, what his name was. Mom didn't keep pictures, and I never searched for them. I didn't need to know who he was. Ansel did. He was all about our ancestry, wanting to know the man our father was and might've been.

"He was supposed to be looking after us," I pictured two, dark-haired infants in a crib. "My mom was out with her boyfriend. The one she was planning on leaving my dad for. She didn't come home till the next day. I only know that because of the police records. A neighbor called the cops when they heard babies who wouldn't stop crying. Cops came. We got taken to the hospital for some malnutrition, nothing serious."

"Jesus Christ," Rowan muttered in horror.

"Yeah, the start to our life pretty much dictated where the rest went." I shrugged. "I have no idea how we weren't taken from my mother right then and there. But she has a way about her. A charisma that she turns on that will fool anyone. Charm anyone."

I'd seen that charm in action many times. With cops. Bill collectors. Men. Anyone she could get something from.

It was impressive.

"All that charm went outward, though. She didn't have any left over for us." Memories rushed through my mind, but I pushed them down. "I honestly don't know why she bothered to fight for us then. She didn't like us. We were nothing but a burden. Except for the benefit checks we provided for her." I shrugged, or at least tried to. In addition to my incision pain, my entire body felt weak and achy. "Anyway, I'm not gonna bore you with the details of our upbringing. Suffice it to say, she wasn't around much." I picked at the hospital sheets with my free hand. "We were left on our own most of the time. I don't remember a time when I didn't have something to worry about. If we were going to have food. If our clothes were clean, if they would fit us. If the heat was going to stay on. If our next stepdad was gonna hate us or like us a little too much."

Rowan jolted upright in his seat, his expression thunderous. I could feel it, his fury, leaching into the air.

"It never went that far," I rushed to assure him. "Not with me anyway." My stomach roiled, and pain speared through my abdomen, pain that had nothing to do with my injuries and everything to do with the scars my brother lived with.

"The one thing my mother did to show she even cared about us a little was shoot that man in the dick when she found out what he was doing to my brother." I remembered the gunshot, how loud it was. The sounds of his screaming. The smell of the blood.

"No charges were made against her, of course," I told Rowan, looking at him but not really seeing him. "And maybe she was a little more careful about the men she got involved with after that. But there were always men. Because my mother did not want to live in squalor. Nor did she want to do the work required to get her out of squalor." I shook my head in disgust, thinking about the woman who birthed me.

246

That's why I'd worked so hard my entire life, why I would never let a man take care of me, lest I have anything in common with her.

"It worked for her, though," I continued. "She married up. Got all the crap she wanted. House. Car. But we were teenagers by the time we got things like health insurance, almost about to graduate high school. It was ingrained in me then, to worry about every little thing. The way that shit manifested was this..." I held my hand out to the hospital bed. "Me thinking that I had something wrong with me constantly. It began when things started going well. Well, being when I got out of my mother's house and never saw her again. I'm conditioned to worry about something being wrong or whatever. So, I've always got pain. But it's in here." I tapped my temple. "I learned how to deal with it since I definitely did not want this overwhelming anxiety to become my identity. Didn't want people thinking I was weak."

I gripped the blanket, looking down in shame. There it was, what I had hidden from Rowan. Which he probably wouldn't understand because it wasn't something comprehensible to a man who was capable, strong and always in control.

Rowan leaned forward to grasp my chin, to tilt it upward so I couldn't escape his penetrating gaze.

"You are not weak," he growled. "Fuck, Nora. You are the strongest person I know. The shit you've been through?" He shook his head. "Fucking hate that you had to live that, baby. That mother of yours has a lot to answer for." His eyes became murderous at the mention of my mother. "A fucking lot. And she'll answer for those sins eventually because karma is real. The life you've given yourself proves that. It wasn't some unseen entity that created it. *You* built it. Literally. You built a life with your bare fucking hands." He lifted our intertwined hands to his mouth and kissed my fingers. "You radiate love, Nora. Warmth.

From your fucking pores. You don't see it because of what that woman did, but there is a light inside you. You attract people. Your bakery isn't as successful as it is just because you know how to make fuckin' great shit. Which you do. It's successful because of who you are. People in this town love you, baby. I love you."

I gaped at him, dumbfounded by everything he'd just said but especially the last three words he'd uttered.

"What?" I whispered.

"I love you," he repeated without hesitation. "I've loved you since the first moment I saw you. And I've only loved you more since I got to touch you, kiss you, make you mine. Every new thing I discover about you is yet another reason why I'm a fuckin' goner. Why I'm yours for life. Hate that you deal with that shit, fuckin' hate it. But you've been dealin' with it alone for all these years. Making you a promise right here, right now... From this moment on, you're not dealin' with anything alone again."

Tears were running down my cheeks by that point. Tears of joy, of disbelief. Though maybe I shouldn't have been shocked. Rowan hadn't hidden his feelings from me. Had repeatedly made it clear how much I meant to him, had told me how long he'd liked me. But hearing it out loud... on top of the drugs, the pain and the overall drama of the situation, I couldn't help the waterworks.

Rowan wiped my tears away with his thumb, not waiting for me to say the three words back. "Gonna need you to make me a promise, though."

"Anything."

"Need you to promise you're not gonna hide pain from me. Even if you don't think it's real."

I bit my lip. That was a hard promise to make. Not just because that would mean exposing a very vulnerable, soft part of me to the strongest man I knew, but also because it took me to a dangerous place.

I'd never looked for sympathy, empathy or attention from anyone when it came to this part of me. Not even my friends. Not even Ansel. Because when I used to talk about feeling sick, worried or weak, my mother would shame me. She would make me feel small and pathetic, and that was a feeling I promised myself I would never experience again.

"See those wheels spinnin' in that head of yours," Rowan murmured with a frown. "I'm guessin' you've done the worrying for the whole household, taken care of everyone, all your life."

I pursed my lips, unable to argue with him. I was the one who'd figured out how to cook, how to wash our clothes, how to patch up my brother's skinned knees, how to treat fevers and colds.

"Yeah," Rowan sighed, taking my silence for the agreement that it was. "Even now you take care of everyone else around you. You're always cookin' for them, feedin' them. Stoppin' on the side of the road and literally putting yourself in harm's way for them."

His jaw ticked with what I guessed was the memory of Ronnie almost hurting me.

"You take care of everyone but have never had anyone to take care of you." His lips brushed my fingers again. "Now, cupcake, I'm gonna brace for a comment on feminism after I say this, but I'm gonna say it anyway. You've got me. You're my woman. I'm gonna take care of you. You can relax your grip on the reins, baby. You can trust that I'm not gonna let you go off course."

He was right... Part of me did want to argue with him. Not the feminist part, though. The other part, the part that had only ever relied on one person: my brother, despite the demons he was still battling to this day. The part that had been let down by

249

everyone who was supposed to take care of her. That part found it hard to trust Rowan. Even though Rowan hadn't let me down. Not once.

"You scare me," I admitted.

His eyes twinkled slightly, and his lip twitched. I figured he wouldn't properly smile until I was out of this hospital bed. "Good," he murmured. "Because you scare the fuckin' shit outta me."

* * *

My recovery was painful. Not so much in the physical sense— although that was also incredibly uncomfortable— but because my diet and eating habits had to change. I was required to eat only small, bland meals while I healed. It was shocking and scary to me that something I'd defined my identity with—my ability to bake—was threatened by me ignoring my body.

I loved to eat, needed to taste everything I was baking when I was experimenting. And I'd nearly stolen that ability from myself. I'd nearly died. It was a confronting reality and something that shook a healthy dose of fear into me.

The bakery did not implode during my absence... which was luckily only about a week when it was all said and done. Tina, of all people, stepped up and did the majority of the baking when our emergency frozen stores ran out.

And although I was unable to eat a lot, all reviews came out great. She'd been helping me out every now and then, and had been with me since the start, so she knew all of the staples and had become an expert at following my chaotic recipes.

Fiona ran the front of the house with the same precision and competence. She'd been there almost as long as Tina and knew how everything worked.

Tiffany came in to help with whatever needed to be done.

It was unsurprising that my friends stepped up for me. They were all by my bedside the second they found out I was in hospital.

Fiona's eyes were red-rimmed when she burst into my hospital room. "Holy fuck, babe! How about you never do that to me again? Scared the absolute piss outta me."

"Ditto," Tina frowned, reaching down to squeeze my hand.

Tiffany burst into tears, leaning against her wife for support for about five seconds before clearing her eyes and jumping into action.

"These sheets won't do," she declared. "And that gown." She screwed up her nose. "I need to go shopping. We need skincare, candles, a robe, PJs... just to start."

No one tried to argue with her because no one was brave enough to do that. So, by that evening, I had sheets, silk PJs, scented candles, and all of my favorite skincare in the small bathroom that adjoined my room.

"Do you want me to call Ansel, babe?" Fiona asked from her perch on the armchair as we all watched Beth and Rip dancing on the ranch on her laptop.

I felt all the blood leave my face, and my body tensed. Since I was half lying on Rowan, he felt the change and turned to me.

I focused on Fiona, thinking about my brother. He'd be here by now if he'd felt anything from our freaky connection. Since he wasn't, he hadn't. And although I would love him near me, I was glad he wasn't here. This would've been a shock to him. And the hospital environment... No.

"I think it's better if we wait until he comes in a few weeks. We'll tell him then. I don't want him to have to deal with all of this." I was being purposefully vague because of Rowan listening to every word, but Fiona understood what I meant.

She grimaced. "He'll be spitting tacks once he finds out."

"He will," I agreed. "But I can handle him being angry over the... alternative."

"Got it."

No one else spoke of Ansel after that, though I knew that Rowan had noted the strained interaction. As he always did. Luckily, he didn't press me on it. I wasn't strong enough to go down that road yet. I would at some point, but not then.

Eventually, everyone left after they assured me they could handle the bakery.

Well, everyone except Rowan.

He stayed.

Practically the entire time I was there. He went home to shower, change, check on Maggie—who was hanging with Kip. But every other moment, he was by my side, touching me in one way or another, as if he were reminding himself that I was still there.

And then when I was discharged, he waited on me hand and foot. He even left Maggie to look over me in his absence. She did not move from her spot on the foot of my bed. I'd reassured him countless times that I wasn't going to die in his absence. He hadn't found that funny.

Rowan had also gone to my house before I was discharged, which was evident when I got home. The place was filled with flowers and food from my friends. But that's not what told me Rowan had been there.

It was the greenhouse off my kitchen.

The last time I'd seen it, I hadn't really seen it at all since there were tarps up between the two spaces. I had been dying to peek, but Rowan had grumbled about a surprise, and I didn't want to face his wrath. Beyond that, I'd *wanted* to be surprised.

When I laid eyes on the greenhouse—the one that looked

almost identical to the *Practical Magic* one with the white wood, the ceiling, the light fixture, the rows of herbs and antique style drawers running along the edge of the structure—I went back on my foot and probably would've collapsed if it weren't for Rowan's arms around me.

"This isn't a g-greenhouse," I stuttered, staring at the space in wonder. "This is an addition to my house. You literally *added another room to my house.*" I turned to Rowan. "How did I not notice this?"

He was grinning. "You've been distracted."

"No one is distracted enough to not notice another room being built onto their home," I retorted, my eyes darting around, overwhelmed by what I was seeing.

"Fiona helped with the styling shit and the herbs," Rowan apprised me, rubbing the back of his neck.

I should've known Fiona was involved in this. I was surprised she'd managed to keep her mouth shut; she normally sucked at keeping secrets. Beyond that, she'd been itching to get her hands on a room in my house since I was too much of a control freak to allow her to make any decisions on my décor.

Yet I'd let Rowan do this without question.

Granted, he hadn't given me much choice in the matter. He'd just... gone and done it.

"Worked all night to get it done. Wanted you to come home to it," Rowan continued, brushing some basil with his fingertip.

The fragrance of it scented the air, among the other herbs thriving in the greenhouse.

"Didn't want you living in a construction zone while you were healing. And I wanted to have it done in time for Ansel's arrival. From what you've told me about him, he seems to be into herbs and magic and whatever."

My heart clenched, unable to handle all of this kindness. This thoughtfulness.

"You better be invoicing me for all of this," I told him in a stern tone. Stern was all I could manage. Tears were prickling the backs of my eyes as it was.

Speaking of stern... that's exactly what I saw on Rowan's face. "You give me a cent for this, we're gonna have problems."

I gulped at his rough tone.

"This is a gift."

I gaped. Opened my mouth. Closed it. Waited for the punchline even though Rowan wasn't exactly a joking kind of guy.

"A gift?" I squeaked. "You cannot build an addition onto my house *as a gift!*" My voice rose then. "I mean, we've been dating like... a month. And this is thousands of dollars of material, labor..."

Rowan surged forward to clasp my upper arms. Not hard. His touch was featherlight, as if I were made of glass, ever since I woke up in the hospital.

"First, you're not workin' yourself up." He scowled. "You're gonna go sit on the sofa."

"No!" I protested, rooting myself in place, even though my stomach was throbbing, and it was exhausting, standing for so long.

A muscle jumped in Rowan's jaw.

"You cannot give me this as a gift," I whispered. "You cannot give me everything I've dreamed of." I looked down so my tears would hit the floor.

Rowan wasn't about to let that happen. His finger lifted the bottom of my chin so I looked upward, into his eyes.

"Cupcake, this is my job." He tilted his head toward the greenhouse. "I get deals on shit, pay Kip in beer, and get plenty of payment in all the things you bake for me. The way you smile at me in the morning. The way you sound when you come."

I was still crying, but desire awakened inside of me. It was an odd juxtaposition.

Rowan caressed my cheek with his thumb. "You give me gifts every fuckin' day, Nora, that are absolutely priceless. Let me do what I can to give you everything you've ever dreamed of."

The tears ran quicker, messier, and I now had ugly little hiccups to go with them too. I was not a pretty crier.

That didn't seem to bother Rowan. Nothing I did nor who I was bothered him.

The man was in love with me.

And I was in love with him.

I almost said it right there and then. Opened my mouth and heart.

But I lost my nerve at the last minute.

Saying it out loud might've made this fantasy disappear. Might've punctured whatever magic it was creating all of this, everything disappearing when I said those three words. And I didn't know how I'd handle Rowan going away.

* * *

My recovery at home was the worst kind of hell. Not because of the pain, because of the muscled man who would yell at me every time I lifted something, was on my feet for too long or tried to get my KitchenAid mixer from the pantry. Which is what I did after about a week.

"I need to bake," I snapped at him.

"You need to heal," he argued, clutching the mixer.

I held fast, though even at my best, my strength was

nowhere near his. "Healing for me is baking," I bickered through gritted teeth.

Rowan's gaze was steely and resolute.

I'd backed down on everything else since I'd been discharged, let him treat me like an invalid, conceded to him carrying me up the stairs—though I did enjoy that. I'd relented on not going to work for two more days... which was killing me.

But because I wasn't back at work, I wasn't baking. And because I wasn't baking, I was quickly coming out of my skin. That afternoon, I'd felt better and thought Rowan was too distracted with his tinkering in the greenhouse to notice.

"Baking is like meditating to me," I ground out, making another unsuccessful attempt to grab the mixer from his arms. "I know that sounds silly, and you likely won't understand, but the smells, the sounds, creating something... I haven't missed a day of it in years."

I remembered the first time I'd baked, having scrounged up the meager ingredients in our small, damp kitchen. How I'd made the house smell like something other than mildew. How I'd filled my brother's belly and made him smile.

"I know I may seem a little intense with my weirdness, and my anxiety is pretty bad now, but you should've seen me before I found baking," I implored into Rowan's resolute gaze. "I need this."

Rowan's face softened some, but there was still determination in his expression. And he didn't loosen his grip on the mixer.

"Fine, you'll bake," he conceded.

I sighed in relief, already feeling less antsy.

Rowan placed the mixer on the kitchen island, not in the spot where I put it when I was baking.

My eye twitched with the need to put it back in front of the recipe books, below the cupboard with organized spices for easier access. The problem was that Rowan's large form was in my way, and I suspected he'd block me if I even tried to move the mixer.

He pointed over to the barstools. "You, sit."

I folded my arms, restraining my wince at the dull throbbing of my—luckily—quickly healing stomach. "I know you're in construction, so this isn't really your specialty, but I actually need to be in this part of the kitchen to bake." I pointed to the floor.

"I'm gonna do the heavy lifting, you're gonna tell me what to do," he said.

I stared at him in shock. "First of all, I don't think a jar of flour is going to be considered heavy lifting, and second of all... what?"

He sighed loudly. "You're gonna sit and rest and tell me what to do. I'll do the mixing or whatever. That way you're still creating but not pushing yourself too hard."

Rowan's tone brooked no argument.

I wasn't really in the place to fight him because, yes, I was tired and sore, and because I was shocked as shit at this turn of events.

"Sit," he ordered.

Still shocked, I rounded the island to do just that.

"Now," he walked to the sink to wash his hands. "What are we making?"

I bit my lip, debating whether I was going to be easy on him with some cookies or brownies or really make him work.

"Lemon meringue pie," I decided with a grin. "Let's see if those muscles can be delicate enough for a light and airy meringue."

His eyes flared with hunger. "Oh, cupcake, I can be delicate when I need to."

My mouth moistened, remembering how long it had been since Rowan was inside me.

Too fucking long.

"Barstool, now," he barked.

I jumped, hopping to his command. Then I settled in for the show.

* * *

I DIDN'T THINK that a man baking could be sexy. Then again, I'd never seen a man baking. I'd never seen *Rowan* baking. Moving around my kitchen as I instructed him how to separate the eggs, when to add the flour and how much. What folding something tepidly meant.

His muscles flexed as he worked the mixture with the wooden spoon, an adorable wrinkle appearing between his eyebrows as he concentrated.

Throughout this process, I'd become more and more enchanted with Rowan and his movements. He was detailed. Careful. Not at all chaotic like me. He cleaned any spills straight away, he inspected the cup of flour to ensure it was level. He did the dishes as he went.

Not that this should've been surprising. Rowan was measured, controlled and sure in everything he did.

"You're so precise," I acknowledged, resting my chin in my hands.

He glanced up at me. "Well, consider it a side effect of the job. You're not precise in the military, someone gets killed. You're not precise building houses, the roof comes down."

"Right," I breathed as he bent over to put the tray in the oven.

His ass looked great in those jeans. More than great.

We had not had sex since before the hospital. Obviously.

Now that I was basically healed—apart from a few aches and pains—I was aware of how sexually frustrated I was. Well, I'd been aware of it for days since I was living in the same house as a sex god and unable to act on my feelings for aforementioned sex god.

"How long does it bake for?" Rowan asked, wiping his hands on the kitchen towel.

"About fifteen minutes." I jumped off the barstool. "Which isn't enough time, but it should do."

His forehead puckered in confusion. "Enough time for what?"

"For you to fuck me." I rounded the kitchen island. The fact that I was comfortable enough to be so brazen with Rowan was a testament to how much I'd grown in the short time we'd been together. Still, heat crept up my throat.

I saw it flash over his face, the naked hunger. The need. Rowan had been in alpha caretaking mode, but I'd still seen his desire when he showered me, when his hands lingered over my breasts long after the soap had been rinsed from them.

And yes, the way his cock got hard whenever he washed me.

But now that hunger lasted only a moment. "No fuckin' way."

"I'm better," I told him, trying to sound sultry.

The determination in his expression didn't falter, unfortunately.

Not to be discouraged, I stalked toward him. He retreated.

"Nora," he warned.

I found myself excited by this reversal of roles. It was not often I got to back my broad-chested, dominant man into a wall. Actually, I'd never backed him into a wall. Which was what hit his strong back when he kept retreating.

"I'm better," I repeated, laying my hands flat on his broad chest so I could go up on my tiptoes and hover close to his lips.

His body tensed even further, but I knew this time it was not from the frustration of me coming onto him, it was from him battling against his hunger for me and the need he had to take care of me.

"Nora, you are not fuckin' better," he ground out.

I narrowed my eyes at him and dug my nails into the fabric of his tee until they pressed into his skin.

He let out a hiss that I knew was not from discomfort.

"I am the judge of whether or not I'm better," I informed him. "And I am. Even though you're still being ultra-protective and over the top and refusing to see it, I'm better. Therefore, I'm better enough for my man to carry me upstairs and let me thank him for what he created for me."

Rowan's mouth flattened into a grim line. "There is no score-card here, Nora. I do things for you because it makes me happy. Not because I'm expecting anything from you."

I wanted to roll my eyes, but he was being far too serious for that. So, I cupped his cheek instead. "I know," I told him solemnly. "I'm going to suck your cock because I want to."

Rowan let out a groan, the veins in his neck protruding.

My wicked plan was working.

"And technically, this counts as taking care of me since I'm medically in need of an orgasm from my man."

Rowan's eyes went half-mast. "You're fuckin' killing me, Nora."

My smile stretched in satisfaction.

"Or..." I stepped back, eyes cast downward. "I can just make you some dinner as a thank you, then I'll go up to my room to satisfy myself."

I barely got the words out of my mouth before Rowan pushed

off the wall and hoisted me into his arms without the kid gloves he'd been handling me with since I got out of the hospital.

My blood started pumping, and desire coursed through me.

"You will not use that fuckin' vibrator without me in the vicinity," he growled.

I let out a delighted squeal.

"And my cock hasn't felt that sweet cunt in weeks, so I'm gonna be using that to make you come," he added as we ascended up the stairs.

It was safe to say the vibrator stayed in the drawer, and I was very satisfied.

Unfortunately, we burned the lemon meringue pie.

CHAPTER
NINETEEN

Recipe: Carrot and Pecan Cake

From 'Dessert Person'

T hings were going well.

Ronnie Cockran had not come to beat me up, kidnap or kill me like Rowan had thought he might. Same with Nathan. We hadn't seen hide nor hair of him.

I had recovered almost fully from my surgery and had been cleared by the doctor for a little over a week. I didn't work until close yet, though—Fiona and Tina took care of that. I still came in in the mornings, with Rowan and Maggie in tow, doing all of the baking and spending most of the day at the bakery.

But the second it hit two in the afternoon, my phone was ringing. If Rowan wasn't physically at the bakery, that was.

"Cupcake," he'd greet me. But not in the sweet, melty tone I had become accustomed to. I'd also become accustomed to Rowan's ability to communicate very different moods with a single word. That single word usually being 'cupcake' or 'Nora.'

The two p.m. greeting was an order. A warning.

"I'm going!" I would say. "I've just got to frost—"

"You ain't frosting shit," he'd interrupt. "You get your ass in the car and get home and rest, or I'll drive myself over there, throw you over a shoulder, make a big fuckin' scene and punish you when we get home."

Whatever variation of argument we had always ended with this or a similar sexual threat. Ones that made my knees weak and my fingers clutch the phone even harder. Ones that made me want to disobey him so he'd make good on that threat.

And it would be really fucking good.

But he had to work. It was unfair of me to expect him to come running in the middle of his workday in order to sexually punish me.

Which he did half the time anyway.

There was no need for Rowan to be spending so much time with me anymore. Sleeping in my bed every night. No need for him to get up with me in the morning or follow me to the bakery. Yet he did all of those things. He was a constant part of my day. My mornings, my afternoons, my evenings. Sometimes Kip would come to my place with him for a home cooked meal— upon my request ever since I found out he relied on takeout and microwave meals.

I enjoyed Kip's company. He was easy to be around, charming. He and Rowan were close. They'd been deployed together, spoke about it a couple of times. Not a lot because whenever the subject came up, Kip's easy smiles no longer looked easy. The light in his eyes went out, and he stopped looking like the happy-go-lucky man he was. He looked... tortured, for lack of a better word.

And although Rowan could not be described as a happy-go-lucky man—he was still positively broody which I had come to find out I fucking loved—something changed in him too. His posture visibly stiffened, and if he was holding on to me, his grasp would suddenly tighten as if someone might try to tear me away.

Rowan hadn't spoken to me about what life had been like when he was deployed. He hadn't told me where his scars came from, though I ached to ask. I'd run my fingers over them while we were in bed, tracing the puckered skin, the question on my lips.

He'd tense beside me, as if he were bracing for the questions. Bracing for me to take him back there. I was desperate to know him in every way I could, but I couldn't do it. I couldn't mar the happiness that we had, couldn't be the reason why he went back to a place that made him tense like that.

The worrier in me, the anxious girl in me, wanted to get the conversation over with. To rush through all of the hard topics because things couldn't possibly be *that* good. But I resisted.

We would eventually go there, that I knew. But I didn't have to rush it. We had time. Rowan wasn't going anywhere. Rowan loved me. He said it often. At the end of every phone call, as I was drifting off to sleep, when he was inside me. Most importantly, he showed it in all of his actions.

It didn't seem to bother him that I didn't say it back. Couldn't was more appropriate. I loved him. Of course, I did. Who wouldn't? But like some heroine in some stupid romantic comedy, I couldn't actually say the words. They were stuck. The truth was, I was worried if I said the words aloud, it would set off some chain reaction, make the bad things start happening.

So, I didn't say it.

Ansel was finally visiting in two days. It was the longest we'd been apart, and I missed him. Not only that, I wanted Rowan to meet him. Maybe that's why I couldn't say the words. Because I needed Rowan to know me entirely. Needed to be complete in that way first. And I truly wasn't complete without Ansel.

So yes, things were going well. Really fucking well.

Things going well usually meant something terrible was coming. I'd learned that. Worrying was my way of coping, my way of preparing. If I wasn't ready, my anxiety serving as an invisible buffer from whatever was coming, the terrible thing would catch me by surprise, knocking me off my feet.

The problem was, I had a man who was making me happy. Healthy. I worried less. A lot less. Especially since I'd told him all about my crazy. He hadn't gone running. Didn't even flutter an eyelash. He took it in stride. Took me in stride.

So, I stopped.

Waiting for the other shoe to drop.

Not completely, of course. I had endured years of trauma, creating multiple layers of anxiety. That didn't get fixed overnight. Or by being with a man I was utterly in love with.

The man who had yet to show any of his imperfections to me beyond his over-the-top, protective, alpha tendencies. Which I didn't hate a bit, even if they didn't align with the feminist I knew myself to be.

I couldn't imagine falling asleep without him. Without my body satisfied from his touch.

Nor could I imagine days when he didn't visit the bakery. I struggled to remember the time that existed before us. We were in a bubble. That magical bubble that was created in the beginning of a relationship, when lust burned hot, and everything was new, special and exciting.

I still got butterflies. Even though he was basically living with me. And they didn't feel like the fleeting kind of butterflies you get when you first start a relationship, they felt permanent.

I knew we had to have some conversations. The kinds of

conversations two adults in a relationship had. Like where this was going. If we were going to live together, where would that be? I liked Rowan's house a lot, but my home was sacred to me. It was something I'd created. Not to mention it now had Rowan's touch on it. I couldn't even think of letting it go in the same way I couldn't let my bakery go.

And if we were going to live together, what did that look like?

Rowan struck me as the kind of man who would insist on taking care of all of the bills, and that would not work for me. I'd grinded, hustled and worked my ass off in order to afford my life-style. To earn it. I wouldn't hand it over to a man. Even this man.

Yes, all sorts of conversations needed to be had.

"You're not allowed to keep coming here," I scolded him, trying to keep a straight face and make my tone firm with disapproval.

But I failed miserably.

Rowan's eyes twinkled as he looked at me like I was the only person in the room. The only person on the planet.

It wasn't something you got used to. And despite the warmth his gaze provided, there was a slice of ice, buried deep in my heart, whispering that this wasn't going to last. That this wasn't how it ended for me.

"Why do I need to stop coming here?" he asked, voice like honey. A rich, masculine kind of honey, though.

"Because," I sighed. "You're much too distracting, and I've got to get work done."

The corners of his mouth turned up. "And you can't work when I'm around?"

"It's exceptionally hard."

"But I'm only here two times a day."

"Three," I corrected him. "You come in the morning before anyone else is here."

"We both do," he teased, leaning forward to coil my hair around his finger.

My whole body tingled from his touch, from the hungry look in his eye, from the memories of what he did when he came in the mornings.

I smiled lazily back at him, leaning forward, not caring whether our public display of affection was unprofessional in my place of business.

The smile froze on my face as my eyes swung toward the door and settled on the person walking through it. My heart stopped beating, and everything inside me turned to ice.

Rowan ceased to exist. The world around me ceased to exist. I didn't remember doing it, but I must've walked around the counter and met her at the door. There was no other explanation for how I was standing in front of her in one slow blink.

There was no reason for her to be here.

She wouldn't come for a visit. Not to see me. Not to see the business I'd created. The life I'd created.

There was only reason she'd be here.

Death.

And still, her clothes were pressed, her hair coiffed into a chignon, her makeup expertly applied. As it always was. Even when there was no money to pay our water bill, there was money for my mother to get her weekly blowout. Her priorities were always crystal clear.

There was a very slight redness to her eyes, but that could've been a trick of the light. Otherwise, she looked like an attractive, upper middle class, sixty-year-old woman who thought she was better than everyone.

Her daughter included.

Her daughter especially.

Normally, that haughty look of veiled disdain, the upturned

chin, the pinch of disappointment and judgment between her brows did something to me.

Though I couldn't say 'normally,' since I hadn't seen the woman in years.

"What did you do?" I hissed, my voice unrecognizable. I realized my hands were clenched, but otherwise, I couldn't feel my limbs.

My mother's lips pursed in what I assumed was irritation and impatience. "Nora—"

"*What did you do?*" I screamed at her.

My mother glanced around. "Nora, we should not have this conversation here."

"Here is the only place we're having this conversation," I snarled. I didn't move. Couldn't move. Because I didn't think my legs would hold me.

There was warmth at my side, a strong presence. My mother's eyes went to him.

Rowan.

He came because he saw my distress. Because that's what he did. He showed up to protect me. Shield me.

But Rowan didn't matter to me. Not now. Not at that moment.

"He's dead, isn't he?" I asked my mother, my tone cold and lifeless.

My mother proved that she had some humanity left inside her by flinching at my words.

She didn't answer me. She wasn't even brave enough to meet my eyes, merely nodded weakly.

"You killed him."

My mother didn't flinch this time, her chin tilted upward as she regained her armor of disinterest. My mother was a lot of things, but she wasn't someone who would take the blame for anything. Especially the things she was guilty of.

"A drug overdose killed him, Nora," she snipped without an inch of grief. "He was a drug addict."

"And what turned him into a drug addict?" I sneered. "*Who* turned him into a drug addict? Who chose her own interests, her manicures, her makeup, her quest for a rich husband, over her son's warmth, over clothes that fit, his childhood?" My fury rose up inside of me, a hot, scalding thing. "You did that." I jabbed my finger at her. "You gave him nothing. Not love. Not a home. Nothing for him to grab on to."

Angry tears were streaming down my face. I was surprised my skin didn't sizzle. Something was tearing inside of me. Something large, something special and irreplaceable inside of me. It was splintering my insides. The pain was unbearable.

"I paid for his rehab," she snapped. "Every single time. I paid for therapists. Gave him a place to live. What did you do, Nora?"

She looked around the bakery. "You ran away. To sell cupcakes." Her words dripped with disdain, the tone shrinking me down like it always did. To make me feel small. Worthless. "You abandoned your brother."

I backpedaled, the words hitting true. I might've actually collapsed on the floor had I not hit something solid. His arms wrapped around my waist, firm, strong. But they didn't do anything this time, merely held me up.

Rowan passed me, delicately, into the arms of my best friend who I hadn't realized had also come to stand by my side. Though she was much smaller, she was strong enough to tuck me under her arm, hold me up.

I stared at Rowan's back as he stepped forward and got right in my mom's face. Even without seeing his face, I knew he was pissed. From the way he held his shoulders. The way he used his size to intimidate the woman. The Rowan I knew would never do that.

My mother, though a lot of things, was not one to be intimidated easily. Or at all. She was the one who was practiced at doing such things. But she shrank back under what I imagined was the force of Rowan's murderous glare.

"You're done."

He said the two words quietly, almost a murmur. But they seemed to boom through the room, bouncing off the walls.

"You get out of here," he ordered, still in that hauntingly soft tone that echoed. "You do not contact Nora. Do not talk to her unless she decides she wants to talk to you. And if I ever hear that vile, that toxic, unforgivable shit comin' out of your mouth again, I'll ruin your fucking life."

In any other circumstance, that tone, that eerie promise would've terrified the crap out of me. Except I had nothing to be afraid of. Not now that my worst fears had been realized.

My mother hated not having the last word. Hated having someone best her, shame her, especially publicly. It probably irked her even more since it was the day her son died. That wouldn't matter to her. What mattered most was that Diane Henderson saved face.

But for the first time I'd ever seen, my mother retreated.

Yet I felt no joy in that.

I didn't think I'd ever feel joy again.

* * *

WHENEVER SOMETHING terribly tragic happens to someone, they often explain how 'everything passes by in a blur.' Now, I'm not going to call those people liars, but I couldn't imagine the universe being that kind after being so indescribably cruel.

Because it certainly wasn't for me.

For me, nothing went by in a blur. Not even for a second.

Everything happened in stark detail. Time slowed down to a crawl. I didn't get a moment of respite. Not one. Even with Rowan's constant presence. I had considered him to be some kind of force of magic, able to fix everything. Able to keep me safe from anything. To bring forth happiness.

But I quickly learned that just wasn't realistic.

No one man, no matter how extraordinary, could fix everything. Could protect me from the realities of life.

But he was there. He was there as I turned my grief into purpose, organizing a funeral, deciding what to do with my brother's apartment, his personal effects.

Fiona was there too. And Tina. They'd taken care of things at the bakery, I think. I vaguely remembered that as Rowan ushered me out, under his arm.

He'd put me in his truck and started driving me home. I'd stared at the road for a few seconds, lost in the yawning chasms of pain that came between every single second.

Then, somehow, I'd wrenched myself out. And I started making calls. Maggie was pressed into my legs when I was stationary and followed my every step around the house.

"Lilies," I told the woman on the phone. "I need lilies." I was pacing on my patio. It was cold outside. Or at least that's what I thought. It was late fall, it was dark. There was wind coming from the ocean that always had a bite that time of night. I was wearing a thin tank and sweats, my hair still wet from the shower I'd taken earlier. Rowan had been in there too, washing my hair like I was unable to lift my arms or do anything for myself.

I should've been freezing.

But I couldn't feel a thing.

"We don't have a good stock of lilies right now," the woman on the phone informed me. "What with the season changing. We can do roses, though." Her voice was strained. Probably because I called her cell approaching ten at night.

I pinched the bridge of my nose. "No, roses won't do. I need lilies. They—"

The phone was snatched from my ear before I could say anything else.

"She'll call you tomorrow," Rowan barked at the florist before he hung up the phone.

"Hey!" I scowled at him. "You cannot just snatch the phone from people."

Rowan did not respond to this. He was too busy sliding my phone in his pocket and lifting me over his shoulder.

"Hey!" I shouted again. "Put me down." I banged on his back for emphasis. Which did nothing. I may as well have been hitting steel.

Rowan closed the door behind us as Maggie followed, still not speaking until he plonked me down on the barstool.

"You're gonna sit there," he cupped my face with his hands, his tone kind but firm. "And you're gonna stay there."

"I'm not a dog," I protested.

"No," he agreed. "You're my woman. And you've lost something important. Part of yourself. You're hurtin' in a way that I can't fix. Can't even take the edge off."

I bristled in my seat, hating that I was being forced to remain sedentary, that he was speaking about the thing I had been avoiding all day. He was making my chest burn and acknowledging that cavernous empty space inside of me unavoidable.

Rowan's hands were firm on my face, his eyes intent. In that moment, I felt a surge of pure hatred toward him. For forcing me to sit there, with my feelings. With my pain.

"I can't do anything to make you hurt less," he said quieter, in a tortured tone that made that hate melt away. "But I can make sure you don't freeze to death outside. He rubbed my arms as if to warm me. As if that were possible. "I can make you somethin' to eat." He stroked my face.

I opened my mouth to tell him that despite the emptiness inside of me, there was absolutely no way I could swallow a single thing.

"I'm not hungry," was what I managed to rasp out. Mere minutes ago, I'd been on the phone talking about lilies, sounding perfectly normal, my voice clear and strong. Yet it was crumbling right now, full of cracks. Frail. I sounded weak and broken.

"I know you're not hungry," Rowan replied. "But I'm gonna make you somethin' anyway. And you can eat it or not. But it'll be there. And you'll have something to draw strength from. So tomorrow you can make calls. So you can do whatever you need to do."

Tomorrow.

Such a benign word. An everyday concept. There was always a tomorrow, wasn't there?

But now there wasn't. There wasn't a tomorrow. Because my brother was lying on a cold slab in a morgue somewhere.

"There's a word for orphan," I whispered. "For widow. But there's no word for this. There's no label to give the woman who lost her brother. But he's not just my brother—"

My voice broke, agony spearing through every cell in my body. Rowan's presence, his touch, usually so strong and reassuring, did nothing now.

"I didn't feel anything," I choked out. "Everyone says that twins have this connection. And we have that—" I stopped speaking abruptly, realizing I could not talk about my brother in the present tense anymore. Because he wasn't alive. "What we *had*," I corrected, sucking in a breath that felt like poison, creeping along my insides. Mixing with all the poison that was already in there.

"What we had was the twin thing," I continued. "I liked a boy at school. I thought he liked me back. He was nice. His friends weren't. And when they found out that I liked him, they told me that I was a freak and to leave their friend alone." I shook my head. "Boys learn to be cruel to women at a young age." I stared into his pale cerulean eyes. "Some boys, at least." I sucked in an unsteady breath. "I locked myself in the girl's bathroom, thinking it was the worst day of my life and that I would die of shame because there was no way I could leave that bathroom."

I smiled sadly, nostalgic for that teenage naïveté when you truly believed the worst day of your life could be facilitated by boys who still washed their faces with Proactiv.

"Ansel found me in that bathroom," I sighed. "We didn't have phones. Everyone else did back then, but not us. Our mother wouldn't dream of spending that much on us. And all of the money we earned from our part-time jobs went to food, bills and clothes."

Rowan's features, which had been soft yet pained, now hardened, his nostrils flaring. "Your mother is really fuckin' lucky I've got a code about committing violence against women."

"Yeah, well, cockroaches can't die anyway," I smiled sadly. "She'll survive the nuclear apocalypse." I pushed away thoughts of my mother, instead focusing on my brother's teenage face in that bathroom all those years ago.

He'd been pissed off. Murderous in a different way than Rowan was because Ansel was just a boy then, but he was feeling a man's rage because it came from a place of love.

"He sat there with me," I whispered. "Redid my makeup for me. At least he tried to. He cursed himself for 'not being that kind of gay.'" I choked out a laugh that sounded empty and cold. "Then he linked my arm with his and walked me up to that group of boys."

Afraid and mortified, I just wanted to go home, and for the first time I could recall, our house actually felt like some kind of safe haven. But Ansel wasn't going to let me slink off and let them win. And though I was still upset, I wasn't scared. Not with my brother by my side.

"He told them off. All of them." A grin tugged at my lips. "He threatened to tell the school which of the jocks were much more interested in staring at his teammate's junk than washing his own. Of course, he'd never actually out someone, but the threat was enough."

I thought about my brother, being unapologetically himself at that school. It was in a small town in Missouri, where being gay was dangerous in and of itself. But Ansel didn't hide himself, who he was. Not for a moment.

"The last time he overdosed, I felt it," I said back in the present. "I felt cold. I felt lost. And I knew, I just knew that something had happened to him."

That day was branded into my brain. The way I'd known that something had happened to my brother. I'd dropped everything and driven an hour back to the house he was living in at the time.

"I had Narcan because even though I didn't want to believe my sweet, strong, unyielding brother had demons inside of him that I couldn't wrench out, I knew that forcing myself to be ignorant could be the reason he died. So, he didn't die. Not that day, at least."

I didn't sleep for a month after that, every time I closed my eyes, I saw my brother, lifeless, covered in vomit, a needle still sticking out of his arm.

"He went to rehab then," I forced out the words, the memories making my skin itch. "Because he felt my pain when he woke up in the hospital. He felt my panic. That was the first time he was sober, stayed that way for almost six months. He relapsed but got sober again right away, staying clean up until... yesterday, I guess."

His sobriety was the permission I gave myself to leave. To study in Paris and eventually settle in Jupiter. Ansel was the one who had urged me to follow my dreams.

"You'll waste away here, honey," he said gently. "And you're only here because of me. But I promise you here and now that I'm okay. And the only way I won't be is if I see my sister sacrificing her dreams for me."

I'd called the hospital where he'd been pronounced dead and was lucky enough to get in contact with the doctor who had treated him. The doctor had been kind. Patient.

"Although I can't be sure, I would hazard a guess that this was the first time he'd used in a long time," he informed me, his voice calm and even on the phone. "The toxicology from his previous overdose shows a much higher concentration." I heard the rustle of papers on the other side of the phone. "What often happens with addicts who have been in recovery a while is something triggers them to relapse suddenly, and they think they can handle the same amount of drugs they did at the height of their addiction. Yet their body cannot metabolize that much."

I racked my brain, for probably the millionth time since my mother stepped foot in the bakery, wondering what could've triggered my brother to relapse. I searched my memory for our last phone call, cursing myself for being so wrapped up in Rowan and not hearing it.

Whatever it was... the thing that would've told me that he was not doing okay. I would've heard it. If I'd been listening for it. If I'd been thinking about something other than myself and my giddiness over my new relationship.

"I didn't feel it," I told Rowan. "He died yesterday at six in the morning. And I was in the bakery. Making croissants. And I didn't fucking feel a thing."

Why didn't I feel anything? Was it the distance between us? Was it because I hadn't seen him in months... the longest we'd been apart?

No, it didn't have anything to do with physical distance or time. Another chasm had formed between us. I'd moved forward in life and love, and I'd left my brother behind. To rot in that town with my mother. Without a shield from her venom.

"It's my fault."

"No, it's fuckin' not," Rowan immediately hissed.

So predictable. He stepped up. Wanted to go to bat for me. Protect me. Even from myself.

"It is," I protested, looking up with dry eyes. I was in too much pain to cry. I hadn't known that was a thing. That your body could be in so much agony that there wasn't a way to expel it physically. "I left him. I made a life here." I waved my hands around my living room. The one I'd been so proud of, my eyes grazing over all the things I was so proud of. Now every fucking thing haunted me, taunted me, showing me what I had and what my brother hadn't. I wanted to tear it all to shreds.

"I was too much of a coward to stay there, be near her. And I wasn't strong enough to get him to leave with me. He was half of me, and I just... left him. To die."

"Enough." The single word was a solid thing, jolting me. "He was half of you," Rowan acknowledged. "And knowing how stubborn you are, I know that you couldn't convince him to do anything he didn't want to do. That he wasn't ready for. You can't take that on. And though I didn't know him, I know that he adored you. Know he'd be really fuckin' pissed off you're laying the blame at your own feet. This is a tragic thing. A fucking horrific thing. It doesn't make sense. It won't make sense. Even the people we're closest to, who we know the best—especially the people we know the best—can hide the truest, darkest parts of themselves from us."

Emotion saturated his tone. And knowing. A knowing that might've piqued my curiosity normally, but not now.

"Please, Nora, can you let me cook for you?" He locked eyes with me.

I wanted to fight him. But instead, I nodded, too tired to do anything else.

CHAPTER
TWENTY

Recipe: Tarte Tatin

From 'Dessert Person'

We flew to Chicago for the funeral.

He would not have wanted to be buried there.

He didn't even want to be buried.

He'd wanted to be cremated, his ashes scattered off the coast of Washington. He'd already told me that. Made me promise to do it for him.

"What makes you think that I'm going to be the one arranging your funeral?" I jabbed him in the stomach.

The atmosphere had been light. Jovial. We were two teenagers, talking about death like we didn't really believe it would ever find us.

But my brother's expression was serious then. Somber.

"We both know I'm gonna get off of this ride early, sis. You're

gonna be the one living the long, wonderful life. Growing old with some husband who adores you. Surrounded by grandchildren."

A cold stone settled somewhere deep inside me, not just because of the words, but because of the certainty he spoke with. He believed this. Truly.

I swallowed a lump and tried to smile. "I know you're into astrology and crystals and all that shit, but you can't see the future, little brother."

"But I can feel it," he replied, still not smiling, eyes far away. "My life is going to be chaotic, messy and short."

My throat burned. With anger. "Stop," I hissed at him. "You are not allowed to leave me here, in this world alone." Tears streamed down my cheeks. "You are not allowed to die."

"Okay, okay, calm down." He held his hands up in surrender. "I promise I won't ever die, and after you do, the government will lock me up and dissect me, looking for the secrets to my long life." He grinned crookedly.

Despite my brother's promises, I'd known somewhere deep inside me, with a terrible kind of dread, that he believed what he'd initially said.

He didn't choose to leave. That I knew. But he also couldn't live his life straight, not with what followed him.

Which was why I fought my mother at the funeral home.

"The burial plot is beautiful," she cooed. I didn't know to who.

She and I weren't talking. She had been on a different flight back to Chicago. I hadn't seen her since the altercation at the bakery. Rowan and I were staying at a hotel. She'd left a voice-mail, giving me the details of this meeting. I was only there at the funeral home because I wanted to make sure my brother's wishes were adhered to.

Rowan was by my side, stoic and stone faced. His hand was on my thigh, staring daggers at my mother.

Though the woman wasn't unnerved by much—she was one tough bitch, I'd give her that— I knew that Rowan was making her uncomfortable.

However petty it made me, I liked that. Liked that my mother wasn't on even footing, didn't sling her venom quite so easily as she might've had my strong, tall, unyielding protector not been constantly by my side.

So, she wasn't talking to Rowan when she talked about the burial.

My stepfather wasn't there. He was working. As he always did. Probably trying to stay as far away from my mother as possible. He wasn't the worst man. Maybe, if I'd had the time to get to know him, I might've even liked him. But we were ships passing. I left the mansion he situated my mother and us in as soon as I could, and never spoke to him again.

There were no Christmas dinners or visits.

But from the scant amount of time I'd known him, he'd seemed decent, and trapped by the viper who was my mother.

"My brother is not being buried," I notified my mother, the first time I'd spoken to her directly since she told me my brother was dead.

"Of course, he is," she replied, not looking at me, brushing imaginary lint from her Chanel suit.

"He isn't," I reiterated through gritted teeth. "He did not want to be buried. He does not believe in burials."

Mom rolled her eyes. "Oh, I know that he had all sorts of things that he believed in, what with crystals and full moons. But that is not important right now."

"What my brother believed and how he wanted to be laid to

rest is the only thing that's important right now," I shouted at her, standing from my chair.

Mom looked anxiously to the funeral director who had not batted an eyelash at my outburst. I suspected that people didn't always behave their best at these kinds of things. Death tended to make people ugly.

"Keep your voice down," Mom hushed. "This isn't seemly."

"Oh, give me a fucking break, Mom. You grew up in a trailer; you have no fucking clue what's seemly."

I reveled at the apples of rage that bloomed on my mother's cheeks.

She pushed out of her seat then too. "I didn't raise you to—"

"You didn't raise me at all," I interrupted. "Nor did you raise Ansel. I did that. For the both of us. You forced that on us. Forced a lot of things on us." I stepped toward her. "Like a man who would change the course of my brother's life forever. I'd bet everything I have that we wouldn't be standing here right now if you hadn't married him."

My mother flinched as if I'd struck her. My palm itched to do just that.

But I'd done all the damage I needed to do with bringing up what happened to Ansel. What ultimately set him on the course to trying to find an escape, the numbness that drugs gave him.

I felt nothing, seeing tears well in my mother's eyes. They weren't real. Nothing about the woman was.

I looked at the funeral director, his expression still impassive. "He'll be cremated," I informed him.

Then I turned on my heel and left, Rowan at my side, where he'd be for the foreseeable future.

* * *

ANSEL WAS NOT BURIED. But Mom kept the plot. It didn't surprise me. She didn't like losing at anything, not getting her way. So, she had to hold on to control wherever and whenever she could. Plus, she needed it for whatever bullshit appearances she'd created. The stuffy circle of socialites she'd managed to elbow her way into.

But appearances didn't matter to me. All that mattered was that my brother's wishes were being respected. That he'd be scattered across the ocean as he'd wanted.

I wondered what my mother had told them, all of the people who had attended the service, most of whom hadn't even known my brother. But some did—the small but lovely group dressed in bright colors, wearing eccentric jewelry, covered in tattoos.

Gunner, a black man with long dreadlocks and a face of beautiful makeup, had informed me that they would be having a different service at the park later... which he invited me to after he'd given me a hug that felt warm and comforting.

"Now, we've got to get out of here," his rich brown eyes surveying the small crowd. "Before all these rich white people get nervous and call the cops on us." He gave me a wink and an arm squeeze. "Ansel talked about you all the time," he added softly. "He loved you so much. He was very proud of you."

My teeth sank into my lip, and I tasted blood.

"Please come to the service," he said. "We would love to have you there, and I know that Ansel would've too." He'd given me one last squeeze before leaving.

I didn't want to go. Here, amongst all of the flowers, the tasteful canapes, the people wearing designer clothing, the stuffy music... I could lie to myself. Tell myself this was not my brother's funeral. This could've been anyone else's, but not my brother's.

It was the last thread of denial I was holding on to.

Oh, how tempting it was to bury my head in the sand.

"We don't have to go," Rowan murmured from beside me. We were on the balcony of my mother's stuffy apartment, where the reception was held.

It was impressive. Had great views of the lake. Was worth millions.

It made me sick.

He was talking about the service. My brother's service. The real one. The one that would prove my brother was truly gone.

"No, we do," I shook my head. "I do." I stared at the lake because I couldn't look at Rowan. Not now.

"I need to say goodbye to my brother the right way." I motioned to the apartment. "*This* is not the right way."

"Okay, cupcake." He kissed the top of my head.

The gesture, the endearment, didn't work as it normally did to make me feel safe, protected. How could it? There was nothing to protect me from anymore.

Rowan stiffened behind me as the sounds of the party suddenly rushed outward with the opening of the door.

I didn't turn to see who it was. I could tell by the fury radiating off Rowan.

"Can I speak to my daughter for a moment? Alone?" My mother's voice was tight, pinched and hostile.

I wanted to smile at how much she disliked him because he wouldn't stand around and let her walk all over me. Because he saw right through her.

"No, you fuckin' can't," Rowan responded, moving in front of me as I turned from my contemplation of the lake.

I placed my hand on his arm. "It's fine," I sighed. I'd known this was coming. My mother was nothing if not predictable.

Rowan didn't move. He stared at my mother for a few more

beats before he turned his full attention to me. His face was creased with worry. "Nora," he murmured.

"I'm fine," I reassured him. "I promise I won't throw her off or anything." I nodded to the balcony. "I wouldn't do well in prison."

Rowan didn't smile. He just looked at me for another long moment before nodding tersely. "I'll be right inside," he said loudly, both to me and my mother before he leaned in to kiss my forehead.

The loss of him was something I felt physically. My limbs went weak. It was hard to keep myself upright. But that also might've been due to all the booze I'd consumed and the canapes I'd ignored.

When my mother walked to stand beside me, I moved to create more of a buffer between us.

Still, I smelled her perfume, her hairspray, my stomach turning.

I held on to the railing with one hand, my glass with the other, staring out at the lake once more, determined not to speak, not to make the first move. My mother was the master at manipulation and gaslighting. When I'd been younger, I'd been more susceptible. But now I was somewhat wiser and had given up my desperate need for her love and approval.

She cleared her throat yet didn't speak.

I waited.

"I would've killed him," Mom stated finally. "The man who..."

"Molested Ansel?" I spoke for her when it became clear she was too weak to say the words. The truth was far too ugly for her lipsticked mouth to utter.

My mother nodded, clutching her crystal glass.

"I wanted to kill him, when I found out," she whispered. "Seeing him screaming, bleeding was good. But it wasn't enough. I was so close to shooting him in the head. Ending his life. But I knew that I couldn't get away with murder. Couldn't leave you both. After..."

Her voice broke, and I wished I could say it did nothing to me, but unlike my mother, I wasn't versed at turning my emotions off when my family was in pain.

And she was in pain. It was the first time I'd heard emotion, vulnerability in her voice. I didn't like it.

"I loved him." She looked out at the skyline. "I know you don't think that's true. But I love both of you."

The only reason I didn't roll my eyes was because I was too tired. Bone tired.

"As soon as I found out I was pregnant, I made a promise to myself," she continued. "That I wouldn't let you grow up like I did. I'd find a way to give you opportunities."

I sipped my drink because the alternative was to hurl it at her head. Was she really trying to twist our entire shitty childhood and her neglect into her working hard to give us more?

Give me a fucking break.

"I don't expect you to believe me," she sniffled.

She was watching me, I could see that in my periphery. I would not give her eye contact. I couldn't.

"It's hard to believe that you loved us and wanted the best for us when my first memory is hunger, my second is constantly being cold, and the third is what crying in an empty house sounds like," I remarked dryly.

"I was a *child*, Nora." My mother's voice was tight with shame. "I'm not going to pretend anything I did was right, but I was uneducated with no role models of my own, and my only advantage was my looks. And being able to talk men into anything."

"Shame you couldn't talk my brother out of killing himself with a drug addiction," I said to the lake.

My mother sighed dramatically. I was used to those sighs. They came when she'd decided I was being too needy, too dramatic, too much for her. Which was pretty much always, in her books.

"I know you hate me."

I didn't correct her.

"Ansel knew, he understood that I made mistakes but that I loved you underneath it all."

His name was a blade, through every inch of me. "He was a fucking marvel," I hissed. "He loved you because love was all he had inside him. He wasn't capable of hating you, resenting you, blaming you like you deserved."

"I know," my mother replied in a small voice. "I know, and nothing will ever bring my boy back."

There was pain in her tone. Agony. A kind that she couldn't mask. A kind that was real.

The worst thing was not finding out your mother was a complete monster.

It was finding out that she *wasn't* a complete monster.

That she was human. That the world had hurt her. And that instead of growing, changing, learning, she'd hurt us. Not because she was evil. Oh, that would've been so much cleaner. If she was just wrong. If I could write her off entirely.

But now I couldn't. I felt empathy for this woman. The woman who had let us go hungry, cold. The woman who had picked me apart like a vulture, finding the loose, fragile parts and tearing them from me.

"It's too late," I exhaled a heavy breath. "For amends. For any kind of relationship between us." I turned to regard the apartment, the windows illuminating all of the people inside. The furniture, the art, all expensive, all impressive... to certain kinds of people, at least.

Rowan was there, cutting a dark shape amongst all of the country club assholes. He was standing close to the sliding doors leading out here. His eyes were on me and my mother, gaze hard and posture rigid. He was ready, poised to run out here, protect me from anything he could.

I tried to give him a reassuring smile, but I wasn't physically capable of such things.

"You did it." I turned back to my mother. "You got the life you always wanted. All you needed to do was sacrifice your son. Steal away our childhood. Now, you've got the money, the things, the husband. But you don't have children. One is gone from this world, and I may as well be dead to you because you're dead to me."

I didn't wait for my mother to say something, to try to get the last word—as she always did. I dropped my glass, letting it shatter on the ground, and walked out, the shards crunching underneath my feet.

CHAPTER
TWENTY-ONE
RECIPE: PISTACHIO PINWHEELS

Recipe: Sour Cherry Pie

From 'Dessert Person'

ROWAN

I kept an eye on her. A close eye.

She was bleeding. Her insides torn apart. It hurt just to look at her. To see the pain clinging to her every cell. And I couldn't do a thing about it. Not a fucking thing. She lost the single person on this earth she'd loved the most, her blood. Her other half.

And though she'd screamed at her mother a couple of times —I'd never met a woman who deserved to be screamed at in the days after her son's death until her—cried at the service and clutched the ashes containing her brother's remains like a life-line, she never shed another tear.

She was doing fucking well at *pretending* she was okay.

She was functioning by taking care of shit. First, it was the

289

funeral flowers. Then it was the service, making sure her brother's wishes were honored. Then it was the ceremony in the park, the one that was filled with colorful characters who'd obviously loved her brother. She spent the whole service comforting them. Then it was straight back here, straight back to work. No fucking pause.

And no way was she listening to me when I'd tried to tell her she should take a break.

She'd firmly said no, though with a tremble in her voice. She was clinging to the edge of a cliff, holding on for dear life. I didn't know how to convince her I could catch her. Didn't know how to prove it to her. Her whole fucking life, she'd had to take care of herself. Her brother. There had never been anyone there for her when she fell apart. She didn't know how to let that happen. She was terrified.

So, I just had to watch. And wait.

Though it was killing me.

Everyone else was worried too. Could see it in their faces.

They loved Nora. Endlessly. Fiona, Tiffany and Tina would jump in front of a bullet for her. But like me, their hands were tied. We just had to stay close. Be there when she fell apart.

I came to the bakery three times a day. Like normal. First thing in the morning when she opened up. Fucked her then. Hard. Quiet. Brutal. I wiped the tears away from her cheeks when we were done, not saying anything. Let her make me coffee while I situated myself on a stool, watching her work.

Her bakery was the only place she didn't shut off from the world. Where she was sure. Confident. It was a fucking marvel to see.

Fiona would come in, swearing like always. But she kept a careful eye on Nora.

While there, Nora seemed herself. Or as close to herself as

she could be with a piece missing. With half of her missing. How the fuck she was going to recover from losing that much was anyone's guess. But I knew she would. Believed she was strong enough.

I was still bracing for her to fall because I understood something had to give. She couldn't keep on like this forever.

And then when I went by the bakery one afternoon, she wasn't there. Fiona looked worried. Really fucking worried.

"She said she was going to pick up something," Fiona said by greeting. Her tone and her expression had me on high alert, the pit in my stomach opening up wider.

"How long ago?" I barked, louder than I'd intended.

Fiona flinched at my tone and probably my expression. I couldn't rein it in. Not now. Not when fear had sunk its talons in.

"About an hour," Tina replied for Fiona, her own face filled with worry. "She's not at home, already been there."

I nodded. "I'll find her."

Tina scowled at me coldly. "You fucking better."

There was a threat there. An unsaid 'or else'.

But the thing was, I didn't need the threat. Because there was no other option but to find Nora in one piece.

NORA

I wasn't well versed in drowning my sorrows. Sure, I might've salved some hurt with a bottle of wine—or even two—in extenuating circumstances, but I wasn't someone to slam countless tequilas. Wouldn't swig from a bottle of vodka while soaking in the tub, though I loved the visual of it, so hardcore and dramatic, yet not for me. I never liked the taste of hard liquor. And I'd always been mindful of the way my brother's addiction had taken hold of him.

I'd always thought if I kept hold of myself, if I didn't give anything too much power over me, it would mean that my brother would be able to get his power back. We were connected after all.

But that had obviously been bullshit.

I didn't know how fucked-up it was to be getting drunk in order to try to deal with my twin brother dying of an overdose. I didn't care much at that point.

That was the wonderful effect of whiskey. The first two tasted like shit, but after that, I barely noticed. I came to crave the burn at the back of my throat.

I was slumped at the bar, staring into nothing, thinking about nothing. It was nice.

But every now and then, memories would rush in. The service at the park. Ansel's friends. Their tears, their laughter, the stories about my brother. They loved him. They knew him. But no one could tell me what happened. What triggered him to go back to the thing that killed him.

"Sometimes there is no answer, honey," Gunner had told me gently. *"Not one we can know. Ansel took it with him. Just know that he didn't want to leave. He just didn't know how to stay, feeling the pain we couldn't see."*

His words had been wise and comforting, but they didn't stop me from staying up, racking my brain, searching for a reason why my brother picked up the needle again.

There was a chasm in my stomach, one that told me Ansel had taken that reason to the grave.

Which was why I was trying to fill that chasm with whiskey.

Night had fallen. I'd left the bakery in the afternoon. Hadn't told anyone where I was going. Which wasn't much like me. They'd be worried.

Normally, I'd care about worrying people. Causing them any kind of harm.

But I couldn't care. I didn't have the energy.

"You haven't come in here before." The smell of cologne and sweat assaulted my senses.

I blinked away from my glass to see a man perched on the barstool next to me. He'd pulled it closer than it had been before. Much too close. His arm brushed against mine.

I didn't like that. Not at all. But moving seemed like far too much effort.

"I would've remembered you," he continued.

The man in question was younger than me. Early twenties, maybe. We lived in a small town, and I might not know every resident, but the bakery was frequented by almost everyone in our town, so I at least knew people on sight.

He wasn't from town, this guy. With his bronzed skin, his Ralph Lauren sweater, the navy pants and the Gucci loafers, he reminded me far too much of Nathan.

"Well, you can forget me," I told him. "I have no intention of being remembered tonight or remembering anything for that matter." I turned my attention back to my drink, pissed off to find out that I had finished it at some point.

I looked down the bar, which had become decidedly busier since I'd arrived this afternoon. The bartender was at the other end, serving three different sets of people. The music was loud, loud enough to drown out the hum of conversation or for anyone to hear me where I sat, tucked away from everyone. My position had been purposeful... I wanted to be alone.

Now that seemed like a bad idea. No one noticed me. No one noticed the unwanted attention I was getting.

The man who obviously was not okay with taking no for an

answer ran his finger along my exposed arm. "How about I buy you another drink?"

My skin felt dirty from the touch. Another man touching skin that wasn't his without my permission launched me out of my contemplation.

"Fuck off!" I screamed in his face.

The music in the place was loud enough that not very many people heard me, and the ones who did were drunk enough to not take much notice.

The man whose face I screamed in did notice and was at least sober enough to rear back in shock.

But the shock in his expression quickly passed to anger, the default emotion for rejected men.

"Crazy fucking bitch," he muttered before walking away.

A girl couldn't even wallow in peace. I sighed and stumbled off my seat to use the restroom.

The ground underneath my feet swayed, but luckily, the walls offered excellent opportunities to catch my balance.

Right up until I was slammed against one wall, that was.

"You fucking *bitch*," Ronnie snarled, holding me against the wall by my neck.

"The second time I've been called that in two minutes," I muttered. "It must be some kind of record."

"You ruined my fucking life," he hissed, leaning right into my face. His breath smelled like booze. Or maybe it was mine. Regardless, his eyes were bloodshot, he was sweaty and needed a shower badly.

He was also mad. Mad enough to grab me by the throat in a busy bar.

Unfortunately, the hall that ran toward the restrooms was not busy. Where was a long bathroom line when you needed it?

Maybe it was because I was drunk or because I was numb to

everything at that point, but I wasn't afraid. What could the guy do to me?

Ronnie slammed my head so it crashed painfully against the wall as if to give me an example.

Black spots danced in my vision, and my mouth tasted coppery from my teeth sinking into my tongue.

"Asshole," I yelled, but my voice was muffled and slurred. Fortunately, the violence shocked me out of the somewhat catatonic state I was in, and suddenly I was very mad. Furious.

There he was, a man who was touching me, hurting me for no other reason than because he was weak. Because he couldn't look in the fucking mirror and see he was the one ruining his own life.

My knee found its way between his legs, leaving me feeling extremely satisfied by the way he cried out in pain.

I never had taken that self-defense class, but a knee in the gonads was always a good go-to.

I didn't get the chance to unleash any more of my fury toward someone who really deserved it since a blur of movement passed by, then Ronnie was on the floor.

Rowan was above him, slamming his fist into Ronnie's face.

I stared at him in shock for a moment, then I waited for him to stop with the punching since it was clear he'd done the hero thing and saved me... yet again.

Eventually, it became clear that he was not in hero mode.

The sound of his fists crashing against flesh and bone was horrifying.

"Rowan," I whispered.

Those wet, crunching sounds kept coming.

"Rowan," I called out, louder this time.

He kept punching.

"Rowan!" I screamed.

He stopped suddenly, his fist midair. Blood dripped off it.

Rowan stayed stock still, like he was frozen in time. The sounds of the bar seemed so far away.

He got up slowly and came toward me. I might've flinched if I wasn't still drunk, if I wasn't so jaded and numb. His eyes were wild and dead at the same time. He didn't look like the man who had treated me so delicately and kindly since we met.

This was a killer.

Rowan's eyes circled, landing on my neck, which was aching and hot. I guessed it was red too because his gaze flared in fury.

"Are you hurt anywhere else?" he asked, the chill in his voice startling as he tentatively stepped forward, like he was expecting me to bolt or cower.

Though this was a rather frightening version of Rowan, I wasn't scared of him. Not what he'd do to me, at least.

I shook my head slowly, deciding not to mention the throbbing in the back of my skull.

We were silent for a long while. Or at least what felt like a long while before he gingerly pulled me into his arms.

I didn't relax, not entirely.

Rowan opened his mouth to say something, but someone entered the hall. Kip, looking worried—likely on my account.

"Holy fuck," Kip muttered, staring at me then Rowan then Ronnie on the floor.

I worried for a second that Ronnie was dead, but then he rolled over, groaning in pain, and I sank back in relief.

Rowan was not relieved, not even a little, holding me tighter.

"Take care of this," he told Kip, angling his head to Ronnie. "I'm taking Nora home."

"Got it," Kip replied without humor for once, staring at Ronnie with a hard, dangerous glare.

"When you say, 'take care of,' you don't mean kill, right?" I clarified as Rowan tried to drag me away.

Rowan's mouth was a grim line and not at all reassuring.

"You need to get home."

I planted myself in place. "You don't mean kill, right?" I asked again, my molars grinding.

"No, I don't mean kill him," Rowan gritted out, sounding somewhat irritated. Which made no sense since I didn't think that asking my boyfriend not to kill someone was a particularly irritating request.

Once I had his word, I let Rowan guide me out of the bar, somewhat dazed and still a lot drunk.

The air outside was biting, causing me to realize I had left my jacket somewhere. Rowan hadn't hesitated to drape his jacket around my shoulders. It smelled like him.

It wasn't until we approached Rowan's truck, so familiar, his hand on my back, that I remembered my plan, that I remembered how I was going to self-destruct.

I stopped moving my feet. Rowan stopped too.

"You can go now," I told him flatly, staring at his face but only seeing the general shape. I was careful not to focus on his eyes. "You've saved the day again; no harm will come to me. Fiona can pick me up."

"What the fuck, Nora?" he growled. "No harm will come to you?" He threw out his hand toward my neck. "Harm has already fuckin' come to you."

I shrugged. "It's a bruise. I'm not dead."

Dead was a heavy word, and it tasted acidic on my tongue, mingling with the aftermath of the spirits I drank.

"Nora, we're going to the police station right fucking now," Rowan bit out, blood leaking off his knuckles onto the concrete.

I noted that absently, same with his demeanor, the violence

he'd unleashed earlier. The violence that had been unleashed upon me. Ronnie was angry. And willing to hurt me. Truly hurt me.

Who knew what would've happened if Rowan hadn't shown up.

That should've scared me more, but it didn't.

"Why are you here?" I asked him.

Rowan stared at me, still breathing heavily. I wondered why he stopped. If he would've stopped if I wasn't here. Maybe he would've killed Ronnie.

"Why am I here?" he repeated, his tone low and dangerous.

I nodded, the world spinning more as a result. "Why are you *always here?*" I was shouting now. I didn't quite know why, but I knew that I'd been holding in a scream for so long, since my mother walked in the door of the bakery. I was physically unable to hold it in any longer.

"Why are you coming here, saving the fucking day?" I shrieked, pointing to the bar while pacing the parking lot. "You're watching me, saving me, getting blood on your hands for me." I sliced a hand toward his fists. "It's like you're waiting for me to break so you can put all the pieces back together."

I spun around, holding my arms out, unsteady on my feet.

"Well, here I am!" I bellowed. "But this isn't me breaking. The pieces aren't neatly scattered on the concrete for you to scoop up in those muscular arms of yours." I glared at the arms in question. "No, those pieces got obliterated, turned to fucking ash the second my brother's soul left this world. There's no saving me here, buddy. There's not gonna be endless assholes for you to beat up. And I can't handle it. I can't have you sitting there, being perfect and handsome and just being there. I can't do it."

I deflated at the end of my little tirade, suddenly tired.

Suddenly so fucking exhausted I had no idea how I was still standing.

"We can't be together," I decided, suddenly more sober. Resolute.

Rowan's lips thinned. "Like fuck we can't be. You're not pushing me away."

"I'm not pushing you away," I rolled my eyes. "You can't know me." I jabbed my finger in his chest. "You can't call me yours. Not really. Not when you don't know all of me. And you never will. Because you can't know *him*."

Though a lot of his palpable fury had retreated, his stubborn, unwavering expression remained.

"Let me take you home, Nora," he spoke gently yet firmly.

"No," I widened my stance, feet planted onto the concrete as if I could embed myself there in the parking lot. It wasn't a good long-term plan, but I wasn't really thinking long term at this moment.

I couldn't.

Long term was a vast, yawning space of future in which my brother didn't exist.

"I'm not who you think I am," I folded my arms in front of my chest, not making eye contact. Eye contact was bad. Eye contact would weaken my resolve.

Rowan being Rowan would not allow that. His fingers grasped my chin, forcing it upward.

"You don't know who I think you are," he grumbled.

I'd been planning on being somewhat childish and cowardly by squeezing my eyes shut when he forced my gaze up, but then I got pissed off. So, I looked at him right in his stupidly hypno-tizing eyes.

"Oh, yes, I do," I snapped. "I know that you think, despite my quirks, I'm something desirable. Something to make yours." I wrenched myself out of his grip. "Something, someone easy." I paced, rage flooding my system, propelling my feet. "Because although men certainly like a challenge." I paused, putting my hand on my hip. "We're taught to play hard to get, not to give the milk away for free or whatever." I waved my hand in dismissal. "I was only interesting to you because I was a challenge. But once the challenge was done, once I was won, you don't want me to be difficult anymore. Well, guess what, Rowan? I'm difficult. Actually, I'm a mess. Especially now." I inhaled sharply, and it hurt. But I sank into the pain.

"I've killed people," Rowan stated flatly.

That jerked me out of my rant.

His face was expressionless. His eyes weren't twinkling. They weren't dark and raging. His features weren't soft or hard. He was just... blank. Like he'd left behind the man I knew in order to convey this information.

"When I was deployed," he continued in that horribly blank, vacant voice. "I saw shit. Bloated corpses that had baked out in the sun. I saw people get their limbs blown off. My friends. Watched a woman carry her dead child along the street. And I killed someone's child. Someone's brother. Someone's father."

Rowan was looking at me, but he wasn't. He was looking above my head. Like he couldn't look me in the eyes when he told me this. Like he was afraid of what he might see on my face.

"Fucked me up for a long time. Fucked me up for life," he continued, still looking above my head. "I've dealt with it as much as a human being can deal with that shit. But it changed me for life, Nora. I'll never be whole. Never be right. Not completely. Which is why I stayed away from you for so fuckin' long. Not because of the ring on your finger. Knew that you didn't belong to that fuck, that you belonged to me before you even knew it."

Despite the horrific subject matter, my heart leaped at that little gem of information. That Rowan had considered me his before I thought he knew I existed.

"I stayed away 'cause I thought I'd ruin you," he peered down at his scarlet knuckles. "Thought that my filth would rub off on you. And you're so fuckin' clean. You smell like fuckin' sugar, for fuck's sake. You're sweet, you're good, and a man like me has absolutely no business bein' near a woman like you."

I struggled to hold back the tears filling my eyes.

"Want to lie to myself and you and say I might've held out, been content in just looking at you, talking to you for a minute a day about fuckin' *Yellowstone* or whatever the fuck." He rubbed his jaw. "But I won't do that. As much as I want to be one, I'm not a good man. Got a code, to be sure. One I live by because it keeps me sane mostly, and because without that code, I'm afraid of who I might be."

My knees shook.

"But you're mine now," he said, his voice no longer even and flat. "And I'm not lettin' you go. I'm yours too, Nora. And I thought you understood me well enough to know that I'm not a man who wants easy. Who wants anyone but you. Thought I'd done a good job of showin' you that. Obviously, I haven't. So, I'll lay it out for you. I fuckin' like that you're a bit broken. I wish I could say that I'd fix you if I could, but I ain't gonna say that because if I did, then I couldn't have you. I need hard, Nora. Want hard, ugly love. 'Cause that's all I'm capable of."

The ground shook underneath my feet.

Rowan had created distance between us in order to give me that part of him, the part he'd been holding back, the part my outburst had brought forward. But now he'd opened up to me, he surged forward, grabbing the sides of my neck so our mouths were inches apart.

He was warm. Solid. Comforting.

"If I could bring your brother back, I would," he murmured. "I would do anything to not see you in this kind of pain. I'd sell my fuckin' soul to the devil." He rested his forehead against mine. "But I can't. Neither can you. You can't drink away the feelings either." He stroked my jaw with his thumb. "But if you want to keep tryin', I'm gonna be at your side, and you sure as shit won't be at a dive bar on your own."

I chewed my lip, not having the strength to try to push Rowan away any further. It had been a futile attempt in the first place. What was my life without this man?

"Are you going to get in trouble?" I asked, looking back at the bar then to Rowan's bloodstained knuckles. He'd unleashed a lot of violence on the man, and he'd deserved it. But not at the expense of Rowan's freedom. My throat dried with the panic of thinking about Rowan behind bars.

Rowan's jaw clenched. "No. I won't be in trouble for that shit. Finn will probably thank me for doin' what he can't."

My interest piqued. "What do you know about Finn and him being into Lori?"

Rowan's eyes went wide. "You're seriously trying to *matchmake* right now, in the middle of all this?"

Though I wouldn't have thought it was possible minutes earlier, I smiled. "Well, I've gotta find a silver lining somewhere, and a happily ever after for two people who deserve it meets the criteria."

Rowan's lips stretched into a grin as he shook his head, kissing me on the nose.

"You and I are the two people havin' a happily ever after." He pulled me close, tucking me into the crook of his neck. "And you're gonna be okay, cupcake. Now let me take you home."

Home.

My house had always just been a place for me. I'd created a pretty one, to be sure. But *home* had always been Ansel. That's why I was at the bar in the first place. Because I was drifting, anchorless. Homeless. But staring at Rowan, I realized that I had a home.

I was staring at him.

CHAPTER
TWENTY-TWO

Recipe: Salted Halvah Blondies

From 'Dessert Person'

My heart didn't heal quickly.

Some days it felt like it didn't heal at all. That I was still bleeding out, dripping crimson pain all over my pink, polished bakery floors.

At the beginning, I lived for three seconds of every day. The three seconds just after I woke up, when my brain hadn't caught up yet, when it still thought everything was okay. When I forgot that Ansel was dead.

Those three seconds were all I got. Then the pain came rushing in, so visceral that I had to bite my lip to stop from crying out.

I might've screamed, maybe, if he wasn't there.

If Rowan's arms weren't around me, if his body wasn't warm and firm against mine, maybe I would've screamed.

Or maybe I wouldn't have. Because maybe if I started

screaming, started vocalizing the pain inside of me, I'd never stop.

So, I didn't scream. Didn't cry. I sank into Rowan's warmth, let him turn me onto my back, uncurl me from the ball I'd coiled myself into and make slow, brutal love to me.

His hands on me, him inside of me... nothing provided complete respite from the pain, but it made it hurt a whole lot less.

After the parking lot blowout, I felt different.

Not healed. I'd never be healed.

There would always be an open, bleeding hole inside of me. I wouldn't ever feel happiness in the same way I had before.

But I also wasn't going to sink into the pit of despair, despite how damn tempting it was. Then again, I couldn't have even if I wanted to since I had friends who wouldn't let me do that.

Rowan wouldn't let me do that.

He was there. Always. His hands on my body, his mouth on mine, making me feel alive. Making me feel excited to be alive.

I did make a statement about Ronnie's assault after he was charged. He didn't make bail since there was no one left in this town to bail him out. He wouldn't be behind bars forever, and maybe he'd come out angry, ready to blame me. But I didn't worry much about that. I had Rowan.

We slept at his place often since it still hurt to be at mine. Not because of the memories I had of Ansel there. A place couldn't hold memories. Only a heart could. Mine was broken. Shattered.

I just liked Rowan's place because it was full of him. Because I could hear the ocean when we laid in bed at night. Because I could sit out on the patio at five in the morning, wrapped in a blanket, cupping a mug of coffee while smelling the salt from the ocean.

Rowan usually woke up when I got out of bed. The man was

hyper-aware of me, but he didn't try to keep me in bed. Didn't try to talk to me. He must've suspected I needed that time in the morning.

Maggie, on the other hand, did not. She got up from her bed in the corner of the bedroom and happily trotted downstairs with me, pressed into my leg as I made coffee then settled at my feet when I sat outside.

Rowan came out eventually, as he always did, holding the coffee I'd prepared for him and left on the kitchen counter.

Most times, we didn't speak. He just lifted me from my spot on the oversized wicker armchair and sat himself down, me half splayed in his lap. I didn't know how this could be comfortable since I wasn't exactly small, but he seemed to like it well enough.

"Want you to come to my family's place for Christmas," he murmured, breaking the usual silence that existed between us.

Thanksgiving had passed. It wasn't much of a celebration, but it was something. We had dinner at my place, Rowan gently suggesting we host Fiona, Tiffany, Tina and Kip.

I hadn't wanted to at first. I'd wanted the day to pass like any other. Wanted to curl up on the sofa with the lights out and a bowl of cookie dough. But even though a part of me wanted to do that, I wasn't a wallower. That's not how I worked. Rowan knew that.

Rowan knew I healed in the kitchen, with busy hands, with flour, sugar, butter. With friends who were really family surrounding me.

And he was right. Though it was a hard day, it was one that was filled with food, friends and love.

Rowan hadn't mentioned his family or if they missed him on Thanksgiving. I hadn't asked about them because I wasn't strong enough to. But I knew they likely missed him. Because they sounded like the kind of people who had big family gatherings. And Rowan missed it.

For me.

"We don't have to go," Rowan stated in response to my silence, holding me tighter. "I want you to meet my family, want them to meet you, but if it's too hard..."

Here he was, giving me an out, to protect me because he did that as easy as breathing these days.

Oh, how tempting it would be to take him up on that offer. To stay where I was safe.

But I couldn't do that to him. To us. And I wanted more of Rowan. I wanted to see where he came from.

"No, let's go," I whispered.

He regarded me for a moment. "You sure?"

I nodded. "Yeah, I'm sure."

We didn't say anything else, just stared at the waves, and I wished, selfishly, that this moment would last forever. That I could live in Rowan's arms, with Maggie at our feet.

But life didn't work that way.

"Why did you do it?" I asked the waves. "Run Nathan out of town." It was a question that had been rolling around in my brain since it happened. One that had been firmly pushed back due to everything I was going through. But I found myself desperate to focus on something else rather than my pain.

Rowan reached up to grasp my chin so I was looking at him instead of the ocean. It always hit me how handsome he was, how expressive those icy blue eyes were.

"Because he was the reason you had a mark on your skin," he answered, voice tight with fury even though the mark was long gone.

I rolled my eyes. "Yes, but you're a scary dude. You could've just threatened to waterboard him or pull out his fingernails and he would've stayed away. That man was obsessive about his nails and manicures."

Not that there was anything wrong with a man getting a manicure. But I had found out I liked a man not afraid to get his hands dirty.

Rowan brushed my bottom lip with his thumb. "He tasted you," he told me, voice husky. "Tasted that sweet pussy of yours." He ground the words out as fury shimmered around him. "Even a coward like that wouldn't leave you alone if he had to know you were within driving distance. I couldn't have that, Nora."

I blinked at the response. "But..." I cleared my throat. "You couldn't have known how sweet my ... pussy was when you run him out of town."

Rowan's eyes flared and my aforementioned pussy pulsed with need.

"Oh yes I fuckin' could've, cupcake," he growled, standing and taking me with him.

I let out a little squeal of surprise.

"So fuckin' sweet I'm gonna have to eat you right here right now to get that bitter taste of that asshole off my tongue," he said, walking inside and laying me on the counter.

And there it was. One of the many ways Rowan distracted me from the pain. Showed me sweet. And being in expert in sweet, I knew that there was no pastry on earth that could come close to this.

* * *

CHRISTMAS CAME QUICKLY. As it tended to do.

I threw myself into work. Baking for the season... themed

cakes, cupcakes and cookies. The bakery smelled of cinnamon, spices, peppermint and hot chocolate. I didn't think too much about the upcoming holiday except when I had a small break-down in the kitchen of the bakery just before opening.

Luckily, Rowan had gone to work, but Fiona was there.

I just started crying while frosting cupcakes. For no reason. Sobbing.

Fiona didn't say anything, just pulled me into a hug.

"I'm a mess," I sobbed.

"You're not a fucking mess," she hissed, holding me at arm's length. "You're the strongest person I know."

"You're telling me I'm strong," I scoffed. "Come on. You're the strongest, most badass bitch I know. Much stronger and more capable at waking, waltzing through life, than I am. I stumble through." I was keeping it light, joking, not quite self-depre-cating—I was really trying to work on that—but pointing out the obvious.

But Fiona, for once, did not match my light, teasing mood. Her gaze was narrow, features tight. "Babe. When I first moved to this country, I had to take the driving test. I was almost a thirty-year-old woman then. Had been driving for almost fifteen years. I'm a great fucking driver. But I failed twice. Twice." She rolled her eyes before narrowing them on me again. "How many times did it take to pass your test as a teenager?"

I pursed my lips, not wanting to answer. "Once. But—"

She held up her finger to stop me. "But nothing. You stepped up. Like you always do. Maybe you thought you had Ebola that entire day, but you pushed through and fucking passed."

I grinned at how well she knew me. It wasn't Ebola but a strain of meningitis, if I remembered correctly. To be fair, there had been a bunch of cases in the area at that time.

Fiona was right. I was a fucking nervous wreck that day. Had a panic attack the night before. But I had to pass because we needed that freedom.

"I rent my house," she continued. "I have never owned a home in my life. This is the longest I've stayed in one place. Because I love it here. Because I've made this place my home. And my fucking visa is going to be up in a year, but there's nowhere else I want to be. As much as I fucking love working for you, and I couldn't imagine being anywhere else, I'm older than you, bitch. And I'm your employee." She pointed at me. "You own a home. You renovated that fucking thing yourself, and I can't even put together flat pack furniture. You created this." She waved her hands around the space. "A business. Filled out whatever the fuck paperwork someone has to fill out in order to start a business. You dealt with a bank. Every single thing you set your mind to in your life, you succeed in." She reached out to squeeze my hand. "You think because you have anxiety, you're weak." She shook her head. "It only makes you stronger. More impressive. That you successfully navigate through life."

Though she was building me up, her words only made me sob harder.

"I love you," I said through my tears.

"I love you more, bitch," she replied with a wink.

It was then I realized I hadn't been living through just one love story but many. That happily ever afters existed in many different ways, and I was lucky enough to have a bunch of them.

* * *

I EXPECTED TO HURT, being around a family when I'd lost mine. And it did. But only because I was in agony every time I inhaled and exhaled. Pain was my constant companion now.

But it was impossible to be bitter or resentful about what I didn't have when I was around Rowan's family. Not when they welcomed me into the family the second I walked through the door of their home.

Well, not even when I walked through the door.

As soon as we pulled into the driveway of the lovely, two-story house with a wraparound porch, a colorful, rambling garden and bright yellow shutters, the front door opened, and a woman burst out of it.

Rowan's hand on my thigh tightened before he reached over to kiss me on the side of the head. "Ready yourself, cupcake," he murmured, undoing my seat belt for me.

I felt a sliver of nervousness then, my only other experience of meeting a boyfriend's family cold and terrible.

But I didn't have long to worry about the temperature of the Derrick family because my door opened.

"You're here!" a woman exclaimed, grasping my hand and pulling me out of the car.

I was engulfed in her embrace the second I was out.

She smelled of vanilla and expensive perfume.

"Well, you're beautiful," she declared, holding me at arm's length.

I guessed the woman was Rowan's mother since she had the same ice-blue eyes and dark brown hair. Hers was longer, brushing her shoulders, framing a lovely face, delicately lined from the years of her life spent smiling, if the crinkles at the edges of her eyes were anything to go by.

She was small, only slightly taller than me and of a much slimmer build, wearing a white turtleneck and relaxed jeans, looking effortlessly put together, and stylish.

"It's nice to meet you, Mrs. Derrick," I replied, grateful my voice didn't crack with nervousness.

"Oh, none of that Mrs. Derrick crap." She waved her hand.

311

"It's Jill, or... Mom if you'd like. I won't force it if it's too odd for you." She gave a wicked smile to Rowan who was rounding the car.

"Jesus fucking Christ, Mom. You're gonna scare her away before she even gets in the front door," Rowan grumbled, but a practiced ear heard the loving warmth in his tone.

She rolled her eyes good-naturedly in a gesture that seemed also practiced and loving before winking at me.

"Oh, as if I could scare her away." She took her son into her arms, kissing his cheek. "Look at you," she squeezed his cheeks.

I couldn't stop grinning.

Maggie barked at Jill, obviously done with waiting patiently for her grandma's attention.

Jill complied, turning to grab the dog by its face to kiss her nuzzle too. "And you, my dear, are even more irresistible." She glanced up to me. "I bet it was love at first sight, wasn't it?"

"Yeah, it was," I answered without thinking. And I wasn't looking at Jill or Maggie. I was looking at Rowan, making it clear what I was talking about.

My cheeks heated with a blush, from the charged silence that came after my words, and from the way that Rowan was looking at me that was totally inappropriate considering his mom was right there.

I cleared my throat, forcing my attention to Jill who was beaming at me. "Rowan told me that you said not to bring anything, but I'm insane and also think I'd probably explode if forced to attend any kind of gathering without bringing something," I explained to her, planning on opening the back door of Rowan's truck in order to get the bags of food I'd baked for the occasion.

But Rowan beat me to it.

I rolled my eyes and didn't battle him as I had when I'd tried to bring them from my kitchen to the car earlier.

"And he will explode if he can't do the ultra-masculine thing of carrying bags of baked goods lest his girlfriend dare strain herself with them," I commented dryly.

Jill let out a warm chuckle and put her arm around me, walking me down the stone path lined with lavender that led to their house.

"If there's anything I've learned in life, it's to let the men do the heavy lifting while we go inside and drink wine," she winked at me. She slowed us before we got to the front door, glancing over her shoulder to see where Rowan was. Maggie was trailing happily behind us.

"I just want to thank you for coming," she said, her tone no longer light and teasing. Her warm expression was sincere and... almost somber. "I am so sorry about your brother. I understand that it may be hard to be around another family, especially during the holidays, especially not knowing us." She reached out to squeeze my hand. "Just know we consider you family already, and though we are arguably all insane, we love fiercely and drink a lot, so there will be absolutely no judgment on this end if you'd like to cope through this holiday with copious amounts of booze."

"So noted," I replied, not feeling cold at the mention of my brother like I had every time I thought about him. Nor was I clutched with the panic I thought I would at the prospect of spending the holiday with a bunch of strangers. Because these weren't strangers. This was Rowan's family.

At that moment, the front door opened, and two children tore out of it. "Uncle Rowan!" they cried in tandem, running toward Rowan with Maggie barking behind them.

"Watch the cakes he's holding!" a woman yelled from the doorway. "I've heard they are life changing." She winked at me and handed me a glass of champagne.

She was tall, like Rowan, with the same dark hair and piercing eyes. Her hair was cut into a blunt bob, and she was wearing minimal makeup, but that only accentuated her soft features. And she looked chic in a cable knit sweater, white jeans and Uggs on her feet.

"I'm Kendra," she leaned in to kiss my cheek. "Those hellions are my children." She gazed lovingly at the kids who were now tearing around the front yard with Maggie barking playfully at them. "Say hello to Nora," she yelled at them.

"Hello, Nora!" they called out dutifully.

"Little savages," she chuckled. "But we love them."

The women guided me inside where I met more people including Kendra's husband, Keith. He was friendly and tall, seemed like he adored his wife and was part of the family.

Rowan's dad, Hank, was the spitting image of his son. A vision of what my alpha might grow into. His dark hair was generously salted as was his beard, which he kept longer than Rowan's five o'clock shadow. He was big, still in great shape, and was a verifiable silver fox. He hugged me in greeting. "My son does know how to pick them," he said once he let me go. "Fucking gorgeous." He winked. "And I hear a successful businesswoman."

I looked down at my shoes, uncomfortable from the praise. "I don't know about successful."

"Shut the fuck up right now. Don't you dare try to deny it," a sharp voice came from the kitchen.

Her heels clicked as she emerged.

She was wearing head to toe black. Leather pants, a designer sweater tucked haphazardly into them, gold and diamonds adorning her ears, neck and wrists. Her heels were at least six inches, and her eyeliner was sharp and severe. Same with her red lipstick and hair that was slicked back to accentuate her angled features.

Again, she looked like Rowan and her sister, but much harsher, beautiful in a different way.

She was intimidating as fuck.

Until she smiled warmly and brought me into her arms like the rest of her family had. She smelled of a perfume so expensive it probably didn't even have a name.

"I've done the research on your bakery, sister," she said once she let me go. "It's hard to open a food business of any kind. In this economy?" She shook her head. "By all means, you should've failed. You're thriving. I could make you millions if you want to franchise." She regarded me shrewdly. "But you don't want to franchise, do you?"

I shook my head. I had already been approached with the offer and turned it down. No matter how much money was promised, I wouldn't do it. I couldn't be at every single location, making sure the exact right ingredients were used, the highest possible quality. People would cut corners. The quality would suffer. It would turn into something cold, big, soulless and utterly unlike what I created.

"Calliope, leave her alone," Rowan scolded, suddenly beside me, glaring at his sister. But I knew Rowan's glares, and this one was all for show. You could see the warmth underneath it.

"Take these, won't you, Dad?" he asked his father, gesturing to the bags. His father took them, but not before leaning in to kiss his son on the cheek.

"Good to see you, son."

It made me feel all melty to see the easy affection displayed by even the alpha males in the family.

"Calliope wants to make everyone rich," Rowan explained, putting his arms around me.

Calliope's manicured brows furrowed. "Why you're saying that like it's a bad thing baffles me."

"I've got everything I need right here," Rowan replied, squeezing me tighter.

Cue more melty feelings.

Calliope rolled her eyes. "Easy for you to say with a construction business making the high six figures with projections reaching the millions in your ten-year plan."

"For fuck's sake, Calliope, stop nosing into my financial shit," Rowan snapped.

Her ruby lips parted, showing her straight white teeth. "Make me, Rambo."

After that, I witnessed what seemed to be a routine for the family. Kendra was the peacekeeper between her brother and sister, who loved to argue yet obviously adored each other. The children, Wyatt and Molly, were, as Kendra said, savages but adorable savages. Keith was quiet but friendly. Hank was much like his son, a man of few words but showed each and every member of his family how much they meant to him as easy as breathing.

Jill was the heart of the household. Running around, adding finishing touches to the meal, sneaking her grandchildren treats, making sure to go out of her way to make me feel welcome.

Rowan was always at my side. Always touching me, kissing my temple, reassuring me that he was there, maybe worrying that this was going to be hard.

And I guessed, in a way, it was. That wound inside of me

throbbed painfully, but not unbearably. And something else bloomed inside of me.

Hope.

Hope that I could be a part of this family.

"You deserve this, sis," Ansel's voice sounded from somewhere deep inside me.

CHAPTER
TWENTY-THREE

Recipe: Classic Kiwi Pavlova

Christmas dinner was wonderful. The Derrick's dining room featured a long table, every seat filled, the entire surface covered in delicious food.

"So, Nora," Calliope said after we'd all sat down. "What was your brother like?"

There wasn't the cliché moment where forks stopped clanging, when everything went still since death entered the conversation. Quite the opposite. People still reached over for this dish and that dish.

Kendra scolded Wyatt for trying to eat mashed potatoes with his hands.

Everyone continued going about their dinner table routines, but they were also listening too.

Rowan's hand clutched my thigh, and I could feel his body tense up beside me. He was coiled, ready to jump to my defense, to protect me from the topic that could send me hurtling back into that pit of despair.

Although the question had surprised me, it didn't unnerve me. Didn't make me feel pain or awkwardness or even pitied. She'd asked the question because she was interested. They all were. They weren't skirting around death, ignoring it. They were finding a way to bring my brother to the table with us.

Rowan, of course, did not see how thoughtful this was because he was in protective alpha mode.

Before he could say anything, I patted his hand and hoped he'd stop giving his sister his death glare.

"He was wonderful." I laid my napkin on my lap. "He believed in crystals, chakras, lost ancient civilizations and was obsessed with UFOs."

"Oh my god, I'm obsessed with UFOs too!" Kendra exclaimed. "We go to all the sights, but Roswell is a big letdown. Would not recommend it. Very depressing."

I smiled because Ansel had said something similar.

"He was once arrested outside Area 51," I chuckled.

"Tell us everything," Kendra demanded.

And somehow, I did. I managed to talk about my brother in the past tense, keeping him alive the only way I could.

BETWEEN DINNER and dessert was presents.

The gift exchange could've been awkward. Maybe with every other family, it would've been, but not with the Derricks.

It wasn't awkward. It was wonderful, watching the children tear into their multiple presents with utter glee. Then when they ran off to play with their toys, the adults exchanged gifts with a little less glee, but not much.

Again, I liked seeing the rhythm of it, seeing the love between them, the smiles, the jokes, the thoughtful gifts.

I didn't expect a gift, not even from Rowan. I'd gotten him a gift. But not one I felt comfortable giving him with an audience, even this audience.

My spot tucked into his side on the large, cozy armchair was pretty much the best place to be. Despite the ever present dull, throbbing pain of grief inside of me—the pain I suspected would always be there, although it might vary in size—I had never felt happier. More comfortable. More... part of something.

I loved everything about the house. I loved the smells, the good quality furniture that was worn... but in the best way. The photos on all surfaces, documenting the life that seemed so full of love.

I envied it, but I also ached to replicate it. To start that kind of life with Rowan.

"Nora?"

I blinked at Jill who was standing in front of me with a wrapped box.

"This is for you, honey."

I stared at the box, wrapped expertly, with a bright red bow.

"Me?"

She nodded, smiling warmly.

I took it from her, holding it in my lap awkwardly.

"Rip it open," Calliope called from across the room.

Rowan's hand found the back of my neck and gave it a squeeze.

"But it's wrapped so beautifully." I ran my hand across the smooth paper.

"Which only makes it more fun to rip open, don't you think?" Jill's eyes twinkled mischievously.

I tore the paper to reveal a silver box, one that looked antique with intricate designs carved into it.

It was heavy, solid and seemed one of a kind.

"It's lovely," I told Jill sincerely.

"Oh, the box is nice, but it's what's inside that counts."

Inside the box were tabs of paper with recipes written in a sloping script.

"My grandmother was a baker," Jill explained as I leafed through the sections. "Neither of these two are interested in baking." She nodded to her daughters.

"We're interested in baking," Calliope argued.

"Eating it doesn't count," Jill returned.

Calliope shrugged and returned to the cookies she was eating.

Me, I only half heard this. There was a staticky ringing in my ears.

"I know it may be a bit old fashioned," Jill said to me.

I shook my head quickly, both to respond and to try to shake away my tears. "It's the most special gift I've ever gotten," I whispered, unable to speak louder.

I cleared my throat and looked up at her. "I don't come from a family where precious things are passed down."

"Now you do," she countered with a warm smile.

Now I did.

As if it were that simple.

And maybe it was.

* * *

CONVERSATION RESUMED EASILY once we sat down for dessert, everyone singing my praises over the variety of things I'd made. I might've gone just a little overboard.

"It's good your bakery is hundreds of miles away," Kendra rubbed her belly. "Otherwise, I'd be in trouble."

"I still don't like that you're so far from us," Jill grumbled, her brows furrowed.

"Mom, we're less than three hours away," Rowan returned, hand still on my thigh. He was eating his cake one handed, as he had with dinner too.

"Well, you could've just stayed here, taken over your father's business so the man could retire," she argued.

Rowan chuckled. "Mom, you know the day Dad retires is the day hell freezes over."

Jill rolled her eyes. "Nonsense. Your father deserves to spend his twilight years doing whatever he wants."

"What he wants is to continue working," Rowan's father cut in. "You know I'd drive you fucking mad if I was here full-time. You wouldn't be ready for all that extra energy I'd have to direct elsewhere," he waggled his brows.

Jill peered at him over her wineglass. "Oh, you think that, do you? Try me."

Calliope groaned. "Can we not have Mom propositioning Dad in the middle of Christmas dinner? Just once?"

"Oh, be happy that your mother and father have a healthy sex life," Jill told her.

"I am happy," Calliope retorted. "I just don't want to have to hear it all the fucking time."

I swallowed my smile as they continued bickering good-naturedly.

Conversation flowed easily and in different directions. Sometimes the whole table was involved, sometimes it split off into sections. No subject seemed to be off-limits or awkward. This was a family that was comfortable with everything.

"Oh my god," Calliope gasped with her mouth full of my lemon meringue pie. "If my brother doesn't marry you, I will."

I grinned at her, my cheeks warming at the praise that had also been uttered in similar ways by the rest of the family.

"Nora, you are supremely talented," Jill gushed, her plate clear and helping herself to my hot chocolate cake. "Your bakery is just what we need here in our town."

Rowan stiffened slightly beside me. "Mom," he said, tone warm, but there was an edge of warning.

"What?" she asked innocently. "I'm just saying that there is potential for her business to do wonderfully here, and that would also mean you'd both be closer, so when you have kids, I'm right around the corner to help."

The possibility of Rowan and I having kids was something we hadn't spoken about since the birth control conversation, but a topic that I'd been thinking of more and more. Especially while seated around this table.

"When we have kids, you'll be driving to Jupiter every damn weekend with or without my permission, and you know it," Rowan replied, not at all perturbed about discussing our future family in front of his own.

His mother sighed. "But wouldn't it be nice for them to grow up close to their cousins? You could move the business back here, merge it with your father's. I know that what happened with Kip was tragic and heartbreaking, but he didn't have to leave town..."

The good-natured smile left Rowan's face, and his expression turned somber. "Mom, no more of that."

The energy around the table changed.

The smiles dimmed, and everyone seemed to take a collective breath.

Jill was not ready to back down, though

"All I'm saying is, it's been five years, and I know his mother—"

"Enough!" Rowan slammed his palm down on the table, and glasses rattled, teetering.

I flinched, but no one else seemed too shaken. Calliope caught her glass before it toppled over then sipped from it casually.

Rowan's father shook his head.

Kendra whispered to her son for swiping through the frosting on one of the cakes. Keith seemed to be looking at some kind of game that was playing on the TV in the other room.

It seemed only I was disturbed by Rowan's sudden outburst. I was the only one out of the loop about whatever it was with Kip.

He and his mother stared at each other a beat longer before whatever it was in the air dissipated.

"What do you use to make this cake so rich, Nora?" Kendra asked, licking the tines of her fork. "I've never tasted anything like this before."

I took one more glance at Rowan, worried and curious, before I answered.

Things went smoothly from there on out, but I shelved the conversation for later.

It was hard to hold on to it, though, surrounded by the sounds of the house. The laughter and easy conversation during after-dinner coffee. With the warm hugs from everyone as they said goodbye. Promises and plans made for the future.

Yes, it was hard to hold on to the one black spot in the day.

Hard, but not impossible.

* * *

We were driving home Christmas night. Even though Jill had urged us to stay, Rowan had firmly said no.

When I'd tried to argue about it, he'd pulled me to the side and said, "Wanna fuck you so hard you scream tonight. Not plannin' on doin' that under my parent's roof."

I did not try to argue any further.

Maggie was sleeping over with her 'cousins' who loved her dearly and weren't yet allowed a dog. The sleepover was a 'test run' of them walking her, feeding her and cleaning up her mess.

They were then driving down with Maggie and the entire family to check out my bakery and spend New Year's Eve with us.

I had been delighted at the news since I found myself utterly at home with each of them and anxious to spend more time with them. But I also had about a million things to do in order to show them the best time.

"Stop," Rowan commanded.

I stared at him in question since I hadn't been speaking.

"You're thinking about spending the next week baking, cooking, decorating, cleaning or whatever the fuck in order to host my family."

I gaped at him. "I knew you were amazing, but I didn't know you were also a mind reader."

He snickered. "Not a mind reader, just know you. Saw your eyes glaze over about two seconds after they lit up in excitement at the prospect of my family comin'." He reached from where his hand was on my thigh to lace his fingers through mine. "And fuck, do I love to see you excited to spend time with them."

"It's pretty easy," I shrugged. "I love your family."

"And they love you," he replied immediately. "Bet my life savings that there's already a million and one texts on my phone singin' your praises."

"It's only because I brought baked goods," I joked.

Rowan didn't smile. In fact, his face turned very serious, his grip tightening around my hand.

"Stop, Nora. It's because you're fuckin' you."

I bit my lip. "Are you sure about me?"

Rowan's head turned to briefly squint at me. "What the fuck are you talking about?"

"Worry is not a state of mind for me, it's a personality trait," I sighed, hoping the darkness inside the truck hid the shame settling over me like sweat. "I'm not like your family, so easy, happy, sure of themselves. I worry that you need—"

I didn't get to finish what I was saying since Rowan slammed on his brakes and pulled the truck over to the shoulder. Luckily, there was no one behind us.

His long, masculine fingers found my chin, tilting it so I was forced to meet those cerulean eyes.

His jaw was stiff, lips a thin line to communicate he was obviously pissed about something, but he was looking at me with a softness that counteracted that sharp jaw.

"You had to grow up fast," he said. "Too fuckin' fast. You had to shoulder shit that wasn't yours to carry, turn into an adult and think about things that you shouldn't have known existed." He shook his head, as if in awe.

"I've watched you bear shit that most people would buckle under," he continued. "And you handled it with such strength, I cannot believe you're real. So, I'm gonna need you to stop sayin' shit like that. Need you to stop questioning whether you're worthy of me when it's me who's gonna spend the rest of my life earning the right to be worthy of you."

Tears burned my eyes.

"Was gonna wait till we got home, but..." He leaned into the back seat, retrieving a small, velvet box from some hiding place.

My heart was hammering.

"It's not a ring," Rowan said when he saw the look on my face. "I'm planning on gettin' you one of those, don't get me wrong, but I have sisters. So, I know that presenting a woman with an engagement ring on Christmas Day and calling it her present is an act of war."

His eyes twinkled as I pursed my lips to hide my smile.

Although his sisters might have been right in regard to other women, or maybe about me with another man, I wouldn't have been mad at all if Rowan had given me the gift of forever with him on Christmas.

I took the box he held out to me and opened it. My shaking hands trailed over the gold necklace and the sparkling green stone in the middle.

"Peridot," Rowan explained. "Your and Ansel's birthstone. I know that he was into crystals and things like that. Know you aren't so much. But I figured this would be a way to carry him everywhere."

My tears dripped onto the gorgeous emerald cut stone, the delicate chain. It was classy, definitely expensive, but subtle.

"Rowan," I chastised. "I've already cried enough over Christmas gifts today."

He was grinning when I looked up, and he reached over to wipe one of my tears away with his thumb. "Happy tears I'm okay with, cupcake. Can I put it on you?"

"You better," I whispered, turning in my seat and handing him the box.

I lifted my hair up to expose my neck, then Rowan reached over, his fingers brushing the skin there. Even the simple act of putting on my necklace did something to me. Awakened my hunger for him that was never far away, the desire that hadn't dulled, not even a little.

"Okay, since we're doing our gift exchange right here on the side of the road..." I reached down into my purse at my feet, grabbing the wrapped bundle at the bottom.

I had come prepared, bringing my behemoth bag that seemed to have endless room.

I handed Rowan the gift, and he did his family proud by ripping the paper off it to reveal Stephen King's *The Stand*. I had combed the internet to find it, a signed first edition.

Rowan's hand carefully and reverently turned the page to reveal the signature.

"I know he's your favorite," I said shyly since Rowan had been silent for a long time.

He blinked up at me, and I will say, I was kind of satisfied I'd managed to shock Rowan Derrick, though I couldn't read his face to gauge whether he was happy or not.

"Do you like it?"

"Like it?" he repeated, voice low, almost a growl.

I nodded slowly.

Rowan carefully and reverently placed the book on the center console—which was sparkling clean, not littered with strange crumbs or sticky with unknown liquids—unbuckled my seatbelt and yanked me over it.

This was no mean feat, even though the interior of the truck was larger than most vehicles. I wasn't exactly small.

But Rowan did it, so I was straddling him in the driver's seat, my dress bunched up at my hips and my silk panties rubbing up against the rough denim of his jeans.

I was instantly wet and wanting him.

Rowan clutched the sides of my neck and kissed me. Not just a kiss, a brutal, magical claiming. One that set my body on fire and had me grinding against the hard cock in his jeans.

"I'm gonna show my baby how much I fucking like the gift which is the most thoughtful, fuckin' precious thing I've ever gotten," he growled against my mouth, lifting my body with one hand so he could free himself from his jeans with his other.

He did it quickly, frantic and furious, pushing my soaked panties aside so he could slam into me, so I could fucking impale myself on him.

I threw my head back in pleasure, Rowan's hand on my hip, pressing me down on his cock relentlessly.

His other hand cradled the back of my head, pulling it down so my eyes met his.

"Yeah, you gonna ride me like a good girl?" he asked, his rough voice enhancing the sensations flooding my system.

I nodded, breathless already. My orgasm built up inside of me as I fucked him furiously.

"You gonna let me come inside you?"

I paused my riding, but only for a split second.

"Yeah," he murmured. "Gonna let me plant a baby in you, Nora?"

My body reveled at the words, shuddering as my orgasm rushed toward me.

"Yes," I rasped without hesitation.

"Milk my fuckin' cock then, cupcake."

My body rushed to obey him. Even as my orgasm bowled me over, I kept going, kept riding as Rowan exploded into me, sending me into another orgasm that damn near obliterated my world.

"Fuck," Rowan breathed as we both came down to earth, my forehead resting against his.

"Didn't think fuckin' you could feel better," he rasped. "But emptying my cock into you?" He shook his head. "Best feeling in the fuckin' world." He clasped my neck so our eyes met. "I'll be doing that every time we fuck until we put a baby in there, and every time after."

What could a girl say to that?

* * *

It wasn't until we got home that I got the chance to talk to Rowan about the moment at the table.

We had showered—together, as usual—so I was bundled up in my robe, and Rowan was wearing low slung pajama pants I got him for Christmas. I made a mental note to get them in every color.

We were sitting on the armchairs in my bedroom, drinking wine, enjoying each other's company.

"What happened to Kip?" I asked Rowan cautiously.

He sighed. "Figured you caught that."

"If you don't want to tell me, it's okay," I said quickly.

"No, cupcake, it's not that I don't want to tell you, it's just..." He ran his hand through his hair. "Fuck, it's not somethin' I've spoken about since it happened. Kip does everything in his power not to think about it. We were best friends growing up," he began, readjusting his position to fully face me. "Inseparable. Both of us knew we wanted to join the Navy. Be a SEAL. He waited till I turned eighteen so we could go together. Figured we'd probably get split up, especially since BUD/S has such a low success rate." He grinned without humor. "But both of us are stubborn bastards and made it through. Before we deployed, Kip came home, married his high school sweetheart. Girl he loved with all his heart. Who somehow understood why he needed to go fight a war half a world away. His family had some fucked up shit goin' on, he had stuff to prove to them and himself. She was steadfast over the years, with us gone more than we were home." He shook his head. "She was a good woman. A great woman. Gave him a beautiful daughter, raised her well."

My heart thundered, knowing this story wouldn't have a happy ending since I hadn't

heard Kip talk about a wife or a daughter. Not once.

"I tried to convince Kip to get out when his daughter was born," Rowan said, his volume lower. "He didn't need to be risking his life when he had everything to live for. His stubbornness runs deep, though, so he stayed. And so did I. Because I didn't have a wife and daughter at home, and because I considered it my job to make sure he made it home to them in one piece. But I had a sick feeling. One I couldn't shake. That I'd be knockin' on their door, telling my best friend's wife that I'd been unable to protect him, that their daughter would never know her father. But it didn't turn out that way."

He gritted his teeth. "They died while we were out on a mission," he ground out. "Car accident. His wife died on impact. Their little girl somehow held on for three days. Three fuckin' days. They knew... our superiors. But they couldn't get us out. Or wouldn't. Don't know which. By the time we got home, they'd already had the funeral. Already buried them."

My heart hurt at the horrors Kip had gone through. Loss I couldn't even fathom someone could recover from. I tried to reconcile that with the Kip I knew... Always smiling, womanizing, never hinting at a past in ruins.

Then I remembered the night when Rowan had left, speaking about needing to pick up Kip from the bar. I thought of the dinners he had alone.

"His family are good people," Rowan continued. "But overbearing. He couldn't be around them, the memories of our hometown. Had to leave. I was more than willin' to go with him. I wasn't exactly in the best place after coming home either. I was not the man my family had known before."

I got up from my seat so I could curl into his arms, unable to be so far from him, hearing the pain in his voice. We hadn't spoken in depth about what he'd told me that night in the parking lot. About the people he killed. What he'd seen. The fact that he'd said it was enough. Uttered words I knew he hadn't said to anyone.

"I love you," I said.

Rowan blinked at me in surprise, which made sense. It was an unusual time for me to finally say it. But I couldn't hold it in any longer.

I ran my hand down the stubble on his cheek. "I love the man you are," I whispered. "Every single part of you. I love what you do for your friends. Your family. I love what you do for me. How you make me feel. I love you."

Rowan gazed into my eyes. "Jesus fuckin' Christ, Nora," he growled, standing us both up so I was in his arms.

"I'm not a fuckin' twenty year old anymore, but you're making it impossible not to have my cock in you after hearin' that." He threw me on the bed.

My robe ripped open, exposing my naked body underneath it.

"But a body like that..." He leaned down to open my legs and expose my pussy. "A cunt like that." His eyes found mine. "And you sayin' you love me." He took off his pants to show his cock, hard and ready. "I'm gonna have to fuck you until you pass out."

Then he did just that.

ROWAN

There weren't many times I was up before Nora. She had an internal alarm clock that defied belief. An energy, a drive that impressed the fuck out of me.

So, the mornings when I woke up, her still sleeping in my

arms, knowing I could wake her up with my mouth or my cock, those were some of my favorites.

But I wouldn't do that right away. I'd spend time just looking at her, tracing the shape of her lips, the freckles covering her nose. She was the most stunning woman in the fuckin' world. And finally, last night, she'd felt safe enough to tell me she loved me. I knew she did. Nora didn't hide how she felt about me. She showed me in about a million different ways.

But hearing the words out loud, it was something else.

There were things about her that I didn't even know I could love in another person. Shit, things I had never even *noticed* about another human.

Like how she had some crazy skincare routine. With tools and stones and a lineup of products that probably cost a bomb because that was her. She liked fancy shit. Liked her routine. And I fucking loved lying in her bed, with her elegant fuckin' sheets, hearing her bracelets clang together as she did that fuckin' routine.

But the thing I loved most was how she'd come out, shiny, smelling good, looking angelic and fresh faced but with a tiny smudge of mascara underneath her eye. How it remained, after all the shit, I didn't know. But I was so fucking thankful. I loved that little smudge because it was her. After doing that long, fancy routine and not being sparkly and perfect... Having a smudge to let me know that.

I loved that the first thing she did when she tripped over or bumped into something—she was clumsy as fuck, and although I was worried that she'd seriously hurt herself one day, that was another thing I loved—she laughed. That was her first instinct. Not to cry out in pain, even if she really was hurt. She laughed at herself. Because that was her.

Even her health shit... her worrying herself about a blood

clot, brain tumor, a brown recluse spider bite. I fucking hated that she suffered, but I understood that was what made her who she was. I hoped that she might one day feel safe enough to feel that worry less and less, but I was more than willing to accept her as she was for fucking ever.

I watched her for a few seconds more, overcome with love and speared with a small amount of guilt. I got everything I ever dreamed of, yet my best friend's life was a nightmare.

My gut clenched at just the thought of losing Nora.

No fuckin' way would I let that happen.

Unable to stop myself, I laid my lips against hers.

Her eyes fluttered open, slowly, still clutched by sleep.

"Hey," she whispered.

"Hey," I murmured back, my hand lowering to her pussy.

She inhaled sharply as her body melted into mine.

And then I started my morning how I planned on starting it for the rest of my life... fucking my woman.

EPILOGUE
FOUR MONTHS LATER

Recipe: Strawberry Cornmeal Layer Cake

From 'Dessert Person'

NORA

It ended with a wedding.

Not ours, mind you.

Rowan hadn't asked me yet.

Not that I was concerned about getting his ring on my finger. Don't get me wrong, I was near giddy at the prospect of marrying the man I loved. But I wasn't in any rush. I didn't need it to be happy, wasn't leaving ring catalogs around the house. A lot of women wanted the ring because they wanted their man to commit. Wanted to know that he was serious and wanted only her. That the man they were with had a future in mind. A shared future. Forever.

Rowan had made it clear since the beginning that he was

serious and wanted only me. He'd never hid how he felt about me. And he was constantly talking about forever type things.

We lived together. I had adopted his dog. We spent almost all of our free time together. He gave me multiple orgasms. Daily.

Marriage, though an exciting milestone in the future, wasn't something that I thought would change anything.

Marriage was changing something for someone, though. Two someones. Changing everything, actually.

"I'm still trying to wrap my head around this," I told Fiona as she topped off both of our champagne flutes. I hadn't touched mine since the first glass she'd poured, and she'd almost polished off the entire bottle on her own.

"What is there to wrap your head around?" she snapped, picking up the glass and taking a large gulp before turning to inspect herself in the mirror.

I frowned at my best friend. "How about the fact that the two of you could barely stand to be in the same room as each other less than a month ago, and now you're getting married?"

Fiona scowled at me in the mirror. "Haven't you heard of the enemies to lovers trope?" she barked in the same defensive tone she'd adopted since they'd announced not only their engagement but their wedding date three weeks ago.

"I have, and it's a great one, but if I didn't know any better, I'd say you were still firmly in the enemies phase," I retorted, running my fingertips around the rim of my glass. "You guys don't seem all that... in love."

Fiona scowled again as she took another sip then leaned in to touch up her lip gloss. She, of course, looked stunning in a simple slip dress that skimmed over her body like a dream and showed off her tanned skin.

It wasn't white. It was bright red. Blood red.

Not that I'd expected Fiona to do anything traditional, but I wasn't quite expecting that. Sure, red could signify love, passion or romance, but this shade was angry. It was almost like a declaration of war.

"Just because we're not all over each other, spouting about true love everywhere like you and Rowan, doesn't mean we don't love each other," Fiona huffed, running her fingers through her hair.

"No, it doesn't," I agreed. "But you don't even seem to *like* the guy. And this is really fast." I looked to my still full champagne glass, considering the reasons why my best friend and Rowan's best friend would need to be married so quickly and so out of the blue. "Are you pregnant?"

Fiona looked at me, genuinely horrified. "No, I'm not fucking pregnant," she hissed. "And even if I were, the last thing I'd do is have a shotgun wedding with the guy who knocked me up. Come on, babe, you know me better than that."

"I thought I did," I countered. "But you didn't even tell me anything was going on with Kip until the two of you were engaged." I tried to hide my hurt, because despite it being the truth, it was her wedding day, and I needed to support her.

Fiona's face softened and she turned around, placing her now empty glass next to mine before taking my hands.

"I'm sorry," she said genuinely. "I didn't mean to hide anything from you. I wouldn't dream of it. This all just happened so fast and... Fuck, I didn't think we'd actually go through with it. I don't even know if he's going to be there waiting for me." She waved toward the doors leading outside.

Fiona had planned on the ceremony happening at city hall, wanting as little fanfare as possible. But she was my best friend, and although she didn't technically ask me, I was her maid of honor. Therefore, there was going to be fanfare, despite how shocked I had been about the whole thing.

Fiona wasn't someone I'd expected to turn into bridezilla, but she'd proven difficult with every single location I'd shown her.

So, we were doing it at the bakery. The only place she hadn't vetoed.

We'd turned my office into a dressing room, my desk cluttered with makeup and beauty products. The cakes were out in the kitchen. I'd gone a little overboard with the catering. Fiona loved anything and everything chocolate, so I made three different kinds of chocolate cake. Kip liked vanilla, so I made a plain vanilla cake with bourbon frosting and a Victorian sponge cake with my homemade jam. Not to mention all the little party favors... cupcakes, cake pops, homemade candies.

Fiona was most worried about the booze.

"He's going to be out there," I assured her, frowning toward the seating area we'd turned into a wedding venue. "He's not stupid. And he knows I'll track him down and skin him alive if he hurts my best friend."

"Oh, I like the bloodthirsty side of you." Fiona winked. "Does Rowan know about that?"

I rolled my eyes but couldn't help but press my legs together, thinking of how I'd handcuffed him to the bed just last night. It turned out my alpha bad boy did love giving up control. To me, at least.

"Does he know about that?" She tipped her head downward to my stomach.

I gasped, looking at her in shock. "How did *you* know?" I asked, cupping my stomach.

"Girl, you've not touched that." Her eyes flickered to my glass. "And that's a $300 bottle of French champagne. One of your favorites. Which I'll not let go to waste." She picked up the glass. "Your tits are even bigger than usual," she added, gesturing to my chest with the glass. "And you've got the whole pregnancy glow going on. You haven't been eating anything in the mornings, just nursing a cup of fucking tea like you're an eighty-year-old English woman. I'm not blind." Her eyes narrowed. "I'm surprised your man doesn't know already. Since his powerful, masculine dominant gaze is always zeroed in on you whenever you're in the vicinity, and he notices every time you fucking blush."

I grinned at her words. She wasn't wrong. Rowan's attention was always on me. Always. He watched me with an intensity like I tethered him to the earth or something. And the feeling was totally mutual. He was incredibly in tune with my body. He noticed tiny things about my mannerisms and expressions that signified I was overly anxious, tired, sad.

But he hadn't noticed the pregnancy.

Granted, I only found out three days ago. But seventy-two hours was long enough to keep a secret from the man I loved more than life itself.

"He's been busy finishing up the job before the wedding," I explained to Fiona. "And I've been here, baking cakes."

I'd planned on telling Rowan last night, but I'd been here late, putting the finishing touches on everything, and was so tired by the time I got home, I ate the meal that Rowan had cooked and promptly passed out on the sofa.

He'd carried me to bed... Something I hadn't noticed because I'd been dead to the world. A state that continued the entire night with Rowan needing to pretty much shake me to get me up, something unheard of.

He could tell something was off then because no matter how tired I was, my internal alarm always woke me. Pregnancy hormones trumped that, apparently.

I didn't want to sit him down and tell him I was carrying his baby at five in the morning; it wasn't something I could blurt over coffee while we were still both half asleep. I wanted to do it right. Wanted to present him with a little onesie that read 'Daddy' and the positive pregnancy test like all the cute couples did online.

I planned on doing that tonight after the wedding. Hopefully he was happy. I was pretty sure he was going to be happy.

This wasn't exactly going to come out of the blue.

"He's going to be over the moon," Fiona said softly, reading my mind. Or maybe the wrinkle in my forehead.

"I hope so," I replied weakly.

"I know so," she replied firmly. "That motherfucker is so in love with you, it would sicken me... If I didn't love you so much and want to see you living out your own little American dream. You have a real one, you know? Not the kind that looks shiny like veneers but underneath there's really just pointed nubs of teeth. The kind with the crippling debt people take on so they can keep up the affair with the secretary, that kind of thing."

I smiled, cradling my not so flat stomach—which had to do with my affinity for sugar rather than the pregnancy. I didn't feel completely at peace, I was still bracing for the bad since I couldn't trust that life could be this good.

I tried to push the negative thoughts away, but while thinking about the worst things that could happen, my mind went to what Rowan told me about Kip.

"Do you know... everything about him?" I asked carefully. Even though this whole thing had been a whirlwind, I figured he'd told her about that life-changing, traumatic event from his past.

Fiona screwed up her face. "I know he's got a six-pack and a prize hog, that's all I need to know." She peered at me. "What do *you* know?"

Shit.

Okay, so he hadn't told her. And it definitely wasn't my place to tell her, even though I thought it was the kind of thing that was way too important to hide from the woman you were marrying.

"Nora," Fiona warned, putting down her glass. "You know something."

"No, I don't," I squeaked.

"You're a fucking terrible liar," she folded her arms in front of her. "And I'm not getting married if you know he's like a secret serial killer or claps when planes land."

"If he was a serial killer and I knew, do you really think I'd let you marry him?"

She put a hand on her hip, regarding me thoughtfully. "No, I guess not," she decided. "But you still know something, and you are duty bound to tell me."

Fuck.

Though it was my duty to share what I knew with my girlfriend, it only went so far.

"I just, um, he was deployed with Rowan. They went through some heavy stuff," I said, not lying. "Has he shared that part of his life with you?"

"No," she sighed. "But I watched *The Hurt Locker.*"

"Fiona," I groaned. "That is not funny. He served this country."

She rolled her eyes. "You Americans are so fucking fanatical about that shit."

I kept my gaze stern. "If you're going to be an American married to a veteran, you better know and respect what that means."

"Yes, Mom." She saluted me.

There was a knock at the door.

"Get the blushing bride out here," Tina called. "We've got an antsy groom, and my own wife is now making noises about us redoing our vows."

I smiled at the faux exasperation in her tone, knowing that if Tiffany wanted it, Tina would give her a hundred weddings.

"You ready?" I asked my best friend.

Fiona looked uncertain for a split second, like she might climb out the window. Which I would help her with. That's what best friends were for.

"I can have the car out back in five," I offered.

Fiona shook her head then drained the last of the champagne. "No, I'm ready." She sounded like she was convincing herself rather than me.

But she didn't give me a chance to ask any more questions. She straightened her shoulders and stomped out the door to get married.

* * *

You wouldn't exactly call the wedding... romantic. Both Fiona and Kip seemed out of sorts. I could understand why he might be feeling conflicted about moving on, but not Fiona. She was not someone to do something she didn't want to.

But she did.

They both said "I do."

And then, when it was time for the groom to kiss the bride, there was a pause. A long and noticeable one. I swear, Fiona was about to hold out her hand for a handshake.

Kip's jaw had been stiff the entire ceremony, his posture rigid. But then he grabbed Fiona by the back of the neck and locked lips with her.

At first, it seemed like she wasn't into it. For about two

seconds. Then I watched her body relax and she kissed him back. Enthusiastically.

Tina let out a whistle, which seemed to jerk them out of it.

Fiona scuttled back with a frown, her fingers going up to her lips. Kip snatched on to her hand and damn near dragged her down the makeshift aisle.

The reception didn't last long on account of Fiona getting very drunk and having to be carried out by her new husband.

And I did not trust my stomach to keep down the dinner, so I asked Rowan to take us home.

Home.

He'd officially moved into my place. Which was our place now. We kept the beach house, which was all paid off. Lucky we did too since Calliope went through some kind of crisis and ended up moving to Jupiter and into the beach house. I had yet to find out what it was about, since she was pretty close-mouthed, but I was almost certain it was about a man. I loved having her around, though and she was often at our place for dinner or drinks.

Nathan had come home after Christmas. I'd seen him. Of course I didn't tell Rowan that. We'd had enough alpha male anger to last a lifetime. Even though I knew Rowan well enough to know I was far from done with alpha male anger.

Nathan, to his credit, had looked sufficiently sheepish when we ran into each other at the store.

"I'm sorry," he blurted as I was frozen in place, not quite sure whether I should run or give him a piece of my mind.

"For everything," he continued as I was frozen in place.

He ran his hand through his hair looking uncomfortable.

Nathan was immaculately groomed, as usual. Designer pea coat, loafers, scarf, expensive haircut. But his eyes were bloodshot, with lines around them I hadn't seen before. Same with the bags. There were strands of gray in his hair. He looked older. Much older.

New York, it seemed, was not agreeing with him.

I should've felt satisfied with that. He deserved some kind of punishment for being an asshole. But instead I just felt sad.

"I was an asshole."

"You were," I agreed, finally finding my voice.

Nathan's eyes flared with surprise. I braced for that expression to change to anger. Instead, his mouth stretched into a smile.

You could've blown me down with a feather.

"You're happy. With him," he said.

I nodded.

"He takes care of you."

I nodded again.

Nathan looked at me for a long time. "I'm happy for you, Nora," he said softly. "You deserve this."

Again, with the feather.

"And I'll take care of my mother," he continued. "Make sure she doesn't keep up with her stupid campaign."

I bit back a smile, wishing I got to be a fly on the wall for that conversation. His mother had indeed tried half assed attempts to 'make me pay'. I'd had surprise health inspections—which I passed because I kept the bakery clean as hell. There had been all sorts of random delays with shipments, permits. But I'd sorted it all out. What I couldn't, Rowan did.

It was nothing more than an inconvenience but I would be glad not to deal with it anymore.

"Thank you," I told Nathan.

He nodded. "Have a good life, Nora," he said, turning and walking away.

Though I had no secrets from Rowan, I figured that interaction didn't need to be shared. We had enough going on.

We had arguments about bills, as I expected we would. Rowan had wanted to take over the entire mortgage... I had fought against that. It might've turned into a sticking point if he hadn't relented, realizing what kind of victory it was for me to maintain my house. So, we went halves.

Though, we'd spoken about combining finances once we were married, and I hadn't argued. Whether it was feminist or not, I agreed with combining finances when you were married. I hadn't realized just how much money Rowan made until Calliope had spoken about it at Christmas. I told him that he needed a prenup when we got married. He'd responded with, "Cupcake, I'm never fuckin' letting you go."

Though that might've been a line from anyone else, it was a vow for Rowan.

"If you want me to sign something, make you feel better about the bakery, I will," he'd offered after that.

I stared at him in shock. "I thought you just said you were never going to let me go?"

"I'm not," he returned earnestly. "But I know how much the bakery means to you. Want to make sure you feel protected. Safe."

"I do," I pulled him toward me. "With you."

That was that. Hard conversations weren't that hard with Rowan.

I shouldn't have been that nervous about telling Rowan I was pregnant. We'd been trying for this. It wouldn't be a surprise.

But I wanted to make it special. Despite my swirling stomach, I planned on presenting Rowan with the little onesie I had hidden in our closet and dressing Maggie up in the 'big sister' shirt I'd gotten her. Though she'd hated it during the trial run.

It would be great.

"Cupcake, what's on your mind?" Rowan asked as he put the

truck in park. I could see Maggie's face in the window beside the front door. She was waiting for us, like she always did.

"You've been quiet the whole day," he murmured, turning to me.

"I'm pregnant," I blurted, unable to keep it in anymore.

Rowan blinked once before he grinned. Ear to ear. "You're carrying my baby."

I nodded.

"You're carrying my baby."

Again, I nodded.

Rowan didn't say anything else.

He got out of the car.

I deflated a little. Rowan was a man of few words with a lot of people. And he was still moody and borderline grumpy. He often didn't react in ways I expected. But I'd expected a little more fanfare.

Before I could get out of the car, the door opened, and he pulled me out, carrying me in his arms.

"Rowan!" I squealed.

"Need to carry you over the threshold," he grunted.

I smiled. "That's for brides."

"Gotta do that too. Get married."

I looked up at him. "Is that a proposal?"

He walked us in the door, Maggie running around his legs in greeting. "Got a ring," he said in answer. "Was gonna do a big thing at dinner at Carlisle's tomorrow."

I laughed. We had both made big plans that went to shit, it seemed.

He shifted his weight in order to reach into his pocket and retrieve a ring.

"You've been walking around with that in your pocket? Without a box?" I gasped, horrified as he slipped it on my finger.

My eyes were wide as I took in the emerald cut diamond. It was vintage, I could tell right away from the look of it, the setting, the cluster of diamonds on either side.

It was the ring I would've designed for myself.

"You would've noticed the box in my pocket." He shrugged.

"But you could've lost it!" I cried. "My gorgeous, perfect engagement ring." I held it up to the light, captivated by the way it sparkled. The way it looked like an extension of my hand.

"But I didn't lose it," Rowan argued.

He grabbed my chin. "You're really pregnant?" he was whispering now. I'd never heard Rowan actually whisper. His eyes were glassy.

I nodded. "I'm really pregnant."

"Best day of my life, cupcake."

I might've burst into tears if he didn't say the next thing.

"And I'm gonna make it even better," he growled, kissing me and carrying me upstairs.

WE WERE LYING IN BED.

Rowan had already gone into ultra-protective, prospective dad, alpha mode. Therefore, when he was done fucking my brains out, he ordered me to stay put while he gently cleaned me then went downstairs to get me some dry toast since I told him I was feeling queasy.

He propped pillows, fussed over me, and Maggie was the same, jumping on the bed and laying her head protectively on my stomach.

But it was only after I got up to pee that I truly thought about being pregnant. I'd been so caught up in telling Rowan, I hadn't thought about the reality of the situation.

"Oh my god," I said as it hit me. "I'm going to be a terrible pregnant person. I'm going to be worrying constantly, thinking something is wrong, and my OBGYN is going to hate me." I put my palm to my forehead, ready to spiral.

But Rowan was around, so he didn't let me spiral. He always actively watched, preventing me from spiraling. He was the anxiety whisperer.

He grabbed my shoulders, steadying me, tethering me to the earth and stopping me from pacing around the room.

"First, there is nothing on this planet you can be terrible at," he told me firmly. "Except parallel parking. You are terrible at that."

I scowled at him, even though I was fighting a smile.

He rubbed my upper arms. "Cupcake, you need more appointments to check on our baby, we'll make more appointments. If your OBGYN gets pissed, we'll find another one."

He said these things like they were very reasonable, logical things. He made plans around my senseless anxiety. Because that's what he did.

"I love you," I whispered, my eyes brimming with tears.

"And I love you, cupcake," he beamed at me, leaning forward to brush his lips with mine.

* * *

ROWAN WAS RIGHT, I wasn't terrible at being pregnant. I wasn't entirely great either. But I didn't think anyone was actually great at being pregnant. Those women who worked out right up until their due dates, who didn't worry about a thing and didn't get fat ankles—I was positive they didn't exist. Or at least I convinced myself that they didn't exist.

Because I didn't work out right until my due date. Granted, I wasn't exactly known for working out. But I did work at the bakery right up until my water broke on the kitchen floor of the bakery. Like the movie scene water-breaking type thing. Rowan was right there because he was always right there with me first thing in the morning. He'd practically moved into the bakery when I got closer and closer to my due date.

Interestingly, I was the one who stayed calmest during the actual labor portion of the pregnancy.

Rowan, "ran around like a chicken with his head cut off," Fiona described later.

He rushed us back to our place to get my hospital bag then raced around the house, muttering about needing our passports.

I had, underneath a laugh, told him we didn't need our passports for me to give birth in the hospital twenty minutes away.

That treated me to an angry scowl. Well, until a contraction tore through my body. Then Rowan dropped everything and went into protective alpha mode, suddenly clearheaded and mission-driven.

My labor was painful. Horrendous actually. Especially since I was the idiot who wanted to do it 'all natural.'

It killed Rowan to see me in that much pain without him being able to do anything but sit there, feeding me ice chips, brushing hair from my face, and holding my hand. He was there, barking at doctors and nurses, kissing me, speaking tenderly.

Then he was there to catch our daughter, Ana Jill Derrick. To be the first person to greet her into this world.

Although it might've been the pain, exhaustion, the emotions, I swore I felt Ansel in the room, right beside me.

"You deserve this, sis," he said. "Your happily ever after."

The wound inside of me healed just a little in that moment. And in the many moments after that, with my husband and my daughter. In our home. With our dog. My bakery. The countless visits from Rowan's parents. The tumultuous marriage between our two best friends.

Though it wasn't without drama or even pain, it was a happily ever after. Mine, at least.

Fiona's was a different story.

RECIPES

The Crisis Cake

- 1 ½ cups flour
- 1 ½ tsp baking powder
- ½ tsp baking soda
- ½ tsp salt
- 1/3 cup neutral oil (I use canola but coconut or grapeseed works too)
- 1/3 cup natural peanut butter (unsweetened)
- 1 cup light brown sugar
- 2 eggs (cooled to room temp)
- 1 cup buttermilk (you can make your own with 1 cup milk & 1 Tbsp white vinegar or lemon juice and let sit for 5 min)
- 1 tsp vanilla extract

Method

Preheat the oven to 350 & grease a 9x3 round baking pan. Or two 6 inch pans for a double layer cake.

Sift the dry ingredients in a bowl and set aside.

Beat together peanut butter, oil and brown sugar until creamy. Add eggs one at a time then add the vanilla.

Alternate adding the dry ingredients and buttermilk to peanut butter mixture. Beat until just combined.

Pour batter into prepared pan and bake for 30 mins or until a toothpick inserted comes out moist and cake springs back.

Let cake sit in the pan for five minutes and then set on a rack to cool completely.

Double Chocolate Frosting

- One stick of butter
- 3/4 cup unsweetened cocoa powder
- 3 snack size Reese's Peanut Butter Cups
- 3/12 - 4 cups powdered sugar
- 2/3 cup heavy cream
- 1 tsp vanilla extract
- Pinch of salt

In a saucepan, melt the butter over low heat. Add in the Reese's until melted. Mix in the cocoa powder, take off the heat and mix until thick.

Transfer chocolate to stand mixer and add 1/2 of the powdered sugar, mixing until combined. Repeat process with half of the heavy cream.

Continue with remaining sugar and cream, adding in the vanilla extract afterward. Continue mixing for five more minutes until smooth.

Frost cooled cake and enjoy.

*Note: the above recipe makes enough for one cake & you can cut it in half for a double layer (make extra frosting) or double the cake mixture and make two separate cakes.

Tan Slice

When we were there last, my husband became obsessed with 'slices'. There were a bunch I wanted to include but this one is a personal favourite of mine.

Shortbread base

- 200g of butter, softened
- ½ cup sugar
- ½ tsp vanilla essence
- 1 ½ - 2 cups flour
- 1 tsp baking powder
- ½ cup chocolate chips

Caramel

- 1 can sweetened condensed milk
- 100g butter
- 2 Tbsp Golden Syrup (I have yet to find Golden Syrup in the US, but I've used molasses as a substitute, and it works great)

Method

Preheat oven to 350°. Line a 8x8 pan with wax paper (or grease well with butter, which is what I do because I'm lazy). You can use a 9x9 in a pinch but that means your caramel layer will be thinner. I like a nice thick caramel.

To make the caramel, combine all ingredients in a saucepan then heat, stirring until melted together (about 8-10 minutes). Make sure not to let the mixture come to a simmer.

Let the caramel cool to room temperature.

While caramel is cooling, make the base. Cream butter and sugar until pale and fluffy. Add in vanilla, then beat until combined. Add in baking powder and 1½ cups of flour then mix. Add more flour until you have dough that stays together but isn't too wet ;).

Press 2/3 mixture into your baking pan, then pop in the fridge.

Add chocolate chips to the remaining 1/3 of your shortbread mixture.

Once caramel is cooled, pour over the base, then crumble remaining shortbread dough over the top.

Bake for 20-25 minutes until golden, and the caramel is cooked and 'wobbly.'

Let cool to room temperature.

French Hot Chocolate

I am a chocolate fiend. I love anything and everything chocolate. And when I was backpacking around Europe, staying at a cheap hostel in Paris, I splurged what was my food budget for days in order to go to the famous 'Angelina'.

It was well worth it.

This is my version of it, which is pretty close to chocolate ganache. This is extremely decadent and not for the faint-hearted. But my chocolate lovers will adore it.

- 1 ½ cups whole milk
- ½ cup heavy cream
- 8 ounces of good quality dark chocolate, chopped (measure with your heart)
- Whipped cream for topping (if you wish)

In a small saucepan over medium heat, heat the milk and cream. Do not allow mixture to boil.

Once small bubbles appear at the edges, take from heat and mix in the chocolate until it's melted completely.

Pour into a mug and top with whipped cream if you wish.

Almond Croissants

So the recipe for regular croissants is in *Dessert Person*. But to make them delicious and almondy, make croissants like normal, letting them sit out for a few hours or overnight until kind of dry.

Once this is done, make the frangipane from *Dessert Person*.

Then, in a small saucepan, combine 1 cup water, 2Tbsp sugar and 1Tbsp rum.

Bring to a simmer, stirring until sugar dissolves and then turn off heat, letting cool to room temperature.

Slice croissants horizontally. Dip each piece in the syrup before arranging on a baking tray, cut side up.

You can also just use an egg wash for the croissants if you don't want to make a syrup.

Spread frangipane on each half (about 2Tbsp).

Add top half to each croissant, spreading about 1Tbsp of frangipane on top then srinkle with sliced almonds.

Bake at 350 for about 15 min.

ACKNOWLEDGMENTS

This book was meant to be light and fun. Personally, I still think it feels light and fun but I wouldn't be me if I didn't add some drama and heartbreak.

It was also meant to be a total standalone.

Then Fiona and Kip happened.

Then Lori and Finn happened.

Then Calliope and her man happened.

Suffice to say, you have not seen the last of Jupiter or its beloved residents.

I'm writing Fiona and Kip as we speak.

Anyway, back to the point.

As always with me, this book turned into something bigger, deeper and longer. Therefore, I turned into what I always turn into during the writing process—a hot mess.

In addition to writing a book, I was also testing recipes. And I'm already a chaotic baker. Try being a chaotic baker on a deadline.

Not pretty.

I had so much fun writing this book. And, as always, it wouldn't be what it is without the people around me.

Taylor. My husband. The man who comes home with flowers, with treats, who treats me gently and kindly when I'm slowly unraveling. The man who taste tested every recipe even though he's 'not a dessert person'. The man who I fell in love with despite that ;)

My biggest cheerleader. My best friend. My soul mate. I'm endlessly glad fate brought me to you.

Mum. You always pick up the phone. You listen to me cry, vent and talk a million miles a minute after many, many coffees. You tell me to buy the purse. You were the one who introduced me to reading. Who told me I could be whoever or whatever I wanted.

Dad. You're not here to read this but so much of who I am is thanks to you. My expensive taste comes from you. My stubbornness. You taught me to do everything a man could do and to do it better. I love you. Not a day goes by that I don't miss you.

Nana. Baking definitely skipped a generation (sorry Mum). My memories of coming to your house and baking with you are so precious. I still call you and ask tips on the perfect pavlova. You instilled my love of baking and ensured the process comes with so many happy memories.

Jessica Gadziala. Yet another beautiful soul who gives me advice, who lets me vent, who gives me a safe space. You are supremely talented and a wonderful friend and author.

Amo Jones. My ride or die. I love you endlessly. We are soul sisters.

Cat Imb. Your light is so bright, your heart is so big and your talent is endless. Thank you for creating covers that make me want to write a book worthy of them. Thank you for being my friend. I adore you.

Annette. You handle my crazy always. I would be so fricking lost without you. I'm so grateful to have you as my friend.

Kim. Yet another badass woman who handles my crazy. Who edits these words tirelessly and is so dedicated to make this story the best it can be. Thank you for all of your hard work.

Ginny. Thank you so much for always being there. For loving my characters as much as I do. For telling me what I need to hear. You are the best.

My girls. Harriet, Polly & Emma. You're half a world away but distance means nothing. You've all gotten me through some of the hardest times of my life and I'm so so lucky to have you as friends, as sisters.

And last but not least, **you, the reader**. Without you, dear reader, I would not be here. I would not be creating stories as a job. Thank you for making my dreams come true.

ABOUT THE AUTHOR

ANNE MALCOM has been an avid reader since before she can remember, her mother responsible for her love of reading. It started with magical journeys into the world of Hogwarts and Middle Earth, then as she grew up her reading tastes grew with her. Her love of reading doesn't discriminate, she reads across many genres. She can't get enough romance, especially when some possessive alpha males throw their weight around.

One day, in a reading slump, Cade and Gwen's story came to her and started taking up space in her head until she put their story into words. Now that she has started, it doesn't look like she's going to stop anytime soon, with many more characters demanding their story be told as well.

Raised in small town New Zealand, Anne had a truly special childhood, growing up in one of the most beautiful countries in the world. She has backpacked across Europe, ridden camels in the Sahara and eaten her way through Italy, loving every moment.

Now, she's living her own happy ever after in the USA with her brilliant husband and their two dogs.

Want to get in touch with Anne? She loves to hear from her readers.
You can email her: annemalcomauthor@hotmail.com
Or join her reader group on Facebook.

ALSO BY ANNE MALCOM

THE SONS OF TEMPLAR

Making the Cut

Firestorm

Outside the Lines

Out of the Ashes

Beyond the Horizon

Dauntless

Battles of the Broken

Hollow Hearts

Deadline to Damnation

Scars of Yesterday

Three Kinds of Trouble

THE SONS OF TEMPLAR - NEW MEXICO

Wretched Love

Wilting Violets

UNQUIET MIND

Echoes of Silence

Skeletons of Us

Broken Shelves

Mistake's Melody

Censored Soul

GREENSTONE SECURITY

Still Waters

Shield

The Problem With Peace

Chaos Remains

Resonance of Stars

THE VEIN CHRONICLES

Fatal Harmony

Deathless

Faults in Fate

Eternity's Awakening

Buried Destiny

RETIRED SINNERS

Splinters of You

THE KLUTCH DUET

Lies That Sinners Tell

Truths That Saints Believe

STANDALONES

Birds of Paradise

Doyenne

Midnight Sommelier

Hush - co-written

What Grows Dies Here

A Thousand Cuts